Nancy Bilyeau has worked on the st[...] *Stone, Entertainment Weekly*, and *Good* [...] a regular contributor to *Town & Country*, *Purist*, and *The Strand*. Her screenplays have placed in several prominent industry competitions. Two scripts reached the semi-finalist round of the Nicholl Fellowships of the Academy of Motion Pictures Arts and Sciences.

The Crown, Nancy's first novel and an *Oprah* pick, was published in 2012; the sequel, *The Chalice*, followed in 2013. The third in the trilogy, *The Tapestry*, was published by Touchstone in 2015. The books have also been published by Orion in the UK and seven other countries.

PRAISE FOR THE BLUE:

'Fascinating details include glimpses of the newly opened British Museum, a Christmas party at the home of William Hogarth, and Madame de Pompadour's residence at Versailles. Historical fans will be well satisfied.' – *Publishers Weekly*

PRAISE FOR NANCY BILYEAU:

'Nancy Bilyeau's passion for history infuses her books and transports us back to the dangerous world of Tudor England. Vivid characters and gripping plots are at the heart of this wonderful trilogy. Warmly recommended!' – Alison Weir, bestselling author of the *Six Tudor Queens* series

'Bilyeau deftly weaves extensive historical detail throughout, but the real draw of this suspenseful novel is its juicy blend of lust, murder, conspiracy, and betrayal.' – Review of *The Crown* published in *Oprah* as a 'pick of the month'.

P 1 8

THE BLUE

NANCY BILYEAU

ENDEAVOURQUILL

AN ENDEAVOUR QUILL PAPERBACK

This paperback edition published in 2019
by Endeavour Quill

Endeavour Quill is an imprint of Endeavour Media Ltd
Endeavour Media, 85-87 Borough High Street,
London, SE1 1NH

ISBN 978-1-911445-89-0

Typeset using Atomik ePublisher from Easypress Technologies

www.endeavourmedia.co.uk

For my father, Wallace Bilyeau, who loved art so very much

Table of Contents

CHAPTER ONE

Amiability has never been counted more important in a woman's character than it is today. Which is why I'm twenty-four and unmarried and without friends or employer, only a grandfather for company. It doesn't matter. Ambition consumes me, an impossible one. It's what delivers me into the back of a hackney carriage on this December night, holding a party invitation that doesn't bear my name as I make my way from Spitalfields to Leicester Fields.

My grandfather and I live on Fournier Street, one of the most respectable in Spitalfields, a street where, never mind the longing and greed and fear that nibble at the souls of a good many neighbors, all say their prayers after supper and snuff the candles. Not so along the route through London to Leicester Fields. From my swaying carriage, I see lights leaping in many windows and hear the shouts and the laughter. London is alive, and so am I.

After more than an hour, the carriage jerks to a stop as it is has many times. But on this occasion, it's not in order to allow another to rumble forward. Thump, thump, thump. The driver pounds his stick. I've arrived.

The carriage door swings open to number thirty, Leicester Fields, the home of England's greatest living painter, William Hogarth.

As I step down, I catch sight of handsome houses rising along each side of the square, illuminated by coal-lit street lamps that stand to attention like tireless soldiers. The largest by far is Leicester House, tucked behind a courtyard, containing whichever Prince of Wales is presently draining the country of gold with his peevish schemes. I know from the newspapers the names of some of the other residents, wealthy doctors and striving merchants and low-rung nobles. But now is not the time to gawk.

I'm not sure what I expected from Hogarth's London home. The solid terraced building, third from the left on the southeast corner, gives no outward evidence of artistic genius. Yet I know I've come to the right place, by the lights bursting from the windows and the roar of many voices. This is the man's Christmas party.

I fully expect the servant at the door to give me trouble. Raising my chin, I try to look as if I belong in the rarefied world of Leicester Fields. Unfortunately, a bitter cold wind envelops me, making my earrings, the only ones I possess, sputter against my neck. I shiver in my dress. I did not bring my winter cloak — how could I? It is too plain, the garment of a modest, God-fearing Huguenot woman of Spitalfields, not the West End. Sober manner and somber dress, such is our creed.

Without a word, I thrust the invitation into the gloved hand of the silver-wigged servant. He does not look down at the card.

"Have you no escort, Madame?"

"None is required."

He peers at the writing and frowns. "This was sent to Pierre Billiou."

"My name is Genevieve Planché and I am his family — his grand-daughter," I reply. My mother died of smallpox when I was eight. My father being dead of typhus three years before that, Pierre has long been my only family.

I say, as casually as I can manage, "Grandfather is ill, but he wished me to convey to Mr. William Hogarth in person his wishes for a merry Christmas."

The servant purses his lips.

I take a step closer. "I'm sure Mr. Hogarth would be most angry to know that a member of the Billiou family was made to feel unwelcome."

A smile crinkles the servant's face. With a mocking flourish, he beckons for me to enter. I straighten my shoulders and follow him, determined to maintain the appearance of being accustomed to such occasions, when the truth is I've only attended two artists' gatherings hosted by my grandfather and they consisted of three or four old friends grumbling about their commissions over goblets of cognac. I've never attended a party among London society in my life.

I cannot help but catch my breath and blink, rapidly, as I walk from the entranceway to a large room, high-ceilinged and brightly lit, yet hazy. Greasy oil lamps sputter on the walls, candelabras and candlesticks flicker everywhere else. The din is ferocious, as if all crammed inside the walls speak at once. After a minute or so, I perceive that every single person in the room is a man. Young and old, fat and thin. They wear frockcoats and wigs, goblets in hand. Wrinkle-faced men cling to long-stemmed clay pipes. A quartet of young men laugh in the corner

A fire crackles in the tall fireplace. Yet a damp-cloud smell of human sweat hovers over this crowd, mingling with the musk oil many men use to conceal their odor — unsuccessfully — and the tobacco smoke and the holly branches heaped around the pink punchbowl, in sole deference to Christmas a fortnight away.

Not one of them speaks to me. I feel gazes drift my way but none move a muscle to include me in their repartee. The man closest to me turns to offer me the expanse of his broad back.

3

Two men who cannot be older than twenty-five share snuff from a crimson box. One pinches his nose afterward to keep from sneezing while the other shakes his head. They glance sideways at me and put their heads together, laughing at some nasty little joke.

I refuse to be embarrassed. They should be embarrassed. From the tempo of this room, no one would know that England is presently at war with France and that young men are dying, horribly, in places like Quebec and Saxony. These gallants don't care about the fact we might not win, that the British banks are strained to breaking point and taxes keep rising along with the cost of food.

But *I* have a more immediate problem. I don't see anyone that matches the description of William Hogarth — and I perceive by the roar of laughter elsewhere that this is but one of several rooms packed with party guests. How am I to maneuver my way through a house of haughty men?

It is at that moment I see it — one of Hogarth's own prints hanging on the wall.

The party guests no longer exist as I make my way toward it. My grandfather owns a book of reproductions of Hogarth's art, and I've seen his paintings mounted at the Foundling Hospital, which he generously finances. But now, with a shiver of awe, I look upon one of the artist's most famous prints: a pretty, innocent young woman from the country, holding the pincushion of a seamstress, inspected by a crone in front of a crumbling London building. Two leering men hover in the background.

"A fine *Harlot's Progress*, wouldn't you say?" rasps a voice.

I whirl to face a man lower to the floor than myself, a hunchback in fact, and not a day under seventy. His bloodshot eyes gleam with amusement under a wig perched precariously on his narrow skull. No doubt he wishes to embarrass me with his question.

"Yes, that is the title of this series of prints," I say calmly. "This country girl arrives in London, seeking honest work, and is taken up by procurers and pimps, determined to ruin her. Which they do, of course. She'll die of the pox in a few years."

A sound emits from the man, half laugh, half sputtering cough. "A prim and proper young lady who tells a tale of a prostitute without a blush?" he says. "I must know your name." He crouches a few more inches in an attempt at a bow. "I am Joshua Holcroft."

"I am Genevieve Planché," I answer, "and I am here to represent my grandfather, Pierre Billiou, who was invited but sadly could not attend."

Mr. Holcroft thinks for a moment. "I am acquainted with Pierre Billiou, a fine painter, yes, but I haven't set eyes on him in five years, at least."

"Grandfather was invited to this party, be assured, Sir."

"Oh, I don't doubt that he was invited. Hogarth casts a large net, as you can see with your own eyes. But Billiou is a Huguenot, living among his people, the silk weavers in Spitalfields, if memory serves. I can't believe a French Protestant would send his own granddaughter here alone, disastrously dressed."

Taken aback, I look down at my best wool dress of darkest green, trimmed with white lace. "Disastrously?"

"My dear, it's not a dress for society."

"I suppose that is why no one has acknowledged my existence here," I say, chagrined. I must make a proper impression on Hogarth himself. Nothing should detract from the seriousness of my request.

"Hasn't your grandfather taught you anything? Even if your frock were acceptable, it's not possible for a man to approach a woman standing alone at a party such as this. Your lack of escort creates an insurmountable problem."

"*You* surmounted it."

"I am old and ugly and —" he holds up his goblet — "more than a little drunk. Perhaps if there were another female present, she could take you in hand and smooth matters over."

"And there are no ladies here, anywhere?"

"Of course, of course, some wives of wealthy art patrons are upstairs, sitting comfortably with Mistress Hogarth or gossiping together. And that is all. There's no place for a young woman in the world of art besides the sort we see here —" His eyes, twinkling with malice, swivel to the wall where *A Harlot's Progress* hangs.

I can feel my cheeks flush at his disdain. This is what I've faced since my teacher chastised me for filling my copy-book pages with drawings of people instead of lessons from Scripture. "Females cannot be artists," the teacher shouted. Tonight, here, I will set matters right. I just need to speak to William Hogarth himself. The man who captures with brilliance the lives of human beings, their sufferings under injustice, will understand.

"Where is Mr. Hogarth now?" I ask.

"Promenading from room to room. He was here an hour ago and should return. His path is not quick. He's weighed down by those who seek to worship at the altar of art — or at least, those who wish to give that appearance. Tonight Hogarth has two lords who perch on either side of the poor man like guardians at the gate. Of course, it's not just him they surround, but also his guest of honor, Joshua Reynolds, the rising sun to Hogarth's waning talents."

"Waning?" I repeat, incredulous, when a commotion at the far end of the room captures everyone's attention.

It is him. William Hogarth, smaller than I'd imagined and older too, but the same round face and short, thick nose I've seen in likenesses published in the newspapers. Next to him is a much younger man, dark countenanced, moving with assurance. This must be Joshua Reynolds. Just as Holcroft described them, two wigged and splendidly dressed men stand close to Hogarth and Reynolds, the lords pressing on either side, as if not to yield advantage to anyone else. One is perhaps twenty, wearing a pale yellow frockcoat and breeches, his delicate face powdered, a beauty spot painted over his lip; the other aristocrat is a little older and taller, sans powder, with grave, dark eyes.

But as the group advances, I catch sight of another face, one that makes my stomach clench.

My grandfather's good friend, fellow artist Robert Drummond, is among the entourage.

I should have thought of this possibility when I filched the invitation, that one of his artist companions would also be invited. Grandfather stopped going to events such as these a few years ago, when his health began to trouble him. He would never countenance my coming to Leicester Fields, for he has tried to dissuade me from my plan of asking a leading painter to sponsor me since the day I first told him of it. Grandfather thinks I'm upstairs in my room in Spitalfields at this moment; thanks to Robert Drummond, he'll know by tomorrow that I lied my way into Hogarth's home.

Why am I such a fool? But it is too late to do anything but go forward.

Mr. Holcroft sidles away, not wishing to be at my side when the host sees me. I have another idea. I dig my fingers into his arm.

"If need be, you will present me as if I am your companion," I hiss in his ear.

"I will not — it's an absurd idea."

"Then I will find a moment to inform our host that you described his talents as 'waning.' The choice is yours."

Mr. Holcroft's mouth drops open in shock and his arm falls limp in my grasp. Which makes it easier for me to pull my "escort" toward the artists themselves.

It is Joshua Reynolds who sees me first. "Holcroft — who have you gang-pressed to our Christmas party?" he asks, laughing. "This poor young woman must be bored senseless, listening to the talk of artists."

"On the contrary," I declare. "Art is my life, and there is no other place I would rather be than here."

The moment arrives. He sees me. William Hogarth looks straight at me, assessing me as if I were a subject to be captured on his easel.

Releasing the sleeve of my relieved companion, I move quickly to stand before him. Other women swoon over the actor David Garrick. For me, there is only this man.

"Mr. Hogarth, I wish nothing else but to learn from you, to be your student in any capacity you would have me," I say, my voice quivering with feeling. "I go about the city, with my sketchpad, as you have, seeking to capture it."

Behind me a man snickers. Another says, "Oh hush, you rascal."

Determined to push on, I say, "My grandfather, Pierre Billiou, has taught me all that he knows—"

"Genevieve, what are you doing?"

My grandfather's friend interrupts. Robert Drummond pushes his way toward me, dismayed.

"Do you know this young lady, Robert?" Hogarth speaks for the first time, a mild voice.

Drummond responds: "Her name is Genevieve Planché. She is the granddaughter of Pierre Billiou, the Huguenot artist, whom many of us in this room have made acquaintance with."

Hogarth nods, as do a few of the others.

"And yes, she has some skill." As if I am not even here, he continues. "She was an apprentice to Anna Maria Garthwaite, painting flowers for design on silk dresses, in Spitalfields. Now her family has made arrangements for her to take a position as a decorator at the Derby Porcelain Works."

Porcelain. Is the whole kingdom obsessed with it? Just the word makes everyone smile — to "ooh" and "ahhh" — as much as it makes me want to scream. The last thing I want is for Hogarth to learn of the position my grandfather pressures me to accept.

Joshua Reynolds claps his hands. "Ah, porcelain, what fantastic creations. 'White gold,' they call it, do they not? People lose their heads over collecting it."

"More than their heads," someone says. "Some poor sods land in debtors' prison."

Reynolds waves his hand, dismissing the image of porcelain-mad bankrupts as unworthy of discussion. "How exquisite the sculpted figures, even the vases and plates can be divine," he says. "And to be commissioned to paint the designs on them, I should think it a great privilege. It seems that this should be more than enough..."

My heart pounding, I look only at Hogarth. I know he must understand. His own training in art was unconventional, limited, yet he persevered to become the best. And he has not devoted his talent to celebrating the wealthy; he paints servants, soldiers, the people of the London streets.

"Would it be enough for *you*, Mr. Hogarth?" I say. "To be shut up in the same room, day after day, painting flowers for silk dresses or for tea cups and plates, and not telling the story of the world with your brush?"

He does not answer me.

"But what else could you aspire to?" asks Joshua Reynolds, once again jumping in. "To paint the stories of the world, you must apprentice to a history painter — and no woman could do that. We learn to paint the human figure through the use of models. No lady of good family could take lessons as an art student, for you'd have to look upon a model barely dressed."

Snickers surround me. My grandfather's friend, Robert Drummond, appears stricken, whether on my behalf or his own, who can say.

"It's not just in England, after all," someone says. "In France they bar women from instruction at the Royal Academy."

"C'est dommage," cries another man. "Les femmes françaises sont belles."

The snickers explode into loud laughter.

While I watch, the faint interest in Hogarth's eyes dims to nothing. He murmurs, "There is nothing I can do for you, Mistress, I'm sorry," and he moves past me.

I cannot believe it. For so long I've imagined myself by Hogarth's side, learning from him, winning his trust — and when the Christmas party invitation arrived, the fantasy promised to crystallize into reality. Yet now that Hogarth has finally met me, heard my voice, and listened to my dreams, it means nothing to him.

I open my mouth, but no sound comes out. The men surrounding Hogarth look at me with pity or with contempt before they, too, move to another part of the room, another conversation. Soon all will be laughing again over some new joke.

"Genevieve, I feel I must —" begins Robert Drummond.

"Leave me alone," I say. My head spins.

"As you wish," he says, and stomps off.

"May I be of service?" says another voice.

I open my eyes.

It is one of the lords who'd been affixed to the side of William Hogarth, the man with the dark eyes. I shake my head, but his hand cups my elbow.

"Allow me," he says, and before I know it, I am maneuvered out of this room, away from Drummond and everyone else and up some stairs. Most everyone we pass nods to the man escorting me or murmurs a greeting, while curious eyes scroll up and down my unfashionable form.

He guides me into a small room, its walls brightened by the roaring fireplace. We're not alone —two ancient and bejeweled ladies huddle on a settee, their faces crumbling with thick powder. I recognize their dresses, made of Huguenot silk in the latest style. With some bitterness, I identify which of the Spitalfields workshops these dresses have passed through. As for their rows of spiraling flowers, pink peonies and yellow roses, adorning the voluminous skirts, they are the handiwork of my onetime employer, Anna Maria Garthwaite. They might even have sprung from my own tiny brush, as I labored in her second-floor workshop on Princes Street, sitting where the light is best. The irony is crushing.

"My friend is not feeling well, and I'm wondering if we may join you," says the man, steering me to a chair by the fireplace. The matrons smile vaguely and return to their iced Christmas cake and sherry.

The old pug resting by the fire toddles over to the man and lays its inelegant nose on his knee. He smiles at the animal, stroking its back, and then smiles at me.

"I don't know your name," I protest, still faint of voice.

"My name is Sir Gabriel Courtenay. I am already apprised of yours."

He continues to smile, but there's no mockery in it. Sir Gabriel is a man of fine features, about thirty years of age. Doubtless other women would be taken with this knight errant, but I want only to nurse my pain in private.

"I must leave this party as soon as possible," I tell him, my voice growing stronger.

His reaction to this is a question. "Mistress, I wonder when was the last occasion you had something to eat or drink?"

I shrug.

"I must insist you have punch. Then I shall make arrangements for you to be taken home."

"I don't care for spirits," I say, clinging to the custom of a Huguenot woman of Spitalfields, though I've behaved as anything *but* that on Leicester Fields. "I appreciate your efforts on my behalf, Sir, but they're not necessary. I've a hackney carriage nearby."

He raises a single finger. A servant materializes out of nowhere; in seconds, I hold a goblet of punch in my hand. Its strong, sweet taste tumbles down my throat. Perhaps after all it would be best to gather myself in this room, for a few moments, before seeking the door.

"I wonder, how did you obtain a coveted spot at the Derby manufactory if you've no interest in the work?" he asks. His fragrance reaches me. He's not like the other men, drenched in musk oils, but wears something dry and subtle, exotic but somehow familiar.

"You have heard of the workshop in Derby?" I ask, surprised.

"Porcelain is all the rage, and everyone has high hopes for the British factories that have opened in the last ten years," he says and folds his hands, expectantly. He's curious about how I came to be offered a position at one.

With some reluctance, I say, "It's my family's doing. My father's cousin was one of the men who founded the Derby business, with his clay designs."

"Ah. Well, in Britain we all recognize the superior skills of the

Huguenots." He pauses. "Perhaps a gathering of the beau monde was not the ideal time to make your case to Mr. Hogarth."

"Is *that* what this is?" I ask bleakly. Of course I do not belong among the beau monde, the pampered pleasure-seekers of London. But neither does Hogarth. This is a group that he once satirized — no, he skewered — in his work. I thought I knew so much about him. How could the man who mocked the heartlessness of the aristocracy in *A Rake's Progress* now cater to them?

Sir Gabriel says, "You must be a talented artist in your own right."

His politeness only pains me. "Not artist. Decorator." The word sours my tongue. "To adorn the lives of my betters, that is the limit of my talent, it seems. I'd thought, quite comically I realize to all present, that Master Hogarth would understand me, he would see why I cannot…" To my horror, my voice breaks. Tears burn in the corner of my eyes.

He says, "What you require now is food. I'll organize it." He eases out of the room.

As I sit there, in an upstairs room of an artist who didn't respond to my heartfelt plea, weeping before a stranger, I've never felt so pathetic. I've bared my soul to a bored gentleman distributing charity. Doubtless, he is planning to escape from this tedium now. I will save him the effort.

I rush out of the room and down the stairs, and push my way through the crowd. The December cold slaps my cheeks, and I am glad of it. The lights in the street lamps burn a smoky red in front of the prosperous square townhouses, as if I'm trapped in a frozen, elegant hell.

I find my coachman, reeking of gin, and in moments I'm swaying in the back of the dark carriage, back to Spitalfields. As the horses clop their way from west to east, I realize two things. The first is that I've lost one of my earrings, fallen somewhere in the house, perhaps in my jostling haste to leave.

The second is, I know now what scent Sir Gabriel Courtenay wears, the man who unaccountably tried to help me. Three months ago, when his gout had receded, my grandfather suggested we visit a conservatory, an experiment in growing faraway plants in a heated, enclosed British garden.

We saw lemons that day, and oranges, and a wondrous variety of flowers. There was one delicate white flower I found particularly lovely and I leaned down to breathe its fragrance. Dry and sweet and subtle.

Before I moved on, I read the neatly written script on the card in front of the flower.

"Jasmine."

CHAPTER TWO

"How bad is it, Daphne?" I ask the next day, sitting up in bed, rubbing my eyes. It is closer to the noon hour than dawn. I wasn't able to fall asleep until very late.

Our tiny housekeeper and cook, Daphne Mortrand, scrunches her narrow nose and purses her lips. That tells me more about my circumstances than her words ever could. I've wrought havoc.

"Monsieur Billiou imparts none of his domestic concerns to me, Mademoiselle," she says.

Now that is not true. I've been party to their long conversations, always in French, so rapidly spoken that I occasionally have a bit of difficulty following.

Setting down the petit dejeuner tray of petit pain and chocolat, she says, "And yet…"

"And yet?"

"The notecards from the other gentlemen, they started coming soon after dawn. Servants knocking on the door all morning long. I think perhaps these notecards concern you."

I slide back into bed, pulling the blanket up to my chin, staring at the ceiling. "There is no 'perhaps.' They do."

Stirring my pot of chocolat, she says, "The only message Monsieur Billiou has for your ears is that we will have a guest for supper. And I should prepare cassoulet."

The choice of dish tells me as much as Daphne's scrunched nose. I know my grandfather, his habits and motives, better than any living soul. Grandfather adores his cassoulet — it reminds him of childhood, savoring the Languedoc cooking of his mother. But I detected years ago that cassoulet is also the dish he wants served when his objective is to impress a purely English guest. The disapproving face of Robert Drummond rises before me.

A family supper, with me sitting in abject obedience, must be necessary to appease Drummond, an important friend. My stomach clenches as tight as when I first glimpsed him last night at Hogarth's home. Tonight should be singularly unpleasant.

Daphne is almost out of the door when I tell her that I will purchase the ingredients for the evening meal. Today is Wednesday, when city laws allow the butchers' stalls to join the sellers of vegetables, roots, and herbs.

"No, no, no, Mademoiselle. It's not safe for you at the market."

"Nonsense, Daphne. You know I shall be fine."

This is our custom, Daphne and I. She protests, I insist. I roll over on my side, reaching for my slice of bread. Today must be faced.

As I force the food down, I listen to Daphne slowly descend the stairs: the shuffling, followed by a thump and the occasional grunt of pain. I have tried so many times to dissuade her from climbing the stairs to the third story of our townhouse. Daphne always shakes her head. I am the gently born daughter of a Huguenot home and so must take petit dejeuner alone in my room. In her, I have met my match in stubbornness.

The truth is, Daphne is my superior in courage.

My grandfather's family, the Billious, came with the first wave of Protestants seeking refuge in England. That diaspora began some seventy years ago, after King Louis XIV issued the Revocation of the Edict of Nantes, outlawing our religion. We made London our new home, bringing our trades and our tastes and our beloved language. On some streets in Spitalfields, English was never spoken. Our numbers were so great that a new word was coined to describe us: refugees.

Daphne's family remained behind in France, as did others. When the persecutions got worse under Louis XV, she was arrested and imprisoned at the Constance Tower of Aigues-Mortes, a prison of great horrors. She escaped, somehow making her way across the Channel to England. My grandfather found her one morning, half-dead, sprawled on the steps of our church. The only legacies of the Constance Tower are her limp and the terrible scars crisscrossing her back.

As I sit at my table, pulling a comb through my long, thick hair, I consider my own looming prison sentence. I will not be starved or beaten or frozen, no, but to spend each day trapped in a Derby manufactory, decorating pieces of porcelain, it is unbearable. Sent far away from London — condemned to decorate the objects of the rich and the frivolous.

I shudder as I recall yet again William Hogarth's expression, weary — and even, if I force myself to be honest, a bit contemptuous. Dropping my comb, I bury my head in my arms. My gamble was a complete failure.

*

"Take George with you to the market," Daphne calls from the kitchen an hour later as I make my way down the stairs. I pass by my grandfather's rooms on the second floor and pause, waiting to hear my name called, half-hoping and half-dreading. The door hangs a few inches ajar.

But the only noises are his beloved canaries, Vermeer and Van Dyke, chirping in their wooden cages.

I push the door farther open with two fingers. It creaks on its hinges. "Grandfather?"

Still nothing. Is it possible he's not in his room after all?

I peek inside. My grandfather, Pierre Billiou, sits in his armchair, looking out of the window, sadness etched in his features, pretending that I have not spoken, that I'm not here. He'd be within his rights, as the head of this family, to exact a terrible punishment, for we women have little say in our lives.

"You didn't trust me," he says, finally.

"I am sorry."

My tone is as close to penitent as I am capable of.

He turns toward me, light hazel eyes set in a face that sags to meet his weathered neck. "And you didn't believe me, that it would be impossible for Hogarth or one of the other great artists to take you as full apprentice. Do you think I'd deny *you*, my grandchild, that opportunity if a woman could pursue it?"

It's true. Grandfather did try for me. When I was seventeen, he invited a history-painting instructor to our home, sympathetic to my pleas to learn more of art. It is impossible to do so without a period of apprenticeship under a trained history painter.

Grandfather's shocked guest remained only minutes after learning of my ambition. "How could a woman do that?" he sputtered. "It isn't just the demands on the intellect or the employment of the models. Females are not meant for it — it's far too dangerous. Their sensibilities are too delicate for art!"

I've been hearing those same criticisms, this refusal to accept me, for the last seven years.

"But it is not fair," I say.

His face darkens with frustration. "So you've said. A hundred times. You refuse to accept that life cannot be what you want, just *because* you want it. And now…" His voice trails away. There's only the noise of Van Dyke, his younger canary, rustling busily in his elaborate cage.

"Now, it would seem, London is not big enough for you, Genevieve," he finishes.

I choke down my words of protest — they'd only worsen his mood. With a nod I retreat, leaving him to his caged birds, and prepare for market.

I know why Grandfather made arrangements with my cousin for me to go to Derby. It is not just a matter of exiling a woman of difficult temperament who demands a career that is impossible to pursue. I do not fit into Spitalfields for more specific reasons, for reasons having to do with the man I thought I loved and the crime he committed. The mistakes we both made. But I cannot dwell on that now. I must banish all thoughts of Denis Arsenault.

"Take George with you," Daphne says when I'm a few feet from the front door.

"I won't have as much to carry as all that," I say.

"You're never as safe as you think you are," says Daphne.

I have no wish to argue with her today. When I step out onto Fournier Street, George is right behind me.

The city tumbles out before me, gray and sooty. A pale sun hovers above the smoke of a hundred thousand chimneys. It is a city of many, many lives, and for each one of them, London is a different experience.

Even on our own street, life is far from the same for everyone. Our closest neighbors are all Huguenots, but the larger, grander houses — gleaming brick, black trim, and red shutters — rising across from us, on the south side of the street, belong to the master silk weavers. They boast four windows across on each floor, compared with our two. The masters' houses even have small gardens behind them, where the most determined wives grow trees and coax red and yellow blooms from plots of ashy, shade-shrouded soil.

After I turn onto Commercial Street and pass a cluster of taverns, the luster of success dims. If you can see beyond the crowds, shut out the cries of the vendors, you'll realize the poor and the despondent hide in every shadow of the East End. Sometimes, I feel as if I'm the only one who sees them.

Prosperous or poor, I look at them all. For years I've practiced a technique that I read Hogarth uses called "visual mnemonics." Hogarth studies the people he sees in public, fixing them in memory to be painted later in his studio. I feel a sharp pang. It's going to be difficult to break myself of the habit of worshiping Hogarth, just as it will be difficult to say farewell to London, the city I've lived in since the day I was born.

George mutters unhappily behind me. If my grandfather was Daphne's savior, Daphne was George's. With her walking stick, she drove off a man beating the ten-year-old boy on Hanbury Street. An orphan, he survived as a mudlark, wading into the muddy shores of the Thames at low tide, scavenging for something of value he could give to his boss in exchange for food. Daphne took him in, hid him, trained him to work in our house.

Even though that was seven years ago, and, thanks to Daphne's cooking, George stands tall and broad-shouldered, he always tenses on these streets, as if waiting for that long-ago boss to reappear.

Daphne frets over my forays into the city, but I never feel strain or fear on these streets. I've walked them all of my life. I know how to spot a phaeton careening too fast and dart out of its path. I know how to maneuver the necessary distance around the deep puddles of filthy water running down the streets' centers. I know how to lower my eyes when an anguished drunk screams. I know how to hide my money from the thieves on every corner, their fingers desperate for something, anything, to give to the "fence men."

A mop peddler, his sticks weighing on his shoulders, veers into my path. "M'lady, wares for sale," he wails, turning his face to profile to hide the fact that half is russet-red, burned. I duck away, heading for my destination.

I haggle with the best of them in the labyrinth that is Spitalfields Market. Haggling is not just a pastime but a necessity, for food prices keep soaring. It is a hardship both of war and poor harvests. Last year was the wettest England ever saw.

Cassoulet is built on beans — now soaking in our cellar — but also on sausages, duck, carrots, onions, and a mixture of herbs. Even if I were blindfolded, I'd be able to find the stalls selling all of these items.

The sausage vendor, after chopping the required lengths, calls out, "That'll be ten shillings and a sixpence, m'lady."

I put my hand on my hip and retort, "You must think yourself quite a mincer, with that price."

He blinks, twice, knocks off three bob, and wraps my sausage.

I make my face a blank; gloating over a triumph in lowering the price is bad form.

I push my way through the thickening crowds to the vegetable and root stalls, George following with the sausage bundle tucked under his arm. I spot a newcomer to Spitalfields, a stall offering odds and ends, including wooden picture frames. There could be a find here for Grandfather, bit of a peace offering.

The frames I see don't meet his exacting standards, but also for sale is a tall mirror, mounted on the ground. I pause before it.

My face is a touch long and my chin a trifle pointed for beauty; I most definitely do not possess the voluptuous figure of an alluring lady of society. "Le coude" was my hated childhood nickname, bestowed on me because of my boniness. My saving graces are my bountiful chestnut hair and my eyes, light hazel like Grandfather's, now sparkling with battle waged and victory won at the sausage stall.

Something about the mirror strikes me as odd, though. A second later I realize why. A man stands six feet behind me. I spot him through a parting of the crowd. He is not the sort of person who commonly rummages through vegetables at Spitalfields Market. He's bulky, bearded, hatless, and wigless, wearing a black frockcoat, staring at the back of my head with great intensity.

When I turn around, a string of workers carrying crates on their shoulders block my view. As soon as they clear, he's gone.

"Is all well, Mistress Genevieve?" asks George, alert to my mood.

"Let's buy Daphne those vegetables," I respond.

The bearded man has unsettled me, though I can't say why. Men have looked at me before on the street or in the market, it's a price we women pay for shopping for goods. There was no lust in this man's gaze, however.

I don't haggle over the cost of carrots and potatoes, I've lost my enthusiasm for it. The church bells clang once, with their usual thunder. We need to hurry back so that Daphne has enough time to prepare her cassoulet. Not many more ingredients to purchase.

While selecting onions from a long bin, I feel an odd sensation. Glancing to the far side of the bin, where shoppers lean in two- and three-deep, I inhale, sharply. The same man stands there, oblivious of any onions. He's watching me.

A quick glance over my other shoulder confirms that strapping George stands close.

This is when my anger erupts. Isn't it enough that I was humiliated before the artistic elite of Great Britain last night, that I am being forced to take a position in Derby I don't want? Now I've a stranger trailing me through Spitalfields Market.

"Follow me, George," I say after laying down my coins and collecting the onions. I don't look for the man's place in the mob; I don't want to alert him about what's to come. When I've walked far enough, I swivel toward the bin. My judgment of the distance is correct. I'm now within reach of the bearded man, whose back is to me.

"Pardon me, Sir?" I call out in my loudest voice.

He doesn't move, though a few people look over, curious.

"Sir — do you hear me? I am addressing you."

Slowly, the man turns, his hands in his pockets. What an incongruous appearance. In the center of his face, a flattened nose. His skin is unwrinkled, yet strands of white shoot through his thick black beard and bushy eyebrows.

At the sight of me, his eyes bulge under those eyebrows. I've taken him by surprise.

"Have I made your acquaintance?" I demand.

His expression shifts from startled to icy. "No, you have not." He has a coarse voice, yet, on closer expectation, I perceive his clothes were stitched by a West End tailor.

At this moment, George tugs on my cloak. "Let's go, Mistress," he pleads.

Just when I need a show of strength.

"No," I hiss out the side of my mouth. Lifting my chin, I say to the bearded man, "If you seek to trouble me, I shall have to call for the bailiff — do we understand one another?"

He eases his hands out of his pockets, to let them hang by his side. On the fingers of both hands jeweled rings gleam, the sort of rings most people would hesitate to wear on the streets of London. He flexes his fingers, slowly and deliberately.

"Yes, I understand you," he says.

"Mistress, we're leaving now," says George, in a panic.

But it's the man who leaves first, leading with his shoulder as he shoves past George and me, his eyes locked on mine. In the final seconds, that stare flashes to hatred. I step back, shaken.

I watch him lope away through Spitalfields Market, his shoulders hunched, until the oblivious throng swallows him.

My most immediate problem is George, in a state of hysteria. "Do you know who he is, Mistress? Do you? Do you?" he demands.

"Of course not," I say. "That was the point, George. He was a stranger, and he was troubling me."

My servant shakes his head in disbelief. "You paid him an insult — and there's nothing worse than insulting a man who's dangerous. Way he walks, his nose, what he wears, the rings, I wager he's a boxer."

I swallow. I'd heard about these men and their brutal matches. "Why would a boxer be afraid of me?" I wonder.

"Afraid of *you*?" he laughs, and then catches himself. "Forgive me, I meant no disrespect. But boxers kill people with their bare hands for money — and not just for money. They take joy in it."

The whole way home, George scans every face, turning around to see if we are being followed. I am wary too, more so than I've ever been while walking through Spitalfields. I look for a black coat and a loping gait.

As George hurries me to Fournier Street, he mutters, "At least the man doesn't know where you live."

I pause to scrutinize every person visible on the street before continuing to Grandfather's house. No sign of him.

"I'm safe," I say to George, as reassuringly as possible.

As it turns out, we are both wrong.

CHAPTER THREE

The front door of my townhouse is within sight when another opens, one belonging to a more prosperous house across the street. The wives of these houses spend most of their lives inside or in the garden. But today, two women emerge, both of whom I know. Their faces are grim. I know that the master weavers complain bitterly of foreign competitors these days.

When they catch sight of me, I expect their faces will turn grimmer.

My neighbor, Madame Parlette, spots me first and turns to her companion, a woman who is tall and wide hipped, like a Dover galleon, and says, "I'm very sorry."

"As am I," snaps the other, Madame Bourgeois. She bestows on me a look of loathing, as intent as that of the bearded man. The difference is, I know why Madame Bourgeois hates me.

I make my way inside my own house, deliver the market purchases to Daphne and help her chop the meat and vegetables in silence. Every day I do my best to not think about Denis Arsenault. Most days I succeed. But after my encounter with Madame Bourgeois, brooding about my onetime fiancé is inescapable.

Denis was a silk weaver in her husband's workshop — until he wrecked it. Two years ago, Denis led a rampage of apprentices outraged by meager wages and long hours and other complaints. They broke into their own workshop at night, destroyed looms, and cut the silk to pieces. It was far from the first riot against grueling conditions in Spitalfields, but it was the most infamous. They call such instigators "the cutters." Monsieur Bourgeois kept his money in a secret place in the wall, and at the end of the cutters' rampage, the money had disappeared, and so had Denis. The magistrate called for arrest and dire punishment.

Yet that was not my first moment of disillusionment with Denis Arsenault. The pain had come earlier. I'd been besotted with him since I was eighteen, thrilled when he first sought me out at twenty, and engaged to him at twenty-one. He was a journeyman with one of the most prosperous workshops, I was apprenticed to Anna Maria Garthwaite. Our future looked golden — for a while.

About two months before the wedding, Denis' behavior turned from erratic to intolerable. He swerved between elation and despair for no reason. He was rarely where he said he would be, and I grew skilled at finding which pub he'd holed up inside and coaxing him out. Spitalfields weavers were known throughout London for fondness for drinking, I kept telling myself. Denis was no different. Would I find him in the Mulberry Tree, the Jolly Weaver, the Little John, or the Throwers' Arms?

But Denis began to disappear for days rather than hours, only to leap in front of me with jealous questions about my own whereabouts. It took effort, but I discovered the truth: Denis was gambling. He played whist, pharo, piquet, tick-tack, or backgammon at table if he could talk his way into a place, a wager over dice rolled on the street if not.

"You could never understand, Gen, never," he said, anguished, when I confronted him in a coffee house.

We quarreled, horribly, and I broke our engagement, fleeing from him, sobbing on the street, which no respectable woman should ever do. By the next day every Huguenot in Spitalfields knew of our scandalously public dissolve.

Which is why, when a month later he led the band of cutters to wreck his master's shop, everyone assumed I knew something. My denials satisfied the magistrate, but not our neighbors. I took a share of the blame. It was as if by breaking the engagement I had set him on the path of crime.

"Why don't you have a wash, Mademoiselle?" asks Daphne, noting my melancholia. "I have supper well in hand."

I trudge upstairs, lugging a large jug brimming with water, past my grandfather's door, shut tight. I light a fire in my room and pour the water into a pot suspended above. Drawing the curtains closed on the windows facing the street, I slip out of my wool dress and pin up my chestnut hair. Sitting cross-legged on the wood floor in my shift, I wait for the water to warm.

Genevieve, think first — think. You must not rush around so, you'll break things.

I hear the voice of my gentle mother, not angry with me, never angry no matter what I did, and I was a difficult child. She holds out her arms and I run into them, press against her soft, yielding body. *Mama, I'm sorry.*

No, these are other memories that are still so raw that I push them away.

I fear not even a wash could help my mood. But I must try. I pour the steaming water into a bowl and sit in a hard-back chair, a silver footbath below. When I dampen the soft cloth, rub in a sliver of rose soap, and press it onto my face, a knot of tension uncoils in my neck. The humiliation of yesterday, the strain and fear of today, the sadness of the last moments — all ease, ever so slightly. I scrub my tired hands. I unlace my shift's bodice, fold it over and over to nestle around my waist, and I dampen my throat, my shoulders, and my breasts.

Creak. Creak.

The floorboard bends above my head, loud enough that I know it's a person's steps.

I drop the cloth.

Our townhouse, like its neighbors, was built not just for living but for weaving. My great-grandfather installed looms in the attic, where a large triangular top floor window afforded the most light. Our looms vanished fifty years ago, when Grandfather turned to art. Ever since I was old enough to hold a brush, the attic has served as my art studio, too. No one else goes up there.

I dry myself, hurriedly, and pull my dress back on. Seizing a large candlestick, I creep out of my room and head for the stairs. I walk the stairs alone, gripping the candlestick so tight that my fingers ache.

My throat is dry, my heart pulses in my chest.

I push open the door to the attic.

Not a sound; no sign of life. As I scrutinize every inch of the shadowy room, I wonder if my mind plays tricks. The late afternoon sun slants through the window, picking up a billow of dust next to my easel, slowly easing to the floor. The sort of billow caused by someone walking across a floor. I realize, with a sickening rush, that a man's muddy boots rest perfectly still, next to the easel. Above the boots, stockings, and trousers, and…

Denis Arsenault sits on a trunk in my attic.

My sharp, pained gasp, verging on a choke, fills the silence of the room.

"It's all right, Gen," says Denis, holding up a hand. "It's all right."

I stumble across the floor, still not believing it is him — and in a strange way, it's *not* him. He looks ten years older than the last time I saw him, just two years ago. He's thinner. There are fresh creases around his mouth and the corners of his eyes. His clothes are worn; his brown hair hangs to his shoulders.

"What is happening?" I say.

He leaps to his feet; his arms close around me. Denis whispers in my ear, "I missed you." I feel the taut strength of his arms and inhale the smell of him: tobacco and sweat and cheap rose soap.

I pull back and slap him, hard, across the left cheek.

"I've missed that too," he says, with a little laugh.

"They'll hang you," I say. "You know it's Tyburn's tree if they catch you."

"Except they won't. I'm only in London for a few hours. To see you and my sister, to say goodbye. I'm going to America — I need to leave London at dawn to reach Plymouth in time. I don't expect I'll ever see England again."

Good. I want to cry, but I can't.

"Denis, where have you been?"

"Ireland." He shrugs. "It's not the place for a Huguenot. America is."

"Everyone thinks you took your master's money at —"

"I didn't," he insists. "You know me better than anyone. I'm not a common thief. It was one of the others."

He returns my hard stare with one of his own. Which doesn't mean he is telling the truth. Denis can be a clever liar. I think of the myriad things he hid from me.

"And how did you purchase passage across the Atlantic, especially now, in a time of war? The gaming tables?"

He sighs. "No, Gen, that's over, long ago. I made the money honestly."

He turns to one of my flower sketches mounted against the far wall. "You're still drawing for Anna Maria Garthwaite?"

"She discharged me," I say flatly. "She didn't want to do it, but to be fair, there wasn't a choice. I am an outcast. I tried for a while to keep a business going, to draw the floral designs myself. I had to stop. No silk weaver would commission my work… because of you."

He throws out his hands, in that passionate way of his. "No! God, *no*. I'm sorry about that, Genevieve. They're wrong to make you pay for what I did. These damn sanctimonious weavers." He paces the floor, running his hand through tangled hair, as he rants about the greed and hypocrisy of Spitalfields. It ends with: "I have to say it — I'm not sorry for bringing down Bourgeois. He deserved it, for his mistreatment."

He focuses anew on me. "So what are you going to do?"

I tell him about my grandfather obtaining a position for me at Derby over my protests, and my attempt to pursue my own dream, of training as a painter under the direction of a master.

Horrified, Denis says, "A porcelain decorator? That would be living death for you, Gen."

I'm so accustomed to people not understanding my abhorrence for porcelain painting that this is heartening, I can't deny it.

Denis continues. "Prettying the lives of the aristocracy. They pay hundreds of guineas for these little dishes while the poor starve. Hogarth might have understood this twenty years ago, but he's one of them, now."

"So I discovered."

"What have you heard of the Levellers — any sign they're growing?"

Denis once haunted the coffee houses of the most radical views.

"I could hardly go to those coffee houses myself, a woman alone, much as I'd like to," I point out.

"What of your own art?"

After a moment, I admit, with a painful shrug, "I've come to the limit of my ability. Grandfather's specialty was posed portraits. I learned flowers from Mrs. Garthwaite. But to compose a narrative, to tell a story with my brush, there's so much more I need to learn."

"You don't give yourself proper credit."

I shake my head. "No, I can't get the proportions of the full figures, much less groups, without instruction from a history painter. I try, but I can't capture what I see on the streets, I can't create the proper composition. It's beyond me."

He reaches for my hand, tentatively, his eyes full of yearning while his cheek bears the imprint of my slap. "There's another way. Come with me, come to America. I'm telling you, you don't need to apprentice to anyone — you are far more talented than you realize, Gen. You can paint what you want to. We will pursue what we wish to do together. I know I don't deserve your forgiveness, but please try."

"Impossible. You've seen me, we've spoken, now go to your sister."

"I still love you, Genevieve," he says softly. "I think of you as my wife."

I know very well what he's thinking of at this moment, for I'm thinking of it too. After we became engaged, he crept into this house, just as he's done today, and we lay together in my bed. He loved me as a husband would, with tenderness and patience and passion. It is my most guarded secret. Some women take marriage vows with babies already started in their bellies, even Huguenot women. But they marry the men. Were anyone to learn — anyone — that I'd given up my virtue without gaining a wedding ring, I'd be worse than an outcast. I'd be a pariah.

Denis reaches for me again, both arms encircling me.

"No," I say, pushing him away while very much aware of how long it's been since I was last embraced.

"Mademoiselle Genevieve."

32

It's Daphne, calling up to me from the foot of the stairs.

When I whisper to him what's planned for the evening, Denis does his best to dissuade me from going down to dinner. "Can't you plead a headache? Stay with me, Gen. I have so much to say to you."

"I *must* do this. After what I did to Grandfather last night, I must."

Slowly, reluctantly, he releases me. "I'll listen to the dinner from above. When they're criticizing you, and blaming you, insisting on what you must do or where you must go, think of me up here, cursing them."

I can't help but smile.

"And we'll talk afterwards?" he says intently. "Later tonight?"

I turn and leave the attic without another word.

*

I think of little but Denis as I dress for dinner, hands trembling. Of course I can't run away to America with a wanted man. It is madness. I should rush down immediately, tell my grandfather, alert the bailiffs, watch as they drag Denis to Newgate.

But I don't.

After all we've been through, I cannot betray Denis today.

When I was a student at the church-run school for Huguenot girls, my classmates used to gossip about the boys attending school on another floor. Although I had few friends due to my turbulent nature, I could hear their whispers. Denis was the handsomest, the most amusing, everyone's favorite. As we grew older and left school, none of those girls chose Denis as a husband, though. He was too wild. He stole kisses when he shouldn't, he cursed in front of polite company, and he drank heavily. Worst of all to my neighbors, he spoke loudly of fairness for workers. Yet that was when Denis and I were drawn to each other. Like moths to each other's flickering flame.

I hear the door to the street open and shut, and muffled men's voices below. I should be downstairs already to greet Robert Drummond, standing next to Grandfather. Already, a mark against me.

I hurry downstairs, smoothing my hastily plaited hair.

They are in Grandfather's library. He holds one of his favorites when I reach the doorway. I recognize the deep red cover of Jonathan Swift's *The Progress of Poetry*. My grandfather loves his books as he does his food and wine.

The man he shows the book to is *not* his old artist friend Robert Drummond. Our guest is a head taller than Grandfather and far younger and slimmer.

"Good evening, Mistress Genevieve," says Sir Gabriel Courtenay, with a graceful bow.

Grandfather, chuckling, says, "I hope you won't mind, Sir Gabriel, that I didn't tell Genevieve you were to join us for dinner. I'm sure she will be delighted by what you found."

Sir Gabriel pulls a velvet box from his pocket and presents it to me, his grave, dark eyes fixed on my face.

I open the box while they watch, feeling self-conscious. My lost earring is inside.

"I found it on the street outside Mr. Hogarth's house, under the lamp," he explains. "I sent it by messenger this morning with a request to present it to you in person, and Mr. Billiou was good enough to invite me to dinner."

Grandfather says, "I'm sure Genevieve was in a hurry to get home, knowing I'd be impatient to hear how the party progressed. I was not well enough to attend." He taps the walking stick he uses during bad times with gout.

So this is how Grandfather wants it to be, the story he wants spread

— as much for his own reputation as for mine. I should be grateful, but it only humiliates me further. Words of denial burn my tongue. I glance at Sir Gabriel, who must surely realize that I went to Hogarth's without sanction from Grandfather. He smiles, encouragingly.

"The box is more valuable than the earring," I finally say. "Thank you."

"It is my pleasure," Sir Gabriel says, and turning to my grandfather, "I was honored to receive your dinner invitation, Sir. I've never been admitted to the famous Fournier Street before. The silk produced by Huguenot weavers is the envy of the world."

I can only imagine Denis' disgust upstairs, if he can hear this.

"This evening, Sir, consider yourself a most welcome spy," says Grandfather.

CHAPTER FOUR

The cassoulet performs its necessary role for Grandfather. The delectable sausage and duck meat, melted into layers of herb-covered white beans, provide the perfect introduction for tales of the Languedoc, our lost home in the south of France. Grandfather brings back to life his beautiful mother, his indefatigable father. They are sugared recountings, of course. Decades ago, when Pierre Billiou told his father he wanted to be an artist rather than a weaver, the old man took the news with disappointment, even contempt. There was a wounding quarrel; a deep gulf separated father and son. But such dramas are not fit fodder for our guest, particularly one such as Sir Gabriel Courtenay.

Why are you truly here?

It's a question I long to ask the man sitting across from me at our small oak table. If I'm sure of anything, it's that Sir Gabriel is a member of the group that convene at Hogarth's home: the beau monde. During the London season, his evenings must be devoted to the opera, the theatre, recitals and receptions for artists and writers, with strolls through Vauxhall Pleasure Gardens. He gambles with gentlemen at private clubs and dances with diamond-laden ladies at balls.

Tonight, however, this man devotes himself to quiet, pious, wary

Fournier Street. He listens attentively to the stories of Hogarth befriending my grandfather, learning through him the details of the careers of the silk weavers. Through Grandfather's connections, Hogarth absorbed enough to depict the fates of two very different apprentices in his series, *Industry and Idleness*. No one makes further mention of Hogarth's Christmas party. It's as if it never happened, as if Sir Gabriel came to this house through some other avenue.

Putting down his fork, our guest comments, "This war with France must be a special hardship for your family."

"Why so?" asks Grandfather.

"It is your own country, one you take such evident pride in. You are French."

"No, no, no, we could not be more English," Grandfather insists. "France is our blood, yes, our history, but we honor and obey King George II. This country has been good to us. The very last thing we would wish is for England to suffer."

Sir Gabriel turns his respectful gaze in my direction. "And you, Mistress Genevieve?"

"King Louis has said often enough he wants to extinguish heresy — how would you expect me to regard someone who wishes to see me extinguished?" I ask. "If I had the opportunity, I'd return the favor."

The corners of Sir Gabriel's mouth twitch, as if he's trying not to laugh. Not the reaction I expect.

"Regicide, Genevieve?" says Grandfather. "Hardly polite conversation."

"I read in the newspaper that two years ago, King Louis was attacked in the courtyard of Versailles by a crazed domestic who stabbed him," I say. "The assassination attempt failed, but you can see someone did *try*."

Grandfather comments that even before the attack, rumor had it King Louis XV had a fear of assassination.

"Perhaps he believes it is his destiny," says Sir Gabriel. "Who can tell?"

Our servant George sticks his tousled head into the room, holding a fresh bottle of Madeira. "More wine, Your Grace?" he stammers.

"No, no, *no*," whispers Daphne, in the passageway, "don't call him *that*."

With a sigh, Grandfather explains to George that our guest is not a duke, and that only a duke or a royal would deserve the title of "Your Grace."

George, his face beet red, puts the bottle on the table and retreats.

There's no question about it. Sir Gabriel makes a sensational impression on our household, top to bottom. Daphne, when she spotted him earlier, gaped in disbelief. And they haven't witnessed him in his full splendor, as I did at Hogarth's party. Evidently, the silver frock coat and embroidered waistcoat were suitable for Leicester Fields but not for Fournier Street. This evening, Sir Gabriel Courtenay wears a dark blue ensemble, beautifully stitched and fitted, but discreet. Something he must have judged seemly for the home of Huguenots, followers of Calvin. Sober dress and somber living.

As Grandfather fills the glasses with Madeira, I return to pondering Sir Gabriel's motives, without success. If this were the plot of a frivolous novel, Sir Gabriel would have come to Fournier Street for love of me. Which is ridiculous. Such a prime specimen of the aristocracy will mate with a woman of angelic beauty and vast fortune, neither of which I offer.

Were his intentions less honorable, the wide gap between us would be unimportant. But no man tries to seduce a woman by flattering her grandfather. All evening he plies Pierre with questions — and not just about the fateful friendship with Hogarth. He expresses great interest in Grandfather's notable portrait commissions, his encounters with rivals. Sir Gabriel is clearly a sophisticated patron of the arts; he tells us that he went on the grand tour at eighteen and saw the paintings and frescoes and statues of the Old Masters in Paris, Venice, and Rome.

At the same age, I realize with a certain bitterness, Denis was a silk apprentice, consigned to long days at the looms that left his vision blurred, his fingers near shredded, and his shoulders and back afire.

It may be unjust to blame Sir Gabriel for the unfairness of the world. But what we hear and see tonight — impeccable manners, pleasing tone of voice — is the product of privileges that people like myself and Denis can't even imagine.

Across the table, our guest picks up on my brooding. "May we enjoy the benefit of your thoughts?" he asks.

Not knowing what to say, I offer, "You are wearing a particularly dark shade of Prussian blue, Sir."

"Is that so?" Sir Gabriel looks down at his clothes and then back at me, smiling.

Grandfather says, "Ah, we must name our colors to please our allies."

I shake my head. "It was named that well before England became allied with Frederick the Great. Prussian blue was invented more than forty years ago by a Berlin chemist, Johann Konrad Dippel."

Sir Gabriel doesn't speak; his expression doesn't change. But beneath the surface of his benevolent, respectful, rather languid air, something stirs.

"You know the history of this inventor?" he says.

"Oh, Genevieve is incredibly knowledgeable about colors," Grandfather says. "Any artist knows his colors. My granddaughter need only glance at a color, in a painting or on a fabric or a piece of furniture, to know the inner workings of each shade, its history. She tapped all of my knowledge years ago, then she moved on to Madame Garthwaite. And she forgets nothing."

Why is he praising me as a farmer with a pig bound for the butcher? It makes me squirm in my chair.

"I would very much like to know about Prussian blue," Sir Gabriel says. His large dark eyes are set in a face that would be perfectly oval if not for a wide forehead. *He has a noble brow*, pops into my head, a sentence from a novel I read long ago. I firmly squash such romantic drivel.

I say, "Keppel discovered, quite by accident, that if he mixed potassium of a certain sort with sulfate it produced a beautiful dark blue that would hold on all sorts of surfaces. He sold the pigment to others, but kept his formula secret for years. Guarded it. Made his fortune that way. I think he was perhaps something of a scoundrel. Finally, another scientist was able to decipher his formula, not just for himself but for all, and there is the story of Prussian blue. The first color brought to us through science."

"How interesting," says Sir Gabriel. There is no mistaking his intense interest, though why, I could not say. "Tell me more."

I take another sip of Madeira. Grandfather set out his very best for our guest. It's heavy and sweet and bears hints of chocolate. I feel a certain aversion to entertaining our guest with my stories.

"Tell you more about what?" I sound ruder than I intend, but Sir Gabriel doesn't flinch.

"About blue." His white and even teeth glitter like pearls in the candlelight. "Far and away my favorite color."

"It's a vast topic."

Sir Gabriel taps the handle of his silver knife with two manicured fingers. "Why don't you narrow it down for me?" he asks.

"Blue," I say, "is the color of death."

"Oh, Genevieve," Grandfather sighs.

"I am not the one who thought of it that way — it was the ancient Greeks," I say. "They'd only use it to depict the underworld. For some reason, people of that time disliked blue, or perhaps — and no one's sure of this — they were afraid of it. They favored reds, *lots* of reds, yellows and browns, along with white and black. Rarely blue. Part of the reason is that it was an impossible color for any artist to obtain. There is no blue found on the earth. You can't take from the sea or the sky to concoct a color for painting."

Warming to my topic, despite myself, I continue: "It wasn't until the twelfth century that blue found a place on artists' palettes, when they began to create it through grinding up certain stones. Every Madonna in a medieval painting wore blue robes, every stained glass window contained blue. It's as if all men decided, at once, that blue was the color of…" I mull the right word… "the divine."

I glance across the table. There's no question: Sir Gabriel Courtenay, solicitous gentleman, is turning into something else. The change is in his eyes, an expression that's acquisitive, even, dare I say, aroused.

Or perhaps it's just the candlelight.

Sir Gabriel says, "I've also heard it said that blue signifies divine contemplation."

Grandfather, picking up on the strange turn of our conversation, says, "We Huguenots are the wrong people to come to for writings on the divine. Sounds Papist."

"Of course, of course," says Sir Gabriel, reverting to light affability. "The Academy of Artists is showing some new painters. I'd be honored to escort you both to an exhibition — perhaps the day after tomorrow?"

Grandfather says, "I'm not well enough for such an outing. But I'm sure Genevieve would like to attend."

Thump-thump.

41

Grandfather, squinting up at the ceiling, says, "Is George upstairs?"

I grip the side of the chair, struggling not to show a reaction. What on earth is Denis doing? He might have moved down to Grandfather's room, to better hear us. Did Sir Gabriel's invitation provoke this movement? He couldn't possibly care enough to risk discovery… could he?

"Monsieur Billiou, it's not me. I'm bringing in the cognac and tobacco now, as Daphne instructed me to," says George in the doorway, gripping a tray.

"Then what on earth was that noise?" says Grandfather, still peering up. "That's not the birds. I wonder if George should go upstairs —"

"I'm sure it's nothing," I say. "George is busy at table."

I feel Sir Gabriel's eyes, studying me.

"He's not so terribly busy as that," says Grandfather.

Desperate to stop this train of events, I turn to Sir Gabriel and say, "I would gladly accept your invitation, Sir Gabriel, but I fear I'll be much occupied with preparations for travel to Derby, since it seems I must take up my new position."

"Ah, of course," Sir Gabriel says. "When are you to depart?"

"As soon as I make arrangements with her relation," says Grandfather, a relieved smile splitting his face. "Her father's cousin Andrew will deliver her personally."

It makes my heart twist to witness Grandfather's happiness. He loves me more than any other living person, and knows me so well, and yet by not understanding my longing to be a real artist — or not *wanting* to understand — he threatens to wipe clean all of the other aspects of our closeness, our bond. We might as well not be family at all.

"But won't it take time to bring him down from Derby, only to turn around again for the journey to the Midlands?" asks Sir Gabriel, puzzled.

Grandfather explains that my father's cousin, having helped to found

Derby Porcelain Works several years ago, is no longer an active part of it. With the money he earned, he moved to London. "To become an actor, of all things," says Grandfather, laughing. "Genevieve's father comes from an incredible family. My daughter married a man possessing unusual talents, as do all the Planchés, but oh, they are unpredictable."

Sir Gabriel's gaze flicks in my direction. I am fairly sure I know what he is thinking.

"Is your father's family from the Languedoc as well?" he asks.

"The opposite end of France," Grandfather says, speaking for me. "The Planchés were from Picardy — the city of Amiens. Silversmiths, not weavers."

Sir Gabriel returns to the topic of winter travel and the challenge it must pose.

Grandfather says, "The roads are bound to be difficult in the depths of January, but the owners of the porcelain workshop insist that Genevieve begin as soon as possible. They've become most particular about their workers. I don't think it's possible for anyone to be hired now unless a founding partner vouches for them. It's only her being a blood relation of Andrew that made the hiring possible. All this vigilance came about after an unpleasant business with a porcelain mixer a few months ago."

"What sort of unpleasantness?" I ask.

"It's nothing for you to worry about, my dear, but I suppose you'll hear of it sooner or later. Some young man from the village nearby, hired to work with porcelain, a 'thrower,' stole a figurine and disappeared."

"Such a shame — honesty is so hard to come by," comments Sir Gabriel, fingering the stem of his glass.

"Pursuit of truth is a calling dear to me," I say.

I sip my drink and continue, "But I suppose a bit of thievery is as close to excitement as can be experienced at Derby Porcelain Works."

"Genevieve!" scolds my grandfather.

Sir Gabriel says, "Is that what you seek, excitement in your work?"

Again I see it, that dark gleam in his eyes. I shift in my chair. Yes, he wants something, I am sure of it. A quick glance at Grandfather, drowsy-eyed, showing the effect of Madeira followed by cognac, confirms he hasn't noticed this aspect of our guest.

"I wish to be interested in my work," I say. "Which seems unlikely."

Sir Gabriel swirls his cognac in the crystal glass. "There are few art forms possessing more allure, more magic, than porcelain," he says.

How ludicrous. "Magic?" I say, not able to keep the sarcasm from my voice.

"Yes, indeed," he says.

"We are Huguenots, as Grandfather said, susceptible to neither talk of the divine nor of belief in superstition, but even if I had not been raised in this faith, I must tell you I doubt there could be magic associated with porcelain," I say. "It's clay and water, mixed and fired in an oven. End of it."

"Do you not find interesting the magnitude of this transformation, from clay and water, as you say, to objects of transcendent beauty? Aren't you curious about the strange facts of its long history?"

"What strange facts?" I say. I resist his charm, but I can't deny my curiosity.

And so Sir Gabriel begins the story.

"For centuries no one in the West possessed the knowledge of how to make porcelain," he says. "The sole place of purchase was China, and everyone had to wrangle with trade intermediaries and pay astoundingly high prices. In the East they'd perfected the formula by the seventh century — whilst we foundered in the darkest years of our Dark Ages. You say it's made of clay and water, and forgive me, but it's a great deal more complicated than that. No one else could make it. When Marco Polo's trade routes opened and the Europeans first held porcelain in their hands, they couldn't believe it. The two things they wanted most from the East were its spices and its porcelain. It was exquisite — so pure and delicate that it was translucent, you could see through it — yet fantastically strong."

Sir Gabriel slaps the table to make his point. Grandfather jumps in his chair, then laughs uncertainly.

Our guest continues. "Of course, the great Renaissance princes started porcelain collections. They competed ruthlessly for the most beautiful figures, the most spectacular bowls, plates, cups. The cost of the objects was so high that only royalty, or the wealthiest nobles and cardinals, could even consider buying it. King Louis XIV built a special room just for his collection."

How he admires the taste of the monarch who persecuted the Huguenots, sent soldiers into homes to force conversion at gunpoint, who finally made our faith illegal. He was the reason my family lost our home, fleeing to England. Now his great grandson, Louis XV — "One king, one faith" — keeps the hate alive, with arrests and enslavement. Huguenot men who refuse to convert are thrown into royal ships and chained, to serve as galley slaves for the rest of their lives.

Sir Gabriel, ignorant of my grief over oppression of Protestants, carries on with his history. "All the time, each country frantically tried to decipher the Chinese formula. They built kilns and hired alchemists to mix different types of clay with glass or chemicals, without success. If it had the necessary delicate appearance to please the eye, it would shatter when someone poured hot liquid over it. Should European porcelain be strong enough to withstand heat, it was not pleasing to look at. The de' Medici family came closest."

"How abhorrent." I am unable to remain silent any longer. "This obsession was — and is — despicable. You realize that a man caring for his wife and children could earn no more than twenty guineas a year in this country, no matter how hard he labors? While a prince tosses hundreds of guineas at a single piece of porcelain!"

Sir Gabriel leans back in his chair and says, "Do you not believe in the proper order of things, Genevieve, that there are some in the world who must be rich and some who must be poor?"

He is simply stating what most believe, what I've heard from the pulpit and read in the newspapers. Yet his indifference chills me.

"Believe me, Sir, Genevieve is not one for the proper order of anything," groans my grandfather. With a start, he seems to remember that the point of this dinner is my rehabilitation. "Tell us," he says, "how the porcelain formula was obtained in the West. You are so very knowledgeable on the topic. Now there are manufactories all over Europe. What is the one called outside Paris? Sèvres?"

"Yes," says Sir Gabriel. "Sèvres is the name."

Grandfather muses, "They say its porcelain is exquisite. How did we reach this level of achievement so quickly? What was the breakthrough?"

Sir Gabriel says, "I'll tell the story only if Genevieve wishes to hear it."

It's as if there is an invisible rope stretching between us at the table. First he pulls me; then I yank it back. But I never have it for long. He grabs hold of the rope again, trying to pull me toward him.

The difficulty of it is, I *do* want to hear more.

"Please continue," I say.

"Some attribute the breakthrough to a French Jesuit who stole a written formula in China while pretending to minister to those in the factory who converted to Christianity," he says. "With a great amount of difficulty, the Jesuit, Father François Xavier d'Entrecolles, was able to smuggle the formula out in letters to Paris. But the true father of it all was a man named Johann Bottger. A German chemist, like your Dippel. He was able to decipher the mystery of porcelain while imprisoned. He was the only one to understand, without espionage, the formula."

"He was a criminal?" says Grandfather.

"Bottger was guilty of having dreams that were dangerous," Sir Gabriel says, turning to Grandfather. But I know he is talking to me. *I* am the one with dangerous dreams.

"He came from a family of shopkeepers and studied to be a chemist, night and day. Bottger was brilliant. In school he stumbled upon texts on alchemy, and that became his fateful passion. He was convinced he could be the one to discover the elixir of life, the philosopher's stone — able to turn base metal into gold. He insisted he could do it, and that brought him to the attention of the most powerful and ruthless men in Germany. Men like Frederick the Great and Augustus the Strong."

"Such names the Germans give themselves," chuckles Grandfather. "Why was he called 'the Strong'?"

"It was said he could break an iron horseshoe with his bare hands," says Sir Gabriel. "There is another reason — he was said to have fathered three hundred children by dozens of women. I apologize for this indelicacy, Mistress Genevieve."

I laugh. "Do you think I'm sheltered from the ways of the world? We all know about Madame de Pompadour, how King Louis XV is enslaved by his favorite mistress."

Sir Gabriel stares at me over the table before saying, "Beauty makes its demands."

"Tell us more about Augustus the Strong," says Grandfather.

"The ruler of Saxony was a man accustomed to spending much more than he had in his treasury. He threw Bottger in prison in Dresden to make sure he didn't escape or get kidnapped while he tried to conjure up gold. The chemist was twenty-three years old."

"Just about the same age as Genevieve," comments Grandfather.

"But why would he do such a thing?" I ask, my heart pounding. "There is no such thing as a philosopher's stone; it's a myth. Bottger was brilliant, you say, so he knew that he could never succeed in producing gold, and yet he made such a rumple."

"Tell us more," Grandfather pleads.

"Augustus the Strong came close to having Bottger executed several times. 'Where is my gold?' he would bellow, but he always spared him, in the faint hope that his captive chemist would succeed. There was another scientist, Ehrenfried Walther Von Tschirnhaus, working in Dresden, conducting experiments in an attempt to duplicate Chinese porcelain. Bottger was ordered to assist him, and that is when he diverted his skills. He was trying to stay alive. At the time, porcelain was as valuable as gold in Europe. It took ten years, but Bottger discovered that the secret to the substance is not the heat of the kiln, or the mixture of clay with other substances, but the *variety* of the clay itself. Through his experiments, he identified a mine for the correct clay in Germany, and the perfect proportions of mixture and… voila! Europe had its first original porcelain and its first true workshop, the Meissen Manufactory, which started production in 1710."

I whisper, "He was forced to do this for *ten years*?"

Sir Gabriel nods.

"But once he had discovered the formula, didn't Augustus free him?" asks Grandfather.

"Eventually," says Sir Gabriel. "Pressure of another kind became a problem — the jealousy of the other princes, and their determination to steal the Meissen formula. Spies were sent from every corner of Europe."

"But he was freed — Bottger was freed?" I must know the rest of the story. It's as if the bars of Bottger's prison pin me back.

"By the time Augustus freed him, it didn't much matter. The imprisonment broke Bottger in body and spirit, he was dead before forty. Some say the man drank himself to death." He must see by my expression how distressed I am, for Sir Gabriel leans across the table, determined to make his point. "Because of his dream, porcelain is worshipped throughout Europe. Workshops throughout Germany, in Austria, France, and here, in England, not just Derby but Chelsea and Bow and Worcester. All determined to come up with the most beautiful pieces."

Grandfather says, "There is always some subterfuge in this porcelain business, then?"

"Yes," says Sir Gabriel, but looking only at me. "Such practices are a necessity for the creation of this beauty, Mistress Genevieve. You see that?"

I rise to my feet. "I see what happens when you lose control of your dream."

Puzzlement tightens Sir Gabriel's smooth brow. "Shall I have the pleasure of your company again before you leave for Derby?" he asks.

"Good night, Sir," I say. "And... I thank you for my earring."

With that, I walk upstairs, to take hold of my own destiny.

CHAPTER FIVE

Just before midnight, that very same night, I tilt my head back and snowflakes rest on my nose, my lips. I close my eyes and flakes melt into my lashes.

"Pull up your shawl, Gen," says Denis.

"No," I say. "I like this." I open my eyes and it's as if we are under a funnel, here on the roof of my Fournier Street home, with snowflakes streaming straight down from a black London sky.

Denis hugs me tighter with his left arm; he grips the side of the chimney with his right. He kisses my cheek, hard enough that I can feel the scratches on his lips. There's exultance in his kiss and a trace of surprise. Here we sit, waiting for our chance to scramble down to the street unobserved, intending to leave London tonight, forever. All I have in my satchel are a second dress and shift and stockings, my paintbrushes, my dead mother's Huguenot cross, my dead father's watch, and, of course, my money.

I am not certain how much I love Denis at this moment. I agree with his beliefs and enjoy his kisses, while my heart stays quiet, well guarded. Still, I'm ready to throw in my fate with his.

"I have family in New York City," I whisper to Denis. "There is a

Billiou who sailed there a century ago. Grandfather told me about a cousin who founded his own island."

"I've friends living in Boston, but if you wish to go to New York, then New York it shall be, Gen." Denis kisses me again. "Just now, though, we must apply ourselves to getting off this roof."

*

Once I'd written my note to Grandfather and gathered my bundle, we had made our escape. All was quiet in the house. The excitement of our dinner had taken its toll on Grandfather; he trudged upstairs shortly after Sir Gabriel left. Listening at my open door, I heard him fussing over his canaries, whispering his good-nights. I even heard "Genevieve." He was discussing me with the birds! That made my heart twist, to think how my running away would cause him grief and worry.

Once the noises of the house had died down, I left my note and we tip-toed down the stairs heading for the door to Fournier Street. That choice of exit was made impossible by the sight of George, sleeping on a pallet near the door. He sometimes does that, after a day of distur-bance. We'd never be able to open the heavy, creaking door without waking him.

Denis, among his other talents, knows how to creep in and out of houses. He climbed in through our window in the back of the attic this afternoon, and now, with great care, we left the same way.

Instead of going down, though, we hoisted ourselves up to the roof to wait our time.

*

"Too many people still on the streets," explains Denis. "It's one thing for a man to be seen climbing about. But we can't take the chance of someone seeing us come down together, particularly on a street where you've lived all your life." And on a street where everyone knows I was once engaged to Denis Arsenault, wanted criminal.

If anyone were to see this nocturnal adventure, there'd be shouts for the bailiff. I'm risking a great deal by running away with him.

Squinting into the snow, Denis says, "There's a perfect span of time, when most every Huguenot apprentice has stumbled home and the night watch isn't patrolling this part of the parish — that is when I'll help you down." He blows into his fingers. "I pray we don't freeze to the bone while we wait."

"Don't worry about me," I say. I barely feel the cold. Climbing out the window, sitting atop my house, the swirling sky above, is intoxicating, an infinitely more potent experience than sipping Madeira with Sir Gabriel Courtenay.

Denis shuffles over to the edge of the roof, peers down. A thin layer of snow covers his dark coat and breeches, making him blend in with the roof. If someone should happen to look out of the window from across the street, they'd not notice anything amiss.

He signals to me, grinning. The time has come.

We don't climb down from my own house. Its sheer brick surfaces, front and back, lack grooves to hang onto. Near the end of the block, within sight of church, is a different sort of building; newer, with wide horizontal ledges. Denis leading, we walk across the tops of four houses and I climb down, face near-pressed to the cold wall, without a stumble, though my skirts threaten to tangle twice.

Tonight, the streets are empty. We take our first steps to freedom. L'Eglise de l'Hôpital on Brick Lane stares down at me. I've knelt in the church pews, hands clasped, saying my prayers, hundreds of times. Yet I've never seen the church like this: not a single candle lit, silent, empty.

Go back, the church intones. Like a silent peal of warning. I shudder. This must be the cold finally settling into my bones.

Denis grabs my hand and, shaking off my nerves, I scurry around the corner — and straight into two men standing in front of a shuttered shop.

"Oooooh," I cry in surprise, spinning back.

"Ha!" cries one of the other men, as shocked as I am.

Denis quickly pulls me back, so that he's half in front of me, a barrier between the pair of them and myself. I peer around him, studying their faces. Even at night, I should be able to recognize fellow Huguenots.

I've never seen either of these men in my life. Both are somewhere between twenty and thirty, wigless and wearing dark clothes; the one who shouted "Ha!" wears a tricorne hat. The other is shorter and stouter.

Not one of us says a word.

Denis is the first to move. He springs into the center of the street, pulling me with him, satchels bouncing on his back. We turn up the street and break into a trot. When Denis pauses in front of the butcher's shop, I look over my shoulder, back toward the church. The two men stand in the middle of the street, dark forms outlined against the snow. Not moving. Not calling out. But watching us.

"Who were they?" I ask Denis.

"No notion," he answers, breathless. "We need to get to Charlotte's."

"I fear there's something wrong. Why are they standing in front of a closed butcher's shop, near midnight? They aren't drunk or…" I turn around again. My heart skips a beat. The two men are now on the move — in our direction.

"They're following us," I say.

Denis curses. We run as fast as we dare, down this street and up another, hugging the buildings, fearing both the men who trail us and the appearance of the night watch. We aren't completely alone on the frigid streets. Other stray shadowy people move in the doorways or the alleys.

"We should circle back to Fournier Street," I say. "This is too dangerous. Those two men may want to rob us — and we can't cry for help because we can't turn to the law."

"Then we'll just stay out of their way," Denis insists. "We must get to Charlotte's tonight and out of London by dawn."

Denis' older sister, Charlotte, a widow with a young boy, lives on the edge of Spitalfields, meaning we still have three or four streets to go. There is no use in trying to persuade Denis to change his mind. He's hell-bent on leaving London.

"Trust me," he breathes into my ear.

I wish he hadn't said that.

Denis leads me past the rows of snow-covered buildings. The streets are unearthly silent because of the white blanket at our feet. We have no choice but to walk slowly. The snow cleanses the streets of their common filth; less helpfully, it obscures those gaping cracks and narrow ditches that could trip one, even break an ankle. Sure enough, in the middle of the street I step onto what feels like hard surface, until the ice breaks and my right foot plunges into several inches of freezing water.

Denis helps me yank free but not before the water seeps into my shoe. My toes burn and ache.

How relieved I am when Denis pauses in front of a vast brick structure. "Almost there," he whispers, and starts to maneuver his way around the corner.

"Stop!" I yank his sleeve, pointing at a yellow glow quivering on the street before us. It must be the lantern of the approaching night watch.

We scramble backward, groping for an alley, an archway, even a pillar to hide behind before the watchman makes the turn. This building is so big, we can't get to the end of it in time. As the glow brightens, I can hear the crunch of the watchman's boots. He's a yard from appearing at the head of the street. Once the lantern shines, we will be visible. Denis flattens himself in a shallow doorway, pulling me in beside him. This is not much of a concealment, but we've run out of time.

I hear a whistle as well as a crunch and the full yellow glow of the lantern emerges. The watchman is here. Denis and I stand absolutely still. I try to still my breathing.

The watchman starts in our direction.

He comes a few feet closer and pauses, his back is to us. He holds his lantern high, peering this way and that. We are seconds from discovery. I reach with my smallest finger for Denis' hand … and brush against a hard, quivering fist. He's preparing to strike.

I pull my hand back. To attack a watchman is a reprehensible crime. We'd both hang for it.

The watchman turns in profile — he has a beaked nose over a snow-tinged moustache — and I wait for him to come around the rest of the way and shine his lantern in our faces, to expose us. We're so very close to him, but he does not know it.

The watchman takes a step in his original direction, and another. The whistle resumes. He walks up the street without ever turning to spot us.

We wait for him to move a safe distance away, and in that moment I think about the route we've taken. It would be vastly dangerous to return to Fournier Street alone, and I'm cold to the bone, shivering, my right foot half-numb, but I don't want to continue with Denis. I cannot countenance violence.

As I open my mouth to tell him I'm parting from him, he grabs my hand with a sharp inhale.

On the edge of the fading lantern light across the street, where the yellow melts into darkness, two forms emerge from a deep archway. It's the men we saw at the church, I recognize one of them by the shape of his tricorne hat. They tracked Denis and me all the way here and hid from the watchman, as we did.

The two men are definitely hunting us.

Denis doesn't need to pull me after him around the corner. I run as fast as he does down the street, narrower than the ones before. I look over my shoulder, but it's too dark to see if they're still on our heels.

This is Charlotte's street, and Denis fumbles at a door. I hear the click of a key turning in a lock and Denis pushes inside, pulling me in behind him. We pant with exhaustion.

I find myself in a small room. As my eyes adjust to the light, I make out a table and two hardback chairs. Denis disappears across the room to peer up the stairs, then returns to lead me across by the hand. "She's awake," he says.

My foot still aching, I follow him up the narrow wooden stairs to a room with candlelight streaming under the closed door, its bottom hanging two inches above the floor.

"Charlotte?" he says, tapping on the door. "It's Denis — and I have Genevieve with me. Charlotte?"

Silence.

"Perhaps she's fallen asleep with the candle lit?" I suggest.

"Not like her to do that," he says. As he grips the doorknob and turns, a sickening shudder runs through me, not unlike how I felt seeing those two men across the street. I open my mouth to say, "stop," but Denis slides inside the room. I can do nothing but follow.

What I see makes me stop short. A tallow candle burns brightly on a small table next to a bed not slept in. A man sits on the edge of it, his legs swung over and hanging off the side of the bed. He wears a green frockcoat, a heavyset man about forty years of age with a mottled red nose, an unlit pipe in his hand.

"Hello, Denis," the man says, setting the pipe down on the bed. And smirks.

As Denis whirls around, someone else, coming up behind, shoves me to the side and I hit the wall, spinning off it. But what happens to Denis is worse. The same man who pushed me grabs Denis by the collar and hits him square in the face. A sickening crack fills the room.

Denis slumps to the floor. With a tremendous effort, he gets to his knees, clinging to the side of the bed, trying to stand.

"Denis!" I start toward him, but the second man grabs me by the arm and pulls me back, smashing me into his hard chest. I don't see his face, but I smell him: The man reeks of gin and rank sweat.

The green-clad man on the bed asks, "Denis, did you truly think you could gammon me at my table and there'd be no consequences?"

"I didn't cheat, Harry," groans Denis, rubbing his jaw, swaying on his feet.

"What is this, Denis?" I demand.

He doesn't say anything, but continues to rub his jaw.

"What have you done?" I shout.

"Ah, the women are always such pitiful fools," says the man behind me, tightening his hold on my arms. I turn to see who it is: a broken-toothed ruffian with filthy blond hair.

Harry chuckles and nods to me — or rather, to the ruffian behind me. While still gripping me with one hand, my captor, with his other hand, sticks me just under the chin with something very sharp.

Denis looks at me, at whatever it is pricking me, with horror. "Don't hurt her," he pleads.

I have a knife to my throat.

Fear and rage fight for uppermost emotion, with fear winning out. I do not move a muscle.

Harry says soothingly, "I'm a gentleman, Denis, unlike you. I've no wish to hurt this lovely young woman. Whether I do so or not depends on you."

Never have I despised Denis more than at this moment.

"You were too stupid to realize it, Denis, but the man you talked to on the first night, at table, the man you thought a friend, works for me and repeats everything said. So I *know* you hit London without a sixpence to scratch with. You told him you planned to wheedle money out of your lady-bird or your sister for your travel across the ocean."

I close my eyes, unable to bear this.

"It wasn't difficult to learn the females' names — you're a famous criminal, after all. Many gabsters have heard of you. Then, even though you already robbed me, I knew you'd be greedy, you'd want more for the big sail. It was just a matter of picking a female and waiting for you to show yourself. Didn't realize you'd bring your lady-bird here with you."

"Where in God's name is my sister?" asks Denis, his voice breaking.

Harry says, in that same horribly soothing voice, "Your sister is unharmed. She was, er, *encouraged* to take her boy and stay with a friend for a couple of days. Now, let's commence with —"

A loud click silences Harry. His eyes widen as he stares at something over my head.

"What you're going to do is lower your knife, slowly, very slowly," says a low, rumbling voice behind me. It's not the one belonging to the man holding the knife. It's a voice new to this room, yet it's one that I've heard before.

The voice continues: "You're in a hobble, my friend. That's quite the knife you brought, you fancy yourself a right busker. But if you don't drop it to the floor, first I will shoot you in the back of the head with this flintlock. Nice spray of brains all cross the room. Quite a mess it will make. Your boss is probably thinking that's no great loss, he can find a way to hurt me while I reload, that I'll never be able to shoot both of you. But the problem with that is… I am not alone."

Harry stares at the blond ruffian, all trace of a smile gone from his face. He nods, once, his lips twisting. Someone else must have appeared behind the gravel-voiced man. This home is filling up with frightening men. Why?

The quivering pinch of the knife is gone. I hear a clunk as it hits the floor.

The deep voice says: "Good. Thank you. Now I need you to step away from the lady."

Once freed, I turn to get a look at my liberators. Two men stand in the doorway. To my astonishment, I've seen them before, though not together. The one holding a pistol is the bearded man from Spitalfields Market who frightened me. The man standing behind him, also armed, wears a tricorne hat — he followed Denis and me here.

"Two of you are wanted downstairs," says the bearded man. While I watch, stunned, his associate takes Denis and ties his hands behind his back, then he does the same to the man who held a knife to my throat. I am not tied, nor is Harry, the despicable gambler. We are the two chosen to go downstairs — but why?

"Gen, I have to talk to you," says Denis. "You can't believe anything that he —"

"Shut up," I say.

"Gen, for the love of God…"

"Shut up. Or else I'll pick up that knife and finish you myself."

Someone chuckles.

The bearded man leads Harry and me out of the room. My plans have collapsed under the weight of lies. Of violence. And yet, I am certain that it is all about to get worse.

Downstairs, in the small sitting room of Denis' sister, flames soar in a freshly lit fireplace. One man sits in the hard-back chair in the middle of the room. I freeze on the steps and nearly stumble.

Sir Gabriel Courtenay, wigless but still wearing his Prussian blue frockcoat, looks at me with those somber dark eyes, set in a pale face.

"What — what are *you* doing here?" I manage to ask.

He smiles. "One of your most singular characteristics, Genevieve, is a complete and utter lack of gratitude."

Harry blusters, "I'd like to know your bloody name and what makes you think you can interfere in my affairs."

My grandfather's dinner guest smiles.

"My name," he says, "is Mr. Sommerville."

CHAPTER SIX

I don't contradict him. I don't say his real name. Instead, I stumble down the rest of the stairs and take the chair that Sir Gabriel Courtenay pulls out for me at the plain wooden table. I'm numb. It's as if a lever were pulled down on my ability to think.

Harry, the gambler, is not invited to sit. With each passing moment, his face turns a deeper shade of scarlet as he snarls his curses, spit flying from his lips. Denis, myself, Sir Gabriel, we are all subjects of his foul names. Some I've heard before, most I haven't.

Sir Gabriel, arms folded, shows no reaction. When Harry pauses to draw breath, Sir Gabriel says, perfectly calm, "I'd like to speak to you as a man of business."

This leads to a round of fresh insults, which Sir Gabriel listens to with perfect patience until Harry exhausts both his repertoire of curses and his breath, and pauses.

Sir Gabriel interjects. "If you would present me with an accounting of Denis Arsenault's theft from your establishment, I'm prepared to compensate you in full."

I do not know who is more shocked, Harry or myself. A transformed man, he eagerly names the figure of seventy-three guineas. I wait for

Sir Gabriel to reject the sum, but he does not. He opens his coat and pulls out a purse of coins for counting.

I wonder whether this Mr. Sommerville, at ease in the criminal world, is the real man and Sir Gabriel Courtenay an imposter. But then I remember how everyone smiled and bowed and murmured greetings at William Hogarth's home, how the artist's pug rested its nose on a trusted knee. He is a man who belongs in that world, the beau monde of London, a world that is impossible to gain entry to without wealth and position. How is this possible?

Paid off, a satisfied Harry struts out of the door, his sullen henchman, the blond ruffian who held a knife to my throat, in his wake.

"I would like to know precisely what is happening," I say, the moment the door shuts behind them. "Why did you follow me here, Sir? Why did you buy that man off? What do you want?"

"You limped a bit on the stairs," Sir Gabriel counters. "What's wrong?"

"It's nothing. Answer my questions."

"You nearly had your throat cut tonight, you're frozen to the bone, and you've possibly injured your foot — this is nothing?"

As soon as I tell him, reluctantly, of stumbling into cold slush outside, Sir Gabriel is out of his chair and kneeling at my feet. He lifts my skirt to untie the laces of my shoes.

"Stop this," I cry, appalled, wriggling away from him.

"Genevieve, listen," he says, showing me as much patience as he did Harry. "I'm no rake. I am interested in your welfare because I wish to offer you employment. The kind of employment that would change your life."

"What are you talking about?" I sputter. "I should work for you?"

"Correct. I was intending to build up to this proposal over a series of social engagements — the Art Society, the opera — but your nocturnal escapade has rather forced the issue."

He hasn't risen. Sir Gabriel sits back on his heels, his assessing stare fixed on me. The fire is behind him, creating a reddish-gold halo around his smooth, dark head.

"What could I possibly do for you?" I ask.

"Take the position in Derby. There's something I need within that porcelain workshop, and you will be ideally placed to obtain it."

On one level, this makes sense. Sir Gabriel Courtenay is an avid connoisseur of porcelain; he was able to summon up the details of its history at dinner. Now that I know of his interest, it explains why he was drawn to me at Hogarth's, and why he contrived to come to Fournier Street the following evening. But the man is obviously wealthy. What could I get for him that he couldn't get for himself, by paying for it?

I open my mouth, but he says, "I realize you have many questions, and I promise to answer them. First I need to tend to your well-being, and second, we really must deal with your friend, Denis Arsenault."

"He's not my friend."

"I'm glad to hear it," he says with a smile. "If you wish to remain by his side after tonight's revelations, you're far too stupid to be of any use to me."

To be of any use to me.

With that, his hands are firmly on my boots, pulling at the sodden laces, easing them off along with the loosened stocking. When my cold, cramped feet meet the bare air, I feel exposed. I pull my skirts forward.

Sir Gabriel rises but only to shift his attention to cleaning my face with a damp cloth, his movements gentle and precise. He is so close, I can smell the faint Jasmine scent clinging to him. "You've been through quite an ordeal," he comments.

I wince when the cloth presses my throat at the point where I was stuck with a knife.

"Are you wearing a necklace?" he asks, pulling at the slender silver-gilt chain that holds my most precious object. I try to pull it away from him, but he's already got hold.

"A Huguenot cross," he says, thoughtfully, looking at its design, its eight points of light.

"It was my mother's," I whisper.

His expression changes. From the way I said *mother*, he must realize the depth of my emotion. Sir Gabriel reaches for the candle and holds it close to examine my ravaged throat. "There's hardly any bleeding," he says. "Still, there's a visible mark." He considers what to do. "You'll have to wear one of those soft velvet ribbons around your throat tomorrow, a wide one, can you manage that?"

I nod, embarrassed by his knowledge of women's things, by his tending to me, by his nearness. But that is nothing compared to what comes next.

Sir Gabriel is back on his knees. He lifts my naked foot onto his lap and cleans it with the warm, damp cloth. The warmth sends a tickling jolt through my entire body. I recoil, crying, "Sir Gabriel!"

He grabs my ankle with his other hand. He's stronger than I expected. "Just a moment," he murmurs.

He finishes cleaning my foot and precisely folds the cloth over, twice, leaving it on the floor, next to a table leg.

Mistaking the source of my discomfort, he says, "You don't have to see or hear from Arsenault again, I'll see to that. He can be dispensed with. I don't want you upset."

"How do you know about our plans?"

"I'm a man who harbors suspicions that often turn out to be true," he says, a smile curling. "I heard someone walking above us at dinner and observed your reaction to the suggestion someone investigate. I'd made inquiries about you, and therefore I knew of the man's existence, though it was commonly believed he had gone into hiding in Ireland. I wasn't sure who was upstairs. But based on the way you said good-night to me at your grandfather's table, I knew something was going to happen, and soon."

"So you waited outside for us to emerge — or rather, your men did."

He nods. "I had to be careful with how I made use of Jimmy after you confronted him in Spitalfields Market." He looks past me. "Isn't that right, Jimmy?"

I look over my shoulder. The bearded man stares back at me, his expression stony. He rescued me from a terrifying fate upstairs, yet I find little comfort in his presence.

"I think you're the first person Jimmy's tailed who called him out — and a woman, to top it," chuckles Sir Gabriel. "I fear he may hold that against you. Now, on to our business. Shall we bring Arsenault down or do you wish this done out of your presence?"

"Bring him down," I say.

Denis doesn't curse when he comes down the same stairs that Harry took. He's rubbing wrists that must have been recently freed, and eying us cautiously.

As I look at my onetime betrothed, the rage recedes and I'm left with disappointment, so bitter it's as if my mouth were filled with cold ashes.

Jimmy tosses Denis' satchel to Sir Gabriel. He pulls out some papers and examines them. "Passage for one on the St Jean de Baptiste, leaving in one week's time," he says. "Presuming you told Genevieve she was going with you, what was she to be, a stowaway? I think it far more likely you would discard her along the road to Plymouth after taking her money."

"Of course not. That's why I needed the gambling wages — to purchase passage for her," Denis counters.

"But if you did that, there wouldn't be much money left. The American colonies are built on slavery and smuggling. They say it's a rich man's paradise and a poor man's hell," says Sir Gabriel. "I find it hard to believe you'd sail there with so few coins in your pocket. You'd be one step up from indentured servant."

"I don't care what you believe," says Denis, turning to me. "Gen, please, you have to listen."

My voice shaking, I say, "You never stop lying. Never."

Denis says, pointing at Sir Gabriel, "And you believe this man is telling you anything approaching the truth? I recognize his voice from the dinner in your house. What is he about here? I've made my mistakes, God knows it and may never forgive me, but I care for you, Gen. He doesn't. He's got some sort of long game."

Sir Gabriel says, dismissively, "I never, ever play games, long or short. Now are you going to leave quietly tonight for Plymouth with your money, or are we going to set you loose on the streets without a shilling? It's safe to assume you'd swing on Tyburn's tree."

Denis says, "Ah, so I'm the bad apprentice, is it? Wouldn't your Hogarth be gratified, Gen? Perhaps he could paint another episode in the story."

I don't answer him. The handsome, bold, intelligent man I loved is gone, replaced by this bitter criminal.

"Very well," Denis says, his voice still defiant. "On to America."

Sir Gabriel says, "My man Edward will escort you — and be sure you board the right ship."

The man with the tricorne hat, who must be Edward, collects the satchel and nudges Denis toward the door. I notice for the first time that his companion on the street, the stout man, is standing in the doorway.

Denis grabs hold of the doorframe and turns to look at me. "Be careful, I beg you," he says. "This business of his, whatever it may be, is dangerous." And then Denis is gone, swallowed up in the snowy night.

I hear liquid hitting glass. It's Sir Gabriel, holding a long bottle. He's already poured himself something. Now the bottle hovers over a second glass. I wave my hand, wearily. "No spirits," I say.

"All the woman has is ale, but I think you may need it," he says. "I certainly do."

I shake my head again.

He downs his drink and says, "No tears. Excellent."

I'm silent. I feel too weary, not just in my body but in my spirit, to weep over Denis.

"I'll give him this — the man possesses bravado," says Sir Gabriel. "What do you say, Jimmy?"

"The sort that'll tighten a rope round his neck, just like he says, Sir," answers Jimmy. The two of them share a laugh, one that I can't join in.

"Now," says Sir Gabriel, "on to the matter at hand. Genevieve, you despise the very thought of being a porcelain decorator. You threw yourself at the feet of Hogarth to escape from it, you were willing to toss in your lot with a wanted criminal to flee England rather than submit to the Derby manufactory."

I swallow and say, "Correct."

"You want to be a true artist. Not one of those timid girls enrolled at watercolour classes at the Academy. Someone following in the footsteps of Hogarth. And there's no one of real stature in England — not the man himself, not a painter of similar talent — who will agree to teach you history painting, composition, the things you must learn to be an artist of significance because you're a woman. Is that correct?"

I nod, not having any idea where the conversation is leading.

"I think it quite possible you could find the life you seek, but not in England," he says.

"But in France they are even stricter about forbidding women from taking lessons in art," I say.

"True. But you omit Italy. I am absolutely certain that in Venice a woman of talent could find a master to teach her, could aspire to the heights of artistic achievement. No one would stop you, no one would disapprove. It's an enlightened city. A licentious city, too, but I think you could learn to cope with that."

I burst into a laugh, as bitter as one of Denis'. "How would I ever be able to travel to Italy and take up residence as an artist?"

Sir Gabriel leans across the shabby table of Denis' sister. "With five thousand pounds in your purse," he says.

"And where would I get *that*?" Suspicion continues to curdle my words.

"From me."

There is no possible response to such an extraordinary offer.

He says, slowly and carefully, "Genevieve, I'll give you that sum of money if first you work for me — in total secrecy — at the Derby Porcelain workshop."

Bewildered, I say, "If you possess such an enormous amount, why hire me to steal from the factory? You can buy any porcelain with that kind of money."

"I don't want an object, Genevieve." His dark eyes burn into mine. "I seek a color."

A shiver runs through me, no less powerful than what I felt outside the Huguenot church hours ago.

I whisper, "Blue."

He reaches across the table and takes my hand in his smooth, cool palm. "I knew that you understood, at dinner."

I pull my hand free. "But I don't — I don't understand you. Blue is blue. There are many different shades, yes, yet the colors are the same for any artist."

"Not the blue created at Derby Porcelain Works," he says, shaking his head, as if in wonder still over something glimpsed.

"And you want me to be your... spy."

"Yes. I do. Very much."

My next question is, how is it possible for Derby to make such a profound discovery.

"They've secured a young chemist who created an entirely new shade of blue somewhere, somehow," Sir Gabriel says. "More than a shade. It's a different way of *seeing* blue."

I couldn't help but scoff at that.

"I would be as skeptical as you, Genevieve, but I've held it in my own hands. The painted porcelain was transcendent. Far more beautiful than the best of the new, modern blues. It's been analyzed, studied, tested — and the source is unknown. Just like the story you told of Dippel, in Berlin, with *his* new form of blue. You said it took years for rival chemists to break it down. I'm afraid we don't have that kind of time."

"Who is 'we'?"

He shakes his head as he says, "There is no advantage in your knowing who my associates are. Suffice to say that color is the next field of battle in the porcelain wars. He who is able to produce the most porcelain in this new revolutionary color of blue will control the market. A vast fortune will be made."

Perhaps it is the lateness of the hour, but I can't make sense of this argument. "It seems to me that if Derby has a chemist employed who's discovered the new blue, then they have won this war already."

Sir Gabriel says, "Derby has talent — and vision — but a small staff and limited capital. And there seem to be challenges with the chemical stability of the color." Sir Gabriel straightens in his chair. "Before I continue with the details of the operation, though, I must have your answer, Genevieve."

There are a dozen emotions warring within me. How could I even attempt to explain? That my admiration for his mixture of high-flying knowledge and base cleverness is undercut by a strong distrust. And beyond my feelings for the man himself, when it comes to the criminal task he offers, I react with an undeniable… distaste. And that would surely offend him.

I look past him, into the fire, and say softly, "A very quaint invisible devil in flesh — an intelligencer."

He reacts in shock. "Are you quoting from the play *The Duchess of Malfi*?"

I nod.

"You are a singular person, Genevieve," he says, laughing. "So I suppose this means that a woman of your background is displeased at the thought of spying."

I blurt, "I should think that it would be an even greater problem for someone of your background."

Something flashes in his eyes — anger? Amusement? Then Sir Gabriel offers a smile. "There are invisible circumstances guiding my actions," he says.

I study him for a moment. "Sir, I shall need to know more about your motives than 'invisible circumstances.' "

Staring back at me, he says, "At your grandfather's table I told you what I believe, that it is the proper order of things that some people must be rich and others must be poor. I take the necessary steps to ensure that I am in the former group and not the latter."

So you're nothing but a mercenary.

I'm not sure why but I feel a twist of disappointment as sharp as when I learned that Denis was gambling again.

"This is how it's done, Genevieve, how businesses are born, fortunes made," Sir Gabriel says. "Almost always, the advantage is gained by spying. The entire foundation of the porcelain industry is built on stealing formulas for the clay mixture itself or the designs. It's not just porcelain, either. In Derby, the same city you're bound for, there's a respectable silk factory, the first one in England, created through means of subterfuge."

"I've heard about it from Grandfather," I say. "They use a machine to do what human hands cannot. It causes some alarm here in Spitalfields."

"As it should. John Lombe, the Englishman who founded the silk mill, based his machine on those he learned about — and found a way to use — in a factory in Italy," says Sir Gabriel. "He copied them and then fled back to England."

A memory stirs. "Grandfather also told me that John Lombe met a bad end because of what he did."

Sir Gabriel tilts his head, regarding me in silence for a moment, before saying, "Yes, he came to a very bad end. He was murdered and almost certainly by poison administered by an Italian assassin. The Italian friends he betrayed, exacted vengeance for the theft."

"I see."

"I know that you despise liars, Genevieve, and so I must be honest with you on this point. In the business of spying, there is always risk. I have resources, I will teach you and provide you with the support and protection you need. Still… there is risk. I hope that you will conclude that the reward is great enough to take the risk."

In this moment I make the decision. For someone to approach me like this, truthfully, presenting me with all I would need to make the decision, including the risks, was almost as persuasive as the large reward itself. Sir Gabriel is right about so many things. I *do* wish to be an artist, to lead a life of significance, to matter, and each time I've tried to pursue this life straightforwardly and honestly it's been denied me. This is my last — and my only — chance.

"I agree," I tell Sir Gabriel.

He gives a great sigh, his shoulders lower, and he closes his eyes. For a moment I wonder at the importance of this color to him. Or perhaps it's purely the amount of money at stake that triggers this depth of feeling.

"What is the next step?" I ask.

"Rest," he says emphatically. "You cannot appear exhausted and upset in your grandfather's house."

"I'm not sure how to return home as if nothing happened."

"But nothing can appear out of the ordinary in your life now. We must find a way to reinsert you into your grandfather's house — and not by way of the roof— before he awakens. And you must act as normally as possible. Pierre may take notice if you've had no sleep at all; he may question you. It is now past two in the morning. Too dangerous to travel with you through the city, even this short a distance. You shall sleep a few hours and then, at dawn, we'll work you back in."

"George is given his errands in the morning, before Grandfather wakes," I tell him. "While he's out of the house I can slip inside. Daphne's domain at that hour is the kitchen below. She won't hear me. I'll slip in then, and destroy the note I left for him."

Sir Gabriel smiles.

"I can see that you are going to be an exceptional pupil."

CHAPTER SEVEN

It is midday and Grandfather sits in his library in his favorite chair, the London newspaper in his lap. I haven't seen him or spoken to him since I slipped back in the house shortly after dawn, exactly as Sir Gabriel and I planned.

As I stand in the doorway, my heart hammering, the velvet ribbon around my throat feels as if it's choking me. "Good day," I say, too loudly, I fear.

Grandfather glances up, returns my greeting, and returns to his newspaper. "I'm greatly worried about the progress of this war," he frets. "British soldiers are sent to colonies far, far away, but French soldiers are close by, fighting across Germany. Once spring comes, what if the battles should come to England — who would fight for us here?"

Taking a seat, I say, "We live on a stoutly defended island. Do you really think the French would attempt it?"

Grandfather folds his newspaper and scrutinizes me. I wait for him to detect a change, to find some proof in my appearance that I endured a terrible night and made a fateful decision.

He says, "You must never underestimate King Louis. And should

France defeat England in this war and gain any sort of control, you know who would be the first to suffer?"

"The Huguenots." I've heard these fears before — they are whispered up and down Spitalfields. Grandfather doesn't usually give in to it. Perhaps last night's wine and food have worsened his gout and darkened his mood.

"The French crown would no doubt like to finish what was begun at the St Bartholomew Massacre," he mutters.

Now this is extreme melancholy, to evoke the massacre. It is something every Huguenot refugee carries in his or her soul every minute of the day, the knowledge that in Paris, Catholics once turned on the Protestant minority and butchered men, women, and children without mercy. But we rarely speak of it.

"Perhaps we can throw ourselves at the feet of Madame de Pompadour and beg the King's harlot for mercy," I say.

It works. Grandfather chuckles. "Genevieve, you are outrageous."

George appears at that moment, holding a sealed envelope for Grandfather. I know who sent it, of course. I do my best to look surprised when Grandfather informs me that Sir Gabriel Courtenay extends an invitation to the Art Academy in three days' time.

Grandfather is far less enthusiastic than I expected. "Are you certain you wish to go with him?" he asks.

"Why wouldn't I?"

"I was under the distinct impression last night that you didn't altogether like Sir Gabriel." He hesitates and then pushes on: "And perhaps that would be best. I am grateful that he returned your earrings and that he seems disposed to speak well of us to others. Overall I found Sir Gabriel an admirable gentleman, an engaging dinner guest, knowledgeable on art, but after all there can't be any sort of ongoing friendship between you, Genevieve. We don't belong in his circle."

"I am aware of that. And I know I spoke dismissively of the Art Academy. But I would like to go."

Grandfather peers at me, openly dubious. I'm failing at this; I'm not a convincing liar.

"Genevieve, your future lies in Derby," he says. "Three weeks after Christmas, your cousin, Andrew Planché, will take you to the porcelain factory."

"I couldn't agree more. My future is in Derby."

He gives a large sigh, relieved, and pats my hand. I wait to feel guilt wash over me for deceiving the person who brought me up. And... I don't. What a curious experience, to learn the truth of one's own character.

*

Those next days, instead of feeling burdened by the knowledge of my criminal compact, I find I move with lightness and freedom, inhabited by a ferocious energy. When Daphne announces she is planning a dinner of beef bourguignon, I insist on purchasing a pork strip at Spitalfields Market and stand by her side, treating the beef, readying it for the wine, onions, and mushrooms. That same day, I stretch canvas for Grandfather, who is, to my delight, embarking on a new painting.

What's strange is I do not sleep more than a few hours at night. My limbs are heavy with fatigue as I lie in the bed, yet I cannot remain sleep. A new destiny hovers, and a destination I had never for a moment dared to think I would see. Venice. In the morning, despite lack of rest, I leap out of bed before Daphne brings my chocolat upstairs.

Time stretches, inching slowly over the three days, but the moment arrives: I am riding in the back of Sir Gabriel Courtenay's carriage, immaculate and freshly polished. Much like the man himself, who sits beside me, all attentiveness. Outside the streets spill over with frantic Londoners. Christmas is but five days away.

"I have a hundred questions for you," I say.

"Of course you do," he says. "But first, your wig."

He places a box on the seat next to me. Removing the lid, I see a plain white wig inside. I do not wear wigs, no unmarried Huguenot woman does.

"For expediency's sake, we need to discuss the Derby plan in my house, where we shall have privacy," he says.

"I know that; I agreed to that. But why must I wear a wig?"

"I own a house on Grosvenor Square, Genevieve. It is daytime. Those who come and go are observed. A young woman would have no reason to come alone, without family, to call on an unmarried man. It would cause conversation among my neighbors. You have memorable hair. We must conceal it."

Before I can say anything else, he is pinning up my hair to flatten it and then lowering the wig onto my head. *Memorable hair.* Is it a compliment, or merely an observation?

"And now... the next step," he says and presents me with a plain wool cloak. "We will halt the carriage two streets from the square and you'll walk the rest of the way, so that you can be seen to carry a box into the house."

"Ah, I'm to pose as your servant."

"I assume you've no objection?"

"None at all."

The truth is, it excites me, to dress up, play a part. Theatricals are discouraged by our church leaders, along with dancing and singing. I've never pretended to be someone else before. Yet when I read the plays of William Shakespeare or John Webster, I enjoy picturing myself as various characters. Up to now, I've only been an actress in my head.

The thrill of the experience dampens when Sir Gabriel tells me Jimmy will meet the carriage.

Reading my expression, he says, "You don't care for Jimmy?"

"I don't think he cares for me."

"Jimmy has a colorful history, he's a boxer who left the sport when certain rules were introduced. A... hmmm, *competitive* man, who lives by his own rules. Don't worry. Jimmy is completely loyal to me, Genevieve."

I find that less than completely reassuring. When I step down from the carriage two streets from the square, there stands Jimmy, wearing his customary black coat. He thrusts a crate into my arms. I fall in behind Sir Gabriel, Jimmy at my side. We walk in silence. A gentleman followed by two servants. My arms ache, for the box is heavier than I'd expected. But I refuse to show weakness in front of Jimmy.

The air is cold; the sun beams bright this afternoon. We reach the end of the street, opening onto Grosvenor Square and its vast park. A statute of George I rises in the center, his notoriously fat, awkward form slimmed into a stone refrain of Hanoverian sternness. A thin layer of snow, edged with brown, covers the ground surrounding the statue. The tree branches are leafless, but regardless, liveried gardeners scuttle around the perimeter of the statue, attending to what I can't imagine.

As for the townhouses on the square, they glitter like new diamonds strung around an heiress' creamy throat.

Sir Gabriel strides up the walkway to a townhouse, while I follow Jimmy to the back doorway that leads down steps to a dim kitchen. There's no fire roaring down here, not a single pot on display. From the looks of it, Sir Gabriel rarely dines at home.

Jimmy whisks the box from my arms, more or less tossing it onto a table, and he points to the stairs at the other end of the kitchen. He will not accompany me; I shall ascend alone.

It's a narrow staircase, and darker going than the kitchen, because there's a door at the top and it is tightly closed. When I reach the top, I hesitate. Am I to knock? That seems rather ridiculous. I'm dressed to impersonate a servant, but I am not a servant.

I push open the door.

I stand on the edge of a tall square of blinding light. A crystal chandelier sparkles above. Its many candles reflect on a smooth, spotless light-gray floor that I realize, with a start, is marble. I rarely have occasion to step upon a marble floor, they are such a luxury.

On one side of the room, an arched entrance leads to a small foyer and, beyond that, the door opening up to Grosvenor Square. But to the right is a very curious wall. It is constructed of dark wood, oak perhaps, with the lower half divided into a series of interlocking panels in the manner of a country estate. Mounted on it is a display of swords, at least twenty of them, crossed at the tips. They are short swords but gleam as if freshly polished. Most of them have elaborate carved handles. It is an astonishing display, like a proud Tudor earl were displaying martial might to the squires of the county.

I am so engrossed that I don't notice Sir Gabriel himself. He's come into the hall quietly, in satin shoes.

"Welcome to my home, Genevieve," he says.

"I am much taken by your… swords," I say, rather stupidly.

"Ah, yes?" he says, a hint of pride in his smile.

He beckons for me to follow him into another room. My steps bring me even closer to the swords. Peering closer at their handles, I realize several of them are carved in the shape of desiccated human heads.

"Are those meant to be skulls?" I ask.

Sir Gabriel's pride deepens. "Not just anyone's skull. That is the head of the martyred King Charles I. Just over a century ago, cavalry carried these swords into battle. They're short, as you see, and intended for close thrusting."

"Close thrusting," I repeat.

"They even have a special name," he says. "Mortuary swords."

A shiver crawls up my spine.

To my relief, Sir Gabriel's parlor holds no more peculiarities. If his wall of swords seems suited to the past century, this room is up to the moment in fashion. The walls, painted dusky rose, are covered with framed oil paintings. A gilded couch is upholstered in the Chinoiserie style: delicate branches, ponds, and pagodas evoke faraway Asia. Most impressive of all, a harpsichord graces the side of the room opposite the fireplace.

Sir Gabriel pulls the servant's cloak from my shoulders but does not remove the wig. He leads me to one of the chairs. Before it is a mahogany writing table with unmistakable clawed feet.

"That is Chippendale," I say.

He nods with a shrug, as if to say, *But of course.*

If I had to name a uniting trait of Huguenots beyond our religious faith, it is our appreciation of that which is well made. The eye of the artisan. Taking another look at the paintings and the décor and all of the furniture before sitting down, I comment, "Everything in this room is of the highest quality."

Sir Gabriel laughs, but it's as if what I said calls forth some particular memory and not perhaps a pleasant one. "Aequalis astris," he says. "My family motto. 'Equal to the stars.' "

Now that is quite a motto.

More briskly, he says, "Today I need to teach you the techniques of sympathetic writing."

He places on the table a tray, bearing sheets of what appear to be ordinary writing paper, a small bottle of yellowish white liquid, and a brush with sharply pointed bristles.

"It is of the utmost importance that you and I communicate, but I fear that the level of secrecy at Derby is such that any letters you write could be read by your employer at the porcelain workshop. So you can't write to me directly and you can't put down on paper anything of importance."

"These would seem unsurmountable obstacles," I say.

"Not at all. You will write to your grandfather once a week, the letter to be posted on Tuesday. Mail between Derby and London is slow, and expensive. But I've worked it out, and we have a method for intercepting the letters before they reach London. But only if it posts on Tuesday. The majority of each letter will be addressed to your grandfather. But you will also write to me—in words that only I can see."

When Sir Gabriel explains that I will use a form of ink invisible to all eyes but his, I fear for his sanity. Seeing my reaction, he takes no offense but instructs me to write one sentence in as small letters as I can manage, on the bottom half of a sheet of paper. I must dip this special brush in the liquid of the bottle supplied. He will not observe what I write — that is up to me.

It takes me a while to think of something; then, as he reads through some papers, I do as he asks, noting that the color of the strong-smelling "ink" is a dark yellow. "Not invisible," I point out, gently.

"We need to wait for it to dry completely," he says. "Then it will reappear." A smile emerges. "Very much like magic. I will make a believer of you, Genevieve."

While we wait, Sir Gabriel tells me all he knows about the chemist employed by Derby Porcelain. "Thomas Sturbridge is twenty-six years of age, from a tradesman's family in Rochester, a brilliant youth from what I've discovered. So much so that his father borrowed the money for him to attend Cambridge at considerable hardship to themselves. To be specific, Trinity College, the same as Sir Isaac Newton. Sturbridge was compared to Newton, by more than one person."

"He sounds quite a paragon."

"Some say a genius. When he was twenty-three, he disappeared. No one knows where he went, and I mean no one. His father died at about this time — his mother was already dead — and some of the neighbors assumed the son was dead, too. Yet eight months ago, his name appeared in connection with the discovery of a new color at Derby. They keep Sturbridge well hidden there, even moving him out of the town on occasion."

"And you have no idea where he works on the formula?"

"No." I can see how frustrated he is to know so little about the Derby chemist. This is a man who gets what he wants with ease. Witness how much he learned about me, how he was able to follow me and anticipate what I would do — all of it within a day of meeting me.

I ask, "What does Thomas Sturbridge look like?"

"He's of medium height, with red hair and blue eyes."

"Well, that is a beginning."

"Hair color isn't much of an identifying principle when most men wear wigs. But we shall work with diligence to find him."

I admire Sir Gabriel's enterprise. We are like partners in a business venture, and that is how I wish it to be. The lies of Denis Arsenault infuriated me, his betrayals hurt. I shall have nothing more to do with men as suitors. I've no intention of becoming lost in Sir Gabriel's dark eyes.

I glance down at the writing paper. It is smooth and blank. "I can't see the writing any longer —it's gone," I exclaim. "How will I be able to read these sentences?"

"Patience, Genevieve," he says. "We have to wait a while longer, until it's completely dry, before I take you to the next step. You're an excellent pupil, I must say. I suspected you would be."

I fight to suppress the surge of pleasure at his compliment. I say, "While we wait, I was thinking more about blue — I have a suspicion that this new shade could be the product of blue dyes rather than blue pigments."

Sir Gabriel encourages me to continue.

"Blue pigment was hard to come by in the Middle Ages because the only sources were minerals excavated from the ground, very costly indeed. For centuries the preferred way to make the blue paint was from lapis lazuli, a beautiful gem that's found in the Afghan Empire and Persia. They'd grind up the gems with binding agents to create the desired pigment. Of course, that wasn't the sole source for artists. Azurite was also discovered and is the main source of blue paint. I assume that the blue you've seen is not a variant of the usual pigment found on ceramics, both here and in China."

He nods.

"But then there's indigo — the leaves of the plant yield the blue dye used in our clothing. Painters often scorn colors that come from the dyes for fabrics, I've never been sure why. But indigo can be lovely. I wonder if a plant isn't the source of the color you seek."

"Genevieve, I wish that could be the answer. The blue in question has been tested extensively. It's not derived from a plant or from a stone in Afghanistan. It's not Azurite. This color must come from some other precious gem deep in the earth, or a combination of chemicals that Thomas Sturbridge alone has discovered."

I straighten my shoulders. "And to discover exactly what he's done, that is my task."

"One that you will be ideally placed to carry out," he says. "You are to discover the formula by the spring, Genevieve. The timing is crucial. I can't emphasize that enough. I must have results from you by the time the sap flows."

For an instant, the amiability of the man drops and I glimpse something close to desperation. He rubs his eyes with his hands, as if to conceal it from me.

I ask a question that's flickered in my head since I walked into this exquisite room. "Are you Sir Gabriel within these walls, or are you Mr. Sommerville?" I ask.

It takes a while for a reply to come. "It's somewhat more complicated than that, Genevieve. I must become Sommerville — and other names too — so that Sir Gabriel Courtenay may exist, even though it is the name I was born with. I hope you can understand."

"I do," I say, although to be honest I don't.

I clamp a hand across my mouth, for I've just realized something. "The boy in Derby who stole a piece of porcelain — that was for *you*," I say. "That's how you obtained a piece of the blue for all of your tests."

Sir Gabriel runs his hand along his harpsichord. "Yes, he worked for me. He was paid well, too."

"What happened to him?"

"He made his way here, to London. He wanted to escape from Derby and I made that possible. Just as I intend to make it possible for you to travel to Venice."

Sir Gabriel points to the far wall and a framed landscape of a river dotted with boats. I gasp as I realize whose work this is and I rush to the wall.

"Is that a Canaletto?" I ask, awed.

"Of course."

Sir Gabriel joins me before the painting. The gondolas seem to slide on turquoise waters, the people of the city strolling down a long plaza. The control of his brush is extraordinary. With his skills, Canaletto has made the people and the buildings appear three-dimensional. And the mood: He depicts a balmy, cloud-kissed sky, one lighter than any horizon I've ever witnessed in gritty London. I yearn to possess such painting skill, as a starving man would yearn for a loaf of bread.

A memory stirs, though, of a criticism in the newspaper Grandfather read aloud to me earlier this year. "They say Canaletto exaggerates the beauty of the places he paints, to meet the expectations of patrons," I say.

"I've heard the same."

"Well, does Venice look like this?" I press.

"Close — very close," he says. "The exaggeration is minor."

Disappointed, I say, "Any exaggeration is unacceptable. It's one matter to make an ugly man handsome in a portrait he's paying for. But to lie about a landscape? Truth must always be the goal."

"Yes," he says. "I remember you said something such as that about truth at dinner."

There's something funny about his tone of voice; I wonder suddenly if he is making fun of me. But he says nothing more on truth.

"You are an expert on Venice then," I say. "How many times have you been?"

"Five times."

"And what is it like?"

"Venice is like no place else. Every year, for months at a time, the people of Venice wear masks. Wherever you go, whatever you do, you wear a mask. You can be someone else. Lose yourself. Whichever you wish."

And why should someone like Sir Gabriel wish to lose himself? I wonder.

"Did you feel so impressed the very first time you saw Venice, when you were on the grand tour?" I ask.

"I didn't see Venice the first time I was on the Continent. I was prevented."

He says the word *prevented* in a voice so bitter, so unlike his customary pleasant tone, that I'm shocked. Sir Gabriel stands no more than five inches away from me, as we both face the Canaletto painting, though I doubt his attention was on it any more than mine was. He is remembering something that happened years ago, that still fills him with fury.

Sir Gabriel turns, walking quickly to the harpsichord, searching among the sheets of musical notes propped before him. "Venice is… ah, here we are, Antonio Vivaldi." He places a bound book of music in front of him. He dives into the music. It's a beautiful piece, light and joyous. Sir Gabriel is an accomplished harpsichord.

But I am having trouble keeping up with these shifts in mood. I wonder if the invisible circumstances guiding his actions are simply financial. There may be more to Sir Gabriel than that.

When he finishes the Vivaldi, not sure what to do, I clap twice.

In response, he frowns. "No," he says. " 'Summer' is celebrated, and well suited for Venice. But not fitting." He searches his sheets again. "Where are you, Scarlatti?"

In a moment another piece of music flows from the harpsichord, lovely and yet muted. Almost sad. When he stops playing, he looks down at the harpsichord keys and says, "That suits better, doesn't it?"

"Suits what — Venice?"

He looks up at me, quizzically, as if surprised I don't understand something perfectly clear to him.

"It suits *you*, Genevieve."

85

I stare at him, suddenly very much aware that there is no other female in the house, no chaperone. The only other person is a man, Jimmy.

"Sir Gabriel, shall we survey the sympathetic writing?" I ask.

"Yes, of course," he says, returning to practicality. "You need a candle to do it. Heat activates the chemical in the liquid." We move to the table and he holds the sheet over a lit candle, making sure to leave a few inches between paper and fire. There's a faint popping noise, and suddenly the words emerge on the surface of the paper, the same ones I wrote. I laugh with delight.

"Didn't I tell you there is such a thing as magic?" he says. His fingers tighten on the paper as he reads my sentence aloud: "Wish me good speed, for I am going into a wilderness where I shall find no path."

He turns paler and demands, "Why did you write this?"

"It's a line from *The Duchess of Malfi*," I point out, confused by his reaction.

"I am familiar with the source. But why did you pick it?"

"I don't know. 'Cover her face; mine eyes dazzle; she died young.' "

"Exactly. You know that it's a play about death, don't you?"

"*The Duchess of Malfi* is a tragedy," I say. "Don't most tragedies end in death?"

"Not always," he says and turns to slip the paper of invisible writing into a large leather book. In a moment he begins another lesson in spying, calm and encouraging. But that can't take away from the glimpse I'd gotten of his face as he turned away from me. And for just an instant, what I saw was something very close to despair.

CHAPTER EIGHT

With my bare finger I trace a circle on the cold glass of the coach window. It is nearly a month past Christmas. I said my goodbyes to Grandfather and stepped into the coach to Derby two days ago. Although it was he who pushed me relentlessly to take the position of porcelain decorator, when it came time for us to part, Grandfather's eyes welled and his arms enveloped me tightly. I didn't want him to ever let go. It was Daphne's compassionate murmur that released us. Her eyes were damp with tears, too.

Now the coach rumbles north on the wide road leading me to my fate. If only the window weren't so thick and smudged, I could see more clearly.

"Put on your gloves, I implore you, Miss Genevieve," trills my fellow passenger, Mrs. Wentworth, pulling up the heavy coach blanket all the way to her plump shoulders. For more than half the length of the journey to Derby, she has sat across from me. More than that; we nudge each other's feet. Our boots are balanced against opposite ends of the coal-filled foot warmer.

"I like the feel of the glass," I say.

"When I traveled by coach as a girl, windows didn't exist — each side was boarded up except for a crack covered by these filthy leather windows," continues Mrs. Wentworth. "And there wouldn't even be a coach in January, heaven forbid. They were taken off the road weeks before Christmas, not to return until after Easter. These new turnpike roads are a miracle. I remember…"

I force a smile as I endure yet another recounting of the history of coach travel according to Mrs. Wentworth. I've learned to give the impression of polite listening while not taking in a word. Sir Gabriel impressed on me the importance of geniality if I'm to be an effective spy. I'm doing my best, but I fear my best is not very good.

Her husband, a tax surveyor, doesn't even pretend. The mustachioed Mr. Wentworth pulls a flask from his end of the blanket and tilts back his head, fastening his lips around the spout. A whiff of brandy fills the coach.

And then come the recitations of my cousin, Andrew Planché, the fourth member of our coach party.

"I follow him to serve my turn upon him. We cannot all be masters, nor all masters cannot be truly follow'd. You shall mark many a duteous and knee-crooking knave, Othello. I follow him to serve my turn upon him. We cannot all be masters, nor all masters cannot be truly follow'd. I follow him to serve my turn upon him."

My cousin is practicing Iago again.

Mrs. Wentworth's reminiscences die in her throat. She settles back into the coach seat, but not before nudging her husband. He blinks twice. I expect when they're alone there is a great deal of gossiping about the sullen young woman and her eccentric uncle.

When he arrived at my grandfather's house to escort me to Derby, Andrew Planché announced that he was preparing for the role of Iago, and the journey would afford him time to memorize his lines. So the rumors are true. My father's cousin, the co-founder of Derby Porcelain, now wants nothing to do with that world. He is consumed with a desire to walk the boards on Drury Lane. Andrew is slight in stature, with sad, thoughtful eyes and a pointed chin, just this side of thirty years old. Not what I would expect of an actor.

As Andrew continues his recitation of Iago, I return to my window. Through the glass I make out the black fringe of treeless branches and low, snow-covered hills. There are few people. I find it hard to get accustomed to, this silent scarcity of men and women after life in London, where every square foot is zealously, loudly filled. It leaves me feeling exposed, as if my own plots were as obvious as those my cousin mutters in Iago's monologues.

Is that why I've grown uneasy on this trip? I've found not a moment of peace. My sense of secret power, which I nurtured while in London these last few weeks, is disintegrating.

I suspect that my unease emanates from the object I carry in my lap, gripped under my shawl. The same object that Sir Gabriel handed me on the day we visited the British Museum — which turned out to be our final meeting.

*

After my lessons in Grosvenor Square, we corresponded by letter, but Sir Gabriel did not want to make too many engagements with me and "push the point." However, the opening to the public of a place of wonder, to be called the British Museum, stirred great excitement throughout London, and it seemed a plausible reason for the two of us to see each other. He was quite keen to meet one last time, in person, before my departure for Derby, now set for January twentieth.

At first, Sir Gabriel treated the outing as not another ruse, but as a true social engagement. "Are you looking forward to our inspection of Dr. Sloan's cabinet?" he asks me, his dark eyes gleaming beneath his white wig.

"Very much so," I say, all too aware of my pulse quickening, and not, I fear, completely due to the prospect of seeing the museum.

"Why do you call it a cabinet?" I ask, quickly.

"Because that's what it is, a collection of books and drawings and maps and coins, and mummified creatures from around the world, donated by Sir Hans Sloan, physician to the king. Such a peculiar notion of his, to pay the government twenty thousand pounds to ensure that the public would set eyes on his cabinet after his death. His estate approached King George first, but he didn't take to the idea, of course. The king is not someone who could possibly appreciate a collection devoted to the arts and sciences."

I'd noticed that before, how he speaks about the king as casually — even contemptuously — as he would anyone else: a merchant, a tailor. Sir Gabriel Courtenay is but a thief, yet considers himself royalty. Above royalty, perhaps.

"I'm hoping for some inventions of science to be on display, the frontier of chemistry," he says. "That should benefit you when you make the acquaintance of a certain Thomas Sturbridge."

So there is a lesson in this outing.

"I know very little about chemistry," I say.

"Few of us do. It's the purview of a select group of men — the new breed of alchemists. Magicians, really."

"Ah, magic again?" I tease, and he smiles back at me.

Our carriage slows. When I peer outside, I see that the street is clogged with other carriages headed for a grand building — a domed red brick palace — set behind a courtyard lined with stiff brown hedges.

Other small groups hurry toward it on foot. Through the glass I can hear their excited chatter.

Sir Gabriel lays his hand on my arm. "I have something for you," he says. "You'll have vital need of it in Derby."

"Then give it to me," I say.

He thinks for a moment. "No, I'd rather you didn't carry it around inside. We'll see the high points of the museum, and then I'll give it to you, with the necessary instructions, on our way back to Spitalfields."

He springs out of the carriage to fetch our tickets from the porter. It seems that "studious and curious persons" must apply in writing ahead of time to be allowed to enter the museum. My companion won't even consider my accompanying him to find the museum porter who holds the tickets. I wait in his carriage, wondering if he confuses me with the fragile ladies of his social circle. I also wonder what he means to give me later.

When Sir Gabriel returns to the carriage with the tickets to the museum, he's plainly irritated.

"The system is not well ordered," he says. I suspect this is one of the worst criticisms he could ever level.

For me, to ascend the wide marble staircase in the museum's towering hall, knowing that so many objects of curiosity await me, is, in itself, worth the trip to Bloomsbury. I can't hide my excitement, which seems to soothe Sir Gabriel's frayed temper. He smiles as we make our way up. A pretty woman walking ahead of us turns, more than once, to gape at him. I notice others, men and women, regarding him with particular interest.

Sir Gabriel seems more interested in the paintings on the wall running alongside the staircase than in fellow museum-goers. The pictures are scenes of classic mythology, painted in the fashionable manner:

mountains of clouds, overgrown gardens, fabrics painted so you could touch them, and all in a rainbow of pastels. Groups of people caught in some ancient tragedy. Every serious artist trains on the classic tales, a pursuit closed off to me.

"It's *The Metamorphoses*," he says, pleased. He points at a painting, filled with frenzied toga-clad figures. "These are stories taken from Ovid."

"Of course," I murmur. With his grand tours and his parade of tutors, Sir Gabriel breathes such knowledge as others do air.

"It's all about transformation," he says.

"Ah. Now I appreciate your interest."

But he does not respond to my teasing, Sir Gabriel is too transfixed by *The Metamorphoses*.

The next painting captures my attention, too. It shows only two figures, facing each other across a smooth pond. One is a handsome man, playing a lute. The other, in the foreground, also holds a lute. But he's not a human — he has the ears and haunches of an animal, a horse or goat.

Seeing my interest, Sir Gabriel says, "Apollo didn't like it when the satyr dared to challenge him in playing the lute, a god. Marsyas was punished severely."

"So *that* is a satyr," I say. My knowledge of mythology is nowhere near his. I hold a frustratingly vague memory that he came to a vivid end. "How was Marsyas punished?"

He tilts his head and says, "I don't think I should tell you. His fate is not for the ladies."

"Tell me," I insist. "You say I'm a singular person, meaning I'm not actually a lady."

He laughs. "Very well. Apollo had Marsyas flayed alive, slowly, for his arrogance." There is a distinct satisfaction in Sir Gabriel's voice.

I am repulsed, as he predicted. But moments later I forget about the satyr. The wonder of the exhibits overwhelms me. From mounted coins and seals of the ancient world to newfangled mathematical instruments — it all swirls around me. Sir Gabriel is keen to see the Harleian Collection of Manuscripts, a display of historical documents that, he tells me with a grimace, passed out of private ownership for financial reasons. "Ah, look at this, Genevieve, an inventory of all that King Henry VIII possessed, his wardrobe, his ships and tapestries and armor, all of the jewels," he says, pointing at a book opened for us. The yellowing parchment is filled with hundreds — no, thousands — of items listed in tiny script.

"Do you think any of the jewels listed here were worn by all six wives, one after another?" I ask.

Sir Gabriel says lightly, "If you can get past all the wives, Henry was a man of astounding taste."

"It's difficult to 'get past' a row of chopped heads," I say.

"Fair point."

We laugh, together. It strikes me that I am having a most enjoyable afternoon when I catch a glimpse of something from across the room. I'd read about it, ached to see it, but never expected to in my lifetime. Dozens of people stand between us and this particular exhibit, but I insist we cross over, repeatedly uttering a "Pardon me" as I pull Sir Gabriel toward it.

"Voila," I say, taking those last few steps toward the tilted exhibit case.

A brilliant blue butterfly, stuck with a pin, stares back at us, wings frozen mid-flight.

I say, "Remember, blue is the rarest color on earth. This is one of the few living creatures the color exists on — a butterfly. I've read about it, but never thought I'd be able to see one."

Sir Gabriel slides closer to the case, but very slowly, as if the butterfly were alive and he might frighten it off, until we are side by side. "Morpho didius," he says reading from the card next to the insect. "A native of the Americas."

"I believe that some butterflies live only two weeks," I say.

"Indeed?"

The light from the nearby window reflects off the delicate blue of the creature's wings, creating a sharp contrast with the ragged black that borders both of the wings. The butterfly is faceless, sightless. It does not seem possible that it ever lived.

At that moment I do not feel that I've agreed to a spying-for-money scheme but something finer, something extraordinary. The quest for blue. And something more. This is our shared obsession now.

"How very beautiful," he says, and his fingertips touch mine, as softly as a butterfly's wing.

Another man's voice says, "They are, aren't they?"

Sir Gabriel jerks his hand away and says, turning, "What a delight to see you here, Sir Humphrey."

Standing a few inches from us is a man, perhaps twenty-eight years old, a little younger than Sir Gabriel, wigless, his blond hair hanging to his shoulders. His face is handsome, square jawed with hazel eyes. He wears the coat, waistcoat, and breeches of a gentleman, but carelessly. Sir Gabriel would never miss a mother-of-pearl button on his waistcoat.

"I wanted to see these fantastical creatures for myself," this Sir Humphrey tells us in a tone of confession, "as part of the naval advance to the West Indies, but I couldn't snare a commission. I expect they harbored suspicions I'd be running through the jungles with my net and not firing on the French."

Sir Gabriel laughs, though not sincerely. This is his beau monde personality. He says, "Sir Humphrey would have us think he's not a serious officer, when the reverse is true. So where will you be posted instead?"

"Nowhere, for the time being," he says. "I'm needed for a bit in Whitehall."

"Oh? That must be terribly interesting."

"And you? I wouldn't have thought a visit to the museum, among the hoi palloi, would be your preferred afternoon. I wager we have you to thank for this foray." He turns to me for the first time; up to now his attention has been tightly fixed on Sir Gabriel. "I am sorry, I don't believe we've ever met." His expression is friendly, but a tension hangs in the air, one I don't understand.

"I'm Genevieve Planché," I say, my words overlapping with Sir Gabriel's apology for failing to make an introduction.

"Lovely name," says Sir Humphrey. "French, is it?"

"I'm of a Huguenot family, our presence is not desired in France," I tell him. I'm accustomed to making this explanation, never more important than now, when England and France are at war.

A glance at Sir Gabriel, though, and I can tell he wishes I had not said so much.

"Sir Humphrey Willoughby is a neighbor of mine," adds Sir Gabriel.

"Not precisely," says Sir Humphrey. "My older brother, Lord Errol, lets a house on Grosvenor Square, which, if I'm not too loud or disordered, I may reside in during the season. It's his house." He smiles and then says, "You know how it runs with families, don't you, Sir Gabriel?"

With a quick bow to me, Sir Humphrey turns and strides into the crowd, swallowed up in seconds.

"Time to leave," says Sir Gabriel, tightly.

"I thought we were here for edification in science."

"There's no relevant science here."

He silently leads me out of the Naturalist Room and down the stairs, now even thicker with excited people surging toward the exhibits. Sir Gabriel is unquestionably disturbed by our encounter with his blond neighbor, but why? Sir Humphrey's parting remark about family seemed harmless on the surface, though as I think about it, I wonder if he was trying to make a point. Something about families. It occurs to me that I'm ignorant of Sir Gabriel's relations, whether he has parents alive or brothers and sisters. His Grosvenor Square house did not seem like a shared place.

He fumes as we stand at the bottom of the stairs, blocked by the jostling, loud crowds from reaching the main door.

"Sir Humphrey Willoughby was right on one matter," I say. "You really do not care for the hoi polloi."

He says, "The founders of this museum take a great risk. These precious exhibits could be wrecked by any violent 'guests' they allow inside."

"Oh, but why should anyone want to destroy museum exhibits?" I protest.

"Ask the silk-weaver whose shop your former fiancé wrecked," retorts Sir Gabriel. "I understand that Denis Arsenault led quite a violent mob."

He is in a temper, and I believe it is due to our meeting Sir Humphrey Willoughby. But I do not appreciate his retort and say, "Those men who rampaged through the shop, they did not wreck it with violence as its own objective. It was a protest against cruel treatment by the shop owner. For those without standing, such actions are the only power available to them."

He nods at once, a smile warming his features. "I am sure you're right, Genevieve. I do apologize." He leads the way through the crowd and out onto Russell Street.

Once we're inside the carriage, he does not give the driver the signal to leave. Instead, from under the seat, he takes a square object, wrapped in a rose-colored cloth, and lays it between us.

Greatly curious, I unfold the cloth. Within is a French Bible of worn brown leather. An early century edition of an Olivétan Bible.

"Why ever did you get this for me?" I ask.

He shows me a tiny lever near-buried in the upper side of the back cover. When he pushes the lever down, the last one-fourth of the bible eases opens to reveal a hidden compartment. A writing instrument and glass bottle containing a yellowish liquid are strapped in.

"This is for your sympathetic writing," he says, and gives the cover of the bible a proud tap.

Dismay hits me as hard as a slap from a brutal hand.

"I didn't expect this — didn't expect it to be like *this*," I stammer.

"Were you planning to order your ink from the village apothecary?" Sir Gabriel says, his voice mocking.

I don't answer, staring at the Bible's cover, so expertly frayed.

"Carry it with you in the coach, don't store it in your trunk, until you get to Derby," he continues. "They say one out of every three coaches is robbed. The trunk could be taken. You absolutely cannot let this book out of your possession. It required the talents of some extraordinarily skilled men."

During the carriage ride back to Spitalfields, Sir Gabriel relays more details of my mission — what exactly he needs me to do, how best to achieve my objective, when I should communicate with him. I've heard most of it before. Some of his words reassure me, a few disturb me. Beneath it all runs a certain feeling, a new one, something that, when I analyze it, hovers between dismay and shame.

The Huguenot Bible. This is what every French Protestant lives for, what some of them died for. I can picture their somber faces in the woodprint drawings put before us in school — the first waves of believers, wearing their plain black suits and white collars. In the pages of the Bible, pored over until they're close to crumbling, we found our direction, our salvation. We Huguenots step forward into the light, even if it means punishment, exile, or massacre.

I am not the most pious person of Spitalfields. Sir Gabriel no doubt perceived that — and he is not wrong. Still... to make a mockery of our Bible, to turn it into an instrument of spying? It is a great deal to ask of me.

And there is more. I remember sitting in my mother's lap, excited to be her grande fille, as she opened her Bible, one that looks just like this one, and read aloud to me. Between passages, she would smooth my hair, pulling gently on a tangle, and kiss my cheek.

His carriage reaches Fournier Street, and Sir Gabriel tugs on his waistcoat, smoothing it out, preparing to escort me inside the house.

"No," I say. "Better not to."

"Why is that? I should like to say hello to Pierre."

"Just... I think it advisable to part ways here."

Sir Gabriel studies me for what seems like quite a long time with those serious, inquisitive eyes, and then leans forward, to take my hand in his. He lifts it to kiss. His lips are warm and firm, pressing on my hand.

"When I next see you in the flesh, you'll be bound for Venice," he says.

He helps me out of the carriage, but his eyes drift to the Bible, wrapped in a small blanket, that I now cradle in my arms.

"Goodbye, Sir Gabriel," I say.

After his carriage turns onto Commercial Street, I stand outside, in the cold, for quite a long time. The sooty gray sky deepens to blackness.

From where I'm positioned outside our windows, I can see into my home. I watch Daphne light a fresh candle on the sturdy little oak table near the window of my grandfather's library. It throws a quivering rectangle of light onto the street. Daphne knows, we all know, that Pierre Billiou always feeds his canaries after sundown and then comes down the stairs, his steps creaking on the sagging wood, the tune on his lips wordless but indisputably French. Before supper, Grandfather likes to read the *London Gazette* while the smell of Daphne's cooking roams the floor and she can be heard chiding George over this or that downstairs. I wait, without moving, for Grandfather to appear in the library and the routine to begin. It's important to me that he do what he's always done.

Down the street, outside of Ten Bells Alehouse, a loud quarrel erupts. "I'll call for the constable," bellows a man. Others laugh. A bottle breaks.

Finally I see a shadow move across the library. It's Grandfather, finding his chair and settling into it. I can see just the corner of his jowly face. He unfolds his newspaper, shaking it with two well measured snaps to work out the crease.

I take a breath, and walk toward the door. But someone stands in my way.

"M'lady, wares for sale," wails the broom peddler, trying to turn his burned face from me. As he does, I suddenly think of the fate of the satyr Marsyas. Because he dared to challenge Apollo, the satyr was flayed alive.

CHAPTER NINE

On the last night before arriving in Derby, we stop at a coach house in a town creeping up the side of a hill. After being shown my small, cold room, one smelling faintly of those who'd slept, loved, or sickened in this bed before me, I am more than eager to meet my cousin downstairs.

The coach house's dining hall smells only a little better, of cooked onions, with a touch of roasted gristle. A couple divide their bread at a table nearest the fire; a young man in the corner nurses a tankard, alone.

Andrew and I choose our table. He looks even wearier than when we emerged from the coach. I can't think that he will welcome discourse on porcelain, a subject he's shown no enthusiasm for discussing over the last days. In the back of my mind I hear Sir Gabriel's instructions in the carriage ride from the British Museum to Spitalfields: *Do not be obvious about your interest in the blue. Use subtle means.*

The trouble is, I've been subtle with my cousin, and as a consequence learned nothing. And I'm running out of time.

"You must be proud of founding the porcelain works in Derby," I say. My cousin nods, and stays silent.

"How did you learn so much about porcelain?" I push on.

"My father worked at the factory in Meissen. I was born in Germany; we came to England when I was eight."

With a shudder, I remember Sir Gabriel's story of how King Augustus the Strong kept a chemist chained up at Meissen until he solved the puzzle of how to make porcelain.

I take a breath and say, as off-handedly as I can manage, "I've heard that Derby is expected to become the best maker of porcelain in all of England. Why is that?"

I long for him to say, "It's because of the experiments in color. Let me tell you everything about the efforts to invent a new shade of blue." Instead, Andrew frowns, looking more displeased than at any time during this journey.

"I have no idea, Genevieve," he says. "I've been gone from Derby for over a year."

Why is he so reluctant to talk about porcelain? I've envisioned a place of sharp-elbowed strivers, tucked in the middle of a dull Midlands town. Yet it's clearly a sore subject.

A roar cuts through the murmur of the room. "Found you, stupid cur!"

A tall, bearded man storms across the room to seize the young man sitting alone. He grabs him by the collar and pulls him off his stool, sending his tankard — and its ale — flying. "Men have been hanged for failing to report to His Majesty's militia," he shouts, as if daring anyone to contradict him. We none of us do; we just watch, stunned, while he half-drags the young man away. At the door, his victim turns to look at all of us, his face a plea, before disappearing into the snowy street.

The innkeeper sets down our meal a moment later: overcooked beef in a lake of grease, encircled by carrots and turnips. The exact same dinner we were served at the tavern the night before.

Pushing the food across the plate, I say quietly, "That boy was terrified."

My cousin nods, staring down at a slab of beef he has no appetite for either. After a moment, he says, "The people in the country remember Bonnie Prince Charlie — and Culloden."

I know that I remember it. I was twelve years old, my mother dead four years, when every French Huguenot was terrified by reports of invasion by the Stuart Pretender, Bonnie Prince Charlie, backed by the French king, come to lead a Jacobite army through England and topple King George II. I was already a child devastated, and then to be surrounded by dread and worries of war… It was so difficult. What would happen if the distant king who hated us, who drove the Huguenots out of France, gained the upper hand in England through his puppet, Bonnie Prince Charlie? Of course, it *didn't* happen. The Jacobite army that fought for the Stuarts was defeated at Culloden. England was safe again, for its French Protestant refugees… for everyone.

My cousin Andrew says slowly, "When I first came to England, when we visited your family, they held a palm over their glasses for a second, right at the beginning of a toast, to symbolize how much they did not support the king across the water."

I smile. "Oh, yes, they still do that all over Spitalfields."

"And do you remember the Huguenot men's march, in support of King George?" he asks. "I wasn't in London, but I heard about it."

Eagerly, I share my memory. I stood at the upstairs window, with Daphne, and watched the French Protestants of Spitalfields, including Grandfather, march together one afternoon, up and down our streets, proving to the English our loyalty, how willing we were to fight the Jacobites, should Bonnie Prince Charlie reach London.

"Your father was kind to me — your mother too — and it meant a great deal to me," says Andrew, reaching across the table to squeeze my hand. "I will do everything I can to help you, Genevieve. I owe them that."

A nasty little voice whispers in my head that this is the time, when family affection warms Andrew's heart, to press him, to learn all he knows about the creation of blue. But I can't. He's summoned up too many precious memories. To befoul this with spying? Impossible.

I sleep little that night. The room grows colder still and the bed is lumpy. It is so quiet here, so very quiet. I'm accustomed to the cacophony of London, diminished at night, but never silent. I never realized how much I depended on those staccato bursts of noise as background to my waking and sleeping. But it's not only the bed or the silence that bedevils me. I cannot banish images from my mind: A blue butterfly, a satyr, the fear of the boy dragged away, the cover of the Huguenot Bible.

The following morning, the threat of more snow hovers. The coachman scrubbed the windows the night before, and I can see more clearly on this, the third and last day of my travels. We pass patches of empty farmland stretching across low hills, and barrel through villages scarce of any inhabitants. The Wentworths both fall asleep. The snow finally begins falling — light, twirling flakes, like eddies in the sky — as our coach readies to cross a long stone bridge over rushing water.

"That's the River Trent," my cousin says. There's something strange in his voice. He hasn't said one word from *Othello* today. I turn in my seat to scrutinize Andrew, and I can tell from his drawn face and red-tinged eyes, that he has barely slept, too.

"We're nearly to Derby?" I ask him.

"Yes." He peers past me out the window and says, "Swarkestone Bridge is famous. This is where Bonnie Prince Charlie turned around twelve years ago. He came down from Edinburgh with his army but only got as far south as this bridge. Lost his nerve, and went north."

I had no idea that the Jacobites made it this far. I shudder at it, to know my body crosses over something touched by the pretender sent by the French.

We reach the other side of the bridge and rattle forward on the road, so close to Derby now, when the question bursts out.

"Andrew, why won't you tell me about what it's like at the porcelain factory?"

After a long moment Andrew says, "Your grandfather asked me to arrange for you to be taken on at Derby in memory of your late father. So I agreed. But you must be careful, Genevieve. Promise me you will be very careful."

"Why?"

He bites his lip, struggling against some memory, some knowledge.

"Please, I need to know what you know," I beg.

My cousin says, "You asked me what set the Derby Porcelain Works apart. It is the reason I left the place, though yes, it was my work, my ideas, that established the manufactory. The men who founded it with me, William Duesbury, the porcelain innovator, and John Heath, the banker, their very lives depend on its success, and they will do whatever must be done to have their way, Genevieve. Whatever must be done. You can never forget that. You are very talented, that is why they're taking you on, but I know yours is a spirited nature. Do not give them cause for irritation or anger or, worst of all, any suspicion."

My heart skips a beat. "Suspicion?"

Mrs. Wentworth wakes with a distinctly unladylike snort, and Andrew breaks off.

I turn back to the window, analyzing his words, his warning. Sir Gabriel told me little about the character of the men who owned the porcelain factory; his focus had always been on the chemist they employed.

The coach slows. The snow has stopped, the landscape is clear. At first I'm not sure what I see. It is unlike anything I've glimpsed so far on this journey. I press my face against the glass, my nose aching.

We are at the top of a hill. Far below curves a river, not the same as was bridged by Swarkestone. A cluster of large buildings rise across the river, tight together, one of them a soaring cathedral that looks more suited to London or York than a town in the middle of the kingdom. But by far the strangest spectacle is a series of large square buildings directly on the river facing the church and the town. Huge wooden wheels attach to two of those buildings, turning steadily in the water. Dozens of workers mill around. They look to be in a hurry and yet there is no chaos in the crowd. Everyone has a purpose.

My cousin sidles closer to me to look out the window too. He points beyond the wheels, to a group of buildings not as large, and without wheels, but surrounded by cone-like structures shooting gray smoke into the air.

"That," says my cousin quietly, "is Derby Porcelain Works."

CHAPTER TEN

"It's better to reign in Hell than serve in Heaven, wouldn't you agree?"

After posing his question, William Duesbury smiles.

He is standing before the yawning door to a kiln of Derby Porcelain Works, the white-orange flames leaping and crackling on either side of him. Standing a yard back, I blink and turn my head, my hands raised as if it were possible to ward off this vigorous blast. I'm standing outdoors in January, but the oven is so hot I feel my cheeks flush and begin to itch.

I have been at my new place of employment for less than an hour. Andrew and I alighted from the coach at mid-day, made our farewell to the Wentworths, and walked a short distance to the George Inn.

My cousin and I found space on a sofa in the inn's busy parlor; Andrew ordered tea and cakes. I leaned back, enjoying the feel of the cushions on bones jolted by three days of travel, and the anticipation of hot, strong tea and sweet treats. But not more than a minute later, a tall, well-dressed man, about thirty years old, strode through the crowded parlor, bearing down on us, calling out greetings in a voice so loud it turned the heads of strangers in this bustling room.

William Duesbury wouldn't put up with any excuse of weariness from the road, or hunger. We must see the porcelain works at once. And so now we stand before an open oven. My cousin Andrew gently moves me farther to the left, so I will not be scorched. I can make out a vase with a carved handle, placed on the center of an iron shelf inside the oven. The vase is swallowed up by the violent flames, yet stands quite still. I feel an urge to seize that pair of long tongs and rescue it, which is quite ridiculous. Firing the vase in flames is the entire point.

Duesbury, standing closer than we are to the open oven door — just inches away from it — does not appear the least discomfited by the scorching flame. Nor does he look at me. His attention is fixed on my cousin, as it has been since the moment he found us in the town.

The porcelain works is clustered off Nottingham Road, not far from those enormous factories I'd seen with their wheels dipping into the water. Sir Gabriel had given me an idea of the layout but still I was surprised by the ambition of it. All of this to produce porcelain? I thought of the old workshops in Spitalfields, crammed with people, making use of every inch. Here, on the riverbank, everything looks new; there is much room to maneuver. I count two large buildings and five separate kilns surrounding them. Three of the ovens are lit, white smoke billowing skyward from their pointed tops.

Duesbury seems filled with an energy so perpetual that he finds it hard to stand still. He shifts from foot to foot, swings his arms, cranes his neck. Now, standing before the oven, he smiles and asks us about Hell.

"Is that Milton you've quoted?" asks my cousin.

"I continue to enjoy *Paradise Lost*, yes. Just because you left, Andrew, did you suppose I would forsake the novelists and philosophers, the works we pored over together, while we built our dream of artistic glory?"

"Of course not, William," says my cousin, wearily. This tour of the factory is another test to be endured by Andrew, and perhaps the most unpleasant one of all. Some of the things Duesbury says contain a barb. My cousin's withdrawal from Derby was apparently much resented, and for him to return in order to escort me is an act of sacrifice, greater than I had imagined.

Duesbury finally slams shut the oven door, the tongs rattling with the force of it, and we all back away. I give a sigh of relief, which he notices. The inner temperature must reach 2,024 degrees to fire true porcelain, he mentions. The oven I peeked inside reached that temperature in the late morning; now it is on the decrease.

What must it be like, I wonder, to work every day in the presence of such infernos?

A long wooden building stretches near the ovens, the next stage of our tour. Once inside, we peer into square pits in the floor holding the different dull-colored clay mixtures. Unpleasant odors choke the room; they resemble rotting vegetables. How peculiar. I hear in my head Sir Gabriel's smooth voice again, weaving his tales of Chinese fortunes, obsessed European princes, a brave Jesuit, a poor imprisoned German alchemist. And to think it's come to a floor pit smelling like spoiled turnips.

A string of workmen scurry about, casting anxious glances at Duesbury as he leads us to the various rooms.

He shows us the grinding room and the mixing room — all the rooms have their own names, it seems. There is no sign of a chemist. Sir Gabriel had said he didn't know if Thomas Sturbridge even worked at the manufactory. "They keep his work a secret from much of the staff," he told me in London.

When we return to the main floor, Duesbury points at two young laborers carrying a long crate between them. Puffed up with pride, he says, "Our crushed ox bones. We've just established a connection with a new seller."

"I'm sorry, but would you be so good as to repeat that? I thought I heard you say *ox bones*," I say. Aiming for the necessary amiability, I have been silent through the tour up to now. My question sounds more challenging than I intend; I honestly assumed I'd misheard him.

Duesbury twirls around to scrutinize me.

"You heard correctly, Mistress Genevieve," he says, mispronouncing my name. "We buy the bones, burn them in order to create ash, and mix them with the clay and the other ingredients in exact proportion. We've experimented with different animals, and ox is best. Those particular calcined bones make the porcelain more… tender."

"I see." Something about his glee over the process repulses me.

"Wasn't it Bow who discovered the value of the animal bones?" asks my cousin.

Duesbury scowls and says, "Yes, Thomas Bow did find a way to turn it to his advantage, producing porcelain next to a London slaughterhouse. But it's no secret, the value of calcined bones. I didn't steal his practice. Others succeed in this business through spying and thievery. I'm not one of them!"

"Of course not," says Andrews.

The name of one of Derby's rivals most definitely stirs my interest, as does his denial of stealing a secret. Do I believe him? I wonder if it's this Thomas Bow who's paying Sir Gabriel — and thus paying me — to ferret out the formula for the new color of blue, as vengeance.

Which brings me to my mission: If the chemist is well hidden, may I at least find this shade of blue for myself and begin to analyze it? I keep my eyes open for any sign of unusual blues.

"On to the next of our buildings, the most extraordinary one of all," Duesbury announces, ushering us outside. I scramble to keep up, Andrew beside me, as the man who is my new employer marches along a path to the building nearest the river. Although it was snowing lightly when we arrived, I don't see a single flake beneath my feet. Someone must be constantly whisking it clear.

Within a minute of entering the next building, there are happy cries of "Mr. Planché! Mr. Planché!" A half-dozen men flock to Andrew's side, all delighted to see him. My cousin's expression lightens. He greets each of the workers by name, with a question about their health or their family. For the first time, I truly grasp that he was once an essential part of Derby Porcelain Works, its co-founder and, I suspect, its heart. What makes it a rather bizarre spectacle is that the faces of the men who surround him are smudged with white, evidence of their work with clay. They look like anxious clowns.

This reception does not seem to please William Duesbury. "I must see to something," he mutters, and strides toward the stairs.

A female voice cuts through the chorus of men's. "And so the prodigal returns."

I take in the sight of this woman, perhaps my age. She wears a dark gray dress of severe silhouette. No plunging bodice or billowing silk, lace or flowers for her. But she's not a humble worker. The dress is made of costly cloth — perhaps a fine wool — and the details of the stitching and buttons show excellent workmanship. Her black hair is dressed unfashionably: two tight braids coiled and pinned; she wears no rouge. Her eyes are dark blue, fringed with black eyelashes. My overall impression is that this woman could be very handsome if she wished to be, but she does not wish it. She holds a plain, dark brown book, tightly.

"Evelyn, hello," my cousin says, unquestionably glad to see her. "How are you faring?"

"Just the same," she says. "We cannot all be talented thespians, walking the boards."

Andrew gestures to me. "I've brought my cousin, Genevieve Planché, who will begin work here as a porcelain decorator. Genevieve, may I present Evelyn Devlin."

I step forward, feeling rather shy but also glad to be making the acquaintance of such an intriguing female. She turns from Andrew to me and her smile vanishes.

"If you will excuse me," she says curtly, and turns away.

While I stand there shocked, and feeling almost a fool, William Duesbury appears to carry the tour forward.

Duesbury resumes his steady patter of explanation as we pass in and out of the throwing room, the dipping room, and the figure-making room, his remarks punctuated by the occasional stinging comment aimed at my cousin. Each time he aims a barb, it makes me wince. Also I can't stop thinking of Evelyn Devlin's display of dislike and wonder what I did to provoke it. I'm surprised at how much this hurts; my belly throbs. Or is that hunger? We've had nothing to eat since breaking our fast early this morning, and Duesbury stopped us from having our tea at the George Inn.

As we stand in one of the doorways, looking at a man hovering over a foot-high slab of unshaped porcelain, Duesbury says, "Geoffrey has the steadiest hand of anyone here in Derby since you left us, Andrew. He's not quite a modeler on your level, but we had no choice but to make do."

How much more of this is the man planning to ladle out? I'm flooded with irritation on my cousin's behalf and can't keep from murmuring, "Is a steady hand so very rare?"

Duesbury stares at me, appalled. "For this kind of porcelain production, only the men with the steadiest hands, the absolute best skills are hired. Do you think we just toss out plates here?"

"No," I say, because it's obvious that is the answer he wants

Duesbury takes a step closer to me, his eyes flaring with genuine anger. "I believe that is what you expected, that we are just another china factory, capable of nothing but imitation, spewing out wares for those with a few guineas," he says.

My cousin says, "William, please."

"When your cousin and I signed the papers to form this company, our plan was to create the most beautiful porcelain in England, works of beauty," Duesbury says. "He has the gift of sculpture, I know everything there is to know about enameling and painting. We produced figurines no one has seen before; they said we would become a second Meissen. There was a judging competition two years ago, and our porcelain was declared indistinguishable from Meissen's. It was in the London newspaper."

Andrew tries to placate him. "William, it is not Genevieve's fault. I've told her very little. I realize that since I moved to London, you've changed the business, made improvements, pursued new directions. I feared to prejudice her."

Waving his hand dismissively, Duesbury says: "Or perhaps she doesn't care to try to grasp the beauty of what we strive for here."

"Of course she cares," Andrew protests. "During the length of this trip, she's pestered me with questions about Derby Porcelain Works. She wants to know everything."

William Duesbury, the man with more restless energy than anyone I'd ever witnessed, stands absolutely still. "Does she indeed?" he asks.

My heart thumps quickly, painfully, as I pour every ounce of effort into maintaining a guileless face. "I want to succeed in my work here, Mr. Duesbury," I say. "I apologize if my words caused any offense."

For what seems an eternity, he continues to scrutinize me in silence. It feels as if he can see into my mind, perceive my true intent. I think of the Huguenot Bible with its hollowed-out compartment, its special ink, and am profoundly grateful that I locked it away in my trunk at the George Inn once we reached Derby.

"Will you stop this, William?" says my cousin, with a sharpness I'd not heard before. "You know quite well you're being unfair."

Duesbury shakes his head and blinks, as if coming out of a dream. "Apology accepted," he says. "Would you like to see the decorator's workshop, Mistress Genevieve?"

"Very much," I say.

Duesbury says, "Then we must ascend."

His unsettling smile is fixed on me now, and there is something in it I do not like. But I've no choice; I must follow.

A flight of stairs takes us to a long hallway with three closed doors on our right. Passing by the first two without opening them, he says, "The glazing room and the gilding room are finished for today."

We reach the end of the hallway, and he pauses before the third closed door.

"If you wish to know *everything*," says Duesbury, "this is the room for it."

CHAPTER ELEVEN

Following William Duesbury into the third room, I am struck by a flash of gold so penetrating that I cover both my eyes with my right hand.

Andrew's arm tightens around my shoulder. "What a remarkable sunset," he says.

I blink until my eyes adjust. The room we've entered boasts an enormous glass window, and outside the window, the sun, wobbling on the western horizon, shoots a thick ray into the river running beneath the building. It's the reflection from the river that blinds.

Now that I've got my bearings, I perceive we're in a room dominated by two fine tables, brand new ones, by the smell of fresh wood. With this much light pouring in from the windows onto sturdy tables, it's a fine artists' studio, perhaps the best I've ever seen. I inhale the familiar scents of oil paint and rags soaked in turpentine. Every artist's studio in England would smell just so.

But no other studio would harbor a new and revolutionary shade of blue.

"The sun this time of day is something to behold," says Duesbury. "Don't you agree, Ambrose?"

"Yes, Sir."

I'm startled; I had no idea someone else was in the room. Someone steps out of the far corner and it's evident why he would blend into the shadow. He's a mild-looking fellow, slight of build, wearing the same somber clothing as Evelyn Devlin but without the stylish flourishes. A colorless man, whose job it is to work with colors.

"I expect you two will have a great deal to talk about," says Duesbury. "Ambrose Stanton is head decorator. He'll be training you."

Training? I suffer yet another jolt, followed by the realization: But of course it would have to be that way. They wouldn't set me loose to paint their ceramics all alone, without supervision or training.

My cousin says, irritated, "Is Genevieve expected to begin work *now*?" Just as he says that, the sunset's glare fades and we're left in a room of the strangest light: a sickly orange, edged with purple.

Ambrose wordlessly bends down by some shelves to fetch something, and there's the gasp of a candle being lit.

Duesbury insists on my having a chat with Ambrose Stanton, dragging my cousin out the door. "Something I must discuss with you, Andrew," he says. "We'll come back for Genevieve in a bit."

The two men leave; Ambrose says nothing. I sense he's waiting for me to ask a question, to begin the training. It's what I came for, to learn about the painting of porcelain. But I find myself nervous, out of sorts; thrown by Duesbury's criticism a few moments ago, perhaps. I'm not ready to begin spying.

I make my way to the window. I can feel the cold pressing from the other side; the panes are edged with delicate ice. The river below gleams from the last rays of sun. The golden hue exudes warmth, but the water must be deadly cold. A stone river bridge of half-circle arches stretches across that water not far from us. I recognize it as the one we used to reach the town.

I see something else, a small stone building that seems to be built onto the bridge, with sparkling windows and perhaps a door peeking out from behind a squat, leafless tree. It possesses a bit of charm for me. I smile, for I'm suddenly reminded of the paintings of Old London Bridge, and all the homes and shops crowded on its top, so high and perilous that they swayed when the wind blew.

"Do you know who lives there?" I ask, pointing at the bridge.

Ambrose joins me at the window. "St. Mary's Bridge? No one." He pauses to think it over. "It's possible someone did once. It was a chapel for many, many years."

"A chapel on a bridge? Why?"

Ambrose removes a handkerchief from his pocket and wipes his nose, quickly and neatly, before folding it back into a square and answering. "The bridge was built centuries ago. I think that the river was always dangerous, even when spanned, and people would say a prayer there first, for protection. I believe… yes, I believe someone said a hermit hid there. But it may have been just a legend."

The last light of dusk withdraws from the river like blood draining from a dangled rabbit; I can no longer see the door or even the windows. The onetime chapel is transformed into a dark block of indifferent stone. But I'm still drawn to it.

"This sounds like a storybook," I say. "The hermit that hid in the chapel."

Ambrose says, "Derby is a modern town, very much at the forefront, but I'm sometimes surprised by the preoccupations of the people who live here, and in the smaller villages surrounding. Full of ghosts and warnings and blessings about this river or that house." His voice sours in disapproval. "Quite superstitious."

He moves away from the window, lighting more candles.

"You are not from these parts, Mr. Stanton?" I ask, following him to the new tables.

"No, I'm a Londoner, like yourself, Mistress Planché. I worked for a decorating house that Mr. Duesbury contracted with for the first few years of the porcelain works' existence. When he decided to have his porcelain painted on the site of the manufactory instead, he made an outstanding offer, sufficient for me and my wife. He loaned us five guineas to move here from London."

As I listen to his story, Ambrose Stanton shifts from a blandly courteous man into something else. What his character is, I can't quite tell yet. He's like a boat pushed off from a bank onto the dangerous river, bobbing and spinning in its middle.

"Mr. Duesbury is a most impressive employer," I say carefully.

"He is a visionary, Mistress Planché, and they don't come along every day." Ambrose's brown eyes flash in the candlelight. "He understands that we have the perfect opportunity here to find the juncture of art and industry. Many people go their whole lives without working for such a man. He was the first to perfect double enameling, you must know that."

"Of course," I lie. I won't make the same mistake twice.

Ambrose produces a porcelain figurine for my examination. It is a laughing clown, and from his facial features and rickshaw hat, I surmise it is meant to be a Chinese clown. "Your cousin, Andrew Planché, sculpted it, for one of Derby's earliest successful series," says Ambrose.

There is absolutely nothing of Andrew's heart and soul in this figurine. It is technically well made and doubtless serves the taste of the buyers, but the absence of artistic connection disturbs me.

"And now Mr. Duesbury hired you to make our flowers more admired, thanks to your special experience," Ambrose says. "It's most inspiring. I am eager to see the drawings you'll compose for us. And I look forward to instructing you on decorating the porcelain directly — it shouldn't take longer than one year before you're ready, if you're prepared to work hard."

It takes me time to absorb everything he just said. So there was a reason for my being hired besides my cousin's sponsorship. My work for Mrs. Garthwaite, painting flower designs for silk, piqued their interest. As flattering as that is, the last bit he said simply cannot stand unremarked on.

"Mr. Stanton, I have been painting since I was nine years old, under the tutelage of my grandfather, a known portrait artist," I say. "At sixteen I became apprenticed to Mrs. Garthwaite. I've been working at my trade since then. So I doubt that it will take one year before I am ready to contribute directly."

He says smoothly, "I was apprenticed as a porcelain decorator at age fourteen and have worked at it without ceasing for sixteen years. It is not like painting on canvas, on walls, or on silk, I'm afraid. The colors are ground into special powders, mixed with oils, and applied on fired clay, objects that are sometimes flat but more often rounded or even pointed. So there will need to be considerable adaptation on your part."

Ambrose Stanton has reached the far shore of Character, and the land is called Pomposity.

"Would it be possible for me to hear more about our colors?" I ask. Why not get to it? No one would find anything suspicious about the new decorator expressing an interest in colors. And I do not much like Ambrose.

"Of course." He goes to the shelf and returns with a tray of powder-paint compartments in one hand and a vase in the other. We take our stools at the table, sitting next to each other.

My eyes rake across the tray, eagerly, until I land on blue. It's a basic blue, the kind I've been using all my life. Perhaps once it's painted, it looks different. I turn my attention to the vase, my throat turning dry. The vase is painted with delicate yellow, a thread of red… and a very pretty — very ordinary — blue.

"These are the primary colors," I say. "You have other shades?"

"Many shades," he says. "You'll learn them all."

"And your sources?" I point at the vase. "That's Prussian blue?"

"Prussian blue is one we use," he says, looking at the vase along with me.

Inside, I am shouting, *This can't be true. I've come all this distance for Prussian blue?* No, Stanton hasn't shared it with me, but the new blue exists. It simply *must*.

I almost ask him about a new source. The question trembles on my lips. Yet Sir Gabriel instructed me not to push too obviously.

Instead I say, "I understand we are to be at the forefront of porcelain decoration."

"At the forefront?" he says, turning to look at me. Only half his face is illuminated in the candlelight. "How would that be?"

"With the designs we paint," I say, losing courage.

He agrees, and launches into a long explanation of the role of oil in how the shades' strengths are deployed, and the challenges of painting delicate designs on objects that are thrust into volcanic heat. I nod, and try to listen, but a part of me is turning over in my head the meaning of not finding a trace today of transcendent blue or its maker. Is Ambrose Stanton hiding it from me, a newcomer; does he himself not know of it; or, most worryingly, does it not exist?

A knock on the door, and a workman informs us we're wanted downstairs.

I find my cousin near the door, standing between two men, William

Duesbury and someone of middle years, florid-faced, wearing a grand russet waistcoat, his boots polished to spotlessness. Duesbury presents me to a man he calls "my partner and benefactor, John Heath." So now I meet the Derby banker. I'm weary of meeting people, but I force myself to greet him with enthusiasm and deference. I don't want to make any more errors.

He smiles, asking about my travels in a distinct voice, and as I answer I catch sight of my cousin Andrew's expression. I can tell from the set of his jaw and his clouded eyes that he is upset.

"My dear girl, you need to say your goodbyes to your estimable cousin now," booms Mr. Heath.

"Why would I do that?" I stammer. "We are returning to the George Inn."

"No, I won't have my new prized decorator — and cousin of a founding partner, Andrew Planché — in an inn," Heath says, as Duesbury murmurs agreement. "You're to live in my home, with my family, from now on. You'll be comfortable with us."

I manage to say, "But my belongings are at the George Inn."

"They've been moved to my house," says Heath proudly and then, to my astonishment, he takes Andrew by the arm and propels him toward me. "It's time for farewell, my dear girl."

My speech deteriorates to babble: "But why? I don't understand what's taking place. Where are you going, Andrew? Will I see you tomorrow?"

Andrew hugs me and kisses my cheek. "I know you'll do your family proud, Genevieve." He pulls back, takes one final look at me, his lips twisting, and then with visible effort, turns and leaves.

In the next moment I, too, leave the porcelain manufactory, led to Heath's waiting carriage. A third person rides with us, a clerk who works for Heath's bank; they talk of business, impenetrably. Sitting across from this smug man, I simply cannot believe I'm to live in his house. That was not the plan. My cousin has made tentative arrangements with a family he was close to when he lived in Derby. I know their names: the Kitteridges. What's become of the Kitteridges? I've never met them, but now their absence seems a crisis.

We reach John Heath's massive square brick house in no time. It stands in the town of Derby itself, on an estate banked by gardens. I catch a glimpse of snow-fringed bushes and empty flower stands on the way inside the grand front doors.

"Welcome to our home, we are so very pleased to have you," says a woman standing inside, in a soaring foyer. Her voice echoes in the space. I'm presented to Mrs. Heath, who seems utterly at ease with my arrival, as if it had been planned months ago. Her husband and his clerk disappear into another room, still talking business.

Mrs. Heath is hardly what I expected. She's around forty, slender and gracious, with black hair arranged in a popular style: tight curls across her head, like a row of black seashells. But what she wears startles me: a scarlet and white and pale blue oriental robe. I'd glimpsed English women in these robes — everything to do with the Far East is fashionable in London. But here, in a Derby house, on an ordinary day of the week? What makes it more disorienting, Mrs. Heath looks familiar to me.

As she leads me to my room at the end of the second-floor passage, I see that the entire house is decorated with Asia in mind, from paintings of distant snow-capped mountains and solemn emperors to red-lacquer trim along the stairs. Large porcelain urns rise in several corners.

"You must be so very tired, why don't you rest a little and then change for supper?" she asks. "I'll send in some tea."

With that, she opens the door to my new room. There yet another shock awaits. The bed in the center of the room is shaped like a giant pagoda, with red, gathered curtains and a black triangular top featuring black points.

Mrs. Heath says nothing about it, as if sleeping in a pagoda were common occurrence.

She leaves and I stand there, my head spinning. There is my trunk in the corner. Yes, I am supposed to sleep in this room.

Utterly confused and bone weary, I sit on the end of this absurd bed and bury my face in my hands. Of all the mistakes in my life, coming to Derby seems far and away the greatest.

I hear a door open on the other side of the room and drop my hands. Mrs. Heath must be back.

It is not the banker's wife who has walked into the room, but Evelyn Devlin, the young woman from the porcelain manufactory, who stands in front of the crackling fireplace.

"What are you doing here?" I demand.

She taps the side of her face with a finger as if mulling a difficult mental equation. "Oh, I don't know, possibly… could it be… yes, I believe the reason is this is my home and you're sitting on my bed."

"I was told this is *my* bed."

"By my mother? That's true. We will be sharing it, now that my sister is married and living elsewhere."

I am appalled. It's true that nearly everyone shares their bed, my solitary room in Spitalfields was the exception rather than the rule. But to share with *her*?

She points at the top of the pagoda in a grand gesture loaded with mockery. "My stepfather ordered it built after reading that the Duke and Duchess of Beaufort obtained one. Cost a fortune. When it arrived, he said he couldn't sleep in it because, well…" she flashes a secretive, contempt-flavored smile… "you've seen him. So it passed to me. Do you like it?"

"No," I say.

"Ah. Don't even think about attempting to have the arrangements changed. I've tried and it is never effective. Only makes matters far, far worse."

A maid arrives with tea, and Evelyn Devlin slips back out the way she came in.

It is only after tea, desperately needed, that I am resolved. I must find what I came here to find and then escape. Of course the secret wouldn't fall into my hands in the first hours in Derby. But Sir Gabriel is no fool. He said he received a piece from an earlier spy. The blue *is* in the manufactory somewhere. I must complete my assignment and propel myself from here.

Supper is surprisingly indifferent. After glimpsing the décor of this house, I'd expected sophisticated fare, not mutton. The dish is served on white plates, sparkling with the unearthly light of true porcelain, gilded with a border of gold-flecked paint… but it's still mutton, over seasoned with cloves. I'm famished, however, and I devour it. Also dining with enthusiasm is John Heath, who does not say a word until he has consumed half of his meat.

Mrs. Heath poses questions on popular styles in London. I do my best to answer them, but I've never set foot in the Royal Academy of Music, I know nothing of the operas she's read about. My knowledge of women's ever-shifting taste in clothes comes from laboring as a link in the chain of people who construct the clothes. After a little while, Mrs. Heath's questions become more general as she correctly comprehends my station in London society.

Down the table, Evelyn picks at her food in funereal silence. I can only assume all family meals pass this way.

When Mr. Heath enters the conversation, it centers on porcelain, of course.

"Your cousin Andrew was a genius," he says. "And having a Huguenot helped us secure our financing."

"I beg your pardon?" I say. "I didn't realize Andrew was ever in finance."

Husband and wife smile at each other knowingly.

"The very first English porcelain was produced in Chelsea in 1744, just fifteen years ago, by a Huguenot immigrant named Nicholas Sprimont," explains Mr. Heath. "He was a silversmith in Soho, managed to recruit some Frenchmen from the factory at Chantilly and began to work. Voila. A factory is born. Ever since then, all the factory owners jostle to hire one and show him off. And not just *any* Huguenot, but the best."

My cheeks burn. He seems to think the comment a compliment, but I feel as if we are like the pet canaries Grandfather keeps caged in his room.

Mr. Heath raises his glass to toast his wife and me — not his step-daughter. "Here's to building our own family traditions at Derby. May we someday be like the Chinese, with their hundreds of years' worth of positions handed down, generation after generation. All of their secrets, guarded with their lives."

On the word *secrets* it seems that Mr. Heath's gaze rests on me. I do my best to look back at him, all innocence.

He continues on, about the Chinese.

"Before the secret of the porcelain formula was stolen from them, they had an entire city set aside for making the porcelain, with kiln after kiln after kiln to supply everyone in the world who wanted it. What did Father François Xavier d'Entrecolles say about Jingdezhen, my dear?"

He mangles the French tongue; I can only wonder if he butchers the

Chinese. His wife reaches across the table. Tapping with her slender fingers, she says, "The whirling flames and smoke which rise at different places make the approach to Jingdezhen remarkable for its extent, depth, and shape. During a night entrance, one thinks that the whole city is on fire, or that it is one furnace with many ventholes."

Taken aback, I say, "You speak as if you were present, Mrs. Heath."

"My wife and I have read the published translations of the Jesuit letters so often that she has them in her memory," says Mr. Heath proudly. "My dear girl, I'd like you to guess how many people worked in those factories of Jingdezhen when the porcelain capital of China was at its height of production."

"I wouldn't know," I say. I try to be as polite as possible, but I detest guessing games.

His voice rising, Mr. Heath says, "You must guess, you must."

"Very well," I say. "Five thousand?"

He scoffs. "Guess again."

"Forgive me, but I've no notion, Mr. Heath."

"Guess, guess, guess!" The man with the moustache pounds on the table like a thwarted child.

"Ten thousand," I say, between gritted teeth.

He laughs, scornfully.

I hear a noise emanating from the other side of the table: a strangled sigh. I turn to see Evelyn, her fingers pressed to her temples as if her head throbs.

"Thirty thousand?" I ask, desperate to end it.

"Correct!" he cries. "Thirty thousand workers, day and night, making porcelain. Just think of it, just think of all…that…" he pauses theatrically — "money." The thick table shakes with the laughter of Mr. Heath, a near-hysterical explosion so forceful I grip my chair.

His wife joins in the laughter, though hers is a light, airy chuckle in contrast to his guffaw. I don't know what to make of Mr. and Mrs. Heath. But then, I've had little opportunity to observe a successful marriage. Perhaps this is what it looks like.

"And how do you judge your countryman's actions?" asks Mr. Heath, his voice still thickened with the laughter.

"Which one?"

"The Jesuit," he says. "Who served King Louis by spying on the Chinese porcelain workers, saying he was saving their souls while taking his notes and writing secret letters. He had the same fever as all the others, didn't he? He sought to discover the formula of porcelain."

Hearing the word *formula* from his lips chills me, and his inability to tell the vast difference between a Jesuit — a soldier of the Pope — and a Protestant Huguenot horrifies me.

"I suppose in his mind he was taking the right course," I mutter.

"Just so," he says, and calls for dessert.

Over chocolate cream, slightly clumped, in fluted glasses, I begin to dread retiring to the same bed as Evelyn. But I am so completely exhausted that the moment I return to the bedroom, alone, I don nightclothes and stretch out on the pagoda bed. Unconsciousness comes at once. My dream is long and complicated and, quite suddenly, loud. People shouting at me.

My arm shakes. No, someone is shaking it — shaking me. And a light burns my eyelids.

I open my eyes to an incredible sight: William Duesbury leans over me, so close I can see every pock mark in his skin. He's the one who is shaking me, saying loudly, "Wake up!"

John Heath stands next to him, holding a candelabra high. "My dear girl, we must speak with you," he says.

Another person is in the room, a rough-faced man wearing a lumpy wig. "Get out of the bed, girl," he growls.

"What is happening?" I ask, my voice a croak.

"Get out of the bed — now," the rough man shouts.

I push back the covers and slide out of the bed, wearing nothing but my night shift, still unsure if I'm even awake. I look at Mr. Heath, the man who welcomed me into his home, who toasted me at his table. He won't meet my gaze now.

"My name is Major Samuel Tarkwell and I am charged with an important task," says the man, moving closer to me. His face is marked by a white-edged deep groove of a scar under his right cheekbone. At the same time there's a dragging thump on the floor. I look down — he has one wooden leg. "I was hired to make sure all is secure at Derby Porcelain Works. But all is *not* secure, and that's because of your presence."

I say, my voice rising, "This is completely outrageous."

"Now you see it for yourself," Duesbury says, with satisfaction, to Tarkwell.

"I do, yes, Sir, I do," says Tarkwell. "What we have here is a French spy."

"What?" I cry.

Tarkwell smiles, making his scar pucker like a hideous second mouth. "Gentlemen, the first thing we're going to do," he says, "is open her trunk."

CHAPTER TWELVE

"Major Tarkwell investigates all recently hired workers at Derby Porcelain," says Mr. Heath.

"And why is it necessary to carry out an investigation in the middle of the night?" I demand.

No one answers.

William Duesbury is the one carrying out the major's order. He throws open my trunk and kneels before it to scoop out the contents. On top are my dresses and shifts and stockings, not yet put away because I was too weary. When I'd arrived at the George Inn, I tucked the Bible deep into a corner of the trunk, under a cloak. It will be scooped out like everything else.

Seeing Duesbury's hands on my clothes, my undergarments, ignites a rage in me I can't control. I charge toward him; Mr. Heath grabs my arm and pulls me back.

"Ask me any question you wish, but why on earth are you searching my trunk, and how dare you treat me in this fashion?" I shout at all three men, struggling in Mr. Heath's tight grasp. "I'm a gentlewoman from London."

"You work for Derby Porcelain Works now, and that means we

can treat you this way," Major Tarkwell shouts back. "This business is riddled with spies. We have our suspicions, and we shall act on them."

"No letters or papers so far," reports Duesbury.

"Keep looking," growls the major. "Check for books; she could have something tucked inside a book."

Fear, cold fear, slices through my rage. I need to think, for it's obvious that flailing and shouting make matters worse. At a glance, the Bible will betray nothing. But sensitive fingers could trigger the mechanism that opens the compartment. As the seconds tick by, and Duesbury's probing hands near the corner holding the Bible, an idea comes to me.

I declare, "If you have any pretense whatsoever to being gentlemen, you will withdraw so that I may dress myself. Then if this outrage must continue, I am plainly powerless to stop you."

Mr. Heath lets go of my arm and says, "After all, Major, we should —"

"No," cries Major Tarkwell, slapping the side of his leg. "I will not be tricked. She could see to her secrets while we're conveniently out of the room. Now I *know* there is something of interest in this trunk."

I have failed.

Duesbury holds up something gleaming to the candlelight. It is my father's watch. "Not bad workmanship," he murmurs.

Tears of helpless anger fill my eyes.

I feel something warm on my shoulders. Evelyn Devlin wraps a long shawl around me. I had completely forgotten about her, I wasn't even aware of her being in the bed when they woke me.

"Thank you," I say, my voice trembling.

"Wait outside, Evelyn," says Mr. Heath.

Silence fills the room for at least five seconds.

"No," she says.

I peer over at Evelyn, her black hair rippled from the undone plait and hanging down her back. She regards Mr. Heath with loathing that is all the more impressive for her display of calm.

Mr. Heath stares back at her but says nothing. I wait for Major Tarkwell to rail at her, to threaten, but he says nothing. Nor does Duesbury, still kneeling before my trunk, peering over his shoulder. They may not like her, but evidently she has standing, for they do not treat her as they do me.

My tears dry. Evelyn's courage, exercised on behalf of someone she barely knows, calls forth something in me.

I say, "State your suspicions. Who do you imagine I spy for? Have I given you any cause at all to doubt me? Tell me which of my words or actions justify this."

Major Tarkwell barks a laugh. "You do not have to say or do anything, girl, you just have to draw air. You are French, that's enough for me. Who knows who you could be spying for? I can think of a dozen scoundrels, in England and on the Continent, who would pay a spy to infiltrate Derby. The French can never be trusted. Sweet Jesus, we're at war with France now. Again. No one needs to tell me about French treachery."

He shakes his head, back and forth, as if he has some form of palsy. "I faced an invading army backed by the French before, at Culloden." He raises his wooden leg a few inches and slams it back down, making a loud cracking noise. "They did this to me, the Jacobite scum. All French are scum."

"You think I am a Jacobite? But I am a Huguenot."

His assumption displays such profound ignorance of politics and religion, it's absurd. What is obvious to me — and to anyone in London — is perhaps not obvious here. What a mistake it was not to explain to the Heaths the differences between myself and a Jesuit at dinner. I must remedy it now.

"We are a Protestant people and for two hundred years the French kings have persecuted us," I say. "We were forced to become refugees — do you know what the word means? We sought refuge from persecution ordered by the French crown. My grandfather was born in France, yes, but escaped here when he was a child. My mother, myself — born in London. I am a citizen of Britain, just as you are."

Major Tarkwell stomps toward me. "You *dare* compare myself to *me*? I served King George in the field — I was ready to give my life, I nearly *did* give my life, you bitch."

"Major," says Duesbury, cautioning him. Ah, so insults and threats are acceptable to my new employer, but he won't tolerate profanity.

A fresh idea of how to save myself springs to mind.

"Mr. Duesbury, I've brought my Huguenot Bible to Derby, I believe it's tucked into a corner, may I have it, please?" I hold out my hand, not imperiously but as a sincere supplicant.

Duesbury pulls the Bible out and frowns at the sight of the worn brown cover.

"Sir?" I repeat, my hand still outstretched, the palm tilted up.

Duesbury lumbers to his feet, and with a half-dozen steps, the Bible is mine.

Gripping it tight, I announce, "This is what we Huguenots fought and died for, to live by the Word; not what a priest says it is, but what we understand through our own reading." I display the inside cover and title pages, and I flip the Bible upside-down, ruffling the pages. Throughout, the secret compartment remains safely closed. "No letters or papers, as you can see, gentlemen. Just God's wisdom."

I turn it back up again, and search for Proverbs, my fingers spinning through the delicate pages. It is silent in the room but for the breathing of those who distrust me. Deuteronomy... Job... Kings...

Where is it? My fingers shake in the search.

I find it. Proverbs 10:2. "Ill gotten treasures have no lasting value," I read aloud, "but righteousness delivers from death."

"Enough," snaps Major Tarkwell. "I'll not be preached to."

I close the Bible and clasp it to my chest.

"I believe your investigation is complete," Mr. Heath says to Major Tarkwell. Duesbury, nodding, says, "I am satisfied." He starts for the door.

"Hold," the major bellows, as if commanding soldiers about to charge. "There's one more thing."

He points at the mantel over the fireplace. "Isn't that small vase made of porcelain?"

Mr. Heath says, "It is indeed. China, Yuan dynasty."

Major Tarkwell turns his finger toward me. "Bring it to me, Mademoiselle." He pulls out the word, emphasizing each syllable. His hatred of the French is implacable.

I place the Bible on the table by the pagoda bed and walk to the fireplace, head high, trying to conceal my dread. It's impossible that the survivor of Culloden would wish to discuss porcelain design. I have no idea what this is about.

I reach for the vase, the heat of the fire racing up the front of my shift.

When I turn around to face them, it is the expression on Evelyn's face that leaps out at me, not the others. Her usual cool composure is gone, replaced by an expression of deep concern.

Major Tarkwell says, "Hold it tight." He comes toward me with his ghastly half-limp, his scarred face twisted in the grin that makes my stomach turn.

When we are but inches apart, he reaches into the pocket of his coat and pulls out a knife at least three inches long with a black handle. He raises it, the flame from the fireplace gleaming on the blade — and

After a moment, I ask, "But still, why did they hire that sort of man?"

"The porcelain business is highly competitive, you must know that," she says. "The minute a new style is mastered, the news leaks and a rival imitates it — any advantage is lost. We must keep our practices secret."

"Yes, I have heard as much. But Derby has been in business for years, why bring him in now?"

"The major is charged with preventing any further lapses," she explains. "We had an incident in October."

"An incident?"

"One of the workers stole something, a valuable piece, and vanished. Not seen again by anyone in Derby. We've had our share of pilfering out the back door, every porcelain manufactory has. But this was something serious, and it's the reason why they instituted their £500 fine."

I remember Sir Gabriel telling me about his experience with an earlier spy, though his name eludes me. It seems that his first attempt to discover the blue will make it extremely difficult for a second to succeed. The warm brandy chills inside me. I will have some unwelcome news to share in my first letter using invisible ink.

"Richard Frederick was such a dull young fellow," she muses. "He was on the sullen side, but I'd have never spotted him for a criminal."

I say, "He sounds like nothing but a base thief. Why did Major Tarkwell go on about spying then?"

She shrugs, pushing her black hair off her shoulder. "There is some other aspect to the theft. They don't share everything with me."

I can detect no subterfuge in her voice or expression, but I have known Evelyn Devlin for less than a day. Perhaps she knows more than she's letting on.

"When I saw you at the manufactory, I thought you one of the workers," I say. "Now I realize that those at the manufactory work for you."

After a pause, she says, "Not precisely."

"Well, if you don't wish to discuss it, I've no desire to pry."

"My stepfather sank a fortune into the porcelain manufactory. He invested thousands of pounds in exchange for one-third of the profits, and that was only the first payment." She balls her hand into a fist and says, "I intend to make sure he doesn't lose it. Not for any love of him, let me assure you, but for my mother's sake. She can't be poor again. She couldn't survive it. So I keep the accounts, mark the expenditures, wages and supplies, and the money we earn when the pieces go up for auction in London. I enjoy mathematics, I always have."

For a female to work as a porcelain decorator is somewhat uncommon. A female manager of a business' finances is unheard of. I'm impressed.

"I think it admirable that you wish to do this work," I say. "Mr. Heath must be grateful."

"Grateful? A man like that? He'd only be grateful if I married one of the strutting fools in this town that he looks on with favor. I keep the books because there's no one better at it, but he's never thanked me for it. He browbeat my sister into marriage, he won't do the same with me. I won't marry without respect."

"I quite agree with your position," I say.

"Do you?" she peers at me. I feel like I'm a row of numbers she adds up in that ledger book of hers. She finally says, "I've heard it said, 'The enemy of mine enemy is my friend,' so I suppose that means we are to be friends."

"What an endorsement." I laugh, and she joins in. Curiously, I find I do wish her to consider us friends. She helped me tonight when I was in need of it.

"I think we should sleep now," she announces. "There will be much work to do tomorrow, for both of us."

She blows out the candles in the room so that only the low flicker of the fire casts any light. Settling under her blanket, Evelyn says, "I hope that our friendship prospers, Genevieve. I do. But I think it only fair to warn you, and I'll only warn you a single time, that you must never betray my trust in any way. Good night — and sleep well."

CHAPTER THIRTEEN

Sir Gabriel Courtenay told me not once but several times that he needs a result from me by spring. I estimate that gives me seven weeks to accomplish my goal. Since extreme caution is warranted, I decide before I even rise from bed the first morning in the Heaths' home that I must be nothing but a porcelain painter for the first fortnight. I will listen; I will watch; I will learn. But I will not ask a single question that raises suspicion.

It is well that I took such a private vow, for the conditions of my work at Derby Porcelain Manufactory cannot possibly be less conducive to discovering secrets.

Each morning, I rise at dawn and ride to the Nottingham Road manufactory in the carriage with Evelyn, glimpsing bits of the town of Derby as we go, reading the signs for street names and gazing at the shops and taverns, until the road swings toward the river, past the enormous silk mill, its prosperity founded on the deviousness of a spy. A few more minutes and we arrive at the porcelain manufactory.

I make my way upstairs to the decorating room, which I rarely have cause to leave for five or six days a week, up to ten hours a day. At Derby there's a five shilling fine imposed on any employee who is found in a part of the porcelain works they have no business being.

Ambrose Stanton gives me my instructions, always in a serious tone, and I follow them. He doesn't speak to me too often aside from that, directing his conversation to his young apprentice, Harry Brown, or seeing to the needs of the other departments.

William Duesbury darts in several times a day, never to speak to me. At the end of the workday, I head down the stairs to meet Evelyn and walk out the door with all the others, the difference being they scurry in the cold for their homes, while we step into the Heaths' carriage for a brief ride to the house.

And so it begins, the position I'd refused, fought off, and dreaded for months, and only agreed to as a pretext for spying. A porcelain decorator buried in the middle of England.

If I'm honest with myself, the work itself is not unpleasant. As promised in my first meeting with Ambrose, my task is painting flowers. For my first three months here, I must produce artwork of various arrays of flowers — roses, peonies, carnations, and lilies — gathered in bouquets or a few blooms intertwined. This artwork will be used to plan decorative designs created by Ambrose Stanton, guided by Duesbury.

"The flowers must be lifelike in every detail but the lightest, airiest, most intoxicating possible version," says Ambrose Stanton, never sounding more somber.

"I see."

Not sure that I grasp his meaning, Ambrose presses it. "You must always convey a light heart."

"Like a fantasy of life?" I ask.

He thinks the phrase over and says, "Yes, just so."

When I worked for Mrs. Garthwaite, I jostled with the other artists for the best spaces in her noisy second-floor studio, divvying up paints and often waiting, hawk-eyed, for the choicest carmine or vermillion to come my way. We raced to finish our work before we lost the sun entirely, even though most days it was a faint presence indeed, due to London's pea soup of smoke and fog.

Here, I have a table to myself, light pouring in from the large window. My medium is watercolor. I must admit, I winced at the sight of it the first morning. Women are relegated to watercolor or pastel crayons; oil paint is only for men. Ambrose explains that it's to make my work go quickly, and I accept this decision in silence. Protest would seem strange from a woman who supposedly came here willingly, feeling herself fortunate to win a post at Derby.

Ambrose supplies me with sheets of wove paper, the best I've ever worked with, a tray with thirty-two cakes of color, and small bowls of water for dampening, diluting, and cleaning. My brushes are excellent, sable-hair tools newly purchased from the leading London supplier. When the wealthy travel on the continent, it's fashionable to take a watercolor box, for capturing a landscape of beauty to be enjoyed after returning to England. I wonder if this was the case for Sir Gabriel Courtenay, on his grand tour. He would have had the best sable brushes. Anything else was unthinkable.

Ambrose and young Harry, painting with oil on porcelain, use top-notch supplies as well: slender white and gray brushes of quivering-straight wild boar hair, manufactured in Germany. Ambrose once told me the pigs grow to be massive in the wild forest, until the day they are driven out into a clearing and speared to death. They die not for their flesh but for their hair.

No expense is spared for the work taking place in this room.

"Do you require certain books of flowers to draw from?" asks Ambrose the first morning. "I will make a list for you of our resources."

"There's no need, Mr. Stanton. I draw from memory."

Ambrose looks highly skeptical. I suspect he wants a fantasy of life, but only one that conforms to an approved book. What he doesn't understand is that no book sketch, even if it employs hours' worth of meticulous detail and color shading, can capture the potent beauty of a real flower. I paint to evoke the feeling of awe and joy of observing a flower.

After he sees my first set of sketches, Ambrose no longer presses me to use a book.

When my right arm begins to throb and my neck ache, I stand, stretch, and look at the view stretching before me: the thriving town and the curving river and the stone bridge. My eyes always linger on the bridge's little house. Even though Ambrose told me it was empty, I wait for someone to emerge in the doorway, a face to appear in the window.

If moments come when I forget the true reason I am here, Major Tarkwell brings it back to me in force. I see him in the morning when I'm walking in or in the late afternoon walking out, and it's always the same. He stands just outside the building, wearing his filthy uniform coat, leaning to the side of his wooden leg, and watches, his eyes tracking me and no one else even if I am part of a sizable crowd. He never speaks to me. A couple times he nods and grins, as if in response to some phantom pouring terrible things about me into his ear.

Major Tarkwell's baleful presence is the reason I remain in the decorators' studio, working steadily and taking my meals there. Lunch is usually plain brown bread and cheese, wrapped in paper, and a tankard of water.

The very first time I sip the water, I am surprised by its taste: bracingly sweet and bitter at the same time, and delicious.

"We're known for our water, here in Derbyshire," says Ambrose's apprentice, Harry, beaming. "People come here from all over England, to take the cure." Eighteen years of age, one year into his seven-year apprenticeship, he has wide brown eyes and curly dark hair that bounces off his bony shoulders. In everything he says to Ambrose, every move he makes, even the tiniest stroke of a brush, he radiates happiness to be here, to have been chosen as apprentice. I think of him as a good-natured puppy, scrambling here and there, tail wagging. All in his life is not joyful, however. Thanks to Evelyn's knowledge of the workers' backgrounds, I know that Harry lives in a humble part of town with his widowed mother and sickly grandmother. His older brother is a soldier of the Forty-Fifth Regiment of Foot, stocked with Derbyshire men, sent to Canada three long years ago to fight the French. The red against the blue.

"It is exceptionally fine water," I agree.

Harry says, "I'll tell my grandmother you said as much. When she was just a girl, she helped make offerings to the water spirit in the well."

"There's no place for superstition at Derby Porcelain," declares Ambrose from his table. "And none for gossip of any kind." Through Evelyn, I'm aware of the background of Ambrose Stanton also. He's a Quaker, a committed opponent of violence, and also of such lesser sins as profanity and idle gossip.

What Ambrose Stanton does believe in is... art. Delicate florals dancing across snow-white porcelain, from vases to plates, cups and fingerbowls, teapots and sugar boxes, seems to be the taste here. One morning during my second week, Ambrose shows me just how extreme such taste can reach. He places on the table for my inspection, with great care, something that, for the first few seconds, looks like a pale pink carnation.

I gasp as I realize this is a piece of porcelain.

The delicacy, the exquisite subtlety of the carved layers of the carnation, leaves me stunned. "Did we make this?" I ask, my hand caressing it as carefully as I would a butterfly wing. If anything could be a fantasy of life, it's this flower.

"Unfortunately not," says Ambrose. "Mr, Heath purchased it from someone in London who himself bought it last year at Sèvres, the factory favored by the king of France."

I pull my hand away.

"So you may observe the high standards of Sèvres," says Ambrose.

Harry pipes up: "We're lucky to have our own French artist in Derby now."

I whirl to face the boy, expecting to see some trace of resentment in his eyes for the sake of his brother, battling the French army across the tundra of Quebec. But there is only honest admiration in his brown eyes.

*

In the carriage that evening, I tell Evelyn about the carnation and also of my personal circumstance. "I'm valued for being French at the same I'm distrusted for being French, while all the while few people understand that a Huguenot living in Spitalfields fears King Louis more than any English person alive ever could."

"It's incredibly confusing," she admits. "And whenever you refer to Sèvres, what you're actually talking about is Madame de Pompadour."

I grimace. "What a time we live in, that a mistress of a tyrant is the most powerful woman in the world."

"Is she?"

"The London newspapers say it was Madame de Pompadour who coaxed King Louis into an alliance with Austria, and declaring war on England," I say.

"In our house, there's little interest in politics," comments Evelyn.

"If you want to set a room afire with enthusiasm, mention the porcelain flower at supper tonight."

*

My curiosity piqued, I tell the Heaths about Ambrose bringing me the porcelain flower to inspect.

Both of them react with passionate enthusiasm, just as Evelyn predicted.

Mr. Heath explodes. "My God, the artistry of it!"

Clasping her hands in front of her, Mrs. Heath says, reverently, "That carnation was inspired by a flower that came directly from Madame de Pompadour's own hothouse. Can you imagine seeing it with your own eyes?"

I exchange a glance with Evelyn, before saying, "Her hothouse?"

"Haven't you heard of it? About ten years ago, King Louis built his mistress a house overlooking the Seine, the Château de Bellevue. She filled it with art and sculpture, but it was in the hothouse that she surpassed herself. It took months to create. She invited the king to see her one day in the middle of a cold winter. When he arrived, he was led to an apartment he'd never seen before: a hothouse. She was sitting in the middle of it, a flowerbed of roses, tulips, peonies, jonquils, hyacinths, blue daffodils. Hundreds of flowers, all of them porcelain. She'd even commissioned essences of oils of the flowers' fragrances, to be released into the air."

"I don't believe it," I murmur.

"Oh it's true," insists Mr. Heath. "The Château de Bellevue was witnessed by certain English nobles before the war broke out."

His wife says: "Everything to do with Sèvres is guided by Madame de Pompadour. The factory has many investors, but of course she and

King Louis are its chief benefactors. The factory itself was moved from Vincennes on the east side of Paris to a building west of Paris, near Versailles, so that the king's mistress could personally supervise. She directs an army of sculptors, decorators, and chemists."

Mr. Heath heaves a great sigh and sets down the knife he's been using to saw his medallion of overcooked beef. "Do you know how difficult it is to compete against Sèvres, a porcelain manufactory with those kinds of resources?" he complains. "In France and in Saxony, the monarchs pour money into the manufactories, but not in England, no. King George cares nothing for porcelain. Here, it's up to the bankers. We are the ones who back the industry — at great risk, may I add — and our nobles, do you think they support what we do in England, by patronizing the porcelain from our fledgling workshops? No, they still prefer to buy from Meissen, and now from Sèvres."

"Wait a minute — we are at war with France and English nobles still prefer French goods?" I ask, incredulous.

Mrs. Heath nods sadly.

Mr. Heath says, "It's against the law to purchase from Sèvres, but they go to great lengths to do it anyway, eager to pay a crippling tariffs. And the merchants and the other people of lesser breeding, do you think they at least patronize English porcelain? No, they turn east and buy from China, thanks to the blasted East India Trading Company!"

It is odd to see him like this, not braying confidence but honestly worried, and with reason, I should think.

Her forehead puckered with concern, Mrs. Heath says, "We shall show them, Mr. Heath."

"Yes, my dear," he says, but his eyes are fixed on the table.

His wife says, "Remember, when it's finally ready, our new porcelain will be the most beautiful the world has ever seen!"

Mr. Heath shakes his head, warningly, his eyes darting sideways to where I sit.

Mrs. Heath, her voice shrill, calls for dessert. I try my best not to show that I took note of what she said — and his subsequent warning. After a minute, I turn toward the other end of the table, at Evelyn, and catch her, too, looking at me with worry.

They know — they all three of them know — about the secret experiments with the color blue.

The realization moves through me like a queasy shudder. I had begun to wonder if the blue even existed, or, if it did, if William Duesbury was the only one aware of the chemist's work and kept him an exclusive secret. But of course Heath would have to know, being the man who backs it all, and his wife is as porcelain-mad as he is, so there'd be no keeping it from her. I'd doubted Evelyn was part of the circle of knowledge but now I see I was mistaken. Heath, while permitting her to keep the books, doesn't like his stepdaughter much, yet somehow she knows about the existence of the chemist, Thomas Sturbridge. I'm certain of it. And they're hiding it all from me.

At dinner's end, Heath rises, heavily, and says, "Mistress Genevieve, you have a letter from London," and pulls it from his coat pocket.

Yet another surprise. I've been in Derby eight days. It would seem too soon to be receiving a letter from Grandfather. I was told that a letter takes at least one week to travel from London to Derby in winter. Moreover, Grandfather is not one for letters. I know that he will write to me — but this quickly?

Alone with Evelyn in the room, I examine it. Sure enough, I recognize Grandfather's handwriting on the square piece of paper, which hangs loose in my hand. Turning it over, I see why. The seal's been broken.

I say to her, angrily, "This is quite a state of affairs, to break seals to read personal letters from a guest's family."

"I think it must be at the insistence of our friend, Major Tarkwell."

"No doubt," I say, clutching the letter close. Grandfather is an honorable man, and I hate to think of Tarkwell's foul hands on the same paper he has touched.

"Aren't you going to read it?" she asks.

Forcing a smile, I unfold my single sheet of parchment paper and read my grandfather's letter. It is very short. He hopes I'm comfortable in my new home; Daphne wishes she had an excuse to make me her morning chocolate; a new exhibit opened at the Society of Art. I am much missed.

I repeat his message to her, out loud. Folding the letter back up, I say, "I miss them all as well." And then: "I shall have to reimburse Mr. Heath the cost of the postage."

Linking her arm in mine, Evelyn says, "Oh, it is the least the man can do. Let's retire to Mother's room."

Have I passed some test? I've never before been invited to join mother and daughter in Mrs. Heath's upstairs parlor. I admit to some curiosity so far about the tenor of these female gatherings.

Mother and daughter do not speak too much during meals. However, it is a completely different matter here. I begin to realize Mrs. Heath's coolness toward Evelyn is for the benefit of her husband. As they chatter, a servant appears to set up the table for a game of faro, spreading the green cloth and laying down the cards.

"You'll join us?" says Mrs. Heath to me, smiling as she taps a chair top her left.

I explain that I do not know any card games; they apologize for even suggesting it. If only it were that simple. It's true that gambling is discouraged by our church elders, but card games can be found all over Spitalfields any day of the week. My aversion springs from Denis' fatal obsession. For a moment the ghost of my rascal fiancé stalks the room, but his tastes ran toward rougher games than faro played for spotted counters.

I take up a novel to pass the time as the two of them play cards. They chat while playing, nothing of consequence, but I note the absence of tension, of pretense. Mrs. Heath does not seek to sparkle; Evelyn does not aim any barbs.

Yet my eyes keep wandering from the page. I'm distracted by some worry; it nags at me like a tooth starting to ache.

Between hands, Evelyn says, "That book doesn't appear to be your sort. It's a shame your grandfather's letter is so short."

Yes, short it is… and with that, the source of my uneasiness comes into focus. The amount of space left blank below Grandfather's signature is precisely what Sir Gabriel recommended in a letter that contains sympathetic ink.

The first Tuesday after I came to live in the Heaths' house, I dispatched my letter to Sir Gabriel in the agreed-on manner: A short, visible message to Grandfather and below it, my invisible message. I used my special writing tools on the first evening that Evelyn spent with her mother, giving me privacy. Within the allotted space on the paper, I informed him that I lived with the Heaths, I had seen no sign of the chemist and doubted he worked within the manufactory, and I'd been threatened by Major Tarkwell.

Is the letter in my hand a reply from Sir Gabriel? I don't see how that is possible, given the constraint of time. But I need to be sure.

"I fear I'm starting a bit of a headache," I say.

"Do you need anything?" asks Evelyn. "I could see to a tonic."

I politely decline and make my retreat.

The Heath servants know better than to let a fire die out, and sure enough, there is sufficient flame in my room to uncover the sympathetic writing the way I was taught. I close the door all the way, and kneel by the fire, unfolding the letter once more. There's not the faintest hint of writing below my grandfather's signature.

I lean closer, hold the letter over the fire, and wait, my fingers nervously clutching the paper.

"Oh!" I cry as two sentences snap onto the bottom one-third of the page.

"Presence of Tarkwell noted. Make every effort to obtain location of chemist's laboratory and relay it without delay."

I fall back onto the floor. How had he done it — or rather, how had they done it? For I see proof of a network of operatives that must have been required to speed last week's letter to Sir Gabriel and for his to hurry back. The knowledge of my daily life at home, the ability to forge Grandfather's writing. All this effort, and cost, for a spy mission that seeks the formula for a color.

How am I learn the location, when I haven't an earthly reason to ask questions about something I should not know about, a secret particularly guarded by a man accustomed to violence? When I'm rarely alone and my movements are watched? I feel a rising panic.

What are the consequences if I fail at this? I had not considered that until now.

A piece of firewood pops loudly, prompting me to do what Sir Gabriel instructed me with a letter immediately after reading: destroy it. I push the paper into the fire. Flames eagerly devour the paper.

A flicker tosses up the piece of paper showing the word *Tarkwell* at the same instant that Evelyn Devlin comes through the door.

"What are you doing?" she asks, frowning at the sight of me, sitting in front of the fire. "Are you burning something?"

Tarkwell disintegrates perhaps two seconds before she glances into the fire. I can't summon up a word to say.

Moving closer, she says, "Was that your grandfather's letter? Why on earth would you burn it?"

I rise, straightening my rumpled skirts, playing for time.

"It's our tradition," I say at last. "Huguenots burn all their letters."

"Why?"

"Something to do with our being refugees."

She doesn't seem to believe me. "I wanted to see if you were feeling better, and you certainly don't look well, but instead of resting, you're practically sitting in the fireplace, burning a letter."

"I suppose I am not myself," I say, with what I hope appears to be a weak shrug. "You should return to your faro game."

"No, I don't believe I will."

Evelyn doesn't say anything more to me. She rings for her maid to help her prepare for bed. I'd insisted from the beginning that I would not require similar attention. I pull off my own dress and put on my shift, and crawl into bed, turning my back to hers and pretending to sleep.

CHAPTER FOURTEEN

The time for cautious waiting is over. I must endeavor to find this blasted chemist.

Blue is a color, colors are used to decorate, those who decorate must know something of such experiments. Sir Gabriel told me efforts have been underway for six months.

When Ambrose Stanton is out of the room, I ask Harry, "We must make our mark with Derby porcelain but do you think pretty flowers painted on the surfaces is enough?"

Harry thinks a moment. "Do you mean we should give priority to the figurines, try for something more original?"

I say, "Hmmm, Harry, it occurs to me that we must be sure to have the finest colors at our disposal. Color could be the next stage of innovation, rather than the shape of the figurine. Don't you agree?"

"Oh, I am certain that Mr. Stanton and Mr. Duesbury order the very best new colors for us as soon as they're in the paint catalogs," says Harry, eyes shining with sincerity. "They follow the developments closely."

Harry knows nothing. I'm sure of it.

Since my first day, I've found a way to explore every room, large or small, in the building I work in — there aren't many — and can safely say there is no chemist here. It would seem Thomas Sturbridge is tucked away in some secret place in the town of Derby. But of course that's only my assumption, based on common sense. He could be absolutely anywhere in England. Once again, panic flutters in my belly. What is the consequence of failure?

Duesbury did not take me everywhere in that large building we first toured. I need to make sure the chemist isn't squirreled away in one of its rooms. Of course I have no reason to be there. But on occasion Ambrose's business takes him to the other building. I wait for another occasion, listening carefully, for two long days. Finally, just after finishing his lunch, Ambrose stands, brushing crumbs off his breeches, and says he needs to take a requisitions sheet for glazes to the mixer.

"May I take it for you?" I ask politely.

My Quaker employer looks taken aback. "Why would you wish to do that?"

"I feel a bit confined here sometimes, and could use a stretch of the legs," I say. "I've only been in our other building once."

"Very well," says Ambrose. "But you mustn't fall behind on your purple peonies."

After reassuring him, I'm out the door and trudging along the path, past the ovens belching gray coils of smoke to meet the sky. A careful look to the right and the left reveals no sight of the hostile Major Tarkwell.

Inside, I'm greeted by a deafening grind. On the main floor, men feed bags of clay into a fearsome machine of turning wheels. I've never seen anything like it in my life.

I find the mixer and hand him the requisitions sheet.

Everyone is preoccupied by the machines, leaving me free to look around the building. My ears filled with roaring and my nose filled with that same scent of rotting vegetables, I peer around. There isn't a quiet corner anywhere; it seems extraordinarily unlikely that a scientist could work here.

"What are you doing here, Mademoiselle?" a voice snarls behind me.

Only one man would use that French honorific. I turn around.

Major Tarkwell stands a few feet away, his face a scowl.

"Explain yourself," he says.

"I needed a walk to clear my head, and Mr. Stanton asked me to deliver a requisitions sheet," I say. "Unless you think I'm here to stir up rebellion."

"You find it humorous, our need for discretion at Derby Porcelain?" he says.

"Nothing about you is humorous," I say, moving past him rapidly to reach the door.

"You're wise to hurry," he shouts after me. "Your purple flowers are waiting."

Heads turn, curious. When I reach the doorway, my cheeks are warm with anger. Halfway down the path to my building, I realize what his parting shot is meant to achieve. He knows what work I'm commissioned to do every day, perhaps every hour, in the decorating room; nothing I do escapes him. He watches me, just as he had vowed to do. Or he has others watch me and report back. It could be Duesbury, Ambrose, even Harry.

In the carriage ride home, Evelyn, who has been aloof ever since the letter burning, comments, "You seem out of sorts."

There is no use denying it, and I say, "It was a trying day."

"It could not be any worse than my afternoon," she says. "Duesbury disputed my accounts again. He overspends, and tries to divert criticism from himself by questioning my competency. He is coming to our house tonight and I will have to defend myself to my stepfather."

She thumps the ledger book on her lap.

"Do you think there is any danger?" I would hate to think of Evelyn removed from her sphere of numbers.

"I don't think so. But I may have to call on Mother in support and I hate to do that," she says, biting her lip. "Duesbury is such a scoundrel to attack my books. What a waste of my time! Every wage paid out, every bit of supply that comes in or goes out, every single address for a shipment, I have it in my book."

The carriage sways as the horses turn up the muddy drive to the Heaths' home. Before the carriage comes to a halt and the footman opens the door for us, I have a new idea for finding the chemist.

Evelyn's book.

A chemist needs supplies. Supplies cost money. Though I have no idea what they could be, if I study the book, I might find a supplies notation for Thomas Sturbridge, and with that an address.

That night, more than any other, supper inches along. As Evelyn broods, Mr. and Mrs. Heath talk of nothing but an upcoming ball they will attend at a place called Exeter Hall. They begin speculating on the guest list, with invitees coming from far and wide. Certain prominent gentlemen are called away to serve on the field of battle in Prussia or Canada, or on ships in the Caribbean, meaning the party ranks may skew toward females and old men. It's a topic that seems of little interest to me.

On that point, I am wrong, for I hear a name on this list that makes me nearly drop my spoon.

"Do you think the Courtenay boy old enough to attend?" Mrs. Heath asks.

"Not a boy any longer — must be fourteen years old," says her husband.

"Still, it's too soon for the mothers of Derbyshire to begin their maneuvering."

"I wouldn't be too sure of that." Mr. Heath barks a laugh.

I need to learn more about the Courtenays before they change topics. I ask, "Why would any mother wish to maneuver?"

The Heaths both look pleased at my apparent interest in country gossip.

"Ralph Courtenay inherited the title of Lord Musgrave and Musgrave Hall when he was five years old," Mrs. Heath says. "The house is at least three hundred years old. It's one of the grandest in this part of the country. Just Ralph and his mother reside there at present, but someday Lady Musgrave will have to make room for a daughter-in-law, much as she will be loath to do so."

The Heaths chuckle together.

"It's a shame that the boy's father died young," I say, trying to keep the conversation alive. I'm still not sure if Sir Gabriel springs from this particular family tree, for "Courtenay" is not that uncommon a name.

"Young?" Mr. Heath's eyebrows shot up. "He died a shriveled old man. Lord Musgrave didn't have his heir until he was seventy years old, with a wife nearly fifty years younger. No one thought him still capable of it, he was so weak after his years of dedication to his family motto, Aequalis astra."

"Equal to the stars," I whisper. So it *is* the same family home. But where does Sir Gabriel fit into this? He is about thirty years old, the wrong age to be younger brother to old Lord Musgrave. Yet he cannot be his elder son, if this Ralph Courtenay inherited everything.

"Genevieve, you've studied Latin?" says Evelyn, impressed.

"Just a bit," I say. It's a lie, of course. In our Huguenot schools, there is no Latin taught; it's the language of the Roman Catholic. I simply must be more careful.

Hearing the name Courtenay gives me pause. The knowledge that his family home rises in this part of England throws a certain peculiar light on my assignment. Why didn't Sir Gabriel mention it to me?

After dinner, Duesbury arrives. Evelyn marches downstairs, her accounts book under her arm, to do battle. While she is gone, I pace the floor, turning over various possibilities in my mind. To get my answers, I need to look through her book, and that will be impossible at the manufactory. She either carries it or keeps it on a table in a small room set aside for her. The room is near the doors, visible to all. I would have no reason to step inside without Evelyn present.

No, I must examine the book here, tonight. If she puts it away downstairs, that should prove a challenge. I'll have to fumble about in the dark, with no plausible explanation should a servant catch me. It would be ideal if she brought the book back up to our room. If she doesn't, and I can't find it downstairs, I may have to think up some other means of finding the location of the chemist. How I'll accomplish that, I've no idea.

I'm wretched with worry by the time I hear Evelyn's determined step in the hallway. She bursts back in the room with a smile on her face — and the accounts book under her arm.

"Redeemed," she announces.

"Very good, very good."

Evelyn sets down the book on a table, pulls out her teacups and brandy, and says, "We shall celebrate."

A moment later, we're clinking teacups. Evelyn sips her brandy and says, "I am touched, Genevieve, that you are this enthused by my victory."

Evelyn is a woman of determination and forthright principle. I'm a liar and a spy, and very much in the wrong.

Concealing my paroxysm of guilt, I ask her questions about Duesbury's criticism and she re-enacts their exchange, and how her stepfather acted as arbiter before he, with evident reluctance, backed his stepdaughter. "He has never liked me — not for a single minute — he thinks my facility for arithmetic unnatural, but numbers are numbers. They don't lie. He cannot dispute them. And he needs me to keep this costly enterprise afloat."

I make a show of paying attention, nodding and smiling, but I'm thinking all the time that tonight I will discover what I need to and then I shall be finished. Enough. Once Sir Gabriel has the location of the chemist's lair, it's up to him to do the rest. He is the practiced spy; he can find a way inside to steal the formula. I'll await the instructions on how to extricate myself from Derby.

Evelyn yawns and I seize on that to say we must go to sleep. It doesn't take long tonight for her breathing to deepen. To be safe, I wait, counting to 1,000. Only then do I slip out of bed, and tip-toe, as silently as I can, to the table where the book lies.

A bit of candle in one hand and the accounts book in the other, I creep down the hall to the chamber-pot closet. I shiver violently for it's quite cold, but donning more clothes might have awakened Evelyn.

Sitting on the freezing floor of the chamber-pot closet, I light the candle, warming my hands before I dive into the book, which covers expenses for the last two months. Page after page, lines of Evelyn's precise handwriting appear, divided into categories. I find the section labeled DELIVERY and the destination of each one. "Nottingham Road" dominates, naturally, with a few references to "Cockpit Hill", which is the place where the raw clay is stored before being brought to the manufactory. Nothing else, as I flip the pages. And since a great deal of what a porcelain factory makes use of are minerals and chemicals, I've no way of determining which could be intended for a scientist instead of the rest of the workers.

And then it leap out at me: "Foodstuffs".... "Seven Nuns Street."

My heart beats faster and, despite the cold in the room, sweat breaks out on my forehead. I've seen a sign for "Nuns Street" in the center of Derby, it's one of the many little streets with Catholic names. There is a Friary Gate, an Abbey Lane. Evelyn explained it once in the carriage, when I commented on the common thread. "Derby was once a bastion of the Roman Catholics. Because of King Henry VIII, the Pope is long gone, of course, but the names live on."

Working and living on Nuns Street, where, as I recall, the houses adjoin one another, would afford privacy, and it's close enough to the porcelain manufactory for ready communication with the chosen few. *Yes, it makes sense.*

I blow out the candle, tiptoe back to my room down the cold, dark, silent hall, and crawl back into bed.

*

Next day, I find a few moments to compose another letter to "Grandfather," and below it I write, "Detected food deliveries to Seven Nuns Street and I believe it is chemist workshop. I will need to suspend spying efforts, too difficult in present circumstances. I await word on manner of departure from Derby."

When I hand that sealed letter to Mrs. Heath to send along with her letters to the post, relief lightens my heart. Venice shimmers on the horizon.

For the next several days, I sleep soundly, eat with more appetite, and draw flowers with greater focus. I attend Sunday morning's sermon at St Mary's Church and listen to the Anglican priest with some appreciation, sharing the Book of Common Prayer with Evelyn. I don't feel completely comfortable in any church besides a Huguenot one, but the priest's words about the importance of humility strike a chord with me.

It's not until Wednesday morning, and our carriage ride to the manufactory, that a disquieting thought occurs.

By studying the street names from my seat at the carriage window, I've been able to find Nuns Street again. Our coach driver never turns the horses up the cobblestone street itself, but we hurtle past it on the way to the manufactory.

The same week I hand the letter to Mrs. Heath, I see a tall man, his shoulders hunched and his hands shoved into pockets, walk up Nuns Street. I twist in my carriage seat, craning to see how far he walks, but in seconds he passes from sight.

There is something about the silhouette of the man, the force with which he shoves his fists into his trouser pockets, that makes me suspect his intentions. He could be the mysterious chemist. And I wonder, for the first time, what Sir Gabriel intends to do with the address I sent to him. How exactly would he steal the formula from the chemist Thomas Sturbridge?

That day, drawing my yellow roses, my brush moves across the paper with steady precision while my imagination runs wild. Will Sir Gabriel send someone to Derby who's practiced in theft? This would be a mission of subterfuge, no question. But what if the thief is surprised and confronts Sturbridge?

My heart thuds, slow and heavy, as I face the prospect of being responsible for a man coming to harm. *I had no idea, I wouldn't wish anyone hurt*, I imagine saying to an accuser.

"Who are you talking to, Mistress Genevieve?" Harry stares at me. "Your lips are moving and your shoulders go up and down."

"No one," I snap. "I trust you have work to do?"

Harry's face turns scarlet and he recoils, as if I'd slapped him. My right hand tightens on the brush until my fingers tremble.

"I'm sorry, Harry," I say. He's the last person I'd ever wish to hurt.

In the next two weeks, as the worst of winter recedes, I listen carefully, at the manufactory and at the Heaths' home, for any hint of a crisis. Should something happen to their precious chemist, it would be difficult for them to hide their distress. But there's no chime of warning, not even a whispered one. Neither do any letters arrive for me from Sir Gabriel. He has not responded to my expressed desire to leave. I am in a state of limbo.

One afternoon I join the rest of the workers at something of a factory tradition: the display of porcelain before it is carefully packed for transport to the Charing Cross warehouse in London, and subsequent sale to well-pocketed buyers. When standing before the rows of creations — the shepherdesses, clowns, cherubs, and other figurines, the plates, the cups, the bowls, the snuffboxes, the candlesticks — I think of how they all began, as foul-smelling clay, and were transformed: thrown, molded, fired in ovens, gilded and painted.

I turn this way and that, to observe the pride that blazes across every face, from the worker who shoulders the crates to the highest-paid sculptor. Ambrose cannot suppress a smile, despite his Quaker soul. Harry trembles with excitement. And I have never seen William Duesbury look this content before, his hunched shoulders and darting eyes calmed before the all-too-visible embodiment of his vision.

I am part of this place, a family in its way. I too gaze with a certain pride at the sparkling porcelain, until I catch the glance of someone looking not at the wares but at me. Major Tarkwell, his scarred face twisted with hatred, glares at me across the room, and I freeze. He's all the reminder needed that I am not a trusted member of this "family." Nor should I be, I'm forced to admit to myself.

A few days later, the snow having melted and dried, Mrs. Heath speaks of an afternoon of shopping in Derby, now that the streets are less disastrous. Evelyn agrees to accompany her and, when I'm invited to join, I leap at the offer. I've found a way into the heart of the town — Nuns Street is not far from the shops. The prospect of setting foot on the same street where Thomas Sturbridge hides away entices me.

After her hiatus from town, Mrs. Heath enjoys warm welcomes from the shopkeepers that afternoon. Evelyn and I trailing her as well as her maid, she makes her way from shop to shop. Of course she orders her clothes and cosmetics and books from London, but she is willing to patronize these shops as well. She enjoys the effusive compliments bestowed, not perhaps realizing that the shopkeepers are well motivated to please the wife of a leading Derby banker. Evelyn and I exchange glances when the sycophancy gets to be too much.

My more significant problem is we are not moving toward Nuns Street but away from it. Mrs. Heath has a shopping plan in mind, and there's no plausible reason for me to push for a diversion. It makes me feel as if I will jump out of my skin. *I'm so close.*

While lingering in the milliner's shop, Evelyn peers out the window and comments on a darkening sky. "It looks like a thunderstorm. Odd for this time of year. But we should find our carriage."

"Allow me to do it," I say, and before she can stop me, I'm scrambling onto the street, lifting my skirts with both hands so I can move faster. I spot the carriage at once but I skirt it carefully, hugging the wall to avoid being seen.

After I've made it around the corner unobserved, I laugh, giddy with success. It's not just evading the notice of the carriage driver. I'm free, not for long, but *free*. This last month I've felt so caged.

It takes a few minutes to reach Nuns Street, which hasn't as many shops as its neighbors. No one gives me, a briskly moving young woman, a second glance, for now everyone is scurrying about, looking up at the sky, apprehensive, as they head for shelter. The sky rapidly darkens yet glows with a distant light at the same time. It's an unnatural gloom.

I walk halfway down Nuns Street and don't see any numbers on the buildings, meaning number seven is hidden. Instead of feeling frustrated by this revelation, I'm cheered. *You're safe*, I think.

A plop of water lands on my cheek; I must get back to Evelyn and her mother. They might already be wondering where I am.

As I turn back toward the top of the street, a light sparks, and I falter. It comes from the second floor of the third house on the left. Squinting, I realize that a figure holds a candle high in the window.

I take a few steps closer, oblivious of two more cold raindrops. The figure is that of a slender young man, wearing a white linen shirt, loose, its collar hanging and the opening slit to mid chest, no waistcoat or coat. It's uncommon to see a man in just his shirt. I feel a little shocked.

He twists his head so that he can look up through the window, toward the sky, and a tumble of dark red hair spills onto his left shoulder. After a few seconds he looks down, at a boy running full tilt across the street, his legs flying as he leaps from one uneven cobblestone to the next. The homely young boy holds a cap on his head with one hand so not to lose it and his other thin arm waving in the air. The man watches the boy's nimble flight, a smile breaking into a laugh, and then he lowers the candle, so that I'm unable to see his face or his red hair any longer. He's nothing but a slim silhouette.

Thunder crackles in the sky. The storm is breaking.

It's a storm that will change everything.

CHAPTER FIFTEEN

Just as I fear, Mrs. Heath lapses into distress at my disappearance, although from inside the dry safety of her carriage, of course. I don't see her or her maid as I scramble toward the carriage. Evelyn stands a few feet behind it, her hand shielding her eyes from the spattering rain as she scans the street for me.

"How could you get lost?" asks Evelyn, relief warring with annoyance once we are all inside.

"I was confused," I say.

"I don't think I've ever witnessed you confused before, and it's a blasted time to start."

Ours is a harrowing ride home, for the thunder terrifies the horses. I can feel them straining and bucking through the cab of the carriage. The driver shouts at them and whips the animals, which only makes matters worse.

After we reach the house, the storm lasts for several more hours, delaying the retrieval of Mr. Heath from the bank and the family's supper plans. Doors slam; servants shout outside and turn fearful inside.

I don't wring my hands over the rain and wind and lightning. I think only of the man at the window on Nuns Street, convinced that he is

Thomas Sturbridge. I've found him, the brilliant chemist whose color experiments have produced a blue the world's not seen before. Yet he isn't what I expected. A man who is at the heart of such a secret, shouldn't he seem more... serious? I keep picturing him: carelessly dressed, the smile that broke into laughter as he watched the boy leap the cobblestones. I can't remember the last time I witnessed such lightness of spirit. He who is the cause of all this drama, evidences none of it. I think of Sir Gabriel's determination to wrest the secret of his work from him. No buoyant spirit could survive that. If the point of laying eyes on Thomas Sturbridge was to ease my fears for him, well, it did not succeed.

*

The next morning, the sun shines bright, but the first fateful consequence of the storm manifests. The Heaths' carriage horses are unfit for at least a week. One hurt himself bucking in the stable for hours; the other demonstrates a glassy eye, suggesting sickness.

Evelyn insists that while the two stricken horses recover, she and I are perfectly capable of walking to the porcelain manufactory, as the rest of the workers do. "I crave the exercise," she says. "It's been such a long winter."

I'm enthusiastic for the walk, but before it's permitted, Evelyn must persuade Mr. and Mrs. Heath, who are opposed because of the rampant crime in Derby. This is a topic I've heard before, and I barely manage to keep from laughing. Derby, a haven of crime? I have witnessed *real* trouble on the streets. To hear Mr. Heath lament the existence of Friary Gate Gaol — how last year it held twenty criminals at one time — is to realize the vast difference between life in London and Derby.

Mrs. Heath is finally persuaded that her daughter and I will be safe if a family servant escorts us there and back. The first day that the plan is put into action, all goes smoothly, as I knew it would. No bloodthirsty vagabonds jump out of their whitewashed houses to attack us. I wish we need never return to the carriage, for I welcome the exercise as much as Evelyn does. My only regret is that our route takes us nowhere near Nuns Street.

The second day, as we return to the house, Evelyn frowns at the sight of a wiry old man lingering outside. "He works for the constable of Derby," she says.

Inside, Mr. Heath's study swings open. A tall man of plain dress emerges, and he is quite a sight: wide at the shoulders, wider at the belly. A giant.

Mr. Heath follows, seeing him out the door, and the man's size becomes even more apparent, since Mr. Heath, no small man himself, is dwarfed by him.

"You will inform your partner, Mr. Duesbury, that I have permission to see all of the employment records," says the man, in a tone of stern reminder.

It's not a tone I've ever heard used before with the banker. But instead of showing offense, Hr. Heath says, "Of course, Constable Campion. Of course."

The constable pauses at the door, held open for him by the footman, and, turning around to say something else to Mr. Heath, he catches sight of Evelyn and me on the stairs. His gaze passes over Evelyn quickly. *I* am the one he studies. Through his entire last exchange with Mr. Heath at the door, his eyes never leave me. With a final tip of the hat, he leaves.

I've had dealings with officers of justice before. A series of constables and under-sheriffs came to the Spitalfields house to question me after Denis committed his crime. When I made firm statement that I, Genevieve Planché, previously the wanted man's betrothed, knew nothing of Denis' whereabouts, they did not bother to conceal their disbelief. Eventually, lacking proof, they went away, the damage done to my reputation on Fournier Street. I hated being the object of their suspicion then, when I was wholly innocent. What would it be like now, to be questioned when I have a great deal to hide? It's not a pleasant prospect — and not even my only concern. I fear that the constable's appearance, his request for worker records, is to do with the chemist Thomas Sturbridge. Something has happened to him.

Evelyn, greatly curious, says to me, "I wonder what one of our people has done, to bring Enoch Campion to the house. He's not one who rouses himself for nothing. Well, my prediction is that my stepfather won't say a word about it at supper. I'll have to worm it out of Mother afterwards."

She's right. Supper yields no words of explanation. But there are clues as to the magnitude of the problem. Mr. Heath says little and barely touches his beef — both are highly unusual. I have no appetite myself, but I force a few mouthfuls down and I attempt to hold up my end of the conversation with Mrs. Heath.

As soon as, mercifully, the meal is finished, I overhear Mr. Heath giving instructions for port to be brought to his study, where he will meet shortly with Mr. Duesbury and Major Tarkwell.

Now I am certain. This *must* have to do with the color blue.

*

When, two endless hours later, Evelyn appears after a night of faro with her mother, I learn that the constable's visit does have to do with the color blue, but not the way I assumed.

"It's really fairly ghastly," she says, excitement gleaming in her eyes. "Do you remember the man I told you about, the one who stole a piece of valuable porcelain last October? His name was Richard Frederick, and, Genevieve, his dead body was found in the River Trent. Imagine it. The violence of the storm dislodged it from a place where someone had weighted it with stones, to stay at the bottom of the river. He was identified by his coat. It still had his initials stitched into the back of his collar, tiny letters, the way mothers do in the village."

"He was found here?" I say, my pulse racing. "I thought you said he disappeared with his stolen piece."

"That's what we all believed. He was gone. The piece was gone. It was assumed he went somewhere to sell it, probably London. Perhaps he spent all the money he received, and came back here?" She pauses. "But that doesn't make sense. Why would Richard Frederick return, crawling back to Derbyshire, still wearing his old patched coat? Surely he could have something better made to wear. He'd not be hired back, he'd be arrested. And who would murder him then, when he had nothing?"

"I don't understand what could be so valuable to lead this worker to such an end," I say carefully. I sit on the pagoda bed and stay silent. I wonder if this is the moment I've been waiting for.

And it is. After a bit more hesitation, Evelyn tells me the truth, or as much truth as she knows.

Lowering her voice to a whisper, she says, "Duesbury found a chemist who was experimenting with color. He'd come up with an amazing shade of blue, like nothing seen before by anyone, anywhere. Duesbury persuaded him to finish his experiments here. The man's had a terrible time with stabilizing certain elements — don't ask me what, because I've never been told, and even if I were, I wouldn't understand. I find scientific matters impenetrable. We have him locked away in town, because it has to be kept an utter secret. If any of our competitors stole the formula for Derby blue and destroyed our advantage, we'd be ruined."

Derby blue. They even have their own name for it. Aloud, I say, "Surely not *ruined*?"

"Do you think hard work is sufficient for success in a business as competitive as porcelain?" she asks. "We desperately need this advantage to stay afloat. Ah, Genevieve, I wish I could be like you, thinking of nothing but art."

She pats my arm, affectionately, as I feel like the worst person in the world.

Evelyn goes on to explain that as the constable investigates Richard Frederick's murder, it's possible suspicion could fall on those at the manufactory who were upset by his theft. Thus far no one has enlightened the constable on the existence of Derby blue. Richard Frederick stole a figurine, but it wasn't anything exceptional, as far as the constable knows.

"You know the truth — do you think that someone at the porcelain works committed murder?" I ask bluntly.

She shakes her head. "They're none of them killers, with the exception of Major Tarkwell, and he wasn't hired here yet. Oh, I do not know what happened to Richard Frederick. Perhaps he didn't sell the piece after all. Duesbury has his sources, and he said no other factory in England is making our blue."

I can only sleep perhaps two hours that night. The actions of Richard Frederick make little sense. Sir Gabriel told me the young man was paid well for his theft, that he was motivated to steal the blue by a burning desire to go to London. The sentence that comes back to me is "He wanted to escape from Derby and I made that possible."

In a few days' time, the post to London will contain a letter from me to him, relaying these developments. But when will I receive a letter from Sir Gabriel? Perhaps this news will finally motivate him to issue further instruction.

Derby is not a small town; yet it is small enough for news to spread quickly. Once I've arrived at the porcelain manufactory, I sense that the staff all knows about the discovery of Richard Frederick's dead body. In the decorating room, Stanton and Harry seem subdued.

With Harry, in particular, the change is stark. I wonder if Harry was friends with the assistant mixer, if he grieves the grisly end of Richard Frederick. There is no possibility of discussing it. Stanton watches us avidly, determined to squelch any syllable of gossip.

My brush keeps going still on the paper. How can I create an intoxicating fantasy of beauty when I'm weighed down with dread?

I make my way to the window. What a gray, sullen day; instead of ushering in spring, the violent thunderstorm sent us back to wintry weather. I look for my little stone house, and find it bereft of company as always. It beckons to me, though. I ache to push open that old wooden door.

Harry stumbles in, his eyes bulging. "The constable is downstairs asking questions."

"This has nothing to do with our work," says Stanton firmly.

Harry takes his seat, and the three of us struggle forward. I wonder if Constable Campion will question Stanton or Harry as part of his investigation. Although neither has said one word about him to me, I have a strong suspicion that each man possesses knowledge the constable would wish to obtain. As for myself, I arrived months after Richard Frederick's theft. Yet I know what no other person living in Derby does: Frederick was recruited to spy on the porcelain manufactory, to obtain the secret of the blue for a serious competitor. And I've infiltrated Derby to finish the job he started.

Finally the sun dips low, and it's time for the three of us to troop down the stairs.

I spot two grim-looking people standing outside of Evelyn's office. One of them is Evelyn, the other is William Duesbury. At first I think they are quarreling again over the accounts, until I realize they're not angry with each other. The focus of their joint displeasure is on the other side of her tightly shut door.

"We can be on our way shortly," says Evelyn, both to me and to the Heaths' servant, waiting by the door, turning his hat in his hands.

The door swings open and a somber young porcelain worker — one of the young men in the Glazing Room — emerges from Evelyn's office, followed by Constable Campion. It seems impossible that Evelyn's small office could contain him. He scans the groups of anxious people waiting and points at Harry.

"You need to come speak with me, Harry."

"Yes, Sir." The answer from the teenaged worker is barely above a whisper.

Evelyn protests, "The hour is late, Constable, and I don't think it fitting to hold our workers here. Surely this can resume tomorrow?"

"Are you interfering with a murder investigation conducted by an officer of the law?" asks the constable, not harshly, but with interest, as if this puts Evelyn into a new light. She stares up at him, putting on a courageous front but I notice her hand fidgeting in the folds of her dark-gray dress.

Duesbury says, "We none of us would dream of interfering. You must continue as you see fit."

Once Harry is behind the door, submitting to questions, Duesbury suggests that the rest of us leave the manufactory while he waits alone for the interview to finish. Evelyn beckons to the servant escorting us home.

Ambrose Stanton turns to Duesbury and says, "I will wait for Harry, Sir."

"And I shall too." The words slip out of my mouth without my giving it more than a second of consideration, and yet I find myself determined to remain.

Evelyn says, "Who knows how long this interview will take? Genevieve, the men have this in hand. Come with me."

"I can make my way to the house by myself," I say, which leads to another round of protests until Stanton offers to see me to the Heaths' home, which I accept.

Evelyn shoots me a last puzzled look on her way out the door. With Duesbury, it is the opposite. He examines me thoughtfully, as if it's time to reassess my character — and favorably. His changing attitude does not extend to my being worthy of conversation, of course. With no effort made to include me, Duesbury and Stanton talk over some matters of design — the new line of carved cherubs — while keeping an eye on the door.

While I wait, half-listening to Duesbury and Stanton, I am near sickened by a churn of emotion. There is a part of me that feels camaraderie, and a protective affection, for Harry. I'm five years older than him. Is this how an older sister would behave? I've no idea; I am an only child.

Or is my desire to wait out the interview motivated by self-interest? Harry might have known Richard Frederick well enough to possess an inkling of his true mission, and he might be sharing that now, even the name of Sir Gabriel. Investigating this murder throws a strong light on matters I would prefer to keep in the dark.

When the door finally opens, the constable is stone-faced and Harry ashen with distress. "I shall have more questions for you after I have confirmed certain things," says Constable Campion. Eying the three of us, he declares, "Let no one pester this young man in the meantime."

Duesbury nods.

The constable, in a softer voice, says, "Harry, be on your way. I know your mother worries."

Harry scuttles out the door, followed by the constable, who, it's clear, isn't done with Derby Porcelain Works.

*

True to his word, Ambrose Stanton escorts me. He selects a different route than the one I'm accustomed to, through the heart of the town, but I welcome it. We walk through the cold in silence; Stanton is much preoccupied, as am I. What does Harry know?

Queen Street is one of the busiest in Derby. This is where the larger coach houses stand, for all the travelers stopping off on the trip from London to Manchester. It is not high travel season, but the street bustles with life nonetheless. Night has fallen, and a row of freshly lit street lamps glow. The inn and tavern keepers have lit their candles inside, too, and we can see much of the goings-on as we pass: people moving from room to room, laughing, drinking, singing a tune. As we approach a corner, one coach house of wooden beams on white stone walls emits the loudest jeering roar. A man stumbles out the door and onto the street, shaking his head. Turning to walk toward us, he starts when he recognizes Ambrose Stanton and then runs to us. I have seen him before, at the manufactory.

He says, "Mr. Stanton, Sir, there's a fight in the Dolphin."

Ambrose says, "I imagine there are often fights in the taverns. Why should anyone from Derby Porcelain Works be a party to them?"

The worker says, "They're trying to give a beating to a man who they say is with the Porcelain Works. He says no."

Irritated, Ambrose says, "Well, and is he?"

"I've never seen him before."

Ambrose waves off the man, and nods to me, suggesting we should proceed. The worker melts away onto the street. After walking a half of a block, Ambrose freezes, mid-stride, as if a thought occurs. Worried, he glances back at the Dolphin.

"Would you mind, Genevieve, if I were to look in?" he says, slowly.

"Not at all."

"You'll remain outside, of course."

Ambrose, his Quaker face tense with distaste, pushes open the door. He's unaware that I'm close behind, not waiting on the street as he said. Tumult-filled taverns are places I'm all too accustomed to, thanks to Denis.

And yes, I find myself in a room indistinguishable from any tavern in London. It stinks of ale and gin and men unaccustomed to soap. Low ceilinged, with wooden tables strewn haphazardly, it is not particularly well lit; smoke from the fire mingles with that of pipes. The laughs I heard are definitely jeers. The patrons are men. The only women I see are two wary-faced servants, handing out drinks.

Ambrose, after scanning the room, darts forward, toward a knot of men I can't make out, who are clustered near a thick square beam running floor to ceiling. I follow him forward, which he still fails to realize in the chaos.

Peering around Ambrose, I see a man on the filthy floor, face down. He's pinned down by another man, a nasty customer, in his thirties, laughing as he presses his foot onto his victim's upper back.

The man on the floor cries out, his voice young, "But you're mistaken!"

This sets off a round of jeers from the group, about a dozen in number, crowding around. "Mistaken?" responds the man standing over him, who I now see brandishes a knife nearly six inches long. "I don't think so! Eh, men?"

"No," they cry as one.

A jeering, wide-backed spectator shifts over, so that I can see the head of the man on the floor, as he tries, unsuccessfully, to rise. While he wriggles under the boot, his hair spills over his coat lapel. His hair is long and red, and I recognize it instantly. The young man on the floor is the man from the window, the chemist.

Thomas Sturbridge.

CHAPTER SIXTEEN

Ambrose Stanton takes a determined step forward and says, as loudly as he's capable of: "Stop this at once. Let him up off the floor!"

The tormentor of Sturbridge whips his head around. "And why should I do that?"

On the floor, the chemist declares, his voice calm: "Don't trouble yourself, Mr. Stanton, I have it in hand."

Mocking laughter rocks the bar.

A sole dissenting voice rises. "Stop hurting Mr. Sturbridge. He's a good man, he is." The man belonging to the protest is white-haired, with watery eyes.

"Shut up, you old fool," shouts the chief tormentor. "I've taken all the insults I'm willing to from these outsiders. They come to our town, build their factories and their ovens and their damned wheels, and hire none of us. None. No, we aren't good enough! They bring 'em in from London. And they come strutting into our taverns, a place like the Dolphin, been standing for 200 years, and insult us!"

Ambrose says, "I'm sure that this man would never insult you."

It is the worst thing Stanton could have said.

"Are you calling me a liar?" the tormentor demands, waving his knife. "You weren't even here! And who the hell are you — another Londoner come to tell us how much better you are? If you want me to take my foot off of your friend, you're going to have to push me off."

Cheers fill the tavern.

Ambrose says, raising his chin, "I'm not a man of violence."

Now the crowd turns completely against Ambrose. Not just the man with the knife, but all of his jeering companions are drawn in. They mock Ambrose, saying to one another, "I'm not a man of violence," imitating his pompous tone.

Meanwhile, I can't see the head of Thomas Sturbridge, pinned down, any longer, just his legs. This is a situation that needs to be remedied — and Ambrose *isn't* the person to do it.

I tap Ambrose on the shoulder, and he winces, as if being struck. When he realizes it's me, he's appalled. "You were told to remain outside."

"You need to go and get help," I say quietly. "Major Tarkwell or Mr. Duesbury. Or even people from the Heaths' home. We need their numbers."

"Leave now? What will they do to him?"

"To Mr. Sturbridge?"

Ambrose's eyes widen with alarm, swiftly followed by suspicion. "That's what the old man called him," I quickly point out. "He's an employee of our manufactory, isn't he?"

"No. Yes." Ambrose is flustered.

Another roar of laughter from the chemist's tormentors fills the room. "Let's seek help," Ambrose agrees, and grabs my elbow.

"No, I will stay here," I say. "My presence may deter them from taking worse action."

"No lady should be here at all," Stanton protests.

"But I'm *not* the only female, there are bar maids here, and ..."

my eyes search the room frantically until they alight on two women huddled with companions on a bench near the window " … you see? Women customers. I can't help you run any faster to get help. But I *could* be of use here."

Ambrose Stanton capitulates, and dashes out the door.

I edge toward the men, carefully, until I'm only a foot away from the elbow of one of the ruffians. Just as I expect, the one on top, the man with the knife, spots me first.

"So 'Not a Man of Violence' runs home with his tail between his legs but leaves his tasty woman in our care?" he cries. "That's generous of the bastard."

He looks me up and down with exaggerated relish, as his comrades snicker their approval.

"I thought you hated we Londoners," I retort, hand on my hip, my speech lapsing into the sport of the East End.

"Oh, I would make an exception for *you*," he leers.

"I'm not here for you or your exceptions, friend, I've come for Tommy," I say and lift up my skirt an inch to point at the fallen Sturbridge with the toe of my shoe.

The men groan in disappointment. The one with the knife cocks his head, in disbelief. "You want *him*?"

"He belongs to me, true enough." I take a step closer. "I'd like to hear Tommy's insult — nothing comes out of his mouth would surprise me."

I hope to explain away whatever Sturbridge has said or done in my new East End fashion.

The head man says, "Your Tommy came in here, bought a topper of ale, as he's wont to do, no harm to it, but then tonight he asks if the stories are true about the doctor sawing up the dead. Those stories are not true, that a doctor lived next to the Dolphin and used a tunnel to bring the bodies in. We don't have any fiends like that in Derby — never had, never will."

Now comes the firm voice of Thomas Sturbridge again, rising from the floor: "Not a fiend. He was a man of science. I respect the lengths the doctor went to in order to learn."

"You hear that?" He digs his boot into Sturbridge's back. "I'm not going to have that swill said in the Dolphin!"

This isn't working. But it would have worked if the chemist hadn't piped up again. The man has no common sense.

"Shut your mouth, Tommy," I shout, loud enough to be heard over the men's shouting. The anger in my voice isn't feigned, I do so want him to shut up. "No one wants to hear that kick and prance!"

At that, the look on the tormentor's face changes from hatred to amusement. "Kick and prance? Ha! I like that. Yes, I do."

He puts his knife back into his greasy coat and looks down.

"He's yours, my girl — or will be when you tell me your name."

"Genevieve," I say, and kneel next to the chemist.

The man takes his boot off Sturbridge's back. Immediately, the red-haired chemist pushes himself up and around, so that we are face to face, no more than six inches apart.

I stare into a pair of light blue eyes under dark red eyebrows. Those eyes are full of surprise; his face is smudged with dirt from the floor. And a trickle of blood runs down his chin.

"Time to go home, Tommy," I say, warningly. "Let me help you up."

"Of course… Genevieve." His face breaks open into a wide, delighted smile. His grin, set in a dirty face, makes him look like a mischievous street urchin.

I grab both his hands. They are surprisingly warm and strong, his palms roughened. We rise together, our gazes still locked.

"Are you all right?" I ask, no longer shouting or warning.

"Never better," he replies, releasing my hand to brush bits of straw from his coat, dampened from ale spilled on the floor. "Shall we be off?"

Half turning his head, he says to his tormentors, "Gute Nacht, meine Herren." It's gibberish to me.

With a light step, he makes his way toward the door, tucking my hand into the crook of his arm. "I can't wait to get home," he whispers into my ear.

My face burning with embarrassment. "Mr. Sturbridge, I —"

A group charges in the door, led by Ambrose Stanton, panting with exhaustion. William Duesbury and Major Tarkwell are right behind, with six men of the porcelain manufactory. They all look relieved to see Sturbridge on his feet, but that look is followed by concern.

"Tom, are you hurt?" demands a frantic Duesbury.

"Nothing to worry about," answers Sturbridge.

"His face is cut," calls out Major Tarkwell.

Hands grab Thomas Sturbridge, breaking our link, and haul him into the street, practically lifting him off his feet. "Go fetch Dr. Gleason," Duesbury orders an underling. With that, they vanish into the night without even a goodbye.

I stand just inside the Dolphin, rather dazed, when I realize they didn't all vanish. Ambrose Stanton says, "Shall I now escort you to the Heaths' home?"

"Please," I say, feeling drained now that the crisis is past.

I glance over my shoulder, taking in the Dolphin a last time, when I catch sight of a bearded man sitting with his back to the wall, to the side of the cluster of ruffians. My heart drops to my shoes.

It is Jimmy, the ex-boxer, the man of the shadows who works for Sir Gabriel Courtenay.

He is not looking at me, he is taking a swig of ale like any other Derby man. While unaccompanied, he does not look out of place, either. I realize he's most likely been here the entire time. Jimmy must have followed Thomas Sturbridge to the Dolphin, I realize.

"Genevieve, are you well?" asks Ambrose.

I nod, saying, "I very much want to leave."

I don't analyze what Jimmy's presence means at first — I can't. Because first I need to decide how to explain the fact that Thomas Sturbridge and I were walking arm in arm across the Dolphin's floor at the moment the rescue party arrived. At some point, Sturbridge is surely going to tell others of my actions and words, so I can't deny them.

"I believe that they were pretty much finished with their tormenting Mr. Sturbridge," I say. "They were ready to move on. That's why it didn't take much for me to persuade them to release him."

"I can't think why he was there at all," frets Ambrose. "He's not a man who goes to taverns."

As I recall, the chief bully said that Sturbridge had been in the Dolphin before, ordering a drink "as he is wont to do." They may not know Sturbridge as well as they think. To the men of the porcelain manufactory, he seems a fragile object. They were in a panic over a cut on his chin, bellowing for the doctor and practically carrying him off. It's odd.

But I don't share my knowledge of Sturbridge's drinking habits with Ambrose. It could further help my standing, to report such facts. I feel I can't tattle on him, though. I'm not sure why.

I hear Thomas Sturbridge saying, "I can't wait to get home," as he presses my hand, and my face burns again. I am relieved that Ambrose can't see me blush in the dark.

We are almost to the Heath house when Ambrose says, "Genevieve, we need to talk about Mr. Sturbridge. He's in the middle of research, valuable research, for the porcelain works. You must know how competitive a business this is. I must ask you not to mention seeing him or repeating anything he said to you."

"He didn't say much of anything to me. And some of it didn't even make sense."

Ambrose slows, touching my arm. "Such as?"

I try as best I can to reproduce the garble he said over his shoulder on the way out the door: "Gute Nacht, meine Herren."

Ambrose Stanton is appalled. "Please do not repeat that phrase — put it out of your mind," he pleads.

I sense that these words, or "that phrase," as he defines it, is a clue to the secret work of Thomas Sturbridge. Devoured by curiosity, I ask, "Do you know what it means?"

"Genevieve, cease such questions immediately," Ambrose says, his voice rising. "It's dangerous to pursue this. Dangerous for you — and for all of us."

"I understand," I tell him.

I do understand. All too well.

*

Inside the Heath house, I glean the mood is just as disordered. I can hear men's urgent voices behind the study doors. If there even was a supper served, it was long ago cleared. I forage for some cold meat and bread in the kitchen before heading upstairs. I need fortification before facing Evelyn. She is too sharp-eyed and shrewd not to wonder why I remained behind at the manufactory.

When I walk through the door of our room, I find Evelyn is not suspicious but happy to see me because she is bursting with news to relay.

"The apprentice in your decorating room, Harry, has been keeping a secret all of this time," she tells me. "He was friends with Richard Frederick, probably the only friend the man had at the manufactory, or anywhere else. He was a sullen boy. One night last September he told Harry that he had met a man, a gentleman, who was going to change his life, set him up in London, and that he would leave Derby and never have to come back."

My stomach lurches. Fortunately, surprise is entirely appropriate in the face of this news. "How did you find this out?" I ask.

"The constable told them not to talk to Harry but of course they did. Duesbury followed him home and questioned him. He was here, telling all to my stepfather, when Stanton came running in. We now know that Richard Frederick was paid to spy on the manufactory, and to steal the piece of porcelain. There is no doubt about it at all. It's a miracle no one else has manufactured it yet, although Duesbury's theory is that it's impossible to replicate without the formula."

"Do they know who paid Richard Frederick?" I ask, my throat tightening.

"No, Harry said he never gave a name, just boasted it was a fine gentleman. Can you imagine? It must have been poor Richard's misperception. He was a country boy, after all. How could a gentleman be involved in all of this? Our competitors are not fine gentlemen, you can be sure of that. And it gets worse."

Evelyn's usual expression, of cool poise, is replaced by agitation. I feel a galloping, nauseous dread.

"How so?" I ask.

"William Duesbury and Major Tarkwell think this mysterious man, whoever paid Richard, is here in town now, trying to learn more, to steal our secret to Derby blue."

"I think," I manage to say, "it's time for some brandy."

Evelyn busies herself with her cups and the pouring, giving me time to think. Jimmy is here, yes. Is Sir Gabriel, as well? Jimmy is never far from his side, so it's a possibility. But why have I received no letter, no communication?

"What did Harry say that led them to believe that Richard Frederick's gentleman is here?" I ask.

"Oh, it's not Harry. Major Tarkwell believes it so based on the fact that someone tried to kill him one week ago."

"What?"

"The major was standing in a crowd on the side of Queen Street, a large coach was approaching, and just as the horses were a few feet away, someone gave Tarkwell a push, someone from behind. The major isn't young, and he lost a leg, but as you've probably noticed, he's fairly spry. He fell forward but was able to roll back, out of the way, just in time."

I hear myself say, "That was fortunate." To hide my face, I go to the fireplace, to poke the faltering embers. "Did he see who pushed him?" I ask, my back to her.

"No, and when he was on the ground, everyone gathered around him, quite concerned, trying to help, it obscured his line of sight. Everyone thought Tarkwell simply fell, being crippled. By the time he got a proper look around, he saw no one suspicious. All he could say, based on how he was pushed, is that he thinks the man was very strong."

The floor of Evelyn's room is rising up to greet me. From far away, I hear Evelyn say, "Are you all right, Genevieve?"

Everything swirls around me, the pagoda bed, the flames in the fireplace, Evelyn's worried face.

It was Jimmy who tried to kill Major Tarkwell, I'm sure of it. "Presence of Major Tarkwell noted," read my last letter. And this is how Jimmy proceeds after learning of the man's presence — he throws him in front of a coach? I had no idea that my letter would lead to violence! I think of Jimmy sitting against the wall, half of a room away from Thomas Sturbridge, and panic heaves.

"I'm fine," I choke out, sucking air into my lungs. "It's been a difficult day."

"Dear me, you don't *look* fine. Another of your headaches?" After helping me to a chair, Evelyn says, "Yes, I heard about the tail end of your difficult day. How in heaven's name were you able to extricate Thomas Sturbridge from the Dolphin? I've never set foot in a place like that, and until tonight I'd have wagered every shilling I possess that you hadn't either."

Don't lie unless it's necessary. That was one of the points of advice Sir Gabriel gave me, back in London. I decide it's time to confide in Evelyn — up to a point.

"I have found myself inside a few taverns in London, and it was because of a man I thought I'd marry," I say, and tell her the story of Denis, our engagement, his falling to pieces, and his arrest. I do not spare her the fact of the violence of Denis against the master silk weaver or his fleeing to London to evade arrest and my subsequent becoming a pariah in the Huguenot community. I do omit the truth of our intimacy while betrothed, and, of course, Denis' return to Spitalfields and his last betrayal. No one will ever know of *that*.

My confession of my stormy past achieves the necessary result. I have diverted her from more dangerous directions. I see no disapproval; Evelyn shows herself all sympathy.

"I do thank you for your honesty, Genevieve," she says. "It explains how you were able to make quick work of them in the Dolphin. And I must say, it also explains other things, such as why you are here at all. No wonder you were keen to leave London. I've felt you seemed terribly out of place at times, but now I understand."

So much for my diligent efforts to blend in.

Evelyn continues, with a hesitation unusual for her, "I wonder if there were some way to tell the others this personal history without your suffering undue embarrassment. I think, particularly at a time like this, we must focus on discovering our true enemy while extending full trust to those who deserve it."

It takes me a moment to comprehend her meaning. "I'm not trusted here? Is it because I'm Huguenot — does Major Tarkwell still think I've a traitorous nature because my grandfather was born in France?"

She spreads her hands, saying, "It is a fraught time that you've picked to come to Derby. Those who would under better circumstances treat newcomers with fairness are not able to exercise good judgment. Now that you've met Thomas Sturbridge, perhaps you have an idea of our challenge."

"He didn't say much to me," I tell her, just as I'd told Ambrose Stanton. "But I perceive that he's... uncommon."

Those light blue eyes, radiating delight, seconds after he'd slithered out from under a ruffian's boot, cut and dirty and abused... No, I've never met the like of him before.

"Yes, uncommon, that's one way to put it," Evelyn says. "Another way to put it is... he is a genius."

"A genius? How so?"

"I've only seen him from a distance, but my mother told me he knows every scientific principle, reads philosophy, understands a half-dozen languages," she says. "I would suppose he fits the definition."

After taking that in, I say, "He did speak a phrase that sounds like a foreign language." I repeat what I heard.

She frowns in concentration. "It sounds to me like German; yes, it could be German, but I'm not sure. After all, *I'm* no genius." She laughs, and I join in while wondering, if it was German, why did the fact that Sturbridge spoke it upset Ambrose Stanton?

Evelyn sits up taller. "Oh, forgive me, I should have given this to you earlier, Genevieve. You have another letter from your grandfather."

The hour is late, and Evelyn drops the menacing topics. After she puts away the brandy and calls for the maid, she talks only of the dance at Exeter Hall this Saturday. She's not looking forward to it, but her attendance cannot be avoided.

After I'm certain that Evelyn is asleep, I slip out of the bed and take my letter and a candle to the chamber-pot closet. I'd read the visible part of it earlier, in front of her. It was the usual innocuous message from Pierre Billiou, with the bottom one-third of the page significantly empty.

When I hold the paper over a lit candle, the real message from Sir Gabriel Courtenay appears: "You must make greater efforts to learn everything about Thomas Sturbridge and the origin of his formula, and the composition of the formula itself. It is not possible for you to leave Derby at this time. Your task is not yet finished.

CHAPTER SEVENTEEN

The next morning, I walk to the manufactory with Evelyn, the same as always. We talk not of spying and murder but of small matters. It is her preference, and I do not question it. Stanton and Harry, too, resume work as usual. Stanton's face is worn with exhaustion and Harry's cheerful nature is subdued. But we three are here to work and we take out our brushes, employ our paints, and complete our designs. I start a series of yellow roses, endeavoring to make them look fresh and uncomplicated, as if their petals opened just moments before I capture them in paint.

Ugly thoughts coil underneath, however. I know that Jimmy is here, I saw him with my own eyes, and I fear it was he who pushed Major Tarkwell into the street. If he had succeeded in killing the major, I would bear the horrible responsibility as the informant. I detest Tarkwell, but have no wish to see him dead.

How could obtaining Derby blue wreak this much havoc? It's true that when Sir Gabriel asked me to spy, he said there were risks. But he also reeled off examples of porcelain businesses built on stolen secrets and said it was the way of the world. Sir Gabriel himself, so cultured and intelligent, can't be directing violence. Nor can I believe he is in Derby. He might not have any idea of Jimmy's murder attempt and, if told, would see it as a gross error. And of course I don't know if it was Jimmy for sure. Someone else might have pushed Tarkwell. Or maybe the man simply stumbled; he does have a wooden leg. I clung to these possibilities in the morning, but as the hours wore on, they seem less and less likely.

One thing is certain: I can't leave Derby. Sir Gabriel made that clear in his letter. Pressure mounts for me to discover the secret of the blue. How am I to do that? Despite my rescue, I know only a little about Thomas Sturbridge: He is intelligent, he is reckless, and he may speak German. That's all. I don't know how to find an opportunity to see him again. Unfortunately, Sir Gabriel could assume I know more than I do after Jimmy reports what happened at the Dolphin.

As the day wears on, I find my thoughts keep returning to Richard Frederick, the assistant thrower whom they found dead — stabbed in the back, Evelyn said — and weighted down to remain hidden at the bottom of the Trent, the same river I crossed in the London coach to reach Derby. Richard wanted a new life and was promised one. He committed a crime to get it. What went wrong, that he ended up back here, facing a killer? I find his naïve hopes, his nasty bit of thievery, and his horrible end unbearably painful to contemplate.

After I force down my luncheon and return to my watercolor roses, William Duesbury appears in the decorating room. I wait for him to launch into a matter of design with Ambrose Stanton but instead his gaze fixes on me.

"You're needed downstairs," he says and beckons, gracelessly.

This cannot be a good development.

I catch a glimpse of Harry's upset countenance as I rise to follow Duesbury. The young man is worried for me. I find it fortifying, that someone who works alongside me does like and trust me, until, halfway down the stairs, it occurs to me with a sad shudder that I don't deserve his trust.

On the main floor, my first instinct is to look for Constable Campion in all of his enormity, but there's no sign of him. Evelyn occupies her office, her neat black head bent over her books. All seems quiet; Major Tarkwell's hostile form is nowhere to be seen either.

"This way," says William Duesbury, steering me out the door.

I gather all of my defenses, to prepare for what is next.

Duesbury does not guide me along the path to Nottingham Road but to the collection of ovens belching smoke.

I can't remain silent. "Mr. Duesbury, what is the purpose of this?"

He stops walking and points, forcefully, to the far side of the farthest oven, his mouth twisted with dislike. Any points gained with him because I stayed at the manufactory last night in support of Harry seem to be gone.

I am to keep walking without him, right off the porcelain works property? I cannot imagine why.

I edge around the oven — and there stands Thomas Sturbridge, alone.

"You?" I say, startled.

"Me." He smiles, not the delighted grin of last night but a rueful one. He looks quite different, wearing a respectably cut coat and waistcoat and proper shoes. The only thing missing is a white powdered wig. His dark red hair is neatly pulled back from his lean face.

I regret that my dress is my worst-fitting and my fingernails are chipped and stained with paint.

"Are you all right, Mr. Sturbridge?" I ask, across the distance.

"Oh, yes." He touches his chin, the place where I saw blood yesterday and now just a nick. "The only significant injury is to my pride."

He tilts his head to glance past me. "Please, William, could you give me an undisturbed moment with Mademoiselle Planché?" When I look over my shoulder, I see that Duesbury has edged forward so he can hear our conversation. Thomas Sturbridge's tone is impatient, and I wait for Duesbury to show offense. But he merely nods and backs up.

"You know my name," I comment.

"Of course. I've been asking everyone about you." He walks right up to me and reaches for my hand. I expect him to kiss it, but instead he shakes it and I feel again his firm grasp. It's quite cold outside, but his flesh is warm. Now that we are so close in the strong light of day, I realize something else: Though he is taller than me by some four or five inches and has broad shoulders, Thomas Sturbridge's face has a certain delicacy. Those light blue eyes, topped by Titian red eyebrows, seem almost too large for the rest of his face, with its hollowed cheeks and cleft chin. He looks as if he stepped from a painting of Albrecht Durer, sensitive and haunted.

He releases my grubby hand without looking at it, thank goodness.

"I have to thank you for what you did," he says. "You were splendid, absolutely splendid."

"It's nothing," I murmur.

"Nothing? You went inside their minds, even though they were strangers, and you knew exactly what you needed to say and do, to motivate them to release me. It was magnificent. If you hadn't been there, Mademoiselle, if William and Ambrose and the major had come charging in, there could have been a terrible fight. Imagine how many people could have been injured, townsfolk as well as porcelain workers, because I asked the wrong question after a tankard of ale."

"They were a volatile group at the tavern," I say.

"And they should not be condemned for their suspicions and resentments," he insists. "Derby is at the forefront of great change in the country, with its new ways of doing business, the silk mill and other concerns, and it causes tremendous concern — rightly. Some will doubtless be left behind."

It's a way of looking at behavior, at life, that I've never considered before.

"And speaking of ale…" His voice trails away and then, he straightens his shoulders and pushes forward. "I had a bit to drink, and between that and the drama of what transpired, I fear I said some impolite things to you, Mademoiselle."

"We shall put it behind us, Sir."

"Very good of you. Thank you."

With that, an awkward silence settles over us. He may think me clever, but my mind has gone blank. Here he is, right in front of me. The man I'm supposed to spy on, steal from. But what am I to say, how to ease into it? Thomas looks as flummoxed as I. The silence goes on; I turn to see if Duesbury is creeping up again, but he's pacing down by the riverbank.

I ask, desperate for a topic, "How ever did you hear about that ghoulish doctor?"

"But he wasn't a ghoul," says Thomas earnestly. "That was the point I tried to make, and failed. He was a doctor who wanted to understand the human body, and how can you, really, if you don't see its inner workings? All this reliance on the humors and the presence of bile, the bleedings, it's nonsense. There was a doctor here, in Derby, who had a tunnel running into his cellar and grave robbers would bring him criminals just hanged and —"

He halts mid-word. "Corpses? This is not what I wanted to talk about with you today. I'm hopeless." He laughs. I join him, and the awkwardness between us dissolves into the frigid air.

I say, "Still, you haven't told me, how did you hear about this particular Derby physician?"

"From Dr. Gleason. He told me about it just as a story to pass the time, certainly not to set me off on a journey of discovery."

Thomas Sturbridge is younger than thirty, I'm sure of it. So why does he pass his time with a doctor? Dr. Gleason was the physician called for in the Dolphin when he cut his chin.

"What I'd truly like to learn more about is you, Mademoiselle," he says and then falters again, his cheeks reddening, perhaps embarrassed at the boldness of his sentence, before pushing on. "You're a talented artist, I hear, like your cousin Andrew. And your grandfather, too? I find that fantastic, a tradition of artistry, and here you are, carrying it on."

His enthusiasm makes me smile. I should correct him in one regard, though.

"Mr. Sturbridge, I thank you but you should know that I don't need to be called 'Mademoiselle.' I'm of French descent, yes, but I'm a member of a refugee family that came here almost seventy years ago. We consider ourselves true Englishmen and Englishwomen."

"Noted. Ah, yes, the Huguenots, such an interesting people," he says. "Here you are, the most talented artisans, yet sprung from the followers of Calvin, who hated all art as papist idolatry…"

Thomas disintegrates into a deep, heaving cough, the sort that is likely painful. I don't know what to do.

The crunch of footsteps. "We should go, Tom," says Duesbury, behind me.

Thomas shakes his head, unable to speak just yet. He seems to be having trouble breathing. With much effort, he waves Duesbury off with a rasping "Go," and my employer reluctantly retreats.

When his voice recovers, he says, "Mistress Genevieve, forgive me."

I inquire as to his health and he dismisses the cough as "nothing," though it obviously is not nothing, and a suspicion, a grim one, is taking root.

He says, "I do wish we could see each other in the future. Right now, it would be a challenge. I'm working on a matter of urgent research for William and his partner, and I need to attend to it every minute of the day and far into the night."

My pulse quickens.

"You weren't attending to it last night," I point out.

His response to that is a smile, the same delighted one of last night, and it brightens his features once more. He leans over, half covering his mouth, and says, "I sneak out once in a while."

"So I gather."

"I hate the feeling of being confined in a space, not free to follow my interests, and I admit I've enjoyed the forbidden fruit of a tankard of ale in a tavern." He shrugs. "It's childish."

"I don't consider it childish, Mr. Sturbridge. It's understandable."

He looks at me, more seriously, holding my gaze. "I wish my work here were not such a secret, that my actual existence wasn't kept secret. I know it's ridiculous, to converse like this while we hide behind an oven." Thomas himself does not seem to appreciate all the precautions made to keep his work secret from rivals. He doesn't uphold the precautions himself.

I must make some attempt to gain information here. "Your work must be important," I say.

"I'm not supposed to breathe a word," he says with a shrug. "Pain of death."

I suddenly think of Richard Frederick, stabbed, weighted down at the bottom of a river.

"Are you all right, Mistress Genevieve?" he asks. "All at once you look... rather melancholy."

"No, no, I'm well," I say, forcing a smile. At that moment, a memory stirs. "You're supposed to be a secret, but there was an old man in the Dolphin who knew your name."

Thomas chuckles. "Yes! Jedidiah was my sole defender until you rescued me. I'm amazed he was in the tavern last night; he lives in the almshouse for the elderly poor, run by St Mary's Church. I go there to talk: they think I'm a teacher, not a chemist. The men are ravenous for discussions of science. In fact I'm expected this Saturday afternoon, it's my only allowed escape from my work, as it's charitable." He brightens suddenly. "Would you care to come along? It's far from sophisticated entertainment for a Londoner such as yourself, but..."

It's not just my hands that feel grubby now but all of me, down to my heart, my very soul. Saturday is the day of the dance at Exeter Hall, opening up a day of unusual freedom for me, unobserved by Evelyn or anyone else. It's perfect. And yet... As he waits, his eyes full of admiration, I have a sudden powerful impulse to snarl, "Stay away from me if you know what's good for you, Thomas Sturbridge."

My turmoil must be evident, for the hope dims in his eyes. "That was a foolish suggestion," he mutters.

Yes, very foolish, I scream inside. And it's a suggestion that I have no choice but to spring at.

I say, "I'd like to join you, Mr. Sturbridge."

Smiling, Thomas tells me the location of the almshouse and then, still embarrassed, asks that we keep our meeting a secret. "They don't want me to talk to you beyond today, that was the condition to the agreement I made with William," he says.

An agreement he does not hesitate to break.

One last smile from Thomas Sturbridge and, moments later, he's on his way back to Nuns Street and I'm once more in the decorating room. Stanton is away, it's just me and Harry for the moment.

"You look pleased about something," observes Harry.

I shrug and dip my brush in the water, just as Ambrose Stanton comes in with a new figure to work on. *Am* I pleased? I should be, for I've found a way to spend time with Thomas Sturbridge, the chemist I've been looking for, for the past month. He makes no effort to hide the fact that he's taken with me. Coaxing information shouldn't be difficult, except for a complication.

I'm rather taken with him too.

He's attractive, brilliant, amusing, rebellious. I came close to warning him off just now. I will need to conquer that particular impulse. I have no future with Thomas Sturbridge. To let myself feel any romantic ardor for him would be dangerous, ludicrous and…

…short-lived. As I paint, I think through the deep cough, his thin frame and warm hands, his luminous blue eyes. I've seen these symptoms before. Thomas, I suspect, is consumptive.

Of course that's the formal name for it. Lung rot, white plague. I've heard the names for those who waste away, coughing and coughing, feverish and weak. I knew a girl in school who died of it before she was twenty.

It would explain some things, such as the need for a doctor, their alarm over his health, the erratic pace of his experiments. It must be the reason why he was sent away for a couple of months last autumn. There are clinics for consumptives, where they can rest and be made more comfortable. But they can't be cured, for there is no cure. Consumptives all end in an early grave.

My fingers tighten on the brush. I need to banish all sympathy, for it will do me no good. As I tell myself this with firmness, my throat swells and I feel tears burning.

Tears? I can't believe it. I rarely weep. I recall Sir Gabriel's approving words after Denis was sent away in the night. "No tears, excellent."

I wipe my eyes furtively, take a breath and go to the window. Staring at the river, my little empty house calms me enough to resume work.

I manage to get myself under control when, once again, William Duesbury appears in the doorway. He beckons for Harry, but tells him to take a walk around the grounds while he talks to me. A pensive Stanton remains.

He shuts the door behind Harry, and then Duesbury turns around, smiling the joyless smirk I detest so much. He slides onto one of the empty stools directly across from me at the table. "I remember these days very well," he says, twirling one of my brushes left on a cloth to dry.

"Tell me what you know about Thomas Sturbridge," he says, putting down the brush.

"What do you mean?" I say, glancing over at Stanton, now positively funereal.

Duesbury abandons his menacing friendliness for simple menace. "Look at me, not him. I am the co-founder of this manufactory. The question is plain! Tell me everything you know, beginning with what you two spoke of earlier today."

"He wanted to thank me, for speaking to the men in the Dolphin who bothered him last night," I say as calmly as I can manage.

" 'Speaking to them.' Ha! I've learned a great many things about you today, Genevieve Planché, and one is how you spoke to them, how you put yourself through a real performance to persuade a drunk man with a knife to turn Sturbridge over to you. For the life of me, I can't think why."

There is only one way out, to brazen my way through.

"I should think you would thank me, not berate me," I throw back at him. "I used a few London expressions to whisk him away, what of it? It wasn't that difficult. I'm not a country girl, and my house isn't Kensington Palace."

Duesbury blinks, three times, and then rallies himself. "No, it certainly isn't. Andrew made me believe you were a proper Huguenot, a modest young lady, and instead we find his little cousin has a shameful past, consorting with a criminal, a man who destroyed his master's workshop and stole his money. If the law finds him, you'll be a hangman's widow. Lurid fodder for the pamphleteers, no doubt." His voice is rising to a shrill bray.

Evelyn. She must have told him — it was a mistake to confide in her. I glance over at Stanton, expecting to see him mirror Duesbury in horror over my immorality. He is somber, but says, quietly, "I was the one who indicated to Genevieve that Mr. Sturbridge is of importance to us here. And… and Sir, I must say she is a fine artist."

This sets off another Duesbury explosion. "There are plenty of good artists, and I could have another one here in a week at half her wages, grateful as hell to be here and cause me no trouble."

"Mr. Duesbury, please," says Stanton. It takes me a few seconds to realize it's the profanity that distresses him.

"Major Tarkwell wanted you out of here the first night and I should have listened to him," continues Duesbury. "Now it's too late."

"Oh?" I say. "Why?"

"Because of how much you know — though *precisely* what you know I can't seem to find out. You're pretty clever, aren't you? But let me be perfectly clear, you are about to tell me everything you know about Thomas Sturbridge, Mistress Genevieve Planché. Here. Now.

Everything. No, we can't send you back to London, but believe me, Major Tarkwell has a whole host of ideas about what to do with you to keep you quiet. For your sake, I'd advise complete honesty."

My mind turns, as frantically as a water wheel, while I try to separate what Sir Gabriel has told me from what I've learned since coming to Derby. I clear my throat and say, "I know he is a chemist and performing important research for Derby Porcelain Works."

"And?"

"He isn't performing his work in these buildings, on Nottingham Road, but in a house in town, in secret."

Duesbury narrows his eyes. "And?" he whispers.

This is the moment. I know that my next words will determine everything, my position here, my ability to spy for Sir Gabriel, my future as an artist in London, in Venice, anywhere.

"Evelyn told me last night he's invented a color blue that could transform the porcelain business. That's what Richard Frederick stole, a piece painted in the new blue."

I brace myself for the rage, the hysteria, the Major Tarkwell-created consequences. But, incredibly, Duesbury nods. "Just so," he says, the anger visibly draining from his face. I made the right gamble. Evelyn must have told him not only my personal history but also the fact that she'd shared the secret of the blue research. If I had denied knowing about it now, I'd be condemned as a liar.

It was a trap, and I evaded it, but barely.

"I didn't want this, but you are now part of the small circle — very small — that is aware of the substance of Tom's research and you must tell no one, not an officer of the law, no one," says Duesbury. "Yes, you are vaguely aware of his work. I am the only one at Derby Porcelain Works who knows what's what." He taps his head. "Even I don't know the answers to it all. Only our precious Thomas Sturbridge does. And now you do, because he likes you. Very much. I hate to stand in the way of a man's fancy, but there won't be any more meetings, planned or accidental, between you two. Or else we will have to take up Major Tarkwell on one of his nasty suggestions. You don't want that, do you?"

"No, I don't."

"Good. Good. We'll say no more. Subject's closed."

His hand is on the door when I stop him. "Mr. Duesbury, I do have one last question about Mr. Sturbridge."

Exasperated, Duesbury asks me what it was.

"Thomas Sturbridge seems a little unwell. Is a recovery expected?"

Duesbury doesn't answer. He pulls open the door and lurches into the passageway, but not without a flicker of a glance at me that is full of a feeling I've never seen in him before. If I had to put a name to it, I would call it sadness.

CHAPTER EIGHTEEN

"I'm so, so sorry, Genevieve," says Evelyn as we walk home. She is in a state. "I've had unpleasant dealings with William Duesbury before, but today was the worst by far. He was so suspicious about you, how you behaved in the Dolphin, that I had to tell him the truth about your background."

"You also disclosed that I'm aware of Thomas Sturbridge's experiments with blue."

She bit her lips. "He forced that out of me, too. But it made him more angry with me than with you. I am the one who couldn't keep a secret."

I say that my confession seemed to reassure him of my honesty.

"So the truth makes us free," she says.

"I believe the passage is 'Ye shall know the truth. And the truth shall set you free.' John 8:32." It was a favorite piece of biblical wisdom in our Huguenot church, recited now with a certain bitterness.

Evelyn says, "Yes, of course." She stops walking, and taps my arm. "You look… strange, Genevieve. Rather grim."

Harry told me I looked pleased, now Evelyn says I look grim. I'm weary of being studied. I say, "Having Mr. William Duesbury threaten and berate me is an experience I would wish on few."

"You forget, I've seen you face down Duesbury, Heath, my stepfather, all of them. This is different."

I profess to not knowing what she means, and we resume walking, though Evelyn's conversation is distracted. I sense that she's trying to puzzle it out, the reason for my change.

At supper, forced heartiness reigns. The talk centers on Saturday's dance at Exeter House, evidently a custom of the season that the Derbyshire gentry look forward to every year. Mr. and Mrs. Heath say absolutely nothing about the murder investigation taking place at Derby Porcelain Works. Constable Campion did not make an appearance at the manufactory today, that I know of. But I certainly don't think he is through with us, any more than Jimmy is through with his surveillance or his violence. And I am not through, either; I'm just beginning. It's a shock to realize that, given my circumstances for coming to Derby, I should be finding ways to aid Jimmy, not praying he will cease his actions.

Outside of this bright, handsome house, over-crammed with luxuries, there are men in the dark, determined men, driven by right or wrong, moving in directions that could collide. At the center of the point of collision is Thomas Sturbridge. I picture the young chemist at the window of his Nuns Street house. Now that I've spoken to him, now that we know each other, he's not a candle-lit silhouette. I see his boyish smile, his angular features and blue eyes.

Shaken, I wrench myself away from the vision and back to the Heath table.

"Some people come not for the music or dancing but so that they can say they've been to the famous Exeter House," comments Mrs. Heath, in her light, agreeable way.

I ask what makes it famous, not that it matters to me, but I am keen to distract my mind.

Mr. Heath jumps in. "People say it's because the house is quite grand, it served the earls of Exeter until two years ago. But if they're honest, they want to go inside because that's where Bonnie Prince Charlie stayed with his officers for three days and two nights, and everyone is excited to see the rooms where the prince lived."

"Bonnie Prince Charlie reached this town and went no farther south," I say, remembering what my cousin Andrew told me on Swarkestone Bridge.

"Charles Stuart was backed by the Jacobites and all those who planned to put the Stuarts back on the throne and throw the Hanovers out," exclaims Mr. Heath. "French money behind him, Papists and Highlanders and all manner of riffraff in his 'army.' He had his council of war here in Derby, right in Exeter House, but then a local man persuaded him that an English army was a few days away and he'd best retreat. It turns out the man was a spy sent by King George's man to infiltrate the enemy and spread false reports. There was no army nearby at all!"

His wife laughs, appreciatively, and says, "Oh, but Mr. Heath that must have been a frightening time for the people of Derby, to be occupied."

"I was away in London, seeing to family business, or else I would have played a large part in saving the town from the Jacobites," Heath blusters.

"It was the spy who saved the town, who saved all of England," says Evelyn, in a rare contribution to the dinner conversation.

Her mother makes a delicate face of disdain. "It doesn't seem fitting to award that honor to a spy."

"There are all sorts of traitors," says Evelyn.

She's right. There are all sorts of traitors, and I am one.

As Saturday draws nearer, Evelyn pleads with me to come to the dance. Had I no other plan, I'd have been willing to go, not to witness the Derbyshire gentry sashay across a floor but to garner details on the Courtenay family. I still wonder about Sir Gabriel's connection to the Courtenays who share his motto. Now, though, I have something more urgent to attend to. I explain to her that Huguenots are forbidden to be anywhere near a dance, and Evelyn accepts it.

I will be free to find my way to Thomas Sturbridge.

On the day itself, Mrs. Heath's maid spends hours on preparing Evelyn's gown, dressing her hair and painting and powdering her face, while my friend looks miserable. I can't blame her, for there is a loveliness to the simplicity of her taste. The present style for fashionable women seems to me to aim for a fussy grandeur, and forcing Evelyn in such a direction does not flatter her. She's wearing a robe à la française with its close-fitting bodice and, in the back, box pleats falling to the floor. Pointing at me, Evelyn cries, "Do something to *her* hair."

"But I'm not going to the dance," I protest.

Still, I don't try to stop her when the smiling maid sweeps my hair atop my head and arranges my unruly curls into tamed tendrils. And I discreetly select my best gown for the day.

The carriage carrying Evelyn and the Heaths pulls out of the drive at three hours past noon. From an upstairs window I watch it disappear, and then turn and make for the back stairs. The servants take little interest in my comings and goings; even so, I don't want my departure to be remarked on. I pull a shawl around my hair – "Memorable hair," as Sir Gabriel put it – so that I won't be recognized by anyone who knows me.

It's a bright day, and as I hurry through the Heaths' garden, I spot the first shoots of green pushing up through the black soil. It's the last week of February. In past years I loved the advent of warmer weather, but this isn't the most welcome sight. "You must learn the formula by spring," Sir Gabriel had ordered. The first day of spring is closing in.

The almshouse is farther that I thought, and I race down the Derby streets, past the market and the shops, before I reach Church Street, where a group of almshouses cluster, one for impoverished widows, one for debtors and their families, and the one I'm bound for, dedicated to sheltering the elderly poor men with nowhere else to go. It has its own name — Dunston's — and once I reach the second block of buildings, I scan the fronts for that word on a sign or carved into stone.

A hand grabs me by the sleeve and roughly pulls me into a doorway.

"No!" I cry.

Jimmy clamps his boxer's hand over my mouth. "Shut up," he says in that gravelly voice. "Does Sturbridge know you're coming?"

I nod, and claw at his arm to let me go.

He removes his hand. "And Tarkwell knows too?"

"No," I spit at him.

"So this is your little secret with Sturbridge?" growls Jimmy.

"I don't have to tell you anything. And you should never, ever lay hands on me."

"Believe me, I don't want to lay hands on you. But you were just about to give yourself away because Tarkwell has the almshouse under personal watch with your boy inside, he's fifty feet down the street as we speak."

Wracked with disappointment, I say, "I have to turn around, then."

"No you don't. There's an entrance through the alleyway in the back. I'll take you. Ready?"

I loathe Jimmy, and I fear him, but without him I can't keep going. I nod.

He holds up a finger, letting me know I have to be quiet, and he leads the way back up to the top of the street, hugging the stone buildings on one side. At the top is a grocer and next to it a narrow opening that I realize is an alleyway. We wait until no one is there to observe us, and then slip into the alley.

It's filthy. The stench of spoiled, discarded food on top of human waste is overpowering. Now I'm the one who holds my hand over my nose and mouth, though it's not enough to block the smell, and I cough. I need my other hand free to hold up my skirts so they don't get soiled. I can't greet Thomas reeking of rubbish. Jimmy looks over his shoulder and snickers.

A few more feet and we reach a peeling gray door.

"This is Dunston's," he says. "Keep going straight through and you'll find the group."

"What if Major Tarkwell decides to look in?"

"He won't," Jimmy says flatly.

"And if he tries, you'll throw him under another coach?"

Jimmy stares down at me. "What coach?" he asks.

I am not ready to give up. "I believe that you tried to kill him."

His stare deepens. A warning quakes at the back of my mind. I shouldn't have taunted him that I'm aware of his attempt at murder. Particularly not in a narrow alley where we are all alone.

"I don't want you to hurt anyone," I say.

"You don't? I'll have to remember that." He jerks his chin toward the door. "Get in there. Do your job and no one will have to get hurt. Otherwise…" He makes a cracking noise in the back of his throat.

Appalled, I step through the gray door, leading to a shabby kitchen without a cook. Just as Jimmy advised, I keep walking, through small interconnected rooms of beds and boxes and shelves. I hear voices ahead and I follow them.

"But what is light? You think you know what it is — but do you?"

That's Thomas Sturbridge's voice. Despite Jimmy's roughness, the threat of Major Tarkwell, and the sundry lies I've told along the way, I smile in anticipation.

I follow the voice into a room. Four elderly men sit on stools, with a plump young man in parson's garb hovering. The room faces the street — there's a window — and in the middle of the room stands Thomas Sturbridge. He's not wearing a coat, just a brown waistcoat over his white linen shirt, with his red hair loosely tied. His arms stretch out wide on either side, as if he's illustrating a point.

He sees me and he stops talking, his arms slowly descending as a smile of relief stretches across his face. Perhaps he was starting to think I wouldn't come. I take a seat near the corner, so that I won't be seen from the street through the window.

"Gentlemen, do you recall that I said a friend of mine might be joining us? Mistress Genevieve Planché is here."

"She's late!" pipes up a high-pitched, warbly voice that belongs to a man I recognize as Jedidiah from the Dolphin.

One of the men says, "You didn't say she was this pretty."

"Didn't I?" Thomas smiles at the men, though not at me. He can't meet my gaze.

"Gentlemen, I am very, very sorry for being late," I say, to the room.

"You're forgiven, my dear," says the same elderly man who called me pretty. His words are enunciated a bit strangely because he is missing teeth.

"Edward," says the parson warningly.

Edward, undeterred, winks at me.

"You missed Mr. Sturbridge stabbing himself in the eye," says Jedidiah.

"What?"

Thomas laughs. "It was in the interest of science, and no I didn't actually stab myself in the eye, you mustn't upset my friend, gentlemen. I pretended to do so. The purpose of my demonstration was to convey what Isaac Newton did." He bends over a box and pulls out a long flat needle and rests it in his other hand, tilting it to show me. "The bodkin Newton used resembled this one."

Edward leans over to say, "Newton stuck that bodkin into the bone next to his eye. He wanted to find the colors."

"Colors?" I repeat, tensing.

"Yes, that's why he did that, very good, Edward," says Thomas. "Newton performed the experiment on himself and when he distorted his eyeball through this undoubtedly excruciating means, he saw a flash of color."

"And what was the purpose of *that*?" I ask.

"The origin of color obsessed Newton," says Thomas.

He holds my gaze just a second too long, before turning to the others. I feel a flush crawl up my cheeks. Is Thomas Sturbridge playing some sort of game with me, to speak of color? Then I remember that this scientific lecture began before I arrived. It must be a coincidence.

"Sir Isaac Newton wanted to understand the true nature of light and color," Thomas says. As we all listen closely, he explains that Newton suspected colors did not exist fully formed all around us to be observed, but began inside our minds as individual perception. Everyone thought — incorrectly — that the sun delivered pure white light and when it reflected on different surfaces, the white light turned into color. Newton proved otherwise.

"Sir Isaac Newton conducted his first white light experiments when he was twenty-three," says Thomas in a tone of voice I might call wistful. I wonder how he felt about studying in Cambridge in the shadow of England's greatest scientist.

Clearing his throat, Thomas says, "The reality is twofold: we understand color because of our mind's innate ability to perceive it, and the colors of the spectrum are in the light."

"I don't understand," I say, and the men of Dunston's Almshouse laugh. "Join us," says Jedidiah. "Indeed," says Edward. The other two also make puzzled sounds.

Thomas, unperturbed, pulls something else from his box. It is a piece of carved many-sided glass attached to a wooden handle.

"Newton used a children's prism," Thomas announces. "His genius was always his simplicity, in tools and in ideas."

He turns to the parson and says that because it's a sunny day and the room faces west, the experiment he'd planned should work. The four men of the almshouse can barely contain their excitement.

The next thing out of Thomas' box is a long, flat piece of wood.

"Mistress Genevieve, could you hold this?" he asks. I rise to take it in my hands as he gathers all of the men to sit on their stools in a semicircle, their backs to Thomas. He stands in front of the window and I face him, holding the wood, the men between us. Thomas twists to close the curtains, pitching us into near darkness. "I'm going to open the curtains," he says, but first glances in my direction. "While holding it, you should look directly down at the wood, so you don't miss this," he says gently.

He slowly and deliberately runs his hands up the curtains again. "What's the boy doing?" one whispers to another.

"Patience, my good friends," Thomas says, affectionately.

With one hand he pulls open the curtains just a bit, maybe a quarter of an inch. With the other he holds up the prism. The minutes crawl by.

A ray of sun peeks through the curtain, hits the prism and then shoots onto the board I hold. Looking down, I see that within the white light radiates a tiny rainbow of exquisite colors.

"Ah," the men of the almshouse cry as one.

I am rendered silent by the discovery of the wondrous rainbow. All my fears and strivings drop away, in view of this beauty.

Thomas, delighted, says, "I think William Shakespeare had it best in *Love's Labour's Lost*: 'Beauty is bought by judgment of the eye.' Do you agree?"

It takes a moment for his audience to recover, for all of us to find our seats again when the curtains are pulled back again and we can see normally. When we do, Thomas puts his objects back in his box and takes one more out. It's something I've seen many times: a color wheel. Many painters employ them as the foundation of our work.

"This is Sir Isaac Newton's color wheel, the eventual product of his first prism experiments," Thomas says. "He determined that there are seven colors: violet, blue, green, yellow, orange, red, and indigo. Those seven make up white light. I must tell you, there's some controversy over the total number. Why seven colors? I favor the theory that, for all of his rational rigor, Newton had in mind certain ancient beliefs."

Jedidiah protests. "Mr. Sturbridge, isn't that an insult to Newton?"

Thomas says, "That's what the more hard-headed scholars say, yes. But it's simplistic to say Newton is the enemy of superstition. What is alchemy but a form of chemistry? I did some reading of his journals when I was at Cambridge, the ones his family hadn't hidden. He was obsessed with Pythagoreanism, a 2,000-year-old Greek cult. Has anyone heard of our friend Pythagoras?"

Heads shake. "What a shame," Thomas says. "The ancient followers of Pythagoras believed numbers were the basis of the universe. To them, seven is the deepest mystery, the number of supreme manifestation, and the vehicle of life containing body and spirit."

I am just as skeptical as the men of Newton's studying theories. He discovered gravity, pushed us forward in exciting new ways. What use could an ancient cult be to him?

"Why is seven so special?" demands Edward.

Thomas, walking back and forth, swinging his arms, says, "God created the world in how many days?"

"Seven," we say as one.

"And then He rested! Quite right. How many days of the week? Seven. How many planetary systems? Seven. And notes in the musical scale? Seven. Maths and music were one to Pythagoras. He wrote that the seven modes, or keys, of the Greek system of music had power over the human mind on one level. Through another level, it was the seven colors."

My head is swimming. "But to return to the color wheel, you're saying that not just the number of colors, but the choice of which seven belonged on the wheel, it is all guided by science?" I ask.

"Of course," he says. "Science and art, they join in the most significant way."

And with that, Thomas Sturbridge looks me straight in the eyes. In front of all of these men, he regards me with such ardor, it's like a thunderclap. The breath catches in my throat, as I stare back at him.

The sound of Edward's chuckle rumbles through the room. The parson, not as amused by this display of feeling, clears his throat.

Thomas pulls himself together, smiling down into his waistcoat. "Yes. Gentlemen. Now I am prepared to speak about any color on Newton's wheel. Which one would you like to hear about first?"

Edward, with another wink, suggests I be the one to choose. "Beauty should have its due."

The cry goes up, I must select the color for discussion. "Yes, please do pick the color you're most interested in, Mistress Genevieve," says

Thomas, holding up the wheel. Again, I could swear I detect an undercurrent in his words. Does he suspect me?

There it is, an inch from the thumb of Thomas' left hand, a narrow triangle of the color blue, the reason I am in Derby, the reason I am in this room. Everything I need to know about it is held within that handsome head.

"My favorite is... yellow," I whisper.

I don't listen to Thomas' explanation of yellow, its principle of light refraction under Newton, or much of anything else until the parson brings in a pot of tea and a tray of biscuits. I'm trying to take in the fact that I had the chance to probe about blue, it was offered to me, and I pushed it away. And yet I am not sorry.

Although Thomas' lecture thrilled them, biscuits are perhaps an even greater treat, for it's the focus of the elderly men, and the parson, while Thomas and I are left to drink our tea, the two of us at a table in the corner, so small I think it intended for children, not men and women.

"I want to thank you again for coming," he says. "And for being such an avid listener."

"I was fascinated," I say, and mean it.

Thomas looks down at the biscuits on the plate before him and then over at me, quizzically.

"What is it?" I ask.

Glancing over at the elderly men, he says in a low voice, "These biscuits are put out very much for my benefit. I'm afraid the parson is a bit miserly otherwise. I pretend to eat my share, but I'm actually squirreling them away. Then I sneak the bundle to Jedidiah or Edward."

I say instantly, "Show me how you do it."

Thomas pulls up a cloth from his lap and then lets it fall back. He picks up a biscuit, brings it to his chin, and then swipes it with the cloth.

After he hands me a cloth, I do the same as he watches, with the mischievous glint in his eyes I first noted that night in the Dolphin.

Listening to Edward and Jedidiah debate a point of science, I say, "Your coming here, it means the world to them."

"They're all intelligent men, given little education but hungry for knowledge and they end here, on the church's charity. It pains me, the injustice."

I say, "I don't believe that some people were born to be poor and have little and there's nothing for it."

Enthusiasm burns in Thomas' eyes. "I have a new book of philosophy I can lend you that transformed my thinking on this, written by a Swiss named Jean-Jacques Rousseau. Have you heard of him?"

So many thoughts and ideas storming in one mind. The light through the window is the softening one of late afternoon, and seeing him like this, Thomas Sturbridge no longer looks ill and fragile. I have not heard him cough once. A fierce euphoria seizes me, until I remember who waits outside the almshouse. Major Tarkwell across the street, and Jimmy just short of the corner. It was a reprieve to be so caught up in what Thomas says, for it made them cease to exist. But it's coming to an end.

Thomas sips his tea from a chipped, stained earthenware cup, completely indifferent to its wretched state. Putting down the cup, he says, "As I'm sure William has told you, or perhaps someone else has, I'm researching a new color for Derby Porcelain Works."

Every muscle in my body tenses. "Yes."

"I now know your favorite color is yellow, but I'm quite close to perfecting a stable version of a new shade of blue. Within the month, it will be ready for production."

There is no undercurrent to his words. He says it as straightforwardly as if he were talking about what saddle to purchase for a horse.

"That sounds quite difficult," I manage to say.

"Ah. Well. Color is the great game. Blue is the hardest to reproduce artificially by far — and then when you have to apply a new formula to a fired and glazed clay?" He shakes his head. "It's a mad quest and always was."

His eyes turn serious, haunted by a thought, or memory.

I say slowly, "You're pursuing this because of the scientific challenge, not to make Derby Porcelain rich or to make yourself rich. You really don't care about any of that."

"You understand," he says. "Incredible." He reaches across the table to take my hand in his.

I can't say a word, I'm too convulsed by guilt. But I don't pull back my hand either. I interlace my fingers with his, thrilling to feel their warmth and strength again, that bit of masculine roughness.

Thomas says, "I've decided. I shall change the arrangement I have with the porcelain works, if necessary. I've never met a woman like you, and I can't let you slip away."

CHAPTER NINETEEN

I manage to make it to the Heaths' house before darkness. I walk alone. Thomas was at first adamant on escorting me, but I told him I'd spotted Major Tarkwell standing watch outside, and if we left together it would cause a public uproar. This news made him vow to go out on the street and declare his determination to see me again this evening. It took a bit of doing, but I persuaded Thomas this might not be the best idea. Should not William Duesbury be told first? As for our immediate challenge, he could leave ahead of me, I'd tarry a few minutes and then leave Dunston's Almshouse separately.

"Mr. Sturbridge, I am, as you well know, a Londoner. For years I walked the streets of Spitalfields and beyond, often by myself. Derby will give me no trouble, be assured."

"I have received proof with my own eyes and ears that you can handle any situation," he says. "I will not insult you by saying you are unequal to this. But I hope you will be willing to call me Thomas? Or Tom? William Duesbury and the others here, they call me Tom."

"I prefer Thomas."

"And I may address you as Genevieve? Or is that too forward?"

"Not at all." I smile.

His face flushed with happiness — and determination — Thomas turns to say goodbye to the elderly gentlemen, the parson and, with a last ardent glance at me, he is off.

When I judge the time is right, I leave the almshouse too. To my relief, there is no sign of Major Tarkwell. Which makes sense. He wouldn't remain on Church Street once Thomas Sturbridge was gone from it. But what about Jimmy? The excitement of my encounter with Thomas, the wonder of his lecture and the thrill of his feelings for me, curdle as I stand on the cobbled street.

If I were a devoted operative of Sir Gabriel Courtenay, I would hurry to the place where Jimmy hid earlier today, to share my news: Thomas Sturbridge has told me himself that he is experimenting with a new shade of blue and he plans to force the heads of the manufactory to allow us to meet in the future.

But how can I possibly serve as a spy now? To coax the entire formula out of Thomas and deliver it to Sir Gabriel, that would be despicable. When I set out to do this, I knew there'd be falsehoods told, but how else was I to achieve my goal in a world that won't accept me? Once here, I found it so difficult to learn of the chemist's location, I never put a great deal of thought into the man himself, what it would be like to trick him. In a way the chemist himself was a blank to me — or I assumed he'd be a person of similar caliber to William Duesbury, John Heath, or Major Tarkwell. Betraying any of *them* wouldn't lose me sleep at night.

But Thomas is nothing like them.

I walk slowly up Church Street, wary of the shadow of a muscular arm, the flash of a sneering face. No sign of Jimmy. Perhaps he, too, left the block once the porcelain works chemist was on his way. With a shudder, I realize what quarry Thomas Sturbridge has become. The man hasn't a notion. And there is no way to warn him.

As I hurry through the town, I compose in my head a letter to Sir Gabriel Courtenay. I've taken this far enough; the spying must halt. I'm sure he will be angry and disappointed. I wince as I think about the lengths Sir Gabriel went to recruit and train me, providing me with the sympathetic writing ink inside the Huguenot Bible.

Your task is not yet finished.

As I expected, Evelyn and the Heaths are not home. My room is cold and dark, and I light the fire and three candles myself, distributing them around the room. I am determined to write my letter to Sir Gabriel now, while I have privacy.

With my regular ink, I write the usual banal letter to Grandfather, leaving space below. I open the compartment of my Bible and take out the dispenser of invisible ink and brush.

For the first time, I begin with his name. It seems necessary under the circumstances. It's the longest letter I've ever written.

"Sir Gabriel, I regret to inform you that I cannot continue to work for you. I'll request no payment. I must also notify you that the dead body of Richard Frederick was found. He was murdered by persons unknown. The constable investigates the crime. The presence of Jimmy in Derby is unwise. Major Tarkwell is aware that someone attempted to push him into a carriage's path."

I wait the recommended time for the ink to dry, I seal the letter, and not five minutes later, I hear voices on the stairs.

"Evelyn, for God's sake, you know that is not true," bellows Mr. Heath.

The door to our room flies open and Evelyn, her eyes flashing, charges in, slamming the door behind her.

"I take it the dance at Exeter House was not a success," I say.

"Why did my mother have to marry that man?" she cries, tearing at the elaborate hair dress. "I've been in Derby for seven years, and every single one has been a misery."

Another second, and there's a knock on the door. The maid is here to undress Evelyn.

"I can't let anyone in," she says, her voice thick with tears. "Will you help me, Genevieve?"

I send the maid away. I unpin and take down her black hair, unfasten her dress, and untie her corset, dampening a cloth so she can remove the powder and face paint. Throughout, she tells me of the dance, which seems to have been an event of many valleys and few peaks. For her mother and stepfather, there was social humiliation. They worked their way into the room where a bishop held court, but when the religious man learned that Mr. Heath backed Derby Porcelain Works, he loudly chastised him. Mania for expensive porcelain was destroying lives, said the bishop. Good Christian men without sufficient means were tumbling into debt, their families ruined. The kingdom should be focused on winning the war with France, not chasing luxuries. The Heaths beat a retreat from the bishop's rant while other guests gaped.

That was not the cause of Evelyn's dispute with her stepfather, though it's likely it fed his subsequent ill temper. Evelyn turned down an offer to dance made by a friend of Mr. Heath's — "the man is repellant" — and a short time later overheard her stepfather apologize to him, saying, "She has the character of a prissy second-rate clerk, I'll never see her out of my house. Who'd take her off my hands?"

I lay my hand on Evelyn's quaking shoulder. "Oh, that is terrible," I say.

"I wish with all my heart I had somewhere to go," she says, the tears streaming down her face. "But to have your own home, you must have a husband. My sister Amelia, she wed someone in order to escape our mother's husband. I can't bring myself to marry someone I don't care for. I can't. And now it's too late. I'm twenty-three."

"That's not so old," I protest. I am a year older than her, and while I realize I must be destined for spinsterhood, it seems of little importance to me. I'm aware that most women do not feel as I do.

"But I *won't* leave, I *won't* give him that satisfaction," she says furiously. "And I know that if I were to cease my work, the factory would run aground. He can't keep pouring money into its coffers much longer."

"That's why Thomas Sturbridge's experiments are so crucial to Derby," I say quietly.

She nods. "You don't know what it is to be penniless, Genevieve. I do. And so does my mother." She pauses. "You never ask me about my real father. I appreciate that. It's something I cannot speak of. Ever." Her eyes fill with tears.

Later, as we prepare for bed and she is calmer, I ask, while attempting to not seem too interested, "What about the famous Courtenay heir? Did he make an appearance?"

"Such a little snob. You'd think he inherited a dukedom. Little Lord Musgrave barely looked at anyone and never smiled. I'm sure that is what Lady Courtenay would want, she was whispering in his ear the entire time. My mother and her friends all despise her, but I think that they're jealous."

"Jealous of what?"

"Lady Courtenay did what most of them have had to do, but she took it to the most extreme place. She married an old degenerate, nearly fifty years older, and got an heir by him. Her boy inherited everything, absolutely everything."

My sleep is not peaceful that night. I see rainbows and needles and teacups, I smell the filth of an alley and the faint lemon scent of invisible ink, and I feel Thomas' fingers, closing around mine. "Sir Gabriel, I regret to inform you… I regret to inform you… I regret to inform you…"

*

What about Venice?

That is the question I wake up with on Sunday. Without Sir Gabriel's fee, living as an artist in Venice is out of the question. The London art world is already closed to me. Even if I wanted to return to Grandfather's house, I'd return to days without much purpose and I'd be a financial drain. If I stay here, the Derby position that to me was merely pretext would become reality. I would at least earn a living. But I'd do so turning out watercolor flowers and fruit, and, if I'm diligent, moving up to designs executed on the porcelain itself. This is the fate I have passionately wanted to avoid.

That Sunday, listening to services at St Mary's Church, walking in the garden, or reading in Mrs. Heath's parlor, I am in an agony of indecision. I don't want to coax information on the blue formula from Thomas Sturbridge and deliver it to Sir Gabriel. Neither do I want to be a porcelain painter. I can't see a solution to this impasse. Evelyn is withdrawn all day, and I feel a kinship with her. We are females that do not fit into the world we must live in.

My sealed letter stays tucked in the corner of my trunk. Perhaps I will toss it in the fire and push on with what I came here to do.

On Monday, working in the decorating room, I cannot rid myself of the melancholy. Working on some leaves in the afternoon, I dip my brush into a dampened cake of green paint, mixed with yellow to lighten. I think of the seven colors of Isaac Newton and the world of strange and wondrous connections that Thomas talked about. Things I'd never conceived of before.

A soft patter hits the window. It's rain, a gray misty rain, the sort that comes in the spring. As I listen to its rat-a-tat on the thick glass of the decorating room, something shifts inside me, falls into place.

That night, after supper, I hand Mrs. Heath my letter for the Tuesday post.

"You're such a diligent granddaughter," Mrs. Heath says approvingly, tucking the letter away in her sleeve.

Once that letter reaches the post, I can't turn back. I am no longer a spy for Sir Gabriel Courtenay.

There's one question that haunts me above all others. What he will do when he learns of my decision?

CHAPTER TWENTY

That night and the next, I sleep more soundly than any other since I arrived in Derby. I take it as a sign that my decision was right. The lies and trickery are finished. It's a smaller future than I desired, but at least it's an honest one.

My newfound sense of peace is shattered on Wednesday morning.

When I come down the stairs ahead of Evelyn, dressed and ready for my day at the manufactory, the three of them stand there, Mr. Heath, William Duesbury, and Major Starkwell, in a grim half-circle.

"We must speak to you, Mistress Genevieve," says Duesbury, quite formally.

I think of the letter I gave Mrs. Heath to post. Sir Gabriel told me to expect them to pry open my letters. If somehow they were able to render visible the ink in my message to Sir Gabriel...

Struggling to appear unconcerned, I follow them into Heath's study. There, I'm informed that Thomas Sturbridge delivered an ultimatum. He must be allowed to see me, or he will cease his work. The men are most displeased. "We can't have him distracted," says Duesbury. "Not now, when he's so close. We hope to start production in a month."

"This is entirely Mr. Sturbridge's idea, so if you dislike it, you should take it up with him," I say coolly.

Duesbury says, "You are not enthused?"

"How I feel about seeing Mr. Sturbridge is my business, not yours. I don't intend to discuss it with you."

Major Tarkwell growls, "That's where you're wrong. It *is* our business."

"We've been given no choice in this, but we do have our own conditions," says Duesbury. "They are meant to protect the nature of his research and your safety. Not just Tom's, but yours."

Looking from one of them to another, I sense something new in the air. "Has something occurred that leads you to believe I'm not safe?"

"We don't intend to discuss it," says Major Tarkwell, mocking my voice.

I take a breath to cool my temper and ask, "What are your conditions?"

Mr. Heath clears his throat and says, "Most couples, when they're courting, like to go out and about. But Sturbridge can only see you here, under the Heaths' roof."

Major Tarkwell interjects. "You may wonder why I permit you to be in the company of Sturbridge at all. I don't trust you. But if we eliminate all of his contact with outsiders except for you, then if there is ever any stealing of his work, if I hear a whisper that another porcelain manufactory has information about color that belongs to Derby, I will know who to blame. And when that day comes, it won't be a matter of fines or penalties or sending the constable after you. I will be with you, Mademoiselle, and not just you. Your cousin Andrew and your grandfather, all related to you will suffer alongside you."

I'm rendered speechless by his vicious threat. I wait for Heath or Duesbury to chastise him, but they don't. At that moment, I realize I've never taken into consideration what will happen if I steal the formula and they discover it was me, what it would mean to my family. I'd honestly not thought that through.

Duesbury says, "Speaking of the constable…"

"Ah, yes," says Mr. Heath.

"What of the constable?" I say.

"He insists on questioning you," says Duesbury.

"Why talk to me?" I demand. "I didn't know Richard Frederick, I wasn't here when he worked at the manufactory or when he was murdered."

Heath says, "I agree, there doesn't seem a link we can see. But we cannot refuse, we promised him we'd give him every cooperation."

"Up to a point," Duesbury says. "Remember, Mistress Genevieve, no mention of the blue."

"When must I talk to Constable Campion?" I ask, anxious for time to prepare myself.

Duesbury looks at his watch. "In an hour he will be here."

"An hour?" My voice rises.

*

In fact, Constable Campion comes early. The men have gone only a few moments earlier, and I've little time to gird myself, to prepare what words I will say. He lumbers into the study, his expression neither accusatory nor friendly. He is a steady blank. I hope I seem the same to him.

"I understand your background is Huguenot," he says.

"Not just my background, I am Huguenot. I've absolutely no loyalty to France or its king."

He permits himself a small smile. "I'm not here to question your loyalty to King George. I am speaking to all porcelain employees hired since last November. Shall we sit down?" He gestures toward a set of upholstered chairs.

After we sit, Constable Campion with a little difficulty, he says, "Your hiring came about because your cousin, Andrew Planché, put you forward?"

I nod.

He seems to be gathering his thoughts for a moment. I spot a greasy streak on his coat — his most recent meal? — and I begin to relax my guard. In conversation, he's nothing like the constables of London.

"Why would a man work that hard to start a business and then walk away from it, just as it progressed toward profitability?" he muses. "It's certainly unusual."

"Andrew wanted to be an actor. He is an actor now, he was preparing his lines for *Othello* in the coach traveling here."

Skepticism twitches Constable Campion's eyebrows. This is a man who does not appreciate the Bard.

"Are you sure," he says, "that your cousin harbors no ill will toward Mr. Duesbury and Mr. Heath? Mr. Duesbury was his partner; Mr. Heath backed the venture. He does not resent their success without him?"

"No." There must be something less than convincing in my voice. I see his blandness recede before a certain intensity.

"Mistress, I must ask you for complete forthrightness. Is there a point of disagreement or grudge on his part?"

"Andrew's my cousin but he does not confide in me," I protest. "Perhaps he's not close as he once was to Mr, Duesbury or Mr, Heath, but I know no details. Haven't you spent enough time with the two of them to perceive why a man of sensitive artistic sensibilities would not be entranced?"

It wasn't the type of answer he expected, I can tell. He shifts in his chair.

"Yet Andrew Planché sends you here, though he is far from entranced?" he presses.

"My grandfather thought it a good opportunity," I say. "I need the position — the wages."

Constable Campion folds his arms across his chest.

"Why are you interested in my cousin Andrew?" I ask.

Speaking deliberately, the constable says, "Because he knew the victim, Richard Frederick, from the time he was here in Derby and may well have thought that obtaining a new piece of porcelain that is superior to other kinds would be essential in starting a competitive business. He'd be in a good position to recruit Frederick, to promise him a new life in London — that's where Andrew Planché had already moved."

"You think that *Andrew* is behind this?" I am so flabbergasted, I laugh.

"Theft and murder aren't light matters, Mistress," he says.

"No, of course not." I try as hard as I can, but his revelation is so misguided, I can't match his somber tone. "You think that my cousin, one of the gentlest of men... forgive me, but you are not on the right path."

"I've been in communication with a constable in Planché's parish in London, to have him investigated, so we shall see," he says.

"I'm sure you'll find out Andrew wasn't in Derby between the time he resigned from the manufactory and when he brought me here in January," I say firmly.

"Perhaps. Or perhaps Andrew Planché is only part of a ring of criminals, and that ring includes you, Genevieve Planché, sent here to finish what Richard Frederick started."

If he sought to extinguish laughter in me, he succeeded. "That is offensive, Sir," I say.

"I know that there's something special to that piece of porcelain Frederick stole, though everyone denies it," he says, pointing at me. "And I am developing a new theory on his murder. I don't think he stole it, made his way to London, and then returned to Derby, to be murdered. I think he was killed the same night he stole the porcelain and he was dumped in the Trent. The clothes bear that out. We can't tell how long a body's been in the water, but it's a fact that there are no witnesses or records for his existence alive on this earth after October seventeenth. He didn't buy a fare on any coach from Derby or buy a horse to ride. After talking to those who knew him best, I don't believe him clever enough to create a false identity. Did he walk 130 miles to London? I don't think so."

I draw back in my chair as a suspicion seizes, like an icy clamp around my heart.

"Why would someone kill Richard Frederick that same night?" I ask, the question for myself as much as him.

"There are many reasons," Constable Campion says. "To take back a reward, to silence him."

The constable spreads his hand, in a somber plea. "Should I be correct in my suspicions, Mistress Genevieve, then whomever is behind this is an extremely dangerous man. If you know anything about this theft or murder, anything at all, you need to tell me. Right now."

"I *don't* know anything about this murder," I say, pouring everything I possess into looking offended, rather than guilty — and terrified.

With a scowl, the constable rises to his feet. "I don't know if I believe you, I don't know if I believe anyone who works for Derby Porcelain. Richard Frederick wasn't a likable young man. It doesn't seem like there are a great number of people who care about his death. But he was a member of my parish, and I will find his murderer."

With that he is gone.

I could not confess to the constable. To expose myself as a spy to everyone — Thomas, Evelyn, Andrew, the Heaths, Duesbury, Stanton, and Harry, and, the most agonizingly of all, my grandfather — was impossible. It would in effect be the end of my life, for confession would not only lose me the love or respect of every one of those people, but I'd also be hustled to Newgate. If Jimmy is the one who killed Richard Frederick, and I am connected to him and Sir Gabriel, I could hang with them. I am not certain the two of them are responsible — how could I be, without proof? — but something inside me says it was Jimmy who stabbed Richard and threw him in a river. And Sir Gabriel knows he did it.

The only shred of comfort I can take from this is that I broke away from Sir Gabriel before my interrogation by Constable Campion. I am no longer a spy. I am a porcelain decorator, right hand to God. Even when I was a spy, I didn't learn much of anything. The only damage done was my informing Sir Gabriel that Major Tarkwell had been hired to protect the porcelain's secrets. I'm responsible for putting the major in danger. That is all.

But my worries and doubts have deepened to pure fear, the kind of fear that burrows into your every waking moment, your dreams at night. It cannot be shed. It is a second skin. When Evelyn tells me that the next Saturday, Thomas Sturbridge is coming to tea, I almost tell her that I don't want to see him. Now that I know how deeply I am involved in a confederacy of theft and violence, I can't face Thomas.

*

And yet, when the door to the Heaths' home opens and he walks in, handing his coat uncertainly to the footman, when I do face Thomas Sturbridge once more, his dark red hair gleaming in the candlelight, I feel glad.

His face breaks into that boyish, delighted smile, and I feel myself smiling back at him.

I confess I hadn't given a lot of thought to how this visit of Thomas' would unfold. But the Heaths have. Thomas is welcomed into the parlor and seated across the little table from me. Joining us are Mrs. Heath and Evelyn.

The maid walks in, solemn, carrying a silver tray loaded with a porcelain tea pot and glittering white cups. Following her is a second maid carrying a tray with a plate of freshly baked cakes: golden brown, pitted with almonds, and sprinkled with sugar like delicate snowflakes.

Thomas sips his tea with ease and talks mostly to Mrs. Heath, who is posing him a steady series of benign questions. I realize his upbringing must have been a genteel one. He had a mother who schooled him in the niceties of society, and I wonder what she was like. Did she have red hair and a lively mind?

If someone were to wander into this room, they might assume Thomas was a country squire come to court one of the daughters of the house. The truth is so much more complicated, so much darker, that I find I prefer the bland façade we're all propping up.

Handed a golden cake, Thomas glances at me across the tea table and picks up the napkin folded in his lap as if he were going to smuggle it out. I burst out laughing, and he joins in.

Evelyn smiles, though she has no idea what is sending me into peals of laughter.

"Sturbridge, my good man!" bellows Mr. Heath as he swoops down on our group.

Thomas rises to shake his host's hand.

"So gratifying to see our resident genius partaking of tea and cake," says Mr. Heath.

Thomas immediately shakes his head. "No, no. I thank you for the kindness and your hospitality, Sir, but it's not the case. I don't fit that description."

"Nonsense. We know your worth. And we appreciate the sacrifice."

Thomas says, earnestly, "In a time of war and poverty, when a man can't be sure his wages will be sufficient to feed his children, no I wouldn't say it's a sacrifice that I commit myself to porcelain experiments."

"The war brings intense grief," Evelyn agrees.

"But it is a noble conflict," Mr. Heath said, reproving her.

Thomas says, "It's difficult to say how noble the war is when for the life of me, I don't understand its origin, what led us to this."

His eyes widening, Mr. Heath says, "You can't possibly think the war unjustified. So much is at stake."

I wait for Thomas to agree, to fall into line. Instead he says, "Everyone talks about how desperately important the war is. But to whom? Does the fur-trading native of Quebec care whether England or France buys his pelt? Or the slave harvesting cane in the West Indies, who suffers under the most brutal conditions on our earth? What could it matter to him? Either country will increase his misery. How about the farmer in Silesia, the territory in Prussia that was the cause of the war breaking out in Europe? Does he care which army strips his land, the Prussian, the Austrian, or the French? The result is the same: he starves."

The Heaths, even Evelyn, are shocked into silence.

"I'd like to show Mr. Sturbridge the garden," I announce.

"In this cold?" murmurs Mrs. Heath.

"Oh, but I love the cold," says Thomas, moving around the tea table, practically knocking over a chair to reach me.

Taking his arm, I guide him to the garden. It is indeed cold, but we are happy to be alone, and free of the Heaths.

We do not walk a straight path. Mrs. Heath read that the fashion in gardens is to do away with straight lines of shrubbery and exactly placed trees and flowers. Last year she ordered many changes, begun in the autumn and to be carried out when we're safely past frost. Following the Oriental style, Mrs. Heath is trying to create spaces of soothing, contemplative nature, barely tamed. Walking paths must coil; floral beds launch surprises. These imperatives are difficult for an orderly English banker's wife to follow, and to me, the garden promises to be a muddle.

Thomas's thoughts are on the tea party he just laid waste to. "The last thing I wanted to do was insult my host, and the financier of my work."

"You were almost as popular in there as you were at Dolphin," I tease him.

"I often say the wrong thing at the wrong time," he agrees, as we make our way down the path, unplanted soil stretching on both sides. "And you are quite clever in all of your rescues." He squeezes my hand. "Genevieve, someday I'd like to rescue *you*."

"I look forward to it."

We laugh together, but then he sighs. "I'm becoming quite the eccentric, a man only accepted by other scientists."

"I accept you, Thomas."

I can't believe I said it, such a bold, stark, shameless statement. This isn't the way young women are supposed to behave with young men who pay a call.

But it was the right thing to say to him. Thomas seizes my other arm and pulls me close to him. "Yes, you do, and I can't believe this is happening to me — happening to us." He looks down at me searchingly. "All that chat about the weather and the war, and I thought I'd go mad. I want to talk to *you*, I want to learn everything there is to know about you."

I take a deep breath, exulting in his feelings for me but consumed with shame too. He will never know everything about me, I couldn't allow it.

He studies me even more closely. "Genevieve, what is it? There's a sadness in your eyes sometimes, and I don't know why."

"Sadness?"

"A far-away look, as if you're distant, no matter our proximity. It's there and then it's gone, and then returns again. I... I think about it."

"Perhaps that is what draws you to me," I say, rather wildly.

He looks around the garden, this way and that. In another moment he is leading me to the only tree in the garden with any life: a large fir. Standing behind it, hidden from the house, Thomas cups my face with his hands and says, his voice low, "*This* is what draws me to you."

His lips are on mine, hungry, curious, and I kiss him back, pulling him to me so tight that I can feel his heart beating. Thomas wraps his arms around me. We mold ourselves to each other, kissing passionately, as if we're trying to drive the world away.

CHAPTER TWENTY-ONE

Nine days later, I'm taken by carriage to Thomas Sturbridge's house on Nuns Street, with Evelyn, her mother, and Mr. Heath escorting me to the door and two coachmen, armed with pistols, above. Waiting for us at Seven Nuns Street is Major Tarkwell, standing against the stone front, leaning hard on his stick.

It's embarrassing to be escorted like this to Thomas' house, to have our fledgling romance under observation by so many people, but there's no other way.

After his visit to the Heaths' house, Thomas insisted on a dinner with me. Once again, there was opposition, and once again, he broke it down. We would not dine alone, of course. The solution: a dinner at Thomas' house, with Dr. Gleason, his physician, as chaperone.

The condition Major Tarkwell and Duesbury insist on is that once inside the house at Seven Nuns Street, I must stay in the front rooms of his dwelling and not venture into Thomas' laboratory.

His laboratory? If Sir Gabriel knew what I was so close to and yet will not enter… I suppress a shiver.

Whether it is because of the constable's disturbing new conclusions about Richard Frederick's murder or the major's deepening conviction that someone in Derby wants him dead, we are all being protected. Tarkwell hired a new round of guards for himself, the manufactory, and its leaders when at home. They are hollow-eyed, tough men, the sort who successfully evaded the recruitment cry for soldiers for the king's army and, more recently, militia companies in the country. It's money that sends them into action, and I can only imagine how much Mr. Heath must summon up for the mercenaries.

These measures have naturally put everyone aware of them on edge. A few days earlier, Mrs. Heath tried to lighten the mood by inviting a few friends over for cake and sherry. It was a mixed success, because the women ended up lost in intense gossip over Madame de Pompadour. They pretended to be horrified but were in reality titillated over rumors that King Louis XV no longer seeks only the Pompadour's bed. The Bourbon king supposedly finds his pleasure in a bordello near Versailles that is stocked with women, most of them young, wild, and poor, called the Deer Park.

"This is part of the reason the porcelain made at Sèvres is so highly sought after," Evelyn says after her mother's guests leave. "You see how obsessed everyone is with Madame de Pompadour? We're at war with France, but the decadence of their court gives the porcelain created under Pompadour such glamour. If someone has money, they'd rather purchase Sèvres, even if it's illegal and far overpriced, than boring English goods. To have any hope of competing, we must produce something wonderful."

The man responsible for delivering the wonder waits for me this evening.

"Try to have fun," Evelyn whispers in my ear as the carriage comes to a halt on Nuns Street. As soon as she learned of Thomas Sturbridge's feelings for me, she'd offered nothing but encouragement. Knowing her own frustration over never meeting a man she can respect, I take this as another proof of her fine character. She insisted on accompanying me to Nuns Street, but her mother wouldn't let Evelyn out of her sight without coming too, and then when Mr. Heath heard… The situation wobbles on the boundary of farce.

I'm like a prisoner running the gauntlet as I pass from the Heaths' hands to Major Tarkwell and his aide. Tarkwell opens the door on the street, shooting me a stony glare, and I step over the threshold into a tiny foyer leading straight up a set of stairs.

Thomas bounds down the stairs.

"Genevieve, at last," he says.

As I murmur my greeting, he's taking my hand as if to shake it but then he raises it to his lips. He kisses it tenderly, his blue eyes alight.

I think of our moments behind the Heaths' fir tree, and my heart skips a beat.

Calling his greetings from the top of the stairs is the promised Dr. Gleason. I see a man in his early sixties with a broad, friendly face. As Thomas, still holding my hand, leads me up the stairs, there is the loud click of a lock behind us.

Thomas and I look at each other. He laughs, and I join in.

"I introduce you to the new protocol," says Thomas, rolling his eyes. "Locked in my home, two guards outside day and night."

And now here I am, inside.

The top of the stairs opens to a short hall, which then connects to a long, sparsely furnished room dominated by an oak dining table and chairs, a window facing Nuns Street on the opposite end. This was the window he must have stood at the first day I first saw him.

I exchange pleasantries with Dr. Gleason and Thomas, looking around the room. There's no evidence of Thomas' character, any taste in furniture or art or signs of preferred comfort. It could be a room in the George Inn.

We sit down at the table. The conversation settles on my job at the porcelain manufactory, which I describe to both of the men as dinner is served. They take keen interest in the workings of the Decorating Department. I don't think Thomas' questions are only driven by his attachment to me, either. His is an innately curious mind. Dr. Gleason has questions too, and I enjoy answering them, for their perspectives on my work are different from an artist's or potter's.

I relax into the atmosphere of the evening, of warm conversation. There's no porcelain or crystal at this table, just ordinary plates and cups, the same as I'd find in my grandfather's house. Another warm reminder of home is the quality of the food. Thomas' cook, a square-faced woman named Matilda, brings out a platter of chicken fricassee roasted perfectly. Daphne would have approved of the sprinkling of parsley and the nestling of juicy yellow shallots alongside the trussed bird.

"Matilda, I must compliment you on this delicious meal," I tell her after she clears the chicken and meat pie to bring out the cheese pot, carrots and radishes.

"Never mind that," she huffs. "You get Master Sturbridge to eat more than a morsel this evening and then you'll have me as a friend for life."

"Matilda!" cries Thomas, in mock-outrage.

"Don't fiddle me with your jokes," she says. "You never eat much and that's a fact."

Dr. Gleason says, "She's right, Thomas. A heartier appetite would be beneficial. I know you're often caught up with your work, but a man must eat."

"Outnumbered," says Thomas, setting down his cup, and a cough erupts. And another. To my dismay, he's convulsed by the coughs. It's worse than when I talked to him by the manufactory kiln, for now he wheezes between coughs. Dr. Gleason, obviously concerned, rises and walks over to where he hunches over his plate.

"No!" Thomas chokes out, frantically waving him off. Bowing his head, the doctor retreats. After a few agonizing minutes of this, the coughing subsides, and Thomas stands.

"Genevieve, I need to get a book for you," he rasps, his eyes watery and bubbles of sweat on his brow. "Will you excuse me?"

"Of course." I'm trying to act as he does, as though the torturous coughs are but a small matter. Yet it's distressingly plain that they aren't.

He leaves the room, quickly. I suspect he needs to be alone, to recover completely, before returning to the table. I glance at Dr. Gleason, who is watching me.

"Doctor, what is the cause of his illness?" I say.

"The last thing Thomas would want is for me to discuss his health with you."

"But I think he will never wish to discuss it with me."

"You're probably right," Dr. Gleason admits.

I lean over the table and say, "Don't you think this is something I should know; whether he has consumption?"

The doctor considers for a moment before saying, "Thomas is not consumptive. He is not in any way contagious."

Relief courses through me, followed by confusion. "What is it, then?"

"It would be unfair, and without ethics, for me to say more."

Thomas returns, pale but recovered, and slips me the book written by Jean-Jacques Rousseau. With determination, he takes up the conversation again, going back to the workings of the decorating room, and I answer more questions about our assignments, our tools, our techniques. The mood of the table is changed, however. He asks the questions, he listens to my responses, but I can tell that he's thinking of something else too. His earlier enthusiasm is gone. He no longer touches the food or drink. Matilda lights candles at the table, and in their reflection, Thomas looks hollow-cheeked. Our dinner finishes on a strained note.

"It was this Mrs. Garthwaite who taught you how to paint flowers with such skill?" he asks.

I don't want to now answer twenty questions about paint on silk and I answer, shortly, "She taught me how to turn art into a lucrative trade."

He tilts his head, picking up on the edge of my temper but not understanding it. On the other side of the table, Dr. Gleason's head droops; he's falling asleep.

"You say that as if art should be something else," Thomas says.

"Of course. Art should be art, a reflection of our society. It should change society. Its purpose is not only decoration."

"Why, then, do you work as a porcelain decorator?"

Thomas Sturbridge looks genuinely puzzled.

"The fact that you ask me this question proves that you don't understand my situation and can never understand it." My words are rude, but something about Thomas' privileged position as resident genius, catered to by everyone, claws at my least admirable quality: my envy of others. But he does not respond with like anger.

"Tell me, Genevieve," he says. "Why is it impossible?"

"I am a woman and — and — that is all. A woman cannot be a serious artist. The men in London and Paris are in utter agreement on that point. My attempts to be one, to learn from a history painter or a master artist as an apprentice, were failures. Abject humiliations. So here I am."

For a second I recall standing in front of the shimmering, golden Canaletto in Sir Gabriel's home on Grosvenor Square and longing to step into the painting. Thinking of Sir Gabriel, and what his seeming sympathy led me to, makes me feel even worse.

I can't stop the words from coming. "Thomas, I need to say something."

"Yes?" He is no longer preoccupied by other thoughts.

"I am not a nice person, or a good person, or a kind person. I am not such as you."

Thomas stares at me and then laughs. Not with delight, but with a surprising bitterness. "That's what you think? Well. I suppose this evening has proven one thing: we do not really know each other at all." He shakes his head, frustrated. "I am not a good man, Genevieve. I am eaten up by selfish ambition; my thoughts are cruel, ugly. I am sure you wonder at my condition, my cough, my inability to breathe. Who knows? You may even have questioned Dr. Gleason here while I was out of the room." His eyes flick toward the doctor, fully asleep. "What would you think of me if I told you that I brought this affliction on myself? It's a punishment, my curse, a deserved one. You suffer because you can't get what you want. Be careful, because I know what happens when you get it."

His speech astounds me.

I say, "I don't believe in curses."

"Of course you don't. A practical daughter of Calvin could never set stock in curses. But Calvin did not know everything." He rises, holding out a hand to me. "Come. I want to show you."

I walk around the table and take his hand. Holding a candle in his other, Thomas leads me back toward the stairs, to a door I missed when I came in. He sets down the candle to reach for a slender silver chain around his neck and pulls it over his head. At the end of it is a key.

"I carry it on me always, it's the only one that exists to the room," he says.

Thomas wants to take me into the laboratory.

I say, "They made me promise I wouldn't go in here."

He looks at me with a half-smile, just four or five inches away. "What about what *you* want? Do you wish to go inside with me?"

"Yes," I whisper.

We stand there, stock still, staring at each other, until Thomas takes a sudden step closer and kisses me. I move my hands across his chest as we kiss. It is even more exciting than the first time.

With effort, Thomas pulls away. "Come with me," he says, his voice roughened.

I hear the key turn in the lock.

The door opens into darkness, and I follow Thomas into the laboratory.

CHAPTER TWENTY-TWO

My first thought is that the laboratory reminds me of the decorating room. It's about the same size. I can make out a long table beneath a window. But in another minute, I become aware of the glass. The room is filled with glass of all shapes: globes and shallow bowls, long and short tubes, and other dimensions I'd never seen before. All of the strange shapes glow in the last rays of twilight. There's a spirit of watchfulness to these inanimate objects; it excites me rather than frightens me. The room has been waiting for me. A faint but sour odor hovers, barely held at bay. I sense that, were it to become stronger, the odor's pungency would overwhelm my senses.

Thomas brings in the candle, closing the door behind him, and uses it to light three others. Once illuminated, this is no longer a table and glass beneath a window. Now the rest of the laboratory materializes, like the moment when the actors without lines join the featured players onstage. Two low bookshelves, crammed with volumes, stand against one wall, under a detailed wall map of Europe; a cabinet rises across from the window. A tray on the table holds jagged pieces of dark, glittering rock. Under the table peek small shelves, holding row after row of tiny labeled metal canisters.

Thomas circles the table. He looks stronger now; I don't know if he draws it from being in his laboratory — a room he belongs in much more than the other — or from our embrace.

"Which colors we see is still the great mystery, and of all the colors that Newton identified, blue is the most mysterious," Thomas says. "I fell victim to it while I was still at Cambridge."

He is going to tell me. I will learn everything, now, at last, when I'm no longer attempting to steal the formula. I should stop him. But all of these weeks of striving and wondering have left me with a lingering ache. I want to know the secret.

"What is the mystery?" I ask.

"It's an essential one. We see blue everywhere in the natural world, in the sky and the sea and lakes, even the little bubbling streams, but what do we *really* see? It's ephemeral. A reflection of something else. The seeming abundance is a trick. It doesn't exist in a tangible form that we can adapt, make into pigment for you and all your fellow artists to use over the centuries. You said your favorite color was yellow, Genevieve. Yellow is so easy. Thousands of years ago, when human beings had discovered fire and lived in caves, man wanted to create art on his walls. So he did."

"Woman did too," I interrupt.

He laughs, appreciatively. "Yes, of course, women painted the cave walls too. But whether they were men or women, only certain colors could be used. Yellow ochre was right there on the surface of the cave floors. Red ochre, too, and brown. They got black from the charcoal in their fires. They used ground animal bones, and blood too."

I suppress a shudder.

"I've seen cave paintings in France, before the war, when English people were freely allowed into the country," he continues. "You're never the same after you see the paintings, and you realize that thousands of years ago, men and women had the same emotions as we do, they feared and loved."

He pauses, with a long, ardent look. I expect him to come to me. There is an exquisite silence, as the two of us waver on the point of abandoning all conversation.

Thomas gives a small shake of his head. He wants — he needs — to keep talking.

"There is a color you won't find in any of their cave paintings. Blue. No blue ochre. It's not in bone, or blood, or bark. There's only one way to obtain a type of mineral that anyone could turn into blue pigment: Beneath the caves. Deep into the earth. Where some say we are not meant to be. It took all of those hundreds of centuries for man to develop the tools to enable him to find blue."

There is an intensity to his voice, containing both regret and anger, though whether it is anger with others or with himself, I am unsure. I am sure of one thing: Thomas Sturbridge went deep into the earth, with his knowledge and tools, and was scarred by it, body and spirit.

I say, "I know that for many years the ultramarine pigment was only possible through digging for a certain stone in the caves in Afghanistan."

"Ultramarine, which means 'across the water,' " he says, frowning. Whatever happened to Thomas, it wasn't in Afghanistan. He continues. "There is one source of blue we know absolutely nothing about. The ancient Egyptians used a gorgeous blue pigment in their art. The Romans gave it the name caeruleum. We still have that blue; we can admire it at our leisure. At Cambridge they exhibit some breathtaking statues and murals. And no one knows how the Egyptians did it! The pigment isn't made with any mineral we know of, excavated from Africa or Afghanistan or China or Europe. The caeruleum formula wasn't written down, or at least not that anyone can find. It's lost. All the chemists who've analyzed it are baffled."

Just as Sir Gabriel says the chemists are now baffled by Thomas Sturbridge's blue.

"What about you?" I ask. "Were you the one who deciphered the Egyptian blue?

"No." He looks down, and I wonder if his desire to go on, to explain everything to me, is cooling. I won't press him, I refuse to play the spy now.

My hand drifts, as if of its own volition, toward the largest piece of glass in the laboratory. It is long and wide and, incredibly, it curves on an angle half way up, and then narrows. A tube attaches to its narrow mouth, and that tube connects to a small wooden barrel. I have no idea what function this all could serve. I see my reflection in it, my skin flushed, my thick hair loosened by Thomas' embrace. I touch the smooth glass with one finger.

"Tell me about this," I say.

In the glass I see Thomas moving toward me, to be next to me. His eyes burn in his lean, handsome face. I want to throw myself into his arms again, and it takes every bit of self-control to stop myself from doing so.

"Do you like it?" he asks.

I nod.

"The name for it is 'distilling apparatus'. This one is based on something invented in Persia by the early alchemists. They were respected, and feared too. There a chemist is a half-step up from an apothecary, steeping anise and cumin to cure a sore stomach."

He laughs, but without humor.

My attention turns to the shelf containing all the canisters, the

243

handwriting beautiful and precise. I wonder if the writing is Thomas'. "These look like spices," I say.

"Spices that could kill you, in terrible agony, if not handled correctly." To my inquiring glance, he explains, "They are my acids." His tone is fond, as if he were talking about his children.

I move decisively away from the acids and toward the bookshelf. There is one wooden object among the books and, when I draw closer, I see it's not only odd but also repulsive. It is a carved wooden figure, half-monster and half-child, grinning spitefully.

"Why do you keep that?" I ask.

"So that I will always remember him." Thomas pulls the carved figure from the shelf and places him on the table. The figure is all the more horrible now — his wooden face sneering — when squatting among the exquisite curved glass.

"Why would you want to remember him?" I ask.

"He is the reason I am here," Thomas says, patting the creature's capped head. "And now that I think about it, the reason why you are here. Many people."

"I don't understand."

"In England we call this fellow 'hobgoblin' or 'sprite.' In Germany he's the kobold, a vicious spirit who lives underground and tries to fool the miners by luring them to their death."

I remember how disturbed Ambrose Stanton was by the fact that I heard Thomas speak German. The reason must be that the source of Thomas' blue comes from that country. In the next second, I make a connection that fills me with confusion.

"For the basic blue and white porcelain, the sort they've been making in China all along, they use a blue glaze called smalt," I say. "I remember someone told me the smalt was extracted from a rock named after a

German devil. It's cobalt blue. But smalt is like blue glass, isn't it? It's not terribly special. That can't be what you're working with."

"You're well informed. The Chinese glaze, the smalt, comes from an impure form of cobalt." Thomas hesitates; I can see he's struggling over whether to say it.

And then he does.

"I've invented a pigment derived from a new, purer cobalt," he says.

My first reaction is not triumph that I've finally learned the origin of the blue but concern at the lasting damage done to Thomas. "How did discovering it hurt you?" I ask.

"I wasn't the one who discovered it," he says firmly. "A Swedish chemist named Georg Brandt, about twenty years ago, announced he'd found a new metal. You may not realize it, but that is a tremendous event in science. It would be the first new metal that man isolated since antiquity. That's what scholars had trouble believing. There've been seven classic metals for centuries…"

"Seven," I say, and a chill whispers along my spine.

He nods, meaningfully, as if to say, *Now you are beginning to understand.*

"The seven are gold, silver, copper, tin, mercury, lead and iron," he continues. "Then Georg Brandt comes forward with cobalt. He said that this dark blue substance, the one that in impure forms can be turned into glazes for porcelain, is a new metal and he has a way of extracting it. No one believed him, but when I read one of his papers, I thought my God, he could be right. My next thought was, What if I could develop a new, richer color blue from Brandt's pure cobalt? I'd be admitted to the Royal Society, write books, be invited to give lectures. I'd be famous."

He invests the word *famous* with a fury of self-loathing.

"What happened then?" I ask gently.

"I traveled to Germany in 1757, trying to find the best source of cobalt for pigment. It's not easy to mine and extract. I went there after war erupted with France. Yes, it was dangerous. I can't tell you how many times I had to skirt Frederick the Great's armies. If England wasn't his chief ally, I'd surely have been arrested and hanged as a suspicious foreigner. I had to keep explaining myself to the police.

"I made my way to the Ore Mountains in Saxony, on the border of Bohemia. That's where the best source of cobalt could be found, deep in the mines. It's strange, from a distance the mountains are so beautiful. But life is harsh, above and below. People who live on the mountains are completely snowbound throughout April, with cattle that freeze to death in their stables. The conditions in the mines? Unspeakable. They found the first silver ore in 1168 AD and now the tunnels run 500 feet! All to extract the silver that makes the Dukes of Saxony some of the richest rulers in Europe."

I say, "Saxony is home of the first European porcelain, in Meissen. It was a duke of Saxony who kept a chemist prisoner until he invented the formula."

He sighs. "Yes, he certainly was. That's where my mission changed. Porcelain is on everyone's mind in Saxony. I wanted to create a blue pigment for use by painters — artists like yourself. I met another English chemist who was more interested in its application to porcelain. He told me color was the next battleground, and we could make our name with something revolutionary for porcelain. It was hard for him to do it all alone, and I hadn't progressed far on my own, so we became partners; I shifted my view to porcelain." He swallows. "His name was Edmund."

"You were friends?"

"We were friends, yes, we shared an obsession with blue, which I've learned is an obsession difficult to survive. We worked for months with hardly any rest or food."

Thomas rubs his eyes, as if reliving that grueling exhaustion.

"I went down with the miners one day, while Edmund roasted a new cobalt sample. We were so sure of closing in on success. Edmund had a contact in England, a man named William Duesbury, who'd invested money in his trip with the understanding that he would have exclusive rights to any invention adapted for porcelain." Thomas clears his throat, painfully. I fear he will sicken again, but he does not. "Do you know why the Germans invented the kobold? Because over the centuries, the miners who were seeking silver suffered if they dug up the ore with the dark blue metal in it. They say that the kobold lives in the rock as we humans live in air. Sometimes it made the men sick and weak; other times they died quickly."

Thomas rubs his forehead. "That's what happened to Edmund. If you aren't careful when heating cobalt, it releases an arsenic gas. Just being around cobalt for a sustained period in a mine can make you sick from exposure to the arsenic. But heating it? That day there was an explosion. You can't imagine what happens to a human being when exposed to gas of that intensity. I see it in my nightmares."

I cover my mouth, horrified. "It killed Edmund?"

"Yes. He was dead, and pulling his body free exposed me to the gas."

Tears prick my eyes. "It poisoned you."

"Dr. Gleason believes the gas caused permanent lung damage similar to asthma. Sometimes I can go for a week with no breathing difficulties. But it always comes back. Last October I collapsed and they thought I would die. William sent me to a clinic for two months and it helped me."

"Oh, Thomas."

He says, "I know it's wrong to pursue your affections when I could be dead in a year. I told you that I am a selfish creature."

"A year?" I say, brokenly.

"It's possible. But it's also possible I could live to an old age. Doctors just do not have answers for me, beyond the fact that there's no cure." Thomas opens the doors to a cabinet. "And I did it all for this." He reaches into the cabinet, then stops, his head sinking. "I shouldn't have kept going in the Ore Mountains after Edmund died. I should have traveled to England, explained to his family, settled his affairs. He was my partner and he was a friend. But I had him buried in haste in Saxony and I wrote to William Duesbury offering my services in Edmund's place. He made all the arrangements to extract the cobalt we needed and to bring it to England. So all that happens to me, I deserve."

Thomas places on the table, a few inches from the candle, a figure of a boy carrying a basket.

The boy's coat and trousers are painted blue, Derby blue. I've tried to find evidence of this color for so long, imagined it, scoffed at it, feared it. Now it's before me. On a practical level, it's a bit darker than I expected: a rich and luxuriant blue, edging toward violet. But that is not what leaves me stunned. It has a life to it that makes every other blue flat and opaque. For the first time, I am seeing a representation of the color blue that tells the truth of the sky and the water: the depth of its dimensions. All that in the color of a boy's trousers.

I feel Thomas' arm circling my waist. "What do you think?" he asks.

There is pride in his voice, but something else too. I cannot give it a name. 'Resentment' is too strong. But there is a complicated feeling for his creation.

"It is as beautiful as they say," I say unsteadily. "You invented this in a German mine?"

"That was the first stage. Extract the pure cobalt, for it must be free of any trace of iron or nickel or the color won't be good. Then I mix it with another chemical, aluminium, in precise ratio. I add a bit of this and that, as well as linseed oil. I must fine-tune to stabilize the elements through firing…" He takes a breath. "And now, yes, we're almost, almost done. The last question that needs to be resolved is on the clay to be used. We may need a new source. Some last tests."

"Thomas, I can see why every precaution's been taken. This is such a precious secret."

"Every day I think about what Jean Hellot would do if he could see what I've done," he says. "You remember how I told you of my ugly thoughts? I fear sometimes I am driven on by my wish to see Hellot's tears when he beholds my blue. He will have to change the name of his prize, celestial blue, because how can it rule the heavens when my blue exists?"

Like someone who hears the first faint peal of a warning bell, I stiffen. With his arm still around my waist, Thomas can feel me tensing. He looks sideways at me, curiously.

I ask, "Who is Hellot?"

"The director of the Academy of Sciences in France and chief chemist of Sèvres Porcelain. Monsieur Jean Hellot. I am able to keep track of the direction he takes all the way from here. William purchases Sèvres' latest colors, painted on small pieces. Discreetly, of course. And he keeps his ears open. There is absolutely no possibility of Hellot being anywhere close to my achievement, even though he has a battalion of assistants and I have no one but myself."

"Hellot is also endeavoring to create a new blue?"

"That's the obsession of Sèvres! New colors. For more than ten years, Hellot has worked on perfecting shades, and far away the most important to him are his blues."

My breathing is coming faster now. "So Sèvres is your real competition."

"Definitely," says Thomas.

The implications of what he's telling me are so frightening that I try to argue them away. "The competitors for Derby Porcelain Works are English; they are Bow, Chelsea, and Worcester, and not Sèvres," I insist. "If anyone were to try to steal Derby blue, the thief would be sent by one of those English factories."

Thomas considers. "I know that's what William fears and I go along with these extreme precautions, but I've never quite believed it. Put it this way, I'd be surprised. From all that I've heard, the other English factories don't have trained chemists, and are stretched fairly thin on investment capital. While Sèvres possesses the scientific and artistic minds, the patronage of Madame de Pompadour, and, through her influence, the patronage of King Louis XV. They're the only ones who could move with swiftness if they wanted to supplant us in producing this shade of blue — *if* they could obtain the entire formula. It's very complex and must be followed precisely." He laughs. "That's why I never write it down. It's locked in my head."

He takes a closer look at me; I can only imagine my expression. "Genevieve, I didn't mean to frighten you. How could Sèvres be a threat to us? We're at war with France. I know that Major Tarkwell insulted you when you first came here, because you have a French name and he doesn't understand the relationship between the Huguenot refugees and France. But he's been corrected on that. Everyone understands that you'd rather die than help the French king."

It all falls into place. The wealth of Sir Gabriel. His sophisticated Continental tastes and familiarity with the countries. His absolute determination and willingness to use and discard Richard Frederick, me, anyone. He *must* be a spy for Sèvres. He serves France. These are his "invisible circumstances".

The enormity of what I've realized, the crime I am guilty of, washes over me, so powerfully that my knees are buckling.

"Genevieve, Genevieve, what's wrong?" says Thomas.

Gripping the table to keep from falling, I say, "Nothing. I'm just… It's a lot to hear tonight, to make sense of. Everything."

"I have frightened you off, I think," he says.

"No," I say, though I've gone cold.

"Mine is a strange world. I wouldn't blame you if you wanted no part of it, of me. What I did to Edmund, my partner, was unforgivable. Sometimes I think he was punished for seeking fame from the discovery of a new metal, beyond the original seven known to man."

"And your punishment?" I ask. "You believe it is your illness?"

His gaze darkening, Thomas says, "No. I feel certain that my real punishment is yet to come."

CHAPTER TWENTY-THREE

I bury the Huguenot Bible in the garden, in the middle of a cloudless night. It would be a sacrilegious act, were not the book already tainted by Sir Gabriel, who has made it into a vessel of espionage.

My first instinct is to hurl the book into the river, but the horrible fate of Richard Frederick proves that nothing stays at the bottom of the river forever. Burning the book in our fireplace would be difficult to conceal from Evelyn and the servants. Destroy it I must, though. I do not want Thomas or anyone else to ever know what I agreed to do for Sir Gabriel Courtenay.

Two nights after seeing Thomas on Nuns Street, I creep down the stairs of the dark, silent house, near the servants' quarters. I weave my way past their warren of rooms to the door leading to the edge of garden. Luck is with me. I am able to unlock the door and step outside, clutching the Bible.

It's cold, yes, but not cold enough to see my breath, and there is a fullness to the air promising spring. It might have to do with the full moon, hanging brilliant, albeit pockmarked and gruel-gray, in the sky.

I know where the gardeners' shed is, filled with tools, across the garden.

I find a hand spade inside the shed. Groping in the shed, I also find a rag for my knees. I place the rag on the cold, damp ground, and kneel before my digging spot. I raise the spade, and a mournful trill slices the air. I lower it, looking around. The sadness of the noise, which must be birdsong, unnerves me.

When Sir Gabriel handed me this doctored Bible in his carriage, I knew what I was doing was wrong, and I should have said no at that moment. Now I will try to make amends. The birds sing louder as I dig and dig, until my forehead is slick with sweat. My breathing is so heavy it drowns out the sounds of the birds. When the hole is deep enough, I place the bible at the bottom and push the soil in.

The Bible safely buried, I rise, my knees wobbly. A wind whispers through the garden, and I'm glad of it. I return the spade and rag, and hurry back across the garden. I know that the servants rise before dawn, and I must be back in the house before the scullery maids light the first fire. And I must find a way to clean up and slip into bed before Evelyn rises.

Halfway across the garden I hear something different, like the snap of a branch underfoot. Fear floods through me, and I clap my hand over my mouth to stop from screaming. By now, Sir Gabriel must have received my letter. What will the consequence be? It cannot be worse than what the law would do to me if I were exposed as a spy for a porcelain factory favored by King Louis.

No human form materializes. I must have heard the wind, or an animal. I force myself to be calm and continue into the house. After scrubbing off the dirt so vigorously my knuckles sting, I ease into bed next to the sleeping Evelyn.

One of the advantages of being courted by Thomas Sturbridge is that Evelyn and the Heaths expect me to be lost in thought. My fear and worry, and resulting fatigue from near-sleepless nights, are mistaken for the torments of a lovelorn woman. I hear that Thomas wants to see me again as soon as possible, and as much as I want that too, I need him to finish his last tests. Once Derby blue can be unveiled before the world and its creator established, we will all be safe. I send word to him that we can be together again in a fortnight.

During that time, I continue to work in the decorating room, traveling back and forth with Evelyn by carriage. I peer out the window as the horses clop-clop their way through town, looking for Jimmy, but there is no sign of him. I even find myself scanning the riverfront from the second-floor window, worried that he will materialize.

My work is my only refuge from ugly thoughts. Ambrose and Harry are too busy with their duties to wonder at my ferocious attention to watercolor. Harry receives no more summons for questioning by Constable Campion. It would be a relief if he abandoned his investigation, but even in my most desperate moments I can't believe that the constable is finished with us. With me.

My other refuge is the book Thomas gave me, written by Jean-Jacques Rousseau. These are ideas that speak to my soul — nature did *not* make men and women unequal. It is society that drives us from our rightful state. Nodding, I read:

"The extreme inequality of our ways of life, the excess of idleness among some and the excess of toil among others, the ease of stimulating and gratifying our appetites and our senses, the over-elaborate foods of the rich, which inflame and overwhelm them with indigestion, the bad food of the poor, which they often go without altogether, so that they over-eat greedily when they have the opportunity; those late nights, excesses of all kinds, immoderate transports of every passion, fatigue, exhaustion of mind, the innumerable sorrows and anxieties that people in all classes suffer, and by which the human soul is constantly tormented: these are the fatal proofs that most of our ills are of our own making."

A week after my evening on Nuns Street, a discovery in the decorating room brings my thoughts on nature into my art. As I take my stool, I see on the wooden table, precisely where I place my paints, a light-brown-and-violet object about two inches in length.

Harry says, "It's a butterfly, Mistress Genevieve."

"No, I don't think so."

"It's a moth," says Ambrose, frowning. "How did such a large one get in here?"

Harry pokes it with his brush, drawing the ire of Ambrose Stanton for dirtying an expensive art tool. "I wanted to make sure it was dead," the apprentice explains.

"If it weren't dead, don't you think it would fly off?" I say. "I just can't fathom why it chose to die here."

Harry grins. "Perhaps it likes you."

Ambrose calls for an end to our moth debate, and also offers to clear the insect from my table. But I insist that I am capable of doing so myself. As the two of them dive into their work, I arrange my paints as a sight barrier between me and Ambrose and Harry.

I don't intend to dispose of the moth. I intend to paint it.

The moth doesn't have the vibrant colors of the butterfly, but it has something subtler to it, something interesting. This is nature, possessing as much beauty as the butterfly. It takes me a few hours to mix the watercolors I need and to master the outline. By the time it comes for us to eat our luncheon, I'm ready to show my work to Ambrose.

"An *insect*?" he says, incredulous. "Do you honestly think that any of the refined customers Mr. Duesbury cultivates would be proud to eat from a plate displaying an insect?"

"Don't dismiss this," I urge. "I think that there is something very expected about a flower, a butterfly, a piece of shiny fruit. I know that we must seek originality in sweeping, bold ways, but to show subtlety, to uncover the beauty in the unexpected, that could impress too."

After a moment, Ambrose Stanton says he will show my moth rendering to Mr. Duesbury, but warns me not to expect him to back it.

Drawing the moth works some sort of alchemy within me, for that evening I end my period of withdrawal from conversation. The Heaths are joined by a friend from London, a portly fellow banker named Mr. Lawson, and the dinner conversation turns to war.

"The tide may very well be turning against France," says Mr. Lawson. "Their harvest last year was catastrophic. It was poor here; there, catastrophic. The French peasants are starving. The war in Canada isn't going as well for the Marquis de Montcalm, because the king can't pay for enough reinforcements, supplies. I heard at the club that Louis may be growing desperate, shaking the cage of Bonnie Prince Charlie."

I shift unhappily in my chair as Mr. Heath sets down his wine to boom, "Nothing bonnie about him now, the man's a drunk old fool! If Louis thinks he can send the Stuart Pretender over to England again and expect any popular support, he must be mad. Louis is spending too much time with Madame de Pompadour, not enough with his ministers."

"They do call him Louis the Beloved," snickers Mr. Lawson.

I cannot stop myself. "The king of France is a depraved monster," I say. "His own people suffer from the vilest despotism, from the king's oppression and unpayable taxes… yet how does he live? Enjoying his luxury." Mr. Heath's eyes bulge, but I keep going. "Should the French triumph in this war, it would not only be a tragedy for England but for the world. We must stop them. I would gladly do so. Hand me a pistol, a sword, a rock. I am ready."

"My God, well said!" shouts the Heaths' guest. "You should speak at our club. Damn shame no females allowed."

The Heaths' footman approaches the master of the house with a letter. Mr. Heath groans. "Not more bad news. Outrageous, that they'd bring it to the house at this hour."

The footman murmurs, "I was told it's from London and of an urgent nature, for Mistress Genevieve Planché. The messenger who brought it waits outside."

All heads turn to me as I feel the blood drain from my face. Would Sir Gabriel send one of his letters with this sort of boldness, hand delivered by a messenger?

The footman comes around the table. My stomach turning over, I take the letter. My name is not in the writing of my "grandfather," and I don't recognize the seal.

I open the letter. Right away my eyes travel to the bottom. The name is Robert Drummond, my grandfather's friend, who chastised me at Hogarth's party.

"My dear Genevieve,

You must prepare yourself for bad news. Your grandfather is gravely ill. Pierre collapsed and he cannot speak or move any part of the right side of his body. The doctor believes it possible there is not much more time remaining to him. Your grandfather's other friends and I have dispatched a messenger to you, a man of my household by the name of Joshua, and we've made arrangements for a flying coach to bring you to Spitalfields after you receive this letter. We shall pray for our friend's health and for you to arrive in London swiftly. It is in the hands of God."

I jump from my chair, sending it crashing, and cry, "No, no, no! Not Grandfather."

*

The next hours are a blur. Evelyn and Mrs. Heath help me from the dining chamber. I meet the messenger from Drummonds' household, a mild-faced, watery-eyed man in his thirties named Joshua who tells me he has already secured the flying coach and will ride atop it back from London the next day. We will leave as early as possible from King Street.

"Mr. Drummond commissioned me to do everything I can to bring you to London quickly and safely, and I shall do just that," Joshua says, wringing his hands. Knowing Drummond's waspish nature, I cannot be surprised his servant is so nervous.

Evelyn, quietly efficient, packs for me. I cannot do anything but repeat anguished prayers for Grandfather, huddled on the bed. I knew his health wasn't good. I received a letter from him last month, a real letter, about not venturing out of the house of late. I should have done more then. It is painful, deeply painful, to think of him suffering, half-paralyzed. I must be at his side, I need to tell him how much I love him.

"Where is your Bible, Genevieve?"

Through the fog of my grief and worry, I hear the sentence. She repeats the question when I do not answer.

"Please, Evelyn," I beg. "Don't bother with it now. If you are my friend, you will do this for me."

She studies me, perplexed, before saying, "As you wish. I have packed the book you have by Jean-Jacques Rousseau."

"Thank you."

For me, the night is near-sleepless, an obstruction to my departure. I rise to dress myself in the first rays of dawn. Evelyn is up soon after. We go down together, to take the Heaths' carriage to Queen Street. That is where my flying carriage awaits.

"I don't know when we will see each other next," Evelyn says. "But that is nothing for you to distress yourself over, whether your position is secure here in Derby. My mother spoke to Mr. Heath and whenever you wish to return, you will have a job as decorator. Duesbury won't replace you."

I thank her, though my position at the porcelain works doesn't seem important right now.

There is only one man I can think of besides my grandfather. "What should I tell Thomas?"

"I sent him a note last night, informing him," she says. "I'm sure that you two will be able to write each other once… once matters are settled."

I wish I could tell him myself. Selfishly, I long for comfort from Thomas.

Evelyn and her mother take me to Queen Street and the flying carriage. As promised, Joshua sits atop, next to the driver, and he tips his hat to me, with nervous respect. The cab of the carriage, freshly painted black, is small, with four horses pulling only me inside. This is the secret to its speed, as well as the frequent changing of horses. We are set to reach London in two days if there is no rain to muck up the roads. As of now, the road south is dry, I'm told. I only pray that it will get me to Fournier Street in time.

The men strap my trunk on top and, after embracing Evelyn, I step inside the carriage.

We start up the street, but come to a halt a moment later. I hear men's cries.

I push open the carriage door to see Thomas shouting at William Duesbury, who tries to restrain him with a hand on his arm. Behind them is Major Tarkwell, his face like thunder.

"Thomas!"

He wrenches himself free from Duesbury and rushes to me. "Genevieve, are you all right? I only heard about your grandfather's illness this morning."

His face contorts with rage as he grips the carriage door. "They tried to withhold Evelyn's note from me, they didn't want my work interfered with."

I leap out of the carriage. "Thank you," I say. "Thank you."

He holds me tight and says, "This must be terrible for you, sweetheart. I should come with you."

"No, you can't. You can't. It means so very much to me that you are here now, that I can say goodbye. You must finish the work."

"Tom, please," pleads Duesbury. "Enough. Do you realize you are in the middle of the street?"

Thomas says, "Nothing and no one can keep me away from you, Genevieve."

"I know."

His depth of caring buoys me. I feel less starkly alone.

Thomas bids me a proper goodbye, our promises to write exchanged, and I step back into the carriage. A moment later I start moving once more. I am on the bridge, over the river, and Derby slips behind me.

*

The carriage is aptly named, for it does feel as if we are flying south on the road to London. We stop only to change horses and to gulp down food and drink. Then the journey rapidly resumes. Looking out the window, I see farmers plowing fields and boys herding sheep. The tree branches are speckled green with buds. I even spot the first pink and yellow wildflowers sprouting beside the road.

I am more than willing to remain in the carriage and ride through the night if it gets me to London more quickly, but Joshua tells me it's impossible. Yes, we can keep changing horses, but we can't change the driver. He needs rest. Moreover, the roads are too dangerous at night. We'd be begging to be robbed.

We stop at a coaching inn that first night, and Joshua and I eat an unremarkable meal. I nod while he drones on about the importance of his pleasing the exacting Mr. Drummond. Joshua is quite the dedicated servant. I barely listen, my thoughts filled with Grandfather... and Thomas. *Nothing and no one can keep me away from you.*

By the afternoon of the second day, I'm relieved to see the farm fields recede as we get nearer to London. The last time we changed horses, Joshua said we should reach Spitalfields well before midnight. I'm grateful to Mr. Drummond for making all of these arrangements, for finding Joshua and paying for the flying carriage, although I recoil at the thought of the cost. I will attempt to offer repayment, but I anticipate he'll refuse. Mr. Drummond is a good friend to Grandfather, and to send Joshua is an enormous gesture. I truly regret my rudeness at Hogarth's party.

"I'm coming to you, Grandfather," I say aloud within the carriage cab.

After another hour or so, the horses slow. I can feel the driver pulling hard on the reins. It must be time for another change of the animals. Or perhaps the horses need water. It's been a hard ride.

The carriage comes to a complete halt. I look outside, and to my surprise, we've come to some sort of town or city, pulled off onto a narrow street. I see an old brick wall covered with dying yellowish vines just six feet away. Why stop north of London now?

The door opens, and Jimmy, Sir Gabriel's man, pushes his way in.

"Don't say a word, just listen," he growls.

My shock turns to fear. I scramble for the door on the other side, but before I can turn the handle to escape, he grabs me by the arm, with much more force than he used outside the almshouse, and yanks me back.

"Calm yourself and listen to me," he repeats.

"Let go," I scream, pulling away from him. "Joshua, help, help!"

Jimmy raises his hand. He's holding something, but moving too fast for me to tell what it is. His hand swings up to my skull, and there's spreading blackness.

Nothing. Velvet silence. And then strange flickering images, too incoherent to be called dreams. Until I begin to fly. I'm out of the carriage, I'm not flying to London in a conveyance with wheels. I am flying. I soar over rooftops, church steeples, rivers.

I look over my shoulder, and I'm frightened, for a monstrous moth chases me, and I soar higher, all the way to the stars, terrified, trying to find a hiding place from it, but I can't, for there isn't one.

The dream disintegrates and I gradually become aware that I'm lying in a bed. It's softer than the wide bed I share with Evelyn in Derby. I can feel a light blanket atop me, followed by the realization I'm wearing a nightgown. When I move under the blanket, I realize the nightgown is made of silk, caressing my skin.

I open my eyes to a ceiling, ivory white and carved. Candlelight fills the room. But which room? When I look to one side, there's the brightness of the candlelight; on the other side is a wall.

I try to sit up, and my head throbs. That's when it comes back to me in a rush: Jimmy broke into the carriage and attacked me. He must have followed Thomas to town, see me get in the carriage, and follow it from Derby.

What happened to Joshua and the driver? Where am I now?

With a concentrated effort, I roll onto my side, and push up on an elbow. After a wave of dizziness, my vision clears. There is a small window high on the wall, and I see darkness outside. I've no sense of how long I've been here.

I realize there's someone sitting in the room with me. How unpleasant to know that a person observes me closely, in silence, while I lie in bed wearing next to nothing. I can't tell who it is, for he sits just far enough out of the circle of candlelight that I can't see his face.

"Who's here?" I ask.

Silence. The man leans forward, into the light. A pale handsome face with black eyes, and straight, dark hair hanging loose to his shoulders.

"So, Genevieve," says Sir Gabriel Courtenay, "I understand you're in love."

CHAPTER TWENTY-FOUR

I've feared and dreaded any encounter with Sir Gabriel for weeks, but at this moment what I feel most is anger.

"How dare you abduct me." I push myself to sit up, holding the sheet to cover myself as I do, for this silk nightgown barely hangs from my shoulders.

"No one abducted you," he says calmly.

"You're saying that Jimmy didn't follow my carriage, hit me on the head? I was there. What did he do to the driver and to Joshua? Sir Gabriel, I know you must be... displeased with me."

Sir Gabriel's eyebrows arch and his lips tremble with laughter, as if what I've said is so outrageous it cannot be believed. I see what a source of anxiety I have proven to be. But I can't worry about that now.

I struggle to sit even straighter. "I must get to my grandfather's house as soon as possible. He's gravely ill." I look around the room. "Where are my clothes? I need to dress and go to Spitalfields. You cannot refuse me."

He holds up a hand, telling me to stop. Then all his fingers drop but one.

"First, Jimmy did not follow your carriage," he says coolly. "He withdrew from Derby two weeks ago, after the security measures around

Sturbridge became impenetrable and you stopped communicating with me. The carriage stopped at the pre-arranged place north of London, where Jimmy was to meet you and, ideally, persuade you to come the rest of the way quietly. According to him, it was very apparent that you wouldn't, so he took measures."

He raised a second finger. "Jimmy never removed you from the flying carriage. Its planned route was always from Derby to here, to my house."

I am deeply confused. "But that was not Mr. Drummond's plan. How did you subvert it? Did you hurt Joshua — did you bribe the driver?"

A third finger goes up. "Robert Drummond has nothing to do with any of this. Though I am pleased that the letter was believable. It means I haven't lost my touch."

At first I'm so shocked, it's like a fist to the stomach. The surprise gives way to a new, blistering rage.

"This was entirely you, a ruse from the start?" I shout. "You put me through the horror of thinking my grandfather was dying with this lie — how terrible."

I jump out of the bed, the sheet falling onto the floor, and I leap toward him, to hurt him, scratch him, anything. But a rush of nausea and head pain stop me. I crumple, and would have collapsed onto the floor if Sir Gabriel didn't catch me in his arms. "You're a bloody stinking devil," I say, the language of the East End curling my tongue as I try to push him away. My weakened hands push against his arms, muscular underneath his waistcoat, to no effect.

"Oh, I don't think that's ever been in question," he says and carries me to the bed, lowering me. He stands over me for a moment, looking down, and I can feel that my nightgown has slipped off one shoulder. My hair, unbound, spills everywhere. I know that someone must have undressed me while I was unconscious, and I greatly fear it was him.

I want to cover myself now, but I can't.

He's never looked at me this way before; not Sir Gabriel, with his perfect manners and tight control.

"I think we could both do with a drink," he says, and steps back from the bed as if forcing himself to take the steps. It requires great effort, no question. He pulls a rope that is hanging from the ceiling.

A moment later Joshua sticks his head around the door. "Sir?"

"Two glasses of… sherry."

"Very good, Sir," he says, his gaze flicking to me but there's no evidence of any remorse for tricking me. His mild, nervous manner has disappeared, leaving the watery eyes, now shifty.

"Crikey," I say to the ceiling.

"Just as Jimmy was a boxer before entering my service, Joshua was an actor," says Sir Gabriel. "And a good one."

Joshua bows, grinning, and leaves.

"Genevieve, I think when you're calmer, you'll realize I didn't have much of a choice. You stopped writing to me. I can't go to Derby, I always told you that. Even if I did, how could we possibly meet? No, I had to bring you here. How else could I do so without raising suspicion? It had to be something of an emergency to justify an extraction. The knock to your head? Jimmy was forced to administer it because your screams would have raised a hue and cry."

He makes it all sound so reasonable.

"Our dealings with each other are at an end, Sir. I'm not your spy any longer."

Sir Gabriel says, quietly, "Resignation is not possible, Genevieve."

I try my best to fight down the fear that surges. I must show him no weakness.

"Why did you stop writing to me?" he asks.

He's not wasting any time with the interrogation. "Could you pick up the blanket and give it to me?" I ask.

He does so and I wrap it around my shoulders. Now I have a thin veil of dignity.

"How long have I been here?" I ask.

"About an hour."

"I am presently on Grosvenor Square?"

"Yes, Genevieve. I said the carriage brought you to my house. And now I would like my answer."

"There was nothing new to tell you," I say with a shrug. "Writing with sympathetic ink was difficult for me. I live in the Heaths' home, I share a room with Evelyn Devlin, Mr. Heath's stepdaughter."

" 'Nothing new,' " he repeats. He studies me for a minute. "You were with Thomas Sturbridge four times, first in the Dolphin tavern, second in an almshouse on a charitable visit, third, at the Heaths' house, and fourth, for hours, in his home on Nuns Street, the home that contains his laboratory. And there is not a single thing to report?"

How did Jimmy know of my visit to Nuns Street, when Thomas' house was so heavily guarded and the street patrolled? I try to conceal my dismay.

Joshua returns with our sherry. I want to throw mine in Sir Gabriel's face but I sip it, playing for time. Sir Gabriel drinks half of his, sets his glass down carefully and leans forward again, his black eyes boring into me.

"Just to be clear, you are claiming you learned nothing at all, Genevieve, about Sturbridge's formula for blue?"

"The content of his work is a matter of utter secrecy, even from me. I didn't go inside the laboratory. That was always understood. William Duesbury and Major Tarkwell made me promise."

He waves his hand, as if dismissing a matter of miniscule importance. "Do you know how close Sturbridge is to perfecting the formula and Derby beginning production?" he asks. I can feel his desperation. Sir Gabriel always was clear with me he needed results before spring, and spring is now imminent.

"No. He was cautious in what he said."

"A couple in love talk about everything, Genevieve. How else can they truly know one another?" His voice edges into sarcasm and something else too.

"Why do you say we are in love?" I counter. "We hardly know each other. A few meetings."

"Sturbridge tackles the carriage as you're departing Derby and makes an exhibition of himself on the busiest street in town, as his keepers work to pull him away from you. That's not love?"

Now we are truly on a chessboard. Move and countermove. But he's the king and I'm no greater than a pawn. Sir Gabriel knows so much about me and Thomas.

He says, "You are an ambitious woman, craving recognition and success, and you cease working for me while knowing all too well that my money is the only way out of England, to fame and fortune in Venice? That is love, too."

Frustration burns. How can I outwit him? I open my mouth to deny it and am bereft of words. The sherry I sipped is incredibly potent too, and I'm having difficulty focusing.

The hardness of Sir Gabriel's face softens. "I should have prepared you for this," he says. "It is my fault. I take responsibility."

"What do you mean?"

"It is a risk a spy runs when tracking someone so intently, someone of the opposite sex. The obsession becomes a... a kind of love. It's impossible to prevent it. And when your quarry is physically attractive and has qualities that would, under other circumstances, appeal? The romance fuses with the pursuit." He holds up Thomas' book, by Rousseau, with evident distaste. "If I'd known that Sturbridge possesses the same sorts of deluded beliefs as Denis Arsenault, I'd have seen the danger ahead and prepared you more carefully. I assumed he was a typical unattractive chemist, toting his minerals. But he's a rebel, isn't he? You have a fatal weakness for rebels."

During his dispassionate analysis, I feel embarrassed and then infuriated.

"That is not true."

"Of course it is," he says. "Or else you would not be so upset now. I should have foreseen that he would fall in love with you if he met you. That was particularly foolish of me."

I manage to say, "Perhaps I developed a certain regard for Thomas Sturbridge and he for me, but that doesn't mean he'd violate all of the rules of the porcelain works to tell me how he makes Derby blue."

" 'Derby blue,' " Sir Gabriel repeats it, caressing the phrase. "He's named it. He's named it, and you know how it's made, you know all about it."

"No," I insist. "No."

Sir Gabriel stands up, with decisiveness. "You are exhausted and require rest, and I have other obligations, ones I must dress for tonight. We will meet tomorrow, talk it all out, and then we'll form a plan for reinserting you at Derby Porcelain, if necessary."

"I am not staying here in the meantime." Pulling the blanket tight around my shoulders, I say, with as much force as I can summon, "I demand that you release me from this room. You have no legal or moral right to imprison me."

He raps twice on the door.

"Sir Gabriel?"

He turns to look at me, his black hair gleaming in the candlelight.

"You can go to the devil."

Sir Gabriel smiles and strides out the door.

After he goes, I collapse back onto the bed, choking on tears of frustration and rage.

My weeping exhausts itself swiftly. He is right about one thing. I'm dazed with weariness after scant sleep for two nights, followed by a knock to the head and a sip of sherry. I can't help but fall asleep. For how long, I do not know. But it seems like a very long time.

I wake up, ravenous, and not long after there's a knock on the door.

A woman enters, dressed in black, her face a watchful sliver of pallor. She carries a tray of food.

"May I know your name?" I ask.

She doesn't answer but sets down the tray and leaves. It is petit déjuener just as Daphne prepared on Fournier Street: petit pain and a tall cup of chocolat.

A bit later the same black-clad woman returns with my clothes from yesterday and gestures for me to take off my nightgown to be dressed. The last thing I want is to be naked in front of one of Sir Gabriel's servants. However, I may be able to extract some information from her the longer we are together, perhaps even solicit help.

I pull off the nightgown, my cheeks burning. She crosses the room, blank-faced, and helps me into my patched white shift and then my petticoat, calico dress and stockings. She takes my hair in one hand and a brush in the other and works it through my tangled tresses. She pulls on my hair so hard, I can feel it through to the roots in my scalp. I endure the pain without complaint. It's important not to show weakness.

"I do think that if you are to tend to me, I should know your name," I say, attempting a friendly tone.

Silently, she keeps working through my hair, section by section, until she's finished.

"What is the time, can you tell me that?" I ask.

She tosses the nightgown over one arm, picks up the tray and makes for the door.

"Ma'am, are you mute?" I ask, losing my temper.

She raps twice on the door. It's opened by someone I can't see, and she edges out. Halfway through, she says, over her shoulder, "No."

So much for soliciting assistance from the servants.

Still, the rest and the food and the return of my clothes bestow a great benefit. My mind works again.

There are various scenarios on offer for me. I can continue to deny knowing anything about the formula. Sir Gabriel will no doubt increase the pressure, and there is an ugly possibility of physical force should his mental manipulation be ineffective. Afterward, knowing me to be uncooperative and untrustworthy, I am not at all sure I will be able to return to Derby — or Grandfather's house in Spitalfields or anywhere else. I know about Richard Frederick's fate. Despite Sir Gabriel's smiles and solicitude, even his looking at me in that unsettling fashion last night, I fear for my life.

It would be a risky course of action for him, though, and that is what I draw strength from. There are people in Derby who'll begin to miss me, when no letters from London appear. Once Thomas Sturbridge or Evelyn Devlin find out my grandfather is not, after all, dying, it will become a matter for the constable. Does Sir Gabriel, a careful man, wish to chance this? Has he covered his tracks? After all, we know each other, my grandfather can attest to it. No one might be able to link him to Richard Frederick, perhaps. But a link exists to me.

What I want is for Sir Gabriel to send me back to Derby in a week, as he suggested. I must regain my freedom. He could do so, it would be prudent for him to do so, but only if he feels full confidence in my loyalty.

How on earth am I to assure him of my loyalty, when I've obviously lied to him, I've cursed him, and I've even tried to attack him?

I pace the floor. There's only one way out. I must tell him about Derby blue, it's the only thing I have to redeem myself with. I don't know the full formula — it doesn't exist outside of Thomas' brain — but disclosing some information should help me turn the tables. The next time I speak with Sir Gabriel, I can't be a scared, angry, peevish girl. I must be like he is. I will use every trick he's taught me, every scrap of advice. Primarily, I will mix truth with lies. Many truths. There's one lie I need to tell that *must* be believed, for everything depends on it. He mustn't know how much I care for Thomas.

A knock on the door. It's the same woman, her arms full of new garments and underclothes, with shoes dangling from one hand, a stringed box from the other. Presumably I am to change from my shabby traveling clothes into all of this. She stares at me, her wary face a question. Perhaps she was warned of my violent, unreasonable character by Sir Gabriel.

"Very well," I say. I pray that if I don this wardrobe, I will be allowed out of the room.

Relief enlivens her dead black eyes. She puts everything down on the bed and leaves, returning with a bowl of water and a cloth. This is most difficult for me. I've not been bathed by anyone else since I was a child. But evidently Sir Gabriel intends to treat me as if I were a pampered lady.

Off go the clothes she dressed me in just hours ago. She dampens a cloth and scrubs my flesh. I realize the water is scented, and the chosen fragrance is jasmine. I'm repulsed. Why does he want me to smell like him? Yet I stand there and allow her to scrub me with his scent.

It's all part of his game, an elaborate one. I've always sensed something twisted in Sir Gabriel.

The funereal maid dries me and dresses me, like a doll. First a silk chemise, followed by petticoats and a corset she laces with pitiless hands. I already have a small waist; she's carving it to nothing. I can barely draw a deep breath in this contraption of bone and cloth and string. Next comes something new: hoops. She ties around my waist a contraption meant to add volume ballooning from my waist. I'm to be like a ship with enormous sails. Over this, another petticoat and finally the gown itself, which has a low cut bodice and is, inevitably, made of silk dyed light blue.

Gazing down at these billowing blue skirts, I recognize the silk weaver shop that the material came from. It's on Fleur de Lis Street. When did Sir Gabriel purchase it? It fits me well. She offers me the shoes, which are also my exact size. The shoes have wooden heels; the color is blue, with tiny sapphires sewn into the material, like stars.

Next comes elaborate hair arranging, with a brush and pins and rose oil. She doesn't hurt me this time, but it requires an eternity. How can other women bear this? I feel achingly restless.

What, I wonder, is Thomas doing and thinking right now? He's probably picturing me at the bedside of a dying man. Although I had nothing to do with this deception, I'm ashamed that Thomas worries for me while I'm poured into a tight gown and scented and brushed. Thomas *should* worry — but not for the reason he thinks.

The last step: cosmetics. I feared she would apply the white powder and circles of crimson rouge I see ruining many women's faces. But there's no powder, just a smidgen of rouge along each cheekbone. She proceeds to pluck my eyebrows, which I've never had done and find more torturous than any of her other procedures. Final touch: she rubs some sort of pink liniment into my lips with her tough, ridged index finger. It tastes of sour wax.

The maid beckons for me to follow her. She raps twice on the door and Joshua opens it. I treat him to a murderous glare as I step out of the room.

With the maid walking right in front of me and Joshua so close behind I can feel his hot breath on the back of my neck, I make my way down a long, wide passageway, closed doors on both sides. The only sound is the clicking of my heels on the wood floor.

The passageway leads to a staircase, its oak banisters polished to a sheen. A portrait of a diamond-laden lady stares down at me, a Stuart baroness, perhaps, with her ample breasts and mercenary gaze.

The stairs lead two flights to the hall of Sir Gabriel's house, and the man himself stands before his wall of carefully mounted short swords. His black hair is nowhere to be seen; he's wigged and powdered and outfitted to his usual standard of perfection. He does not wear blue himself — no, that would be too crude, somehow. His waistcoat and breeches are a pale, shimmering gray, with a waistcoat embroidered in threads of dusky rose, green, and gold.

His eyes travel from my shoes to the top of my head as I come down the stairs and his lips curve. I do not smile back; nor do I glare. I will not allow him to intimidate me.

Taking my time, I reach the bottom of the stairs. A small window next to the door to the street reveals it's still daylight, though late in the day.

Something seems called for and I dip a deep, and insolent, curtsey.

"You look beautiful, Genevieve," he says. "Shall we eat?"

CHAPTER TWENTY-FIVE

We don't dine on porcelain plates in Sir Gabriel's home, and that is fitting. Porcelain is sacred to him, not something to touch gravy or gruel. In his dining chamber, a long room, I do spot one object of interest on a side cabinet: a handled vase sporting two cherubs, little demi-gods, sitting on a voluminous cloud, their dimpled knees swinging in the sky. The airy, delicate beauty of the drawing makes me think it was created in Sèvres — that and its deep turquoise color. Perhaps the shade is one of the latest creations of Jean Hellot, master chemist of France.

I say nothing about the vase to Sir Gabriel. He leads the conversation, telling me what everyone at the Royal Society of Arts is discussing these days: the prolific talents of Joshua Reynolds. I remember how the night I first laid eyes on Sir Gabriel, he was standing inches from the artist. He continues to follow Reynolds' career closely.

"He is able to paint anyone, absolutely anyone, in an hour," says Sir Gabriel. "The question is, can he be *good* at that speed? I have to say, based on the work I saw last week, the answer is yes. I can't stop thinking of his portrait of Georgiana, Countess Spencer, and her little daughter."

"What are the features of interest?" I ask.

Sir Gabriel tells me it is the artist's ability to capture the subtle attraction of the countess: graceful, assured, a trifle plain, wearing a black ribbon around her throat, as she embraces her daughter, also named Georgiana. The daughter stands on a platform of carved wood, the mother embraces her below the waist, with a dog on the other side.

"It's Reynolds' use of light and shadow, of nature and a room mingling, that is most impressive," says Sir Gabriel, thoughtfully. "The mother and child are in front of a deep red curtain, but it opens onto a field, a dark one, as if a storm were coming."

"A storm breaking over the woman?" I ask. I don't want to hang on his every word, but it's impossible to be blasé when he brings up art. I'm hungry for the latest news. The last time I discussed art, I defended the merits of a watercolor moth.

More silent servants appear to serve us dinner. A bottle of champagne is slipped into an ice bucket. I wonder about the expense of his life. His staff: cooks, maids, lackeys, even an assassin. Sèvres does pay well.

The first course is mussels in sauce blanche and a soup I've never tasted before. It's thick and white but there's no cream I can taste. It's a bouillon made of capon and mushrooms with the strong flavor of almonds. Both dishes are extraordinarily delicious.

"Genevieve, I do hope you enjoy the potage à la reine," he says with his usual exquisite courtesy.

"Queen's soup? I see. Ah. Yes, it's quite good." I pause to reflect on the flavors. "The touch of lemon balances the almonds."

Sir Gabriel laughs.

"Why are you laughing?" I say coldly.

"You are so French, Genevieve. You think like a Frenchwoman. You act like one. Until recently you did not dress like one. I've remedied that."

"Am I supposed to thank you?" I ask, setting down my spoon. "For the clothes or for your comment, which gives me little pleasure, given my family history. I am what I am, but I harbor no sympathy for the kingdom as it is, or its king." I pause and then take the plunge. "You know that quite well — you wormed it out of me at my grandfather's — and I suppose that's why you never chose to tell me I'd be stealing Derby blue for Sèvres."

I watch him closely for reaction and am rewarded with a quick flash of surprise.

"And what brings you to that conclusion?" he asks.

"No English porcelain factory could afford to pay its spy this well," I say, gesturing at the food, the cherub vase on the cabinet, the champagne chilling in a silver bucket.

"I do not serve one master, Genevieve. I've always told you that. What else feeds this suspicion of yours?"

I say evenly, "Thomas knows that Monsieur Hellot of Sèvres is his chief competitor."

A gratified smile spreads across Sir Gabriel's face. "Very well. Yes. I work for Sèvres. And am proud to do so, as it is the preeminent porcelain manufactory in all of Europe. Monsieur Hellot created a porcelain dinner set of celestial blue — more than 100 individual pieces! To see it is to weep. You would be proud, too, if you were not so hampered by your prejudices."

"Prejudices? You call my religious faith *prejudices*?

He does not answer but studies me. "I do realize now that these conflicts within you were sufficient for your breaking off from your assignment. Am I, though, to assume you intend to cooperate with me again?"

I nod.

"And you do not believe yourself to be in love with Thomas Sturbridge?"

Looking straight at him, I tell the lie. "No, I do not."

"You have no idea how much that pleases me. I feared you lost your head to this chemist but at the same time I know you to be an intelligent woman, a practical woman."

"I've not 'lost my head', as you put it, but I do admire Thomas Sturbridge and yes, I would have to say he is obviously fond of me. But that is a recent development. I decided to cease spying for you because of the conflicts caused by your dishonesty, Sir Gabriel."

He blinks, twice. "About Sèvres?"

"We could be arrested for what we're doing, not just for thievery but for treachery. Don't you think I deserved to know I worked for the factory favored by the king now making war with England?"

"Oh, Genevieve, all the wealthiest English families buy from Sèvres. The government knows it. Do you think William Pitt cares? He has far larger concerns. If you and I were caught, perhaps a fine. That's all."

"If I were caught, let me assure you that the owners at Derby would not shrug it off with a fine. Myself, my grandfather, and my cousin would face terrible censure."

Instead of calling for the servant to fill his glass, Sir Gabriel pours himself more champagne. I shake my head no when he half-rises with the bottle; my head must be clear.

"I would always do everything in my power to help you," he says.

"From Grosvenor Square? You sent Jimmy, who I can't believe would ever lift a finger to help me, to Derby. All he did was push a man with one leg in front of a coach."

Sir Gabriel grimaces. "Major Tarkwell, yes. The scum who tells people he is the hero of Culloden."

" 'Tells people?' Wasn't he there?"

"Oh, he was there. But he didn't lose his leg on the field, that came the year after. He was at the forefront of those who marched under the king's son the Duke of Cumberland, the 'Butcher'. What happened after the battle is a stain on civilized history. Cumberland pursued the defeated army of Bonnie Prince Charlie, you must be aware. I'm sure the children are taught that in schools. But that's not what really happened. It was far more horrific than the English public was ever told. Tarkwell committed atrocities, Genevieve, acts that are expressly forbidden by the code of war. He stabbed wounded men to death, defeated officers and common soldiers. As they pleaded to surrender, he bayoneted them. He found a hut of wounded Highlanders and helped to set fire to it, with its door jammed."

"My God," I whisper.

"Yes. It's documented. And do you think the cruelties were confined to soldiers?" Sir Gabriel demands of me, growing heated. "Tarkwell marched through the Highlands with others of his ilk, and he became a torturer of the Scots for months on end. I cannot tell you, for you could not bear to learn the details, what he did to the old people, the women and the small children, except that death, when it came, was a blessing."

There's no response possible. I am filled with horror, and despair, over the savagery of men.

"Do you see now that it's not so simple, not so black and white, to say who is in the right?" Sir Gabriel demands. "Why do you think Tarkwell's not been given a commission? There's another war on. But for a few infamous officers of Culloden, their actions were too disgusting. Cumberland is under a cloud, and so are they. And this is who William Duesbury hires to provide security at a porcelain factory? You can see why I felt decisive action was warranted. I wanted to protect you from this monster." His lips tighten. "I had no notion it would make you turn against me."

This is not going as I planned; I feel the high ground slipping away beneath me. "What of Richard Frederick?" I say. "Jimmy killed him, didn't he? And you must have found out. Perhaps you were there."

There's no surprise at this, only sadness. "It was necessary but most regrettable."

"He was thrown in the river, found near the Swarkestone Bridge," I say. "The same bridge where Bonnie Prince Charlie turned around the year of Culloden. I don't think it's coincidence."

Sir Gabriel shrugs. "The choice of rendezvous was a bit of a private joke, I admit it."

"This is a man's life, not a joke," I cry.

"When I selected the meeting place, I didn't expect him to betray my trust. I don't want people to be hurt or killed, Genevieve. But I can't permit anyone to betray me."

I feel the warning chill of his last words. "I have not betrayed you," I say, with as much calm force as I can summon.

"I know you haven't. Or we would be having a different kind of conversation."

After a moment, I say, warningly, "There is a Constable Campion investigating the murder with all diligence. He knows Frederick died shortly after committing the theft, and suspects it was at the hands of his master."

Sir Gabriel smiles. "I'm not worried about a Derbyshire constable."

Servants clear our soup and mussels and bring out the next course, leg of lamb and an enormous lobster swimming in burnt butter. I don't know why Sir Gabriel isn't bringing up the blue. It can only be because he's waiting for me. This is part of his game.

"I suppose," I say, "it's time to pay for the food."

"I beg your pardon?" Sir Gabriel is startled.

"The work of Thomas Sturbridge."

He looks down the table, his black eyebrows arch as delicate triangles under his white wig. "Yes, well, Genevieve, if you would be so good as to share your findings, that would be appreciated," he says in his driest voice.

I dig my nails into the palm of my left hand to force myself forward. Telling Sir Gabriel about Thomas' work is a monstrous act. I do it safe in the knowledge that there's little he, or anyone at Sèvres, can do now. Thomas' Derby blue will be first, his reputation secure.

"He spoke of the color first at the almshouse," I say. "Not the pigment, but the color."

"Be specific."

"It won't be easy to be specific, for it was hard for me to keep up with his conversation. He talked of the true nature of light, of color, starting with Pythagoras and leading up to Sir Isaac Newton."

"How very erudite," says Sir Gabriel. Is that edge to his voice one of jealousy?

"Blue holds a mystery to Thomas that I believe tantalizes him, draws him forward, even when he wishes he could stop," I say slowly. "He sees the color as having a mystical power."

"He does?" Sir Gabriel tenses in his chair. It's as if I've confirmed something dreadful. "What sort of power?"

"Based on it being so terribly difficult for man to re-create as pigment for centuries on end."

Sir Gabriel looks strangely relieved. "Tell me about his pigment, Genevieve. Everything."

I take a deep breath and say, "Derby blue is derived from cobalt blue, a purer form of the metal discovered twenty years ago by a Swiss scientist named Georg Brandt. Thomas located the best source of the cobalt deep in the Iron Mountains, in Saxony. It has to be completely free of iron or nickel or the color won't be good. He brought the treated cobalt back to Derby, where he combines it with aluminium, oil and minute amounts of other minerals to form the pigment. The stability gives him troubles and he hasn't been able to solve it. Consistency is what delays him."

Sir Gabriel rises from the table, his black eyes blazing, his lips parted. I can't tell if he is angry or elated. He moves quickly toward me, crashing into the table as I back into my chair. I've never seen him like this.

"Genevieve, oh thank you," he groans, seizing my hands. He kisses both of them, turning them over to kiss the palms and my wrists. "My darling, darling girl, you are my treasure."

To see him like this, awash in joy and gratitude, like a boy given the most superb gift in the world, one he's hoped for with all his heart, startles me, to say the least.

"So Sturbridge has not mastered the problem with stability?" he asks eagerly, still holding my hands.

"I think that if this were pigment paint for paper and canvas, he would have a finished formula," I say. "It's the color on clay and the firing that gives him trouble."

Sir Gabriel tightens his grip; my news makes him even happier.

"Dare I hope that you know the precise formula, the ratio of chemicals?" he asks.

I shake my head no, and he says, "You've given me enough," and kisses my hand a last time. He strides out the door, I hear him calling names, Jimmy and Joshua among them. There is a steady murmur of men's voices.

I take my first sip of champagne, for though I need to keep my wits about me, I also feel deeply confused. I twirl the glass, the feel of his kiss still on my hands. Thomas has become a pure soul to me, as pure as the cobalt, laboring in creation. While in the last weeks, Sir Gabriel was transformed into someone greedy, deceitful, and violent. Yet I perceive that the quest for the most spectacular blue has reached into Sir Gabriel's soul too, in a different way. He does this for money but for other reasons too. I have still not gotten to the truth of his invisible circumstances.

Everything is topsy-turvy right now. Thomas did, after all, invent a new blue pigment to make a name for himself in the scientific world, not for the aesthetic magnificence. Sir Gabriel seems more like a knight on a quest, in comparison. This makes my head spin.

When Sir Gabriel returns, he is still aglow. "Saxony is a challenge, of course, but it was among Hellot's theories of the color's mineral origin. We will be able to advance with all speed." He sits and drains his glass.

I say nothing and he takes a closer look at me. "You are experiencing some guilt, I know. It's to be expected. This is your first assignment. I know you have genuine feelings for this chemist, along with unhappiness over the rival turning out to be Sèvres. You don't want to be paid by the French, the persecutor of your family."

Sympathy was the last thing I expected from Sir Gabriel Courtenay.

He holds out his hand. "It's been a terrible time for you, my darling. But the worst is over. Come. I need music."

I assumed he called me *darling* earlier because he was caught up in excitement. I am taken aback that he continues to call me that now. With my return to Derby not yet set, though, I have little choice but to answer to it.

His hand in mine, he leads me to his study, the room where I learned to write with sympathetic ink. He takes a seat at the harpsichord, and I stand where I did before, listening to the flood of music that pours from his fingers. His head goes back, his eyes close, as he plays; he barely needs to read the sheets of notes.

When finished, he sighs. "George Friedrich Händel. Presently dying, not far from this very house. It doesn't seem that the man who composed this could ever die, does it, Genevieve? With such gifts, he'd be immortal."

"No."

Sir Gabriel looks at me. "Tell me what you're thinking. Whatever it is, Genevieve, share it with me."

"Will Hellot now claim credit for inventing the blue?" I ask.

"I suspect he will. But Hellot will need to make it his own in some way, to justify the claim. Sturbridge could challenge, and with his previous history of digging in the mine, many will believe him. I expect it will come down to countries. As in so many other things, it will be the French versus the English. The debate will still make Thomas Sturbridge's name, believe me. A quarrel between chemists over the rights to a beautiful color? An irresistible story for the newspapers."

I cannot imagine Thomas peddling his story for newspapers, begging for supporters. He would never degrade himself like that.

Sir Gabriel studies me. "It suits you, this poetic aura. Melancholy for your genius. Did Denis Arsenault, your other rebel, touch you this deeply? Most likely not."

I don't want Sir Gabriel to probe any deeper into my true feelings for Thomas, nor to compare him to Denis. Uncomfortable, I turn away, toward the Canaletto painting.

"You are exquisite in that dress, Genevieve," Sir Gabriel says, coming up behind me.

"No, no, I know that I'm much too thin," I protest nervously, wishing I had a wrap to throw over my décolletage. "It's the fashion to be plump."

"Slender women hold the most appeal," he says. "Madame de Pompadour is tinier than you are."

"You've seen her?" I say, surprised. I shouldn't be. Isn't he in service to Sèvres?

"I have."

He stands next to me, looking at the Canaletto. We are side by side. It's as it was before, yet so much has changed between us. He doesn't trust me. And I don't believe in his compliments, his endearments. I wonder if this is all just to pull me closer to his side again.

"I'll work out all the letters and arrangements for you to go back to Derby, long enough to remove any suspicion from yourself," Sir Gabriel says. "When the time is right, we'll create the necessary excuse and you're off to Venice, the city where you can become an artist without peer."

I feel such relief. My plan has worked. Once I'm free of Grosvenor Square and returned to Derby, I'll help Thomas produce his Derby blue as swiftly as possible. Somehow I will put the perplexing Sir Gabriel far, far behind me.

Sir Gabriel says, "I will take you to Venice myself."

I whirl to face him. "Take me there? Why would you do that?"

"A change is necessary in my life," he says, looking at me intently. "I have been thinking about it for a long time yet unable to take the steps necessary. Now I know why I was hesitating. I was waiting for you."

Sir Gabriel kisses my forehead. I freeze as he takes me in his arms and draws me close, kissing my cheeks.

"Are you doing this to make me more loyal to you?" I whisper.

He takes my face in his hands. "No. There's something genuine between us, from the beginning. You know it as well as I do."

He kisses me, lightly, his lips wander to my throat, to my earlobe; he nibbles it, his tongue darting in my ear. No one has ever done that to me before. He presses me closer to him. "Genevieve, Genevieve," he moans.

His lips are on mine, not curious and ardent like Thomas, but now demanding. Something quickens, some response I can't control. My arms snake around him, moving up his waistcoat, under his shirt, holding on to his lean back.

It's like a signal for him. His kisses my throat and moves down .

I am not Genevieve Planché any longer. I'm a person watching Genevieve make love to Sir Gabriel Courtenay, all of the feelings — the bursts of dark pleasure, the curious groping — happening at a strange distance.

He scoops me up in his arms and then lowers me down, onto the floor. He's tearing off his waistcoat. He pushes aside my petticoats, his fingers finding my legs, tearing loose my stockings.

With a jolt, I am brought back to myself. I am the one flung down onto the floor by a man I do not trust. "No, no, not this, I *can't*," I protest.

But it is a sharp rap on the door that makes him stop, not my words.

"Damn them," he groans. And then, hoarsely shouting, "Wait."

He kneels beside me, out of breath. A few seconds later, he's helping me to my feet as I numbly arrange my bodice and try to fix my stays. "Sit here," he says softly, leading me to the settee and kissing me on the cheek, with much more tenderness than his touch moments ago. He puts his waistcoat back on and hurries out the door. I hear Jimmy's gravelly voice.

I stare down at my lap, clutching my hands. My knees under my skirts tremble. I can't take in what just happened. No woman better than a harlot would behave like this.

"Darling, there are so many things to attend to, I'm sorry," Sir Gabriel says, from the door. "I will be with you as soon as I can."

I nod without looking at him.

The black-clad maid returns, beckoning.

"Where are you taking me?" I ask.

"Where you're meant to go," she snaps.

I don't want to go with her, but where do I want to be in this house? I'm at a loss.

The maid leads me upstairs, to the second floor rather than the third. We're not going back to the small room with a bed and a table. She opens the door to a vast room, a canopy bed in the center. When I stand in the doorway, hesitant to step inside, she gives me a nudge, and closes the door behind me.

This is Sir Gabriel's bedchamber. I am to wait here until he finishes his business and comes upstairs, to make me his mistress. Who can blame him for assuming I'd willingly share his bed? I couldn't stop myself from responding to him. *There has always been something between the two of us*, he insisted. If I'm honest, I can't deny it.

But I cannot do this to Thomas — and even if it were not for him, if he did not even exist, I still cannot do it. A spy sleeping with her master. What could be more sordid, more contemptible?

If I stay here for the next week with Sir Gabriel, sharing his bed, I've no doubt I will return to Derby, as we always planned. But I will be forever changed. I could not face Thomas after this. I could not sit in the decorating room painting my flowers next to fellow artists; I could not share a friendship with Evelyn. And I realize right now that I *do* want those things. Not only my budding relationship with Thomas — *all* of it.

Sir Gabriel has the origin of the formula for Derby blue, and that's all he shall have from me.

I listen at the bedchamber door and hear not a sound. I turn the doorknob — to my relief, no one locked it.

A moment later I'm out on the passageway. I hurry down it, back toward the stairs, cursing the clicking sound of my heels on wood.

Standing at the top, the stairs below me are empty. The hall is empty. I see a streak of movement. It's the maid again, moving around in the study. If I come down, she will see me.

As I wait, I hear men's voices in another part of the downstairs. They must be making their plans, now that I've given them the secret.

I wait until the maid walks out of Sir Gabriel's study. This is my opening. I may not have another one.

I run down the stairs.

CHAPTER TWENTY-SIX

The sun has set when I open the door to Sir Gabriel Courtenay's house. I'm wearing only this thin silk dress and dainty shoes, and the cold March air hits me like a blow. Trying to look nonchalant, I make my way down three marble steps and onto the walkway between the houses and the park.

Unfortunately, the street lamps are lit, making me highly visible. Anyone glancing out the window of Sir Gabriel's house would see me. And thanks to the length of the street, with few other people on it, if anyone realizes I'm gone and runs outside, I will be visible for a good while longer. I need to get off the street, fast.

I dart into the park, where I hope the darkness will envelop me.

It is deserted. Ahead of me rises the statue of King George II. I hurry toward it, the rich, bitter odor of freshly turned earth everywhere. The park gardens are being planted, and twice I nearly stumble and fall into mounds of planting soil.

My relief over escaping Sir Gabriel's house fades as my predicament comes into focus. What am I to do now? I have not a shilling. Traveling to Derby is impossible without money. My only option is to make my way to Fournier Street, but what am I to say to Grandfather when I get there? He thinks I'm in the Midlands, usefully employed, and I appear on his doorstep in the middle of the night, dressed like this? My steps slow, well short of the statue.

I stand, shivering, as I debate going to Spitalfields. How will I explain my presence without telling Grandfather about Sir Gabriel? How can I upset him like this? The news of his health breakdown was false. Learning that his granddaughter is a spy for Sèvres could make it true.

I rub my arms, cursing these flimsy, flouncing sleeves. It's quite cold. But unless I want to turn around and make my way back into Sir Gabriel's house, I'd better start walking to the East End. It's not cold enough to kill me.

I hear a man shout to my right, on the street running alongside the park. Surely Grosvenor Square is not a place for shouting. I squint to see what's happening, the first stirring of fear in my belly. I am in the middle of a park with no lamps within. It couldn't be Sir Gabriel's men. I'm invisible.

Under a glowing lamp, I see him. It's Joshua, Sir Gabriel's servant… and he's pointing right at me.

"She's here!" he calls again.

I look down at my dress, horrified. The pale blue silk must shimmer bright enough to mark me as a target in the darkness. How could I be so stupid?

I hear running feet behind me. I whip around to see a man running full out, right for me.

I pick up my skirts and sprint, as fast as I can, my heart hammering with panic. I swing around the statue of King George II, and keep going, heading for the far end of the park. My feet ache in the shoes; my lungs are on fire from running in a corset.

I glance over my shoulder. The man chasing me through the park gains on me, and I can see now that it's Sir Gabriel himself.

I run even faster, a stitch in my side becoming sharp as a knife. I can't go much farther.

I'm almost to the other side of the park when I spot a group of people, men and women, assembled on the street as if waiting for a carriage, under the street lamps. If I can reach them, I am safe. Sir Gabriel couldn't possibly drag me back to his house in front of them.

The footsteps behind me grow louder. None of the people on the square have seen me yet. Sir Gabriel is certainly capable of silencing me if he can get hold of me first.

"Help me," I cry, but I'm so out of breath it's nothing but a gasped squeak.

I leap over another dirt mound.

"Help!" I cry, louder.

A head turns in the crowd. A man nudges another. They see me now, I'm no more than twenty feet from them.

A hand seizes my arm and pulls me to a halt.

"Stop," says Sir Gabriel.

"No," I try to tear himself from the grip of his hand.

"Your grandfather," he says, his face rigid with rage. "Jimmy will kill him and everyone in the house on Fournier Street if I give the signal in the next minute."

"No. You wouldn't. You couldn't."

"No matter what happens to me, or to you, they die, if I give the signal," he says, every word emphasized. "Jimmy cuts their throats."

A man calls from in front of us. "Pardon me, but are you in need of some help?"

The entire group, six men and women, have formed a concerned cluster. One of their party, who has selected himself spokesman, is out in front.

Sir Gabriel tightens his grip on me. "We're going to talk to these people now. The two of us. Remember what I said."

Still breathing heavily, I step over the last mound of earth, and turn onto the opening in the park that leads to the street, his steps matching mine.

Sir Gabriel waves to them, in sheepish greeting. "I am so very sorry to have disturbed you."

The young man out front says, in disbelief, "Sir Gabriel Courtenay?"

"We've had a bit of a disagreement, my friend and I," Sir Gabriel says. "But it's resolved."

An older man in the group, heavier than the others, a matron on his arm, says, deeply shocked, "My good fellow, running in the park? Our park? What kind of lover's quarrel could account for it?"

His wife clucks disapprovingly on his arm.

"I beg your forgiveness, Lady Errol," says Sir Gabriel, with all sincerity.

Another young man pokes a fashionably dressed woman in the side, his hand over his face, to conceal laughing. Her eyes are so wide they may pop out of her head.

"I'd like to hear from the lady, if she says it is now resolved," says another man who steps forward. I know his face and voice, he is Sir Humphrey Willoughby, the person who spoke to Sir Gabriel that day at the British Museum.

Sir Gabriel says to me, "Tell him the truth, darling. But remember, we're late to Pierre's. Do you want me to have to send that messenger on ahead?"

He peers meaningfully off to the side. Following his gaze, I see Jimmy, twenty feet away, poised to take flight.

If I don't go back to the house with Sir Gabriel, Jimmy will rush to the East End to murder my grandfather and Daphne and George. Even if I shout out the truth to Sir Humphrey and the others at this moment, Jimmy will run, and who could stop him? By the time I'd convinced anyone of the dangers I'd endured, of Sir Gabriel being a spy, a paid agent of Sèvres Porcelain, Grandfather would be dead.

"All is well, Sir," I say, my voice less than steady.

"You're certain?" Sir Humphrey scrutinizes my face in all seriousness. Is it possible that he remembers me from the museum? He has not said so. Yet he takes great interest in my welfare.

"I am sorry to have caused this scene," I say, and force myself to turn to face Sir Gabriel. "Can you ever forgive me?"

"Of course," he says, taking my hand and kissing it. His lips barely graze my skin.

"Ahhhhh," says a delighted woman in the group.

Sir Gabriel bows, takes me by the arm, and leads me onto the street, turning back toward his house. Jimmy is still standing near the corner. I look up at Sir Gabriel, who shakes his head, and Jimmy relaxes his stance.

"How romantic," I hear a young woman say.

"Who was she?"

"At least we have our conversation for tonight."

We walk more quickly now up the walkway along the park. I can't hear any of their voices any longer.

"Is my grandfather safe?" I ask.

"Yes," he says tersely.

"How could you threaten him like that — how?"

"Because it is the only thing that could stop you."

I realize that it is not Sir Gabriel's criminal side that most terrifies me, his history of duplicity marked with violence, but his utter pragmatism.

Now he looks over his shoulder and says, urgently, "Did he recognize you? Did Sir Humphrey Willloughby recognize you?"

I stay silent.

"Answer me."

"I don't know," I spit at him. "I don't think so. What does it matter?" A few more steps and I say, "Ah, if Sir Humphrey knows who I am, then if you murder me tonight, you'll be suspected."

He says, chillingly, "If only that were my most serious problem."

We walk in silence until we are almost to his house.

"Genevieve, wait," he says, pulling me to a stop on the street. "Was that panic sending you into the park, or were you lying to me the entire evening to relax my guard so you could escape? I assumed the latter when I found you missing, but I can't believe hiding in a park is any intelligent woman's idea of an escape plan."

"I suppose this proves I'm not intelligent."

"You panicked, then?" He's not as angry as he was moments ago. He seems genuinely confused, even, I realize, rather hurt.

I don't know what to say, so I say nothing.

He says, "I only wish in so doing you hadn't exposed yourself to so many people, to these particular people. Your actions will have serious consequences for both of us." He takes a closer look at me. "What about the source of Derby blue? Is that a lie?"

"What I told you about Derby blue is true, Sir Gabriel," I say.

He leads me into the house, Jimmy coming up behind us. Joshua and two other men await us. I recognize them as the ones who followed me and Denis that night in the snow.

The maid appears to take me upstairs, not to Sir Gabriel's bedchamber but to the other room. Undressed and changed into a plain cotton shift, I crawl into bed to consider my fate.

The uncertainty of what is to happen hangs over me, waking or sleeping, for the next six days. I only know how much time has passed from watching the sun rise and fall through the small window of the room. The maid brings me food and takes away the chamber pot. She does not speak one word, of course.

I am sure that the fact of many people seeing me run across the park protects me. But after I tried to run away, no matter how much he wanted me physically, he can't trust me. He can't send me back to Derby. What will Sir Gabriel do? I can't stay here forever. How long until Thomas and the others in Derby begin to wonder about me? This is the question that gives me faint hope for freedom, until I remember that Sir Gabriel is an expert forger. Who knows what "my" letters say? He could keep up a fictitious story for weeks.

*

I'm awoken one night by a noise. Again I open my eyes to see Sir Gabriel sitting by the bed, watching me.

I'm stunned by his appearance. He wears only his breeches and a loose white shirt. Black stubble darkens his chin; violet shadows pouch his eyes. I've never seen him like this; without his beautifully tailored clothes, less than clean shaven.

"What do you want?" I ask, sitting up.

"Genevieve, I want to give you another chance."

How his words offend me.

"Chance at what?" I say. "Chance at taking you on in your bed? This room suits me fine, thank you."

I expect him to take offense, but instead a wry smile stretches his gaunt countenance. "I don't know why I like it so much when you behave as if you're from the gutter," he says, thoughtfully, as if he actually sought to understand an interesting problem. "It's a quirk of mine."

Disgust rises in me, and an immolating rage over all that this man has done. "So you want to dress me up again? Shall we play lord and lady of the house? You fancy a tumble on the floor, in the bed, who knows, maybe the harpsichord is next. Sure, let's have at it. But you know what? Better be careful, Sir Gabriel. Because next time I won't be running for the park. First chance I get, I'll be taking a knife to you. Just like you threatened to do to my grandfather. Don't think I can't carve you to pieces."

His eyes widen throughout my speech.

"My God," Sir Gabriel says to himself, "what's to be done with her?"

I pull my legs up to my chin, hugging my knees like a little girl. "That's your problem," I say.

"You talk to Thomas Sturbridge like this?" he asks, wonderingly.

"None of your business."

He sighs. "I suppose that at the end of the day I'm like King Louis. I prefer them wild."

"If you think comparing me to Madame de Pompadour will win my heart, I fear for your sanity."

"Wild? Jeanne Antoinette Poisson? Not at all. You'd never meet a more genteel and cultured woman who happens to be living in double adultery."

I press my forehead to my knees and say, "When I think that I am helping these evil people, giving them an advantage with knowledge of the blue, I'm certain that God will punish me."

Sir Gabriel says, "And now your other side emerges, the holy Huguenot, clutching her Huguenot cross. I much prefer the side of the passionate artist."

"All of my sides would like you to leave, Sir Gabriel. If you won't free me, than leave me be."

Neither of us speaks for a minute.

"Oh, Genevieve," he says. "I've felt so close to you; our spirits understand each other, don't they? When we're fighting for the blue, fighting to win it? I know that no one else could understand what we have been through."

It is the only thing he could say right now which could reach me.

"I need you," he says, his voice raw, stripped of all of its carefully schooled polish. "I need you to save me, Genevieve."

I still find myself unable to speak, to move.

"Let me try to make it right between us. I won't force you. I have never forced any woman. You don't have to share my bed. You don't have to do anything. Come with me now, out of here, so we can talk to each other."

He stretches out his hand. I could take it; I could go with him. If I had never met Thomas, I might move toward him now with pleasure. But I *have* met Thomas. I close my eyes.

"Go away. Please, Sir Gabriel, go away." I say it as if I were a helpless little girl begging the bogeyman to disappear.

After a moment I hear him get up and leave, the door closed — and locked — behind him. For the next day and more I think of everything he said, every gesture, and my responses too. Over and over again, until I fear I'll go mad with it. I am desperate to think of something else. I pick up my Rousseau book, my present from Thomas. I read its wisdom, those insightful, provocative sentences, and yet when I reach the end of each paragraph, I don't remember what came before. I don't give up. I force myself forward, and after the seventh or eighth time I try reading, I'm able to take in Rousseau's philosophy.

*

The following day, everything changes.

The door swings open and Sir Gabriel steps in, followed by Jimmy. He has shaved and put on his best clothes once more. His face is a blank, pale and circumspect, except for his eyes, cold and flickering. I know instantly he is quite angry.

"Read this," he says, thrusting a letter at me

I unfold it carefully. When I see the signature below — Thomas Sturbridge — I feel a leap of happiness that I do my best to hide.

"Dearest Genevieve,

It has not even been a fortnight since you left and I miss you. It was a tremendous relief to receive your letter and learn that your grandfather improves. Please, as soon as you can, inform me of his progress and your plans. I also have news. I told you production of the porcelain was set to commence shortly. There is an unfortunate development. We are unable to solve a difficulty with the porcelain substance itself. William has a contact at a different clay foundry in Devon, and I will go with him to run tests on the site with my equipment. It should not take too long to complete the tests. William says a month at the most. I will send letters to London and Derby. Wishing that I were with you now.

Yours, Thomas Sturbridge"

My heart pounding, I look up from the letter to Sir Gabriel's face. He quotes one sentence from it: " 'I told you production of the porcelain was set to commence shortly.' "

Sir Gabriel slaps me across the cheek. The pain is hot and stinging. Stars explode in front of my eyes.

"You lied to me," Sir Gabriel says.

"You've lied to *me*, from beginning to end," I throw back at him.

"You want to go back to Derby, Genevieve? You want to reunite with him? Fine. You're going back. Within a fortnight there will be men in France working on Sturbridge's formula, but we will be hopelessly behind if Derby starts production in a month. You are going to make sure that doesn't happen."

"How?"

"You'll lure Sturbridge out of his house for the night, and while he's out, Jimmy will break in."

"No, no, you can't," I protest. "He'll know if anything is missing."

"I would think so, since we plan to empty the laboratory."

I'm so stunned, I can't take it in. "But he'll know it was to get the formula right away, and Duesbury and Heath, they'll go to the constable."

"We're past that," Sir Gabriel says.

Another terrible realization sinks in. "If it happens during the night that I lure him out, Thomas will know it's me, too, that I'm part of it." I shake my head. "No, you'll have to find another way."

"Oh, there is another way, Genevieve. Jimmy and the men will break into the house, kill Thomas Sturbridge and whoever else is there, and then empty the laboratory."

"Have you gone mad?" I whisper. "Murder a whole group of people, not just Thomas? He has a cook and housekeeper, a good woman. She should die for this? And the guards?"

Sir Gabriel stares at me, implacable.

I implore him, "Sir Gabriel, listen. Put aside your anger with me and listen. How could a porcelain color possibly be this important? Even if it's the most beautiful in the world, if it makes Sèvres' fortune, it can't be worth committing such a slaughter."

Sir Gabriel shakes his head, unmoved. "If you want to save his life, you'll draw him out for the night."

"Wait until he leaves Derby and the house is unoccupied, and then rob it," I plead.

"You just read the letter, he's taking equipment with him. I'm sure his samples of cobalt and key acids and chemicals too. No, we need everything."

"Even if I agree, how am I to do it?" I demand.

He steps forward and takes my face by the chin. "You have something he wants, Genevieve. You know it as well as I. You'll figure a way. You're quite clever when you want to be."

He must be angry to be this crude. This close to him, I can read the warring emotions in Sir Gabriel's eyes: besides the anger, there's frustration, resentment, jealousy, and also a trace of fear. How could he be afraid?

"There is something more to all of this," I say slowly. "Something you've not told me."

All emotion is extinguished.

"You will do this, Genevieve. You will do as I tell you, exactly how I tell you to do it."

"And afterward?" I ask. "When you've ruined Thomas' life and I'm under arrest, what's to stop me from telling William Duesbury and Constable Campion absolutely everything about you? I won't have anything to lose."

"Let us be perfectly clear. You breathe my name, or Jimmy's or Joshua's, or a word about anything or anyone about Grosvenor Square at any time, you forfeit your grandfather's life," says Sir Gabriel. "And you know me capable of it."

Vicious threats wielded again. I'm backed into a corner, a terrible corner.

I run my hands through my hair. "Why are you doing this?" I ask. "Why?"

In the doorway, he half-turns and says, "Be of good cheer. You won't have to keep your mouth shut forever. In six months' time, matters like a theft or murder in a Derby porcelain factory won't be uppermost on anyone's mind. We will be living in a new world, and you'll be the toast of it."

I have no idea what that is supposed to mean. But Sir Gabriel is gone, and I'm left to face my future.

CHAPTER TWENTY-SEVEN

Evelyn is pleased to have me back in Derby, but she's as surprised as the rest of her family when I arrive on their doorstep at nine o'clock that Tuesday night in April, and she's alarmed by my appearance.

"You look utterly exhausted," says Evelyn. "And you're even thinner than when you left. Why didn't you send us word when you'd be back?"

"I just wanted to be here," I murmur. "The day I decided to return was the day I left, so a message couldn't have arrived before me."

*

The reality is, Sir Gabriel arranged another flying carriage to take me to Derby. His goal was to return me to the town as soon as plausibly possible, in hopes that I would be able to lure Thomas from his home before he traveled to Devon. If I arrived after they'd already gone, there was nothing to do but wait until they came back to Derby and execute the plan.

Jimmy rode in the same carriage as me, sometimes sitting across but more often on top with the driver. I'm sure he found my presence as abhorrent as I found his; we exchanged no more than a handful of words. My understanding was that Sir Gabriel's other operatives followed. Soon Derby would be crawling with them.

Sir Gabriel drilled me on various protocols, including the method of communication with Jimmy. When I had a plan in place for spending the night with Thomas away from his house, the morning of the day we were to be away, I was to place a red flowerpot under a yew tree in the northwest corner of the Heaths' garden.

Sir Gabriel repeated, for the tenth time, that I must arrange my nocturnal rendezvous with Thomas as soon as possible. An inn in a nearby town, posing as husband and wife, was his advice.

"Thomas could well refuse a lewd proposal. Will you then kill a man for being moral?"

"He won't refuse," said Sir Gabriel, shortly.

*

Now, back in Derby, I wait nervously until I'm up in our room, and we're alone, to ask Evelyn about Thomas.

"Oh Genevieve, you just missed him. Such a pity; I know that he was so worried about you and your grandfather. On Monday he left for Devon with William Duesbury and Major Tarkwell to see about a new clay supply."

Sir Gabriel will be spitting mad with disappointment over the news. But I'm not sure how I feel. Relieved that I have more time before executing my final betrayal? Or regretful, because more time will only increase my mental torment over the inevitable?

As I put my belongings back into their places in the room, Evelyn asks me about my grandfather's health. I spin the lies fed to me: a miraculous recovery, followed by Pierre's insistence that I return to the position I love.

"The truth is, Genevieve, I have some news of my own." Evelyn's face is flushed; I've never seen her like this.

"I met someone at church," she says. "He's come up from London on business with the silk mill and will be here throughout the spring and into the summer. I've seen him twice in three days. He's quite… nice."

In six months' time, matters like a theft, or a murder, in a Derby porcelain factory won't be uppermost on anyone's mind. We'll be living in a new world. I don't know why that disturbing prediction of Sir Gabriel's runs through my head yet again. Perhaps it's because I sense there is some larger meaning to it — something that might explain much of what I've endured — but I can't grasp hold of it.

More immediately, through all of my misery, I can see the happiness radiating in Evelyn and I am glad of it.

"This is quite encouraging," I say and squeeze her hand.

Evelyn finding a young man she likes is the only bright spot in my dark world. I am exhausted, Evelyn is right. I can't remember when my sleep wasn't riven by horrific nightmares. The following morning, Evelyn says I look ill and urges me to stay in bed, but I won't hear of it. As much time as I have left, I intend to spend it being useful.

Ambrose Stanton and Harry are glad of my return to the decorating room, although their solicitous tones indicate they're as concerned as Evelyn over my pallor and lost weight.

"Mr. Duesbury has gone with a small party to Devon," says Ambrose, "but before he left I did show him your drawing of the moth. I had to wait for the right moment. He is a gentleman of… variable temper. And do you know what he said? 'It's a creative and promising idea.' Mistress Genevieve, you are to be congratulated on your first innovative design."

"Ah, that's wonderful — wonderful," cries Harry, clapping.

Looking at their kind faces, the tears come, rolling down my face.

My colleagues are concerned, and confused, by my weeping, even though I choke out the excuse that it's because I'm so happy. It takes me a few minutes to gather myself, but I manage it. Sitting at my table, working steadily with my paper and watercolors, yields a little happiness that day. And as we eat our luncheon, Harry tells me his good news. His family has had a letter. His brother is alive and well in Canada with hopes of an English victory against the Marquis de Montcalm. The war continues, across the globe.

The three of us are summoned to the main floor three hours before the end of the work day. There stands the massive form of Constable Campion, with a new question to pose to everyone. One by one we must file into Evelyn's office.

The constable is the wild card in the game I'm forced to play, and I approach my interview with trepidation.

After saying he heard about my grandfather's bout of illness and expressing the usual wishes for his full recovery, Constable Campion says, "There is a development in the case of Richard Frederick. I've learned that Richard met with no stranger in Derby at any inn or tavern or coffee house — I've canvassed them all — but he did meet last September one Sunday with a stranger, a well dressed gentleman, in Nottingham, not far away. The man registered at the Flying Horse Inn under the name of Sommerville. Now, have you ever heard that name?"

He discovered the alias used by Sir Gabriel.

"No," I say.

"You didn't seem to me to give the question proper consideration. Not here, not in London?"

I pretend to think harder and then say, "No, Constable."

He gestures that I'm free to go. I make my way toward the door but a desperate curiosity slows my steps.

"So there is progress in your inquiry? I ask.

He strokes his beard and says, "We are making progress on several fronts, Mistress; the other lines of inquiry I must keep confidential, you understand. But I believe I will be making an arrest soon, and it is as I have suspected from the first. This Sommerville is part of a ring of criminals."

"A ring," I repeat.

"Yes, and I fully expect to see them all hang."

He looks me straight in the eye, a triumph flashes, and then he picks up a paper.

I back out of the room, nearly stumbling into a nervous Harry who is edging in next.

I barely notice him. I am no longer on the main floor of the porcelain factory, I'm not in Derbyshire. It is a summer day, and I am nineteen years old. Denis thought we should make a day of it, going to Tyburn with a group of apprentices to see a murderer hanged. It had been nothing but thieves and forgers for weeks, ordinary criminals swinging from the rope. Now a real murderer had been caught and condemned. We brought wrappers of beef sliced thick and ate them as we waited for his execution at Tyburn, with the rest of the crowd. I can still taste the edge of the fatty slice of beef, washed down with warm beer. Then a cry went up, as the condemned man approached. I caught a glimpse of a cart rumbling toward the triple tree — not a real tree, of course, but interlaced wooden gallows — and a chaplain, his head thrown back in song, sitting next to the condemned, who slumped, a rope already around his neck. I found I couldn't watch the hanging when the moment came, I could only listen to the din of excited jeers. I was sorry when I opened my eyes some five minutes after he dropped, because the murderer wasn't dead yet. His legs and arms shook as he dangled, and in the most shocking moment of all, I saw how spindly his grayish-white limbs were. How could he have ever summoned the strength to take another man's life? It seemed impossible.

I hear the cheers and curses of the Tyburn crowd as I make my way to Evelyn. Surely my distress — my raw fear — must show on my face, but Evelyn does not seem to notice.

"I know it's a great deal to ask, but I have need of the carriage," she says, her eyes bright. "My friend from church invited me to tea in the parlor of the George Inn. I recruited a fine fellow here to walk you home, and could you also tell my mother I'm working late on the account books? If I have the carriage, she won't worry. And I can fix it with our driver to back my story if need be. He'll do anything I ask. Would you do me this favor?"

I tell Evelyn I'm agreeable to all she asks. She rushes off, and I walk home with my porcelain-works escort, respectfully silent the whole way. The fullness of spring thickens the early evening air, trees sprouting leaves, shopkeepers calling out to last customers.

I seek out Mrs. Heath once I reach the house and deliver Evelyn's explanation of lateness. "Oh, I wish they wouldn't demand so much of her," Mrs. Heath fusses. And then: "I have a letter for you, Genevieve."

It is from Thomas, and I hurry upstairs to read.

"Dear Genevieve,

A fine situation I find myself in. While standing in a clay pit or measuring chemicals, I see your face and I hear your voice. I've been corrected more than once by William when I grow distracted. Genevieve, I regret to say we will be here for at least another two weeks. The longer I am parted from you, the more I think of you. Sleep is becoming elusive. The only comfort I can draw from this is that I will insist on seeing you as often as you are willing to tolerate my presence. I trust to find an embrace as soon as I come back to Derby and to you, my sweetheart.

Thomas Sturbridge, written by hand at the Inn of the Dove, Fremington"

I cannot count how many times I read his letter, huddled on the bed, listening to Thomas' voice. It is a source of both solace and pain. I am not selfish enough to harbor regret over losing Thomas. He is lost. My pain is for him. I won't go through with my part in the plan to trick and rob Thomas — our imminent arrests will take care of that — but he will be devastated when he learns the truth about me. I fear Thomas will never be able to trust another woman for as long as he lives. *I* did that to him.

The door opens; Evelyn has come home. She doesn't say anything as she moves around the room, and I wonder if her tea was not what she hoped. I must rally to comfort her. I sit up and look for her, but I can't see her. I've only lit one candle and there's no fire.

"Genevieve," she says from the foot of the bed. "Have you been crying?"

I touch my cheeks; they are wet.

"I suppose I have," I murmur. "I'm sorry. I know I am poor company."

"What are you reading?"

"A letter from Thomas," I say, caressing it.

Evelyn comes closer and she looks strange. It's like the first time we laid eyes on each other, when Andrew introduced us and she turns away, disdainful.

She glances down at my letter, which rather surprises me since it is so clearly private, and then resumes her scrutiny of my face.

"What's wrong?" I ask.

"Nothing." I can see how troubled she is, however.

"Did you not enjoy your tea?" I ask gently.

"I did enjoy it," she says quickly. "Very much. He is… is a fine man.

But I'm late home; I'm sure Mother is hysterical. I'll need to spend time with her."

And with that, she is off to her mother's parlor, and I return to my letter. I fall asleep before she returns.

*

The dawn comes and with it a fine rain, and the promise of nothing but more of it. We step quickly from the front door to the waiting carriage. The footman covers Evelyn's head with a parasol; I welcome the cool spattering. I like the softness that the gray rain bestows on Derby, and I look forward to seeing the drops quiver on the surface of the river from the window of the decorating room.

It appears I've found a strange calm. I shall enjoy the place for as long as I have left. Today, I officially begin my moth series. I do not expect to be able to execute too many of these, so I want the ones I do paint to impress.

The challenge draws on my focus to a remarkable degree. But the end of the work day at Derby Porcelain Works comes early, for Evelyn says we are needed at home. There's no sign of Constable Campion when I come down. I am reprieved for one more day.

Evelyn and I hop into the carriage for the ride home. The rain has just stopped, and the sun peeks from behind a shred of low lying cloud. Looking out the window, I see the puddles shrinking and the tree's first leaves glow a more vivid green because of the day's soaking.

The carriage rumbles down a street I don't recognize, and I say, "Are we trying a new route today?"

"Yes, I thought Babington Street would make for a change," says Evelyn.

The carriage slows to a halt in front of a very high wall running between the street and a building whose top I can barely see. Taking a closer look, the wall is made of two parts. The lower half is centuries old, on top the bricks are much newer. Someone built the top part to conceal this particular house from view.

"Why do we stop here?" I ask.

"Genevieve, there's someone we need to speak to."

"Here? Who?" I say, taken aback.

The figure of a man appears at an opening in the wall. I've seen him before, but for the first few seconds I cannot place him. He's handsome, rather young, wearing a wig. He walks up to us, signaling to the driver to bring the carriage in, and I recognize his square-jawed face.

It is Sir Humphrey Willoughby, the neighbor of Sir Gabriel Courtenay. I can hardly believe it.

Evelyn says, "Genevieve, this is my friend."

The carriage turns in, and immediately rocks back and forth, up and down. Sir Humphrey opens the door for us and I step out, looking down. The drive is pitted with large holes. If the carriage went any farther, it could break a wheel. The house looms above; it is vacant, crumbling, even disintegrating. A streak of sun breaks through a hole in the roof, I can see it streaming down through a gaping window.

I turn from this ravaged mansion to the Londoner standing before me.

Sir Humphrey says, "Hello, Genevieve Planché. I am very glad to see you"

That settles one thing. He *did* know who I was at Grosvenor Square; he remembered me from the British Museum.

"Why have you come here?" I ask.

"To learn why you ran across a London park, in terror of your life, only to go back into the house of the man who terrified you," he replies. "And all the while your Derby friends believed you to be in a house in Spitalfields, tending to a sick relative."

I open my mouth, then close it. What response could I make to this? I glance at Evelyn.

"How did you know to come here?" I ask.

"I had your name, and that you are Huguenot — you told me that at the British Museum. I went to Spitalfields, where the Huguenots live, and it took less than a day to locate your grandfather and learn where you'd gone."

Evelyn takes a step closer to Sir Humphrey. So this is the man from London she spoke of, the one doing business with the silk mill? But that's far from true.

"You work for the government," I say accusingly. "I'm sorry, Evelyn, but this man is not what he told you he was."

"I know what he is," she says quietly. "He told me yesterday."

They look at each other, and some emotion passes between them, nothing to do with me.

"Will someone enlighten me?" I say.

Sir Humphrey says simply, "I work for a man, and that man works for the prime minister."

I say, incredulous, "How could my affairs possibly be of interest to Whitehall? That's absurd."

"As much as I care about the well being and safety of any Englishwoman, it isn't *your* affairs that brought me here," he says. "It's the affairs of Sir Gabriel Courtenay."

Hearing his name spoken, and in front of Evelyn, makes my stomach turn over.

"Who?" I ask.

"Come. You know Sir Gabriel, you know him very well indeed. And we're going to talk about him. Shall we?" he says, pointing at the vacant building behind us.

"Is that an abbey?" I ask. "Why should we go inside?"

"It is not an abbey, no," he says. "And I believe it will be instructive."

I follow him, most reluctant, as he pushes a rotted wooden door swinging on its hinge and into a soaring space that was once a grand room. The wood floor sags and splinters away. Wet moss clings to the walls. Worst of all is the smell: foul, like a damp, reeking crypt.

"This house belonged to one of Derbyshire's leading families 200 years ago," says Sir Humphrey. "They were celebrated not just in Derbyshire — in all of England. Their name was Babington. Do you know of them?"

"No," I say.

Evelyn says, "No one ever talks about the Babingtons in Derby even though they were a leading family. The son of the house, Antony, committed an infamous crime in the reign of Elizabeth I and the family was utterly destroyed."

"What crime?" I ask, not having any idea why they're talking of centuries-old history.

"High treason," says Sir Humphrey. "In 1572 Antony Babington conspired against Elizabeth, going so far as to plan her assassination. He was arrested, condemned and executed. The manner of execution for traitors was prescribed: hang him, cut him down before he is dead and disembowel and castrate him, burning his private parts while he is conscious."

This is worse than being hanged at Tyburn. "Why are you telling me these horrors?" I say, looking from Sir Humphrey to Evelyn.

He studies me before saying, "Have you ever heard of Le Secret du Roi?"

"The king's secret? No. Which secret do you refer to? Is this from the age of Elizabeth as well?"

Evelyn says, "You see, Sir Humphrey? Genevieve doesn't know."

"Know *what*? Please tell me." I'm so frustrated my voice breaks. He's already mentioned Sir Gabriel, why take this roundabout journey now?

Sir Humphrey says, "King Louis XV has for the past ten years used his own private network of spies, reporting only to him. They are known as Le Secret du Roi. A handful of men operate in France, of course. In Italy. We know of one who was sent to Russia. They are of similar type: men from the ranks of the nobility and well educated, but impoverished. Sophisticated tastes. Not men who are too respectable; we could call them dissolute. The Russian spy dressed like a woman and impersonated a lady in waiting — successfully. They are able to mix without suspicion at the highest levels of society, learn things useful in politics and war and convey these findings to Louis. Their ostensible position could be diplomat. Or perhaps their focus is artistic."

With the word *artistic*, I take a step back.

Sir Humphrey reads something in my face. "I know that Sir Gabriel sent you to steal the formula for the blue pigment that Thomas Sturbridge invented here in Derby," he says.

I look between him and Evelyn, horrified. How could she tell him that Thomas was working on the blue?

"You cannot deny that you know Sir Gabriel," he presses. "I've seen you with him, twice."

"Sir Gabriel is not responsible for my being here," I insist. "My grandfather, Pierre Billiou, made arrangements with my cousin Andrew Planché to secure the position."

Evelyn says, "Oh, Genevieve, stop lying, I beg you. I took note of your secret letters, of your burning them. Of your disappearing Bible."

"I believe it possible your original hiring was honest, but somehow Courtenay learned of it and he recruited you to commit a criminal act," says Sir Humphrey, whose manner grows sterner by the minute.

"Even should that be true, and I am not saying it is, I cannot believe that you, that the prime minister, that anyone should think it of such great importance what color porcelain is painted when we are in the midst of a war," I say, flailing and desperate.

"We don't care a whit about the porcelain — we care only about the color," says Sir Humphrey.

"What?"

"It's the color of France, Genevieve. Blue has been the color of the French monarchy, the sacred symbol of France, for six hundred years. King Louis must want the color desperately, for once he gets the formula for this extraordinary shade — whether it's for his porcelain, his art, his palaces, the uniforms of his soldiers — it will give France a crucial advantage. And Courtenay, as a member of Le Secret du Roi, is desperately trying to get it for him."

CHAPTER TWENTY-EIGHT

It takes quite a while for Evelyn and Sir Humphrey to calm me. When I realize what I've done in telling Sir Gabriel the basis of Thomas' formula for Derby blue, that I could be aiding the war effort of King Louis XV, the greatest enemy not only of England but of the Huguenot people, I become hysterical.

Once I'm capable of it, I confess my involvement to Sir Humphrey, omitting only the love making on the floor of Sir Gabriel's house. I am too ashamed to speak of that. I tell him everything else, including how I tried to end my part in the spying and how I was tricked into returning to London, where he imprisoned me and forced me to resume. Since Sir Humphrey witnessed my attempt to escape, the story seems to ring true to him. I finish with the warning that my grandfather will be killed if I ever betray Sir Gabriel.

"That's reprehensible," bursts Evelyn. She was silent during my confession, but cannot hold back on this.

"I will send word immediately to have Pierre Billiou and his household protected," promises Sir Humphrey.

I thank him through my relief. At least I have secured this for my family, one act of goodness in this whole sordid business.

"How did you know about Sir Gabriel?" I ask. "It seems you have suspected him for a long time. And I think he is aware of it. At the British Museum, he was snappish after talking to you, something you said about family upset him."

For the first time, Sir Humphrey smiles. "I'm happy to hear it, for that was entirely intentional. I sought to provoke him. Sir Gabriel is sensitive about his family, and with good reason."

"Why is he so sensitive?" asks Evelyn.

"You know the Courtenays, you told me so yesterday," he says, turning to Evelyn. "What you probably don't know was that Gabriel was heir to the title of Lord Musgrave, the property and family seat and all of the money, from the time of his birth until he was twenty years old. His father, who died when Gabriel was a boy, was the much younger half-brother of old Lord Musgrave. His mother, who died when he was a child, was of such a good family that he inherited his title through that line, but they had no money to give him. No, it would all have to come through his uncle, and he designated Gabriel as the successor and he was groomed and educated as such. Until Gabriel's uncle married a very young woman. While Gabriel was on his grand tour, the new Lady Musgrave gave birth to a son, and he was recalled from Europe. It was not… well handled. Gabriel was given a little money to continue his schooling. But after his uncle died, the widow cut off Gabriel entirely and ordered him off the family estate. He had a noble title, but that was all he had."

Sir Gabriel's home on Grosvenor Square with its peculiar wall of swords, his bitterness and brooding over the past, I begin to understand him. But I don't comprehend how family grievances could lead him to turn traitor to England.

"Is he a Jacobite?" Evelyn asks.

I remember his passionate hatred of Major Tarkwell, enemy of the Jacobites, and I wonder the same thing.

"Perhaps, but I doubt it's his prime motivation as a spy," says Sir Humphrey. "It's to reclaim his heritage, the privileges of his birthright. That is the man's weakness. If Sir Gabriel led a quieter life in London, he might have escaped our speculation. He needs to be in London during the season, to maintain his contacts and gather information, but no one lives off Grosvenor Square without a fortune to draw on. When we became convinced that Louis XV had injected a spy into London society, his name kept coming to the top of the list of candidates, because no one could understand how he lives like an earl without income."

"He's not a military man and there are no battles taking place in England," I point out. "What could Sir Gabriel learn that would damage His Majesty's war effort?"

"A very great deal," Sir Humphrey says with a wince. "It is the peers of the realm who lead the armies, who hold critical positions in government. Their fathers, brothers, sisters, wives, friends — they know what's happening, they receive letters, and all are in London during the season. If a man were to move among them every day and far into the night, a man who was trusted and accepted by all as one of them, he could do the kingdom a tremendous amount of harm should he pass all he hears along to Versailles."

Evelyn says, "So you believe that this man has been spying for Louis XV for years — but it's only recently that Sir Gabriel's aim became stealing the formula for blue?"

"That is correct," he says, in his brisk way, as if he were in a room full of army officers.

I say slowly, "Color is part of my life, my work, but I find it hard to believe that possessing blue would turn the tide of war."

"Because you don't understand the mind and will of a soldier," Sir Humphrey says. "What drives them forward is duty to king and country, but also inspiration that can seem to come from the divine. It's… mystical. Look at our ally, Frederick the Great, quite often outnumbered. His soldiers fight like none have before while singing a song. The power of words, of song and color, it wins battles. At Leuthen the Prussians killed 22,000 Austrian soldiers in three hours, while singing!"

My blood runs cold at his exaltation of such butchery.

He continues. "The French are not winning this war, but neither are we. Not yet. And that makes them more dangerous to us than ever before. We have information that the Duc de Choiseul met with Charles Edward Stuart, the old man still called by the ridiculous name of Bonnie Prince Charlie, in February, to discuss yet another attempt to put him onto the English throne. Stuart would be the puppet king for Louis XV; France would rule England. You must not repeat this, either of you, but the prime minister is gravely concerned about the possibility of a French invasion. Our army and our navy, our resources, are concentrated in America, India, and the Caribbean. We are vulnerable at home. A spy in England could learn of all the weaknesses in our defenses."

Something about the way he phrases matters — "could," "would have," "speculates" — gives me pause.

"You do have some real proof of Sir Gabriel doing these things, of being a traitor to England?" I ask.

Sir Humphrey laughs. "If we had proof, he'd be in sitting prison right now. No, he's very clever; the man is meticulous and cautious. We can't positively link him to any official secrets being learned. But secrets have made their way to Versailles. We caught a spy for France early last year, a pitiful man, a Dr. Hensey, who was paid a paltry sum by the French ministry to pass along intelligence of our naval and army preparations. He knew next to nothing and was easily caught. We believe he was sacrificed, tossed into our path to hide the identity of a far more dangerous person. Sir Gabriel Courtenay best fits the criteria."

Best fits the criteria?

My spirits flip from shame to anger.

"You don't *know* if he's a spy for Louis XV, or that he has passed along military secrets, all that you know is he recruited me to steal the blue formula for money and he says that the client is Sèvres — and that comes from my telling you just now," I say heatedly. "You told me you already knew it was him, just to trick me."

Evelyn jumps in to say, "Once they question Sir Gabriel, and bring pressure to bear, he will admit to it, I'm sure."

Sir Humphrey is silent.

"Aren't you going to question him, Sir Humphrey?" Evelyn asks, tentatively.

"Not yet," he says, straightening his shoulders. "Courtenay is no Dr. Hensey, he has an excellent barrister on retainer and could lodge a defense that would send us in circles for a year. We need to trap him in the act of stealing Thomas Sturbridge's formula and dispatching it to Paris."

Dread growing inside me, I say, "Just how do you plan to do that?"

Sir Humphrey says, "I want you to carry out the mission just as Courtenay instructed you to. When Sturbridge returns, you'll ostensibly spend the night together somewhere — you won't actually have to do anything improper — while Courtenay's men empty the laboratory. We will track them from there."

"Thomas and I are to be bait?" I cry.

He shrugged a yes.

"I don't agree to this," I tell him.

"I'm not offering a proposal for you to consider," says Sir Humphrey. "This is what you will do, exactly as I instruct you."

An hour ago he didn't know of Sir Gabriel's plan. Now he's commandeered it. I find I cannot believe how much he sounds like Sir Gabriel at this moment. In London, he said to me, "You will do this, Genevieve. You will do as I tell you, exactly how I tell you to do it." Now it's someone else using these words.

I don't appear to have any choice — that much is clear. But I can at least be the one to break it to Thomas when he returns from Devon, to share with him the truth at last.

When I tell Sir Humphrey as much, he shakes his head. "It's important that Sturbridge learn of the situation officially. You're not to go near him until I've briefed him."

"I must explain it to him, please, can't you allow me that?" I plead.

"My chief concern is not your romance," says Sir Humphrey, bluntly. "You need to understand your position, Mistress Genevieve. Only by carrying out my orders will you hope to escape arrest. You've been tricked and manipulated, yes, but the fact remains that you agreed to spy here at Derby for a fee. This is a crime."

It takes all of my strength not to collapse before him, begging for mercy.

"I'm very well aware that I face severe penalties," I say. "Constable Campion could arrest me in connection with the murder of Richard Frederick before you arrest me for espionage."

Sir Humphrey dismisses the indefatigable Campion with a wave of his hand. "This is not a matter for him. I represent the Crown. I'll speak to Campion tonight. There is only one man who can bring down Sir Gabriel Courtenay, and that man is me."

It dawns on me that Sir Humphrey has his own obsession.

A worried Evelyn says, "It is your duty, Genevieve, to cooperate. You hate the king of France, you've said so many times."

"Unless you wish to see French soldiers coming onto English shores wearing uniforms dyed the color blue that Sturbridge invented, you'll cooperate," says Sir Humphrey with all force he can muster. "Sir Gabriel Courtenay must be stopped."

"Yes," I say quietly, "he must be stopped."

Looking relieved, Sir Humphrey says that he will come up with a plausible reason to meet at length in the next few days, so that he can interrogate me about Sir Gabriel's plans, his house, and the men who work for him.

"You have been in the company of some formidable criminals," he says. "The backgrounds of these men makes for disturbing reading. A boxer who killed an opponent, and left the sport when new boxing rules were established that prevented him from displaying unbridled savagery. An actor who has repeatedly tricked and defrauded those who trusted him."

That must be Jimmy and Joshua. Chilled, I say, "And you are sure that my grandfather will be safe from repercussion?"

"Oh, yes," he says, with utter confidence. I wish I could share it.

We bring this talk to a close, for we're losing the sun, or as much sun as one can see inside a mildewed mausoleum. Arriving home late could draw attention, and Sir Humphrey said he suspects that the Heath house is under surveillance. I know that it is, but I will wait for this longer briefing to tell him those details.

I wait in the carriage as Evelyn and Sir Humphrey talk together, just the two of them, on the broken Babington drive. Most likely their conversation is not devoted entirely to my misdeeds but to their feelings for each other. I have other things to contemplate.

Once we are back in the carriage, just the two of us, Evelyn says,

"What a terrible nightmare this has been for you. To think that this Courtenay practiced such deceptions, tricking you into doing what he wanted."

"As Sir Humphrey deceived *you* into doing what he wanted — finding his way to me without drawing notice," I say.

Evelyn recoils as her face turns red. "Genevieve! What an offensive comparison. I can't believe you'd equate Sir Humphrey with a man who's a criminal and a traitor."

"I am sorry," I murmur.

But I'm not. Not really. I've been pressured, deceived, insulted, threatened, struck, sneered at, and strong-armed by a long line of men, with Sir Humphrey simply being the latest. Perhaps my flaws in judgment and character have brought this on. Perhaps not. The fact remains that only one man treats me with honest affection and regard. And he's going to hear from someone else of my lies?

I can't allow that to happen. I feel deeply shaken by what I've learned today, and drained, but a cold resolve spreads through my entire body.

That night, while Evelyn is elsewhere, I take all of my wages earned at Derby Porcelain Works and pour the coins into a small purse. I wear the purse in my skirt pocket when I leave for the factory the next morning, next to the tightly folded letter from Thomas.

Halfway through the morning, Evelyn pulls me away from the decorating room to tell me something in private. Her face is tense and fearful.

"Sir Humphrey sent word to me that a messenger arrived from London to report that Sir Gabriel Courtenay has disappeared," she says. "The house on Grosvenor Square is empty; all the servants are gone."

My first response is relief. If Sir Gabriel is gone from London, it makes Grandfather that much safer. But then I think through other implications.

"Does he think Sir Gabriel is bound for Derby?"

"Sir Humphrey believes that his family being known in these parts — he lived at the family estate for years — has kept him away this long. But you are so important to him, he may be willing to risk it."

Just another reason to pursue my own plan of action.

After luncheon, I excuse myself from the decorating room. Downstairs, everyone has a task. No one thinks twice about my crossing the floor. I spot Evelyn in her office, bent over the books, and quicken my pace.

With Major Tarkwell and William Duesbury away, it couldn't be easier to walk off the property. I smile and wave at those I pass as I follow the path past the fiery ovens. Victory in war is all about being inspired, Sir Humphrey says. I'm inspired to convince these people that there's nothing unusual about my walking to Nottingham Road when the sun is high in the sky.

More serious of a problem than porcelain workers are the operatives of Sir Gabriel and the man himself. I keep careful eye as I walk off the manufactory property and across the bridge, into town. I spot no one of concern. And my presence on these streets draws absolutely no notice from the people of Derby. It's a beautiful spring day, and many people are about their business.

I recognize the friendly and efficient man at the George Inn who assists guests. He is happy to take me to the other man, who is in charge of arrangements and schedules with the coaches going in and out of Derby.

I fetch my purse, bulging with every coin I have in the world, and say, "I need to pay for the fastest possible coach to Devon."

CHAPTER TWENTY-NINE

Fremington is a village in the heart of the clay pits of Devon, so it is no surprise that Thomas and the others would find lodgings there. Five days after I walked away from Derby Porcelain Works, I reach this village in the back of a cart. I'd left my coach in Exeter and hired the cart to take me the rest of the way.

It was a grueling trip, of jostling coaches, shared beds crawling with bugs, and burnt or spoiled food. What a luxury that first coach to Derby was, in comparison. Last night, knowing I was closing in on Fremington, I washed my dress in a bucket and left it to dry in the open window, praying in the darkness that my only dress wouldn't be stolen. God answered me, and it hung where I left it at dawn. I cleaned myself with a hard scrap of soap and wished I could do something with my hair.

I have bigger worries than looking like a ragamuffin when I find Thomas. If someone in Derby suspects I've gone west, they could be in pursuit. As soon as the day's work ended at the porcelain factory and I was found missing, the hunt would begin. They might think I've fled to Sir Gabriel; that could win me some time. Unfortunately, Constable Campion is capable of locating the coaching agent at the George Inn. I gave a false name, but he'll remember what I looked like. And then there's Sir Humphrey and all of the resources he can draw on as a man of His Majesty's government. But they cannot get around the fact that there isn't any way that a man from Derby could overtake me, not with a half day's start at least and the speed at which I've moved. But someone could, just possibly, arrive on my heels tomorrow.

I honestly don't care what they do to me. If they wish, they can fight over who gets the honor of arresting me. I've completely wrecked my life; I have no future. All that I care about is seeing Thomas and telling him how sorry I am.

"That's the Inn of the Dove," says the man driving the potato cart, pointing at a two-story whitewashed building next to an orchard, set back from the road.

I pay him, leap out quickly, and find a tree across the road to stand behind. It's a fine old apple tree, but it's months too early to gobble down any fruit. A shame, because the sun is low in the sky and I find I'm hungry.

Holding onto the tree bark, peeking from behind it, I see the three of them trudge up the road: Major Tarkwell, William Duesbury... and Thomas.

"Oh, oh, yes," I say into the scratchy bark, seeing Thomas for the first time in nearly a month. He's dressed like a laborer, his shirt open like the very first time I saw him, but wearing good shoes, his black boots. He's nodding at something Duesbury says, and his skin is a little more golden. He must be outside in the sun, and it's doing him good.

I want to run across the road. But I can imagine the reaction from the other two men at my arrival. I'd not get my chance to speak to Thomas alone. No, I must wait.

Twilight comes, and I watch a woman light the candles in the front room of the inn. Through the window I can see the back of someone's head at a table, but it's not Thomas'. I wish I could see him. I realize with a smile that this is how it began for me, after all: Thomas Sturbridge in the window.

I force myself to wait until night truly falls, when the frogs in the ponds and the birds in the branches begin their serenade. The candles burn inside the inn, but out here it's blacker than black. I can barely see my hands in front of my face.

I slip across the road. The first challenge: what if the door is locked? The second: what if the door is guarded? No respectable inn allows an unmarried woman to go upstairs alone. All someone has to do is make a loud inquiry and Major Tarkwell could hear. For all I know, he is lingering downstairs.

The advantage of a country inn is that no one sees me cross the road and sidle up to its side window. I peek inside — and see a stout, blond woman sitting just inside the door. That settles the frontal approach.

I hurry to the back, checking doors as I go. I find two, also locked. Why did they have to select the Devonshire inn most conscientious about doors? I look up at the second floor. Six windows, three of them with candles lit inside. I've no idea which is Thomas'.

There's only one solution.

Up I go, climbing the wall, gripping a trellis, until I can grab a ledge and hoist myself to the second floor. I can't make my way across the inn, peering inside each window, for there's nothing for my feet to hold onto. Perhaps I should have ascertained that before climbing? I clutch the ledge, my arms aching. Turning to look the other way, I see a shuttered window, flung open. I might just be able to manage it.

Will I be leaping into the room of William Duesbury, instead of Thomas Sturbridge? Or some poor stranger, soon to have a heart spasm?

It turns out to be neither. The room that I climb into is empty, although candles are lit and the bed turned down. I see a dress hanging. Definitely not Thomas'. Perhaps this woman guest is using the privy.

I scramble out of the room and into the narrow hall. No one in sight. I move as quietly as I can, wondering desperately which room is Thomas' until I spot black boots, caked with clay, in the hallway. I'm sure they are his.

I push the door behind the boots open just an inch, and see him sitting alone, at a writing desk, a quill in his hand.

He turns at the creak of the door, I nudge the door open farther, and his lips part in shock at the sight of me.

"Shhhhh!" I rush toward him, holding my finger to my lips, frantic for quiet. "I have to see you. I have to talk to you, Thomas. But no one else can know I am here."

"How is this possible?" he asks. "I haven't received a letter."

"No. You wouldn't, for I didn't send one. I took a series of coaches, I told no one."

I thought he'd be suspicious and confused from the start. Instead, he reaches for me and kisses me, passionately. "I don't care why you came, it's like you're a dream come to life," he murmurs.

My heart leaps as it always does when he touches me. But still, I pull away and say, "You will care, when I tell you."

Stroking my hair, he says, "Then tell me."

I fear I'll fail at this moment. He's touching me, my handsome Thomas, his eyes are full of adoration, how can I speak the words? My mouth is dry as dust. But I must force myself forward.

"Thomas, I wasn't honest with you at first. I came here tonight to be completely honest, and then I will go."

"Go?" For the first time, a worried line etches his forehead. "Where would you go tonight?"

"Truth is, I haven't gotten that far in my planning." I take a deep breath. "I obtained the position at Derby Porcelain Works through my being the cousin of Andrew Planché. He and my grandfather made the arrangements. But before I left, I met a man at a party in London, a party at William Hogarth's house, and he made me an offer. He'd reward me with a large sum of money if I went to Derby on his behalf. Large enough so that I could leave England, in a place where I can never be accepted as a real artist because I'm a woman."

"I know how much it angers you, that you are blocked from furthering your career as an artist," says Thomas. "It is most unfair."

My throat tightens. Why does Thomas have to be so kind? I would much prefer his anger right now.

In a rush, I say, "The man's name is Sir Gabriel Courtenay. He told me to go to Derby to steal the formula for blue. Only if I gave him that, would I receive the reward."

Now, finally, I see the hurt, the beginning of pain, in Thomas. His eyes shift focus, and he pulls back from me.

"Do you have the reward in your possession now?" he asks quietly.

"No, Thomas, no. Once I met you, I knew I couldn't do it, and I tried to stop spying for him, but that was not… acceptable to him. When I received word about my grandfather's having a stroke, it was false. He forged the letter and sent the coach to bring me back to London, to force information out of me. I didn't know until the coach reached the city."

Thomas' eyes widen. "Force you? What sort of a man is this?"

I say slowly, "I suppose he is the worst sort of man there could be, although I didn't see it that way for a long time."

Thomas says, horrified, "Did he hurt you, Genevieve?"

Did Sir Gabriel hurt me? I find I can't answer this question, for suddenly I see him, sitting across from me, his face darkened with stubble, his eyes mournful, saying, "I need you to save me."

I can't save you, Sir Gabriel, for I must save myself.

"No," I choke out. "He didn't hurt me."

Thomas turns away from me, leaning over his writing table with one hand, tapping with the other.

I had planned for this, girded myself for this, yet as I watch Thomas at the point of disillusionment, seconds before he rejects me, it is agony.

Thomas finally says, "I knew there was… something. From the first night in the Dolphin. Something that was driving you toward me beyond care for my well being, besides any sort of affection."

Astonished, I say, "Why did you seek me out then, the next afternoon and after that too?"

"Perhaps I wondered, deep down, if you had come to stop me."

"But that doesn't answer my question — why then did you seek my company?"

His mouth quivers in a half-smile, half-grimace. "Perhaps I want to be stopped."

CHAPTER THIRTY

"No one wants to stop you, Thomas," I say, stunned. "Everyone wants the blue — everyone." I tell him the rest: Sir Humphrey's suspicion about what Sir Gabriel would do with the blue, that he could well be a spy for Louis XV and how obtaining this extraordinary shade could give France a critical advantage. About the plan to rob his laboratory after I'd lured him away.

Thomas begins to pace the small space of his room.

"And after all this, you don't think my work *should* be stopped?" he asks, incredulous. "Look at who has died — my friend Edmund in the Ore Mountains, that poor spy Richard Frederick in Derby — and look who has suffered. My health near ruined and at times my sanity too. I launched this adventure ..." his voice curdles on the word *adventure* "thinking it would be my first step into the scientific brotherhood of chemists. It's been years of little but pain and toil, and I fear I shall never be free of this bloody color."

Thomas points at me. "Think about how much happier your life would be if you had never met this Courtenay and been persuaded to go to Derby."

"Don't say that," I cry.

"Why?"

"If I hadn't come to Derby, I wouldn't have found you."

Thomas leaps to me and I kiss him with a desperation I can't hide, for after tonight I know I won't see Thomas again. His kisses grow more passionate, I press myself against him.

He pulls away and whispers, "Soon I won't be able to stop."

"I don't want to stop," I say. "Please."

Thomas takes off my dress and my petticoat, my stockings, as if he were unwrapping a precious gift. He kisses my shoulders and the hollow in my throat. His fingers tremble on my buttons. I help him unfasten them. My dress is gone, and my petticoat. I stand before him in nothing but my shift.

Thomas begins to tear at the buttons of his shirt. "Let me," I say. I take off his shirt as if I were the one unwrapping a present I'd hoped for and dreamed for. I bury my face in his chest, kissing the silken knots of hair. He tastes like sweat and sun.

I take a step back and pull my shift off, over my head, and toss it on the floor.

Thomas blows out the candle and leads me to his bed and we lie on our sides, facing each other. His fingers move all over me, exploring. "Genevieve," he moans, again and again, until he can't speak any more. We move together, finding a harmony.

When, with a cry, I collapse onto Thomas, my head buried in his chest, I tell him what I've known for a long time. "I love you."

"I love you, Genevieve."

"We have tonight," I say after I've gained my breath. "In the morning I will tell William Duesbury everything. It's possible that Sir Humphrey or Constable Campion are in pursuit. We just need to wait for events to catch up to us. I'll go quietly."

"No." Thomas kisses my shoulder. "An hour before dawn, we will both go."

I shake my head in the darkness. "Where? How?"

"Genevieve, I can't possibly cooperate in any plan that brings about your arrest."

"But Thomas, you can't disappear. You absolutely must continue this work you've pursued. Once they've removed Sir Gabriel Courtenay from this game board, you'll be safe. The Derby blue will make your name. Everyone will know you're a genius."

He groans. "I'm no genius."

"No?"

"Definitely not."

"When I first heard your name, I was told some people considered you the next Sir Isaac Newton."

"Oh, I've already proven I'm no Newton."

"How?"

"Isaac Newton died a virgin."

We laugh, holding each other tight.

"There's a fishing village I saw when I was a boy, on the coast of Devon," Thomas says when our laughter is spent. "It's called Clovelly. I want to take you there. I love the coastline."

Stroking his long hair, I say tenderly, "This is your plan? With all of England, including the prime minister's man, searching for us, we go fishing?"

"Genevieve, there is only one thing I am sure of in this world and that is — I love you. So yes, why not? I have enough money with me to get us started. It would be a terrific place for you to paint. I can write, read. Once all this business with the blue has died down, I can teach."

Remembering the almshouse, I say, "You are a wonderful teacher."

Thomas asks me if I have ever seen the sea.

"When I was small. My mother took me to Brighton, just the two of us. I remember those waves, those incredible blue waves." I take a deep breath. "She died the following year."

Thomas props himself up on one arm. "That must have been very frightening," he say. "And sad."

"I would say that, most of all, I was angry for a very, very, very long time."

"Until when?" he asks.

I pull his mouth to mine before saying, "Until tonight."

Thomas kisses me deeply. I take his face in my hands... and freeze when I hear a floorboard creak on the other end of the room.

"Stop," I whisper.

"What?" he breathes.

We hold each other, tight, listening together.

"I do hate to intrude, but I'm afraid we're all going to have to leave," says the voice of Sir Gabriel Courtenay.

"What the devil?" says Thomas.

"No!" I cry.

The flare of a match reveals Sir Gabriel and Jimmy standing in the room. Jimmy holds the candle, and Sir Gabriel holds a pistol, pointed at us.

"Lower your voice, Genevieve," Sir Gabriel says. "And Mr. Sturbridge, I'd advise calm. I know this is not a comfortable situation."

Staring into the muzzle of the pistol, Thomas says, "We're not going anywhere with *you*."

"No?" Sir Gabriel takes a few more steps toward us, the pistol still aimed; Jimmy sets down the candle and remains by the door.

"You are Courtenay, correct?" says Thomas. "Genevieve has told me everything."

"Has she indeed?" he asks with a slight smile.

Rage singes every inch of me.

"You followed me here," I say.

"Of course. The minute you bought the ticket at the Derby inn, we knew where you were going," Sir Gabriel says, smoothly. "And we already had the name of the inn Mr. Sturbridge stayed in. It was just a matter of all parties converging, so to speak. I believe Sir Humphrey Willoughby will be here by tomorrow afternoon, but we'll be long gone by then."

Thomas says, "*You* will be gone. Not us. I know what you want from me and I will give it to you, the exact formula. After which Genevieve and I will leave, the two of us together, but not to return to Derby or to seek out legal authority. You won't have to worry about either of us. But do put down your gun. I abhor violence and there's absolutely no need for it here."

I seize Thomas' hand, feeling dismay and fear but, most of all, intense pride.

Sir Gabriel says, "I appreciate the sentiment, but that's just what it is. Sentiment. You two are coming with me now."

Thomas says, "It's out of the question."

Sir Gabriel moves much more quickly, reaching the bed and aiming his pistol directly at my head. "You'll come with me, Mr. Sturbridge, or I will shoot her."

Thomas snaps, "And that would end my motive to comply."

Sir Gabriel smiles. "It's nice to discover that some reputations are built on reality. You're an intelligent man. But are you reckless, as reckless as our mutual friend, Genevieve Planché? Do you want to test my will and see her brains splattered all over the bed? It's true, I'd have little reason to keep you alive after that if you refused to come with me. That was always an option, you realize. If we kill you, then England doesn't have its Derby blue."

"But France won't have it either," I say, the words tumbling out. "He won't shoot you, Thomas. He wants the blue too badly, and he can't be sure of it without you. The blue owns him. It rules him."

"Quiet, Genevieve," says Sir Gabriel.

"He won't shoot me, because then he doesn't have you," I say, staring at the long pistol muzzle, inches away.

"Shut up," says Sir Gabriel. His imperturbable mask slips and he speaks with more ferocity than I've heard before.

"No," I throw at him. "You can't trick me any longer."

Thomas says, "Genevieve, we must —"

"Shhhh," Jimmy hisses. "Outside."

A few seconds later, "Hello, Mr. Sturbridge, is all well in there?" says the voice of Major Tarkwell, from the other side of the door.

Sir Gabriel grabs me by the shoulder, and jams the barrel of the pistol against my skull. He mouths to Thomas: "Get rid of him."

Swallowing, looking at me, Thomas says, loudly, "Yes, Major, I'm perfectly all right."

Silence on the other side of the door and, holding my breath, I wait for Tarkwell to retreat. That door isn't locked, unless Sir Gabriel somehow locked it behind him.

The doorknob turns. Jimmy shoots a quick look at Sir Gabriel, who nods.

Before Major Tarkwell is all the way into the room, Jimmy has torn open the door and pulled him inside. Major Tarkwell grunts with surprise at the ambush, and his eyes bulge as a sickening slicing noise fills the room.

Frozen with horror, I watch Jimmy yank his long knife out of the stomach of Major Tarkwell. The major stumbles and begins to go down, but with a jerky spasm, he pulls the knife out and turns to slash Jimmy's throat with a last wild flail.

Only then does Major Tarkwell collapse to the floor, his wooden leg crashing. Jimmy staggers and falls onto the foot of Thomas' bed. The blood spurts from a deep crevice, pouring down his neck and chest. He reaches out a hand to Sir Gabriel, but cannot say a word. A hissing gurgle is the only sound. Thomas and I can only clutch each other and watch this horror, frozen like statues.

Sir Gabriel is the first one to speak. Turning to us, he says, "Get dressed."

Thomas and I do not move.

"*Get dressed now*," he says, his voice terrible.

I glance at Thomas, and he nods. We put on our clothes as the two wounded men die on the floor, gasping and gurgling. I wait for William Duesbury to charge into the room, or for those below us to appear in the doorway, for surely the noise was loud enough to raise alarm. But there's no one.

Once we're dressed, Sir Gabriel tosses us a burlap sack and orders Thomas to stuff his papers inside.

"You are leaving, Mr. Sturbridge," he says. "Be assured I will shoot Genevieve if you do not comply."

I grab Thomas, ready to defy Sir Gabriel once more, but he says, "No, Genevieve. We must cooperate. I won't risk your life."

A moment later, the three of us are hurrying out to the hall and down the stairs, the pistol against my head the entire time. There's no sign of Duesbury. I can't figure out how Sir Gabriel and Jimmy were able to come into the inn late at night, until, next to the door, I see the blond woman, a blindfold around her eyes, tied to her chair by the door.

Outside, Joshua and the two others wait with a large carriage, and we're bundled into it, with Sir Gabriel. Thomas says nothing; I believe he is still struggling to come to terms with the murders. As am I, who caused their deaths. It was my arguing with Sir Gabriel that must have brought Tarkwell to the room. He was a frightening man — they both were — but their deaths leave me sickened.

The carriage sets out. Sir Gabriel has pulled in Thomas to sit next to him, with me opposite. I can't make out the expression on either of their faces in the darkness, but in the faint moonlight streaming through the window, I see the gleam of the pistol on Sir Gabriel's lap.

"Where are we going?" asks Thomas, speaking for the first time since we left the inn.

"Out of England," Sir Gabriel replies. "Thanks to Sir Humphrey, there's no longer any choice."

My heart stops.

"What do you mean, out of England?" I say. "Where are you taking us?"

"To Sèvres."

"No, no, you can't," I cry.

"Oh, I can, Genevieve. And I will. You're going to France."

CHAPTER THIRTY-ONE

I burst into a protest of fury and panic in Sir Gabriel's carriage. Nothing he says can still me. In fact, I even, in hysteria, beg him to shoot me rather than send me into France.

"Genevieve, you must compose yourself," says Sir Gabriel.

"Compose myself? After being made party to spying and treachery, and then to witness murder? Now we are kidnapped? To France. France!"

"Say no more, Genevieve, not tonight." Thomas speaks for the first time. "It will achieve nothing."

"Thank you, Mr. Sturbridge," says Sir Gabriel.

With that, I am quiet, though I have to clamp my hand over my mouth to achieve it, my hand continuing to shake. I'll say no more if Thomas asks that of me. I cannot see his expression in the dark carriage but in his voice I hear great strain.

We ride in silence for a long time. I cannot make out either of their faces; they are but darker outlines against the back of the carriage. Only thing visible is the gleam of the pistol.

In this dark and wretched wordlessness, listening to the wheels creaking and the horse hooves pounding, I think of the kingdom that has meant exile and fear for me since I was old enough to speak, to listen. France. They want Thomas for his skill, one they cannot match at Sèvres, and I am going only as a means to force him to work. But what happens when the French realize I am Huguenot?

A weariness comes over me, draining my bones of strength. I hear a steady, deep breathing from the left corner and realize Thomas has fallen asleep. I am not far behind. There is no noise or movement from the right corner. It is possible Sir Gabriel dozes.

At that instant an idea explodes in my head, and all fatigue vanishes. Killing Sir Gabriel Courtenay.

His death will deliver us. It is a terrible solution, I shall be a breaker of commandments, beyond God's grace, it's true. Yes, God may condemn me, but will any legal court in England? If I am the one who kills Sir Gabriel, Thomas cannot be blamed for anything, and I don't expect to be condemned too harshly. I killed a spy, a traitor. And even if I were to suffer arrest, it doesn't perturb me. Thomas must be saved; he is the one who matters.

I will seize Sir Gabriel's gun as he sleeps, when his grip of the weapon is loose. He sits but a few feet from me; he'd die quickly.

I've come such a sorry distance in the last five months. On that snowy London night, I was horrified that Denis Arsenault might hurt a night watchman. In Derby I was tormented with guilt over someone being hurt by my spying. Yet here I am, coldly plotting murder, the breaking of a sacred commandment. It is Sir Gabriel who drives me to this, I think, and it is he who shall pay. I feel nothing but hatred for him.

As I turn the idea over, an obstacle occurs. I don't in fact know how to shoot a pistol. I have seen them brandished but not fired, and my impression is that it's a bit difficult. How will I manage in a dark, swaying carriage? The only way this can succeed is if I'm quick.

Another obstacle occurs to me: Is there not a chance of hitting

Thomas in error? That gives me serious pause, leading to the forming of a fresh plan. I will seize the pistol and threaten to shoot Sir Gabriel, giving every assurance that I am capable of it. I can hold the pistol and point it at his head, surely. Once I have the upper hand, I can order Sir Gabriel to direct the carriage, come dawn, to a place well occupied by people. Thomas and I will, before witnesses, get out of the carriage, hurry away, and then report Sir Gabriel to the authorities.

Now all that remains is to ascertain whether Sir Gabriel is safely sleeping before I lunge for the pistol. I wait, and listen for some change in his breathing, a telltale sign.

He's utterly still and silent, like a phantom.

How could any man be awake and not move a muscle for so long? He must be asleep. I'm tempted to rush him, but a scrap of uncertainty holds me back.

There is a faint lightening, meaning the first rays of dawn are coming. As I sit in the rumbling carriage, the darkness continues to retreat and before not very much longer I can make out Sir Gabriel's face.

Those eyes, somber with an edge of cynicism, bore into mine. He did not sleep a second. Frustration claws; will I ever get a chance to overtake him, to get the better of him?

The faintest smile deepens at the corners of Sir Gabriel's mouth, as if he knows what I am thinking.

Not too many more minutes and the carriage jerks to a halt. Thomas wakes, blinking rapidly in confusion as he looks at me and Sir Gabriel. I open my mouth to speak to him but close it a second later. How can I wish Thomas a good morning?

We are taken out of the carriage in the light of morning. Joshua takes charge of Thomas while Sir Gabriel escorts me down a short, narrow lane, his pistol still in hand. We are in the shadow of taller buildings;

I hear hooves clopping on brick to the right and behind us, too. This is a city of some size.

We walk to a small cottage at the end of the lane, a pungent smell in the air. It is not the odor of London: coal and rotted food and unwashed men. This is unfamiliar.

Tightening his grip on my arm, Sir Gabriel says, "You hoped to shoot me in the carriage, didn't you, Genevieve?"

My heart skips a beat. *How am I ever to get the better of him?* I wonder. Aloud, I say, "Yes, I did."

I expect him to be angry, to punish me.

"Good." I swear I detect a note of pride in his voice. It makes me so angry that I wish I had shot him, and he'd died slowly.

Inside the cottage, Thomas and I are given bread and meats to eat and cider to drink. Although I would like to throw the meal onto the floor, I'm truly lightheaded with hunger and can't help but devour it. I'm glad that Thomas eats too, for he's pale. While he is the one who slept for a few hours in the carriage, Sir Gabriel has the advantage over him in vigor today, I am sorry to see.

Looking around us, I take note that the cottage is skimpily furnished, the curtains tightly drawn. It must be a place that Sir Gabriel leases as part of his enterprise of spying. Sir Gabriel and his men swarm all around us, bringing in boxes and long crates, busying them for something. I wonder fleetingly if the men all know of Jimmy's death and if his loss troubles them. It doesn't appear to.

Thomas leans over and whispers, "I believe we're in Portsmouth."

"How do you know?"

"We're definitely close to the sea, I can smell it. Judging by the distance we traveled from the inn at Devon to reach here, I calculate that he will…"

Thomas breaks off. Sir Gabriel looms over us. If only he'd given us another few moments. I'm desperate to hear more from Thomas, who hasn't been silently raging against me, as I feared, but using the time to analyze our situation.

"Pardon me," says Sir Gabriel. He's no longer armed with his pistol, but of course with so many of his operatives present, it's unnecessary. "I trust the breakfast was adequate."

Thomas straightens on his shabby stool, and says, formally, "Sir, the time has come for me to discuss certain matters with you."

"Mr. Sturbridge, we do indeed have much to discuss," responds Sir Gabriel with an amiable nod. "However, now is not the most opportune time."

He turns, beckoning to his men, and they advance toward us, ropes and handkerchiefs in their hands, their faces grimly set.

I leap to my feet, as does Thomas. He puts his arm around me. "I protest this action," Thomas says as I push back the rough hands that seize me, tearing me away from Thomas.

Joshua, the one I hate the most, ties a cloth around my mouth so I cannot say anything intelligible. He then drags me to the wall of boxes, Thomas behind us, also gagged. Two crates sit side by side, opened, half filled with straw.

Sir Gabriel says, "You two will need to be smuggled aboard our ship, but I present you with a choice. Step into a crate and allow us to make you as comfortable as possible. Or you'll be put into your crate the other way; not so comfortable."

Looking down at this long crate, I recoil. It looks like a coffin.

"No, I can't," I cry, but it sounds like a gibberish bleat through the gag.

Thomas, waving frantically, manages to persuade them to remove the gag. Once off, he speaks to me, only to me. "Genevieve, we have to cooperate — it will avail us nothing to resist and I don't want you to be hurt."

"Very sensible, Mr. Sturbridge," says Sir Gabriel.

I shake my head no at Thomas, at all of them.

"We don't have time for this," Joshua says to Sir Gabriel, who frowns but says nothing.

Thomas keeps trying. "Genevieve, will it help you if you see me get in first? That way, you can know that you will be alright."

He looks down at his crate, takes a breath, and steps in. Lowering himself to sit, he says, "You see? There is no ill consequence."

One of the men re-ties the handkerchief around Thomas' mouth. Another kneels at the foot of the crate, to tie his feet together.

Sir Gabriel turns to me and says, "Genevieve, if you please?"

I take a step toward my own crate, and then another. When I reach it, looking down, I have a flash to the worst day of my life. I am eight years old, at the graveyard, my Grandfather's hand on my shoulder, as we watch them lower the long wooden box carrying the body of my mother into the ground.

I whip around, and run for the cottage door, not with any sort of plan but in a raging panic. I do not control my arms and legs, the panic does. I must escape. They are upon me six feet short of the door and pull me down. If I could scream, I could raise the alarm, for there are other houses close by. But of course they'd gagged me ahead of this — now I know why.

I'm on the floor, on my back, with these men holding me down. An even stronger panic seizes me.

"So regrettable," sighs Sir Gabriel Courtenay, standing behind them. "To business, gentlemen."

They tie my feet together, tight, and then turn to my hands, binding my wrists in a thick knot before me. Lifting me like a plank, they carry me back to the crate. Someone jokes about how light I am, wishing all his burdens were no greater than this.

"Do not be fooled by her slightness," says Sir Gabriel. "She's not fragile."

I lose control again as they begin to lower me. I can't see the crate carrying Thomas any longer. I am alone, and completely at their mercy. I twist and turn, bucking and shouting into my gag. But my struggles do not impede their effort. I am thrust into my crate, straw scratching my arms and legs and face. I beat my bound limbs against wood.

"She could crack it, Sir," says a voice.

"You shall be still and silent, Genevieve," says Sir Gabriel, from above and behind me, unseen. "There are several ways to render you senseless if you do not, and each of them carries risk of, shall we say, *lasting damage*. I'd rather not proceed unless you give me no choice."

I cease my most violent thrashing, more from exhaustion than obedience. But I cannot be still — it's impossible. I rock back and forth as tears slide down my cheeks.

"Withdraw, gentlemen," I hear Sir Gabriel say, as if it were a parlor on the West End. This strikes me as so blackly ludicrous that laughter mingles with my tears.

The men's faces disappear as a scraping sound grows louder.

Sir Gabriel sits in the chair that's been dragged over for him. His face looms over me, somber, and he says, "Genevieve. I've admired your spirit, and still do. But there are limits. What am I to do here? Reason and sense, which Mr. Sturbridge responds to, thank God, are just not effective with you."

I stop laughing. I don't like his bringing up Thomas' name.

His eyes flicker as he seems to perceive my response. "Allow me to explain your situation, in case you haven't surmised it. If you make any noise during the transport, if you seek to escape, I'll have to hurt you. And if it appears that we are soon to be discovered, no matter whether you are the cause of it or not, I won't have any choice but to have you and Mr. Sturbridge killed. Immediately. Do you understand? Both of you."

I do not doubt for an instant that he is serious.

"Nod if you understand me."

I swallow, painfully, through the gag... and I nod.

Sir Gabriel rises and beckons to his men. Minutes later, my confinement becomes even more terrifying. A long, dark wooden lid hovers above me — and then descends. They fit the lid onto the crate, hammering it shut with fierce, crashing blows on nails. The lid is so close to me that I cannot bend my elbows and reach up to my mouth.

The lid is not solid; slats provide some air and a little light. Regardless, I am now trapped, and if I move or utter a sound, they will do worse.

It is as if Sir Gabriel reached into my soul and found my most terrible nightmare of childhood and made it real.

I am buried alive.

CHAPTER THIRTY-TWO

I fight to breathe in this dark box, the kerchief choking me. The difficulty feeds the panic. I have such a desire to lash out, to flail. Because I am bound, I cannot bang on the lid with my hands or kick with my feet. This must be why they tied me up. I realize it would be fruitless, resulting only in worse pain, to struggle. But the urge to do so is nearly overpowering me.

I assume Thomas is not similarly tied by hands and feet, since he showed himself calm. I worry about his breathing in a closed box of straw, gagged. Sir Gabriel does not know anything about the particulars of his health, of the damage done to Thomas' lungs in Germany.

The men's voices grow louder, along with a rise in banging noises. They all seem hurried, and I wonder if it's because they fear pursuit. By now, the dead bodies of Jimmy and Major Tarkwell had to have been discovered, as well as Thomas' disappearance, and my being at large. William Duesbury must be distraught. He would not know what to do next, but, should Sir Humphrey Willoughby have tracked me to Devon, to the inn, he could suspect that our next destination would be out of England.

My heart lurches when they lift the crate I'm trapped inside.

Peering through the slats, I can tell that the sun holds in the sky. Long slivers of yellow reach inside the crate. They load me onto a flat surface. I've no idea what surrounds me, but Thomas must be close by; I hope he is none the worse for his entrapment.

The wagon begins to move. Streets are bumpy in Portsmouth, if Portsmouth this is, but the pain is dulled by my bed of straw. I can make out the outlines of a few taller buildings as we rumble down the streets, and I hear the cries and laughter of men surrounding us. Other horses clatter by; street peddlers shout; bells ring. It is the smell that comes through strongest: that same sharp odor I noticed before, which must be that of the sea. It's tinged with rotting fish, or something very like.

Our wagon comes to a halt. Nothing happens as the minutes crawl by. Men converse a short distance away, but I can't make out the words or identify the speakers.

What if by a miracle Sir Humphrey Willoughby or some other agent of His Majesty's government were to discover Sir Gabriel here, in Portsmouth, planning to set sail? Would they insist on inspecting his cargo and discover us? I am torn between hoping for rescue and fearing it. Would Sir Gabriel have us killed, here, in these crates as the authorities closed in? I feel a growing skepticism, but I wouldn't dare any escape attempt, not with Thomas' life in danger.

I hear a new sound, one that I find strangely comforting: seagulls screeching overheard. I haven't heard gulls since I left London. Between the warmth of the sunlight bleeding through the slats and the birds' mournful cries, a heaviness descends. I wouldn't have thought it possible, fearful, tied and bound, itching from the straw, but... I fall asleep, into a deep, fathomless dream.

*

The next thing I'm aware of is my name being called, over and over.

"Genevieve, are you alright? Make a sound, something. Please!"

It's Thomas' voice. I try to answer, to move toward him, but I'm immediately thwarted by my gag and ropes.

"I hear her," cries Thomas. "Enough of the harsh measures. Damn it, man, open this crate, or there will be hell to pay."

There's a ripping sound as the lid of my crate is removed. The warmth and light of the docks are gone; I'm in a dark, dank place. Joshua cuts loose my binds with a short knife and removes the gag. My mouth and jaw ache, as do my arms and legs. With that, Joshua's gone.

"Genevieve, by God, are you hurt?"

I shake my head as Thomas pulls me to my feet. We two are being held in a small corner of a low-ceilinged room, lit by a lantern affixed; a wall of boxes seal us off except for the narrow opening Joshua used to slink out of. Once Thomas helps me step out of my crate and onto the floor, my limbs aching, I feel something worse — truly terrifying: the floor moves. The very room tilts.

"What's happening?" I say, my voice as hoarse as a frog's.

"It's the boat — we're below deck, Genevieve."

At that I break down, sobbing. We were not rescued; we may now be beyond rescue, inside a boat controlled by Sir Gabriel, sailing in the Channel, bound for France. Thomas expresses no fear over our dire situation, only a desire to comfort, his lean arms wrapped around me. That almost makes it worse.

"I am so sorry," I gasp into his shirt. "So sorry."

"There's no point in regret or recriminations," says Thomas. "We must put our minds to coping with what comes, with developing a strategy."

Thomas, through his eavesdropping and own power of observation, believes we are in a boat posing as one conveying supplies to a high officer of the English fleet. We two will be kept out of sight, that much he was told by Joshua already. Our journey will not be direct but follow a course charted by the captain, a man Sir Gabriel has clearly done business with before. Our destination is the Port of Le Havre, but before that the goal is to reach French waters for escort. Should we be boarded by someone of our country first, and the below-deck searched by the suspicious, we could be rescued — or we could be killed before discovery.

"I do not wish to distress you," I say, "but we are hardly out of danger in France. I don't foresee long lives for either of us after we reach Sèvres and you have created Derby blue for them. Once you've served your purpose, they don't need you anymore. We'd be a liability."

Thomas shows no alarm at that; he must have concluded as much himself.

I say, "We shall put our minds to planning our escape should we reach French soil alive."

Thomas slowly, deliberately, takes my hands in his and squeezes. "Genevieve, I need you to listen to me. You must not attempt escape. Nor should you provoke Sir Gabriel or our captors in any way."

"What?"

"We have no money, not a shilling, no travel papers, and while I can speak French, I fear I possess a strong English accent," he says. "Escape from Sir Gabriel has a remote chance of success. But how are we to get out of France afterward? It is impossible."

I cannot believe what I'm hearing. "You intend to join their effort *willingly* at Sèvres, to cooperate with England's enemy?"

"Genevieve, my loyalty is to my country, you must know that. But I'm not meant to serve in a military capacity. I'm being pressured to work as a chemist — with other chemists. I expect I will meet Monsieur

Jean Hellot, one of the greatest scientists in all of Europe. These are not killers or men of war or perpetrators of espionage. I will deliver us from this crisis by forging a connection built on science."

I do not know whether to embrace Thomas or shake him.

I say, "These men you will work with at Sèvres may well be scientists, but more than that, they are French. They will hate us for being English — and for me they will harbor a special hatred for being Huguenot."

"You say that because you don't understand what it is to be a scientist, the brotherhood it forges," he says.

I take a deep breath. "I know, Thomas, that you admire the advances made in France, you've told me of their chemists and engineers and doctors. But an admirable intellect does not correspond to an increase in courage, and they would need courage, tremendous courage, to defy the wishes of their king. I know that precious few Catholics in France ever tried to defend a Huguenot."

"Religious hatred is not a privilege held by the Catholic," Thomas says. "Think how unfairly the Protestants have treated their Catholic neighbors in England. Or look at Ireland."

A cold dismay throttles me. "Thomas, Thomas! It is not the same."

Our debate grows more heated and we seem headed for a full-fledged quarrel, when nothing less than the Channel itself intrudes. The boat's steady swaying turns to a forceful rocking. "A storm must be rising," says Thomas. No one comes to tell us anything, but I can hear men shouting to one another above deck, and feet running.

"Do storms sink boats like this in the Channel?" I ask.

"I have no idea."

Amid fears of drowning, I begin to sicken. I've not felt well in the belly since I woke, and now the nausea overwhelms as I sit on a stool on the floor of the boat, helpless, eyes closed. I fight off the act, but after a time I've no choice. I vomit into a bucket.

"For the Huguenot slaves, it would always be like this," I groan afterward to Thomas, as he strokes my back. I am grateful for his solicitousness, though embarrassed he continues to sees me at my worst.

"Slaves?" Thomas repeats.

I fight my way through the nausea to tell Thomas that when French police captured Huguenot men who refused to convert, they were imprisoned or sent to the West Indies as indentured servants, or condemned to serve as galley slaves, rowing below deck. I tell him of the prison for Huguenot women that Daphne escaped from, which left its longtime inmates blind and crippled.

"I won't let them put you in prison," says Thomas, thrusting out his chin.

"How can I make you see that you won't be able to stop them?"

Before we can pick up the debate, my sickness worsens, and I spend hours in wretchedness. Finally the boat ceases its most violent rocking. The storm seems to subside, and with it I return not to health — I feel too dizzy and exhausted for that — but a stable stomach at least.

I lie with my head in Thomas' lap, as he strokes my hair with incredible gentleness.

"That feels nice," I murmur.

"I used to dream about going on a journey with you, just the two of us," he says with a little laugh. "Perhaps we can pretend that's what is happening?"

I reach for his hand and kiss it. But too much has occurred for me to join him in this sort of fantasy. And, a bit later, peering at his troubled face in the dim light, I suspect that he, too, is full of fear and dread.

"What are you thinking about?" I ask.

"Of the porcelain factory, of its owners — my employers — and all its workers. What is going through their minds. They are doubtless wondering if we are dead, or being held against our will. But also I'm sure they're thinking about my formula, how all the precautions and the expense and the effort came to this. I made provision for this — I've left them a formula for a blue that they can use without need of me, a simpler formula. It will be very attractive but…"

His voice trails away and I finish: "… it won't be wondrous."

Thomas shakes his head and sighs.

I say, "When I think of Ambrose and Harry being told the truth about me, that I was a spy, it's quite… unbearable."

"Were you fond of them, and of your work there? I thought not, after you told me how much it distressed you that being a true artist was forbidden because of your sex."

After a moment, I say, "I loathed the thought of being a porcelain decorator, but when I came to Derby, it wasn't quite what I thought — in many ways. The others who painted porcelain, they were artists. And to earn their respect, I discovered it meant something."

"Tell me."

Haltingly at first, and then with more enthusiasm, I tell Thomas of the work we did in that artists' workshop, of the standards reached in our painting, and of how it felt to be respected by Ambrose after weeks spent there. When I reach the point of telling him of my idea of painting the insects, I find I've grown quite tired and we both fall asleep.

When I wake, the boat no longer rocks a bit, and I'm better, but I take no comfort in it, for this, the second day, is when Thomas weakens.

The coughing fits come, ones that leave him short of breath, sweating and trembling. Joshua appears with food and drink for us. Or some semblance of it. I hold a biscuit hard as a rock. There's nothing that could be of less appeal to me, but for Thomas' sake I nibble the biscuit, made of nothing but flour and salt, and turn to him, coaxing him to eat. The nourishment doesn't give him strength, though. I try to conceal how much this frightens me.

When Joshua returns in the afternoon, his gaze lingers on Thomas, slumped on his pallet.

"Are you not well?" he demands.

"A bit of seasickness, nothing more," Thomas answers, sitting up, forcing vigor into his reply.

Once Joshua retreats, Thomas stretches out on his pallet again.

"Why did you lie?" I ask.

"There's nothing that *he* can do," he murmurs. With the emphasis on that single word, I know it refers to Sir Gabriel. And that despite all his reasonable talk of science, Thomas hates him.

Joshua has left us water and I dampen a cloth with it, cooling Thomas' forehead. After a time, he falls asleep. While I am glad of it, the sound of his heavy, labored breathing, propped on his side, fills me with distress.

Our conditions below, the stale, fetid air, must be worsening his health. When Joshua next appears and sees Thomas unconscious, he stares at me, his face a question. I hate that Joshua views me as a compatriot of any kind. But I must put aside my distaste.

"Please ask Sir Gabriel if I may come up to speak with him," I say.

One eyebrow shoots up. Joshua appears to think it unlikely my wish will be granted.

He backs away, only to reappear two minutes later.

"You're to follow me, at once," Joshua says.

CHAPTER THIRTY-THREE

I follow Joshua through the warren of boxes and crates, to the narrow stairs leading up into blackness. I did not realize. There is no day or night in our below-deck corner, only the filthy lantern.

When I reach the top of the stairs, I pause, and it's not for lack of strength. Above me stretches a tapestry of shimmering stars on velvet. I rarely saw stars at night in London for the coal smoke, and was kept indoors most nights in Derby. The intoxicating sight of all these quivering stars—their elaborate and magical assembling — leaves me reeling.

"What may I do for you, Genevieve?"

On the side of the boat and toward the bow, next to a fluttering sail, stands Sir Gabriel, in ordinary seaman's clothes: long trousers and a tight shirt open at his throat. With an arm flung back on the rail, he looks like a boy. I'd not have known him, but for his voice.

And that voice is nothing but courteous so far. I've requested an audience and he grants it, as a gentleman would a lady — that is the tone taken. How I loathe Sir Gabriel's flawless manners. His air of perfect breeding deceives us all, like a thick crust of sugar encasing an apple that is brown and soft with rot.

"It is not for myself I've come — it's Thomas," I say. "He's unwell."

"Tell me," he says, walking toward me, the wind lifting his long black hair off his shoulders.

"He needs to breathe the air above, *this* air." I spread my arms into the bracing breeze, which is definitely restorative for me.

"But what precisely is the matter with him? It's not seasickness." Sir Gabriel comes closer to me. "You were sick during the storm, and he sickened after the storm passed."

"Isn't it enough that I'm telling you he needs the air?" I would not betray Thomas' confidence.

"No, it's not. I must understand this. Why forestall me? You care about the health of your lover, I care about the health of the prize for the King. Our reason for said interest diverges, but that does not make it any less urgent."

I can feel my cheeks redden at the word *lover*. I am insulted by its use, yet he is not untruthful. We have bedded, as Sir Gabriel knows all too well.

"Is Mr. Sturbridge consumptive?" presses Sir Gabriel.

"No," I say. Only then do I explain, reluctantly, what happened to Thomas, the explosion in the mines that damaged his lungs, the need for him to be sent to a clinic late last year.

Sir Gabriel takes it all in without comment. I'm about to demand a response when I spot a light shooting across the heavens, and my head turns to follow it.

"It's remarkable, the sea at night," says Sir Gabriel.

I agree, though I refuse to say so. I still resist sharing a moment of appreciation with him. This is a man I hoped to kill two days ago, a man who had me bound and gagged one day ago.

"I had the opportunity to join the Royal Navy," says Sir Gabriel. "A family friend would have made the connection for me. I was nineteen."

Because of Sir Humphrey, I know what happened when he was that age. He also told me of Sir Gabriel being orphaned when young, as I was. But I won't allow myself to feel sympathy for him now.

"Most successful officers begin their service aboard ship at twelve or thirteen," he continues. "I did not think I could properly advance, starting so late."

"So you decided to advance through treachery on behalf of France, instead."

"Correct," he says, and smiles, the moonlight gleaming on his even white teeth. "You once quoted me a line from *The Duchess of Malfi*, Genevieve, but not the one that follows: 'Why, a very quaint invisible devil in flesh, an intelligencer' is followed by 'Such a kind of thriving thing I would wish thee; and ere long thou may arrive at a higher place by it.'"

"You think you've reached a higher place?" I ask, incredulous. "By that you mean Le Secret du Roi?"

He runs his hand along the side of the ship. "Ah. So Sir Humphrey used that phrase with you?"

I nod.

He is silent for a time. "There is a certain irony to this; I've been pondering. King Louis changed the rules when he created his own service. Up to then, his intelligence was gathered by a vast department of letter openers, the cabinet noir, similar to how it works in England. The postal department is open to the prime minister's men, and any letter of diplomacy containing a cipher is sent to the Bishop Willes and his idiot sons to decode. Then there are the spies of the field, men of humble birth stealing a tidbit of information, here and there, to sell for a quick fee. Louis' secret service is something else entirely, made up of men answerable only to him, changing the destinies of countries, who decide the outcome of war. For years the English had no idea of us, they were still obsessed with Jacobite sympathizers, trying to eavesdrop in coffeehouses or infiltrate the Hellfire Club. A gaggle of fat, old degenerate drunks, plotting their orgies in a cave. Do you think King Louis XV in need of support from such a quarter?"

Sir Gabriel laughs, hard and contemptuous.

"Time and again, William Pitt and his men failed to grasp the larger picture," he says. "Only in the last year have the English government enlisted anyone of real ability to oppose Louis' designs — and created their own secret service to track us down."

How proud he is of his crimes. He's a different man entirely to the one who came to me, disheveled, in his London house, and pleaded with me to save him.

"Sir Humphrey has uncovered you," I point out, with satisfaction.

"Yes, he proved quite adept at exploiting my weakness."

"Weakness — you?" I say mockingly. "Surely not."

He says nothing, and in the moonlit darkness I can't read his expression. I feel uneasy, as if I am hovering at the brink of some frightening truth, and to break the silence, I say, "You've got Thomas but at a very high price. You can't go back to England."

"Can't I?" The wind gusts and sends his black hair whipping across his face, and he pulls it back.

"Sir Humphrey knows that it's not just porcelain that you care about — that the color blue is synonymous with France, and you'll use the formula for everything, not just porcelain but uniforms, to increase the prestige of France."

He swivels away, looking out over the water, and says, "So that's what Sir Humphrey thinks."

"Is Sir Humphrey wrong?"

He lapses into silence again. But he definitely does not seem as upset as I assumed he would be.

"It's time to return below deck," I mutter, edging away.

"Yes, and you can bring Mr. Sturbridge up now, we're safe from observation at night and the Channel is calm."

I say, hesitantly, "When he wakes, I will tell him that it's possible."

He takes a step closer to me. "Do you mean he knows nothing of your coming to speak to me, Genevieve? I'll have Joshua go down in the morning as if you had nothing to do with the request. It will not be a good development if he's woken and found you missing. It could only feed his suspicion."

"Suspicion of what?"

"Why, that this is a ruse, our despising each other — that we planned it all along, for you to flee to Devon and leap into his bed, for me to pretend to threaten your life, all in order to force him to come to France."

I feel as sick as when I lunged for the bucket below to vomit. I stammer, "Thomas would never... *never* think that of me — that I would be so vile."

"Oh, really? I know that I would suspect as much, in his position. I've treated you harshly only to keep him from suspecting that we are in league. However, I fear he is a perceptive man."

"But we are no longer in league! And let me be clear — let me be perfectly clear — I shall never, *ever* be in league with you again. Even if I were willing to play traitor to England, I'd be an utter fool to trust you for a single second."

"Yes," he says. "For now, that is the best role for you to play."

I back away, stumbling, desperate to get away from him.

*

Thomas is still asleep when I return. I sit next to him, my legs drawn up to my chin, shaken. Sir Gabriel implied that this was part of his plan from the beginning. But he must be taunting me. It can't be true, I pray it isn't true that he predicted every action of mine since I returned to Derby — and even earlier than that — in order to get Thomas on a boat to France.

Yet the more I examine the chain of events in the last week, I realize that it's only with me as an active part of it, seducing Thomas, that he could have been induced to leave England. Once Thomas went to Devon, with the authorities closing in on us both, did Sir Gabriel manipulate circumstances to drive me on? Devon is far closer to the Channel than Derby is. And a willing Thomas Sturbridge, working at Sèvres in order to protect me from harm, is far superior to stolen, incomplete formulas.

My mind goes round and round until I collapse onto the pallet in confusion. I, too, fall asleep, only to be woken by Joshua. It must be time to bring Thomas onto the deck, as agreed. But Joshua brings unexpected news.

"You are to move to another boat," he says.

I wake Thomas, and press on him a biscuit to eat. He seems a little improved by rest, although his eyes are glassy and his forehead damp. But he is able to sit up and, when Joshua comes to fetch us, to stand. I know it is difficult for him to walk, but pride propels him forward.

When we go to the top of the deck, it is bright morning, with a most unwelcome sight awaiting us: a ship of three masts anchors alongside us, flying the flag of France. There is no sign of Sir Gabriel. A row of at least thirty sailors stands on the larger boat, watching us. I can feel the weight of their curiosity as we two, bedraggled and tense, are led to the ladder flung over the side, climb down, and are ferried the very short distance to their boat.

Once we've climbed the ladder onto the ship, Joshua leads us toward two white-wigged officers standing on a platform above all the others. When we are fairly close, Thomas stops, grasping my arm.

Following his gaze, I realize that one of the two men is a wigged Sir Gabriel, erect and immaculate. His uniform is dark blue — yes, the color of France — and trimmed with gold, a long row of sparkling buttons running down his coat.

"Bienvenue," he says.

Even for Thomas, whose plan is to go along, this is hard to face. Both of us gape at Sir Gabriel, appalled, before Joshua and a young Frenchman take us below deck of this ship.

Our next "home" is a small but well furnished cabin, with a single bed. Someone laid out a change of clothes for Thomas and me on the bed: for him, a waistcoat, shirt and trousers, and for me a pale-lavender dress. I have no idea how they could have secured such a dress on a boat in time of war. I can see at once it's too large for me, but at least it's clean.

A soft knock sounds on the door.

It's the ship's doctor. He is all politeness, saying he heard that we experienced a rough voyage on the other boat. Under his persistent questioning, the condition of Thomas' lungs is slowly revealed. While Thomas does not know it, I am certain that Sir Gabriel repeated to the doctor what I told him last night and the doctor now pretends to discover what he was in fact previously told. His line of inquiry is too specific for it to be otherwise.

Yes, I definitely recognize Sir Gabriel's role in this. I've betrayed Thomas. But if I hadn't, he would not be receiving the ministrations of this doctor. I look out the cabin's round window, at the churning waves, full of confusion.

As treatment, the doctor burns some herbs in a bowl, tosses a towel over Thomas' bent head, and exhorts him to inhale.

"Yes, that is much better," says Thomas afterward, grateful.

The next step, the doctor says, is for Thomas to take the air. The two of them are gone for quite a while. I remain in the cabin, for the doctor says firmly that it would be "disquieting" for the crew to see a young woman walking about.

When he returns, Thomas' color has improved. His eyes are bright and clear. The doctor's assiduous attention works wonders.

That night, Thomas and I are served a first-rate meal of roasted fish and stewed beans with a bottle of wine, a cabin steward addressing us throughout as "Monsieur" and "Madame."

After the steward leaves, Thomas says shyly, "He believes we are married."

"Yes, I suspect the whole crew has been told I'm your wife. To learn otherwise would be far too... disquieting."

We smile at each other, and Thomas rises to latch the door.

"I think this is our last night on the ship," he says, his back to the door, holding on to that latch. "And it could be our last alone for quite some time."

I rise and unthread the laces of my borrowed gown.

His lovemaking is tender, almost reverent, as he kisses my lips, my throat, my shoulders. "I love you," he murmurs. I tell him I love him too — and I mean it — but I find I cannot exult in this sweet fantasy. It is all contrived to an end: the comforts, the fine meal, the privacy. I can feel Sir Gabriel's hand in this, almost as if he were standing in the corner, watching. Sir Gabriel wants Thomas to love me, to worship me. It helps *him*.

Afterward, Thomas falls asleep, his head on my breast. His breathing is peaceful, not the tortured rasps of the night on the other ship. I stare out the window, loving him — and despising myself — more than ever.

When morning comes, the doctor returns to examine Thomas. He peers into his eyes and down his throat, listens to him cough. "You are greatly improved," he exclaims.

Thomas shoots me a quick glance and reddens.

The doctor pauses at the door to say, "We are close to the Port of Le Havre. Expect to disembark soon."

This unlikely interlude of ours is over.

The doctor gone, Thomas says, in a rush, his hands lightly on my shoulders, "I fear they will separate us before long. I must now have your promise, Genevieve, that you will do nothing on your own. Wait for me to resolve this — and I swear, I *will* resolve it."

"I simply can't understand how you can be so sure that other scientists will risk their lives to help us."

"For one, look at the ship doctor, what a decent, honest, and straightforward fellow he was," he says earnestly. "There will be more like him."

I stare into Thomas' handsome, sensitive face, and my shame and guilt burns the back of my throat, like the bile of a murderous sickness.

"Please, Genevieve, I know that trust is difficult for you."

Is it? I wonder, while knowing he is right.

He tightens his grip on my shoulders. "Genevieve, will you trust me?"

"Of course."

"Then will you promise to wait for me to resolve this?"

My heart breaking, I say, "I promise, Thomas."

A knock on the door. The last man I'd wish to see now is Sir Gabriel Courtenay, so of course he is the one who escorts us, still wearing the blue uniform of the enemy of England, to the deck. I don't speak to him, nor do I meet his gaze.

It is another sunny day, with the warmth and light now enveloping the land of my ancestors, the kingdom of France. How should any refugee react when forced to return? Curious... afraid... angry... wistful. I feel all of those things, but such emotions recede before something else, as I take in what spreads before me in the large harbor.

Ships. *Hundreds* of ships. Large and small. Sitting in the water or on land, half built. I see spines of wood with curved boards arching upward, like the dry skeletons of fearsome animals. As we draw closer, even I, ignorant of the sea and the navy, perceive that many of them are not graceful sailboats. They are flat-bottomed boats, the sort that would be ideal for transporting large numbers of men across the Channel.

Sir Gabriel says, "I give you the invasion fleet."

Now I understand it all. Why he expects to return to England someday, and what he meant when he said those words: "In six months' time, matters like a theft, or a murder, in a Derby porcelain factory won't be uppermost on anyone's mind. We'll be living in a new world."

CHAPTER THIRTY-FOUR

Thomas is right. There are no more nights with the two of us alone. There is little rest, body or spirit, on the roads to Sèvres, a journey of one hundred miles.

I thought I'd known swift travel before, to Derby or Devon, but it is nothing compared to how Sir Gabriel drives us forward. We ride in two carriages, changing horses at regular intervals. Thomas and I sleep and eat in the carriage, unable to speak freely, because the loathsome Joshua rides with us, staring with those watery eyes. We ride through the night, too. It's not because French roads are free of highwaymen. At the port, Sir Gabriel took on a dozen new operatives, hard-faced men gripping pistols and swords, presumably as defense. We travel as a small army, and since the roads are hard and dry, we hurtle to Sèvres without challenge.

All of this effort is made to convey a single chemist to a French porcelain workshop. I've seen the invasion boats made ready at port; I've heard many a tale of the viciousness of the French army. England shall soon be attacked. Yet the substance of clay and the color blue are of paramount importance to King Louis and one of his most trusted spies? It seems impossible to me, a farce, but even the most biting farce contains humor, and none exists in this.

I cannot demand answers from Sir Gabriel, for he never rides in our carriage. We hear him, calling out orders in perfect French. But we rarely see him.

Once, while the men change horses, Thomas tells Joshua that he insists on speaking with Sir Gabriel. A few minutes later, our captor materializes at the carriage window. I can see the rigors of travel in his face: the grime of the road layered on his cheeks, the shadows pouching beneath his eyes.

"Yes, Mr. Sturbridge?" he asks.

His fingers taut against the carriage door, Thomas says, in his much more hesitant French, "I must talk to you about the conditions under which I will be compelled to work, the expectations of that work, and what accommodations are being made for Genevieve."

"Such a discussion is regrettably premature," says Sir Gabriel smoothly. "Arrangements are being made for you as we speak; I sent word on ahead. I can assure you that of course you'll be made comfortable."

"And Genevieve?" presses Thomas. "Will she be made comfortable?"

Sir Gabriel's eyes flick over me, but he says nothing. With a short bow to Thomas, he turns on his heel.

Thomas draws back into the carriage and makes a frustrated noise in his throat. He worries more for me than for himself.

For my part, I am certain that a prison of some sort awaits me. A cold dread thickens inside me, but I try to hide it from Thomas as our carriage resumes its journey. I divert myself by imagining our carriage will be robbed by brigands that night, and Thomas and I will flee into the forest in all of the chaos. It's a childish fantasy, and hardly a solution, since, as Thomas pointed out, we have no money or papers. But I enjoy the dream of hiding with him in the deep, mossy wood, or finding an abandoned cottage to live in. It's a blurry vision plucked from a storybook my mother might have read to me years ago.

Later that same day, our carriage comes to a halt. I wait for the usual shouts to ensue, the calling for fresh horses, but there is none of that.

Someone bangs on our carriage door; Joshua leaps out and then comes back for us. He signals for us to get out of the carriage.

I've seen glimpses of the countryside for two days, enough to confirm that France and England look much alike. But as I step onto a cobbled street, I find myself in a place not quite like any I've been to before.

It is a town: tidy, handsome, and very old, judging by the large church casting a violet shadow on the street rimmed with flower pots. The church is made up of a tall, round tower, adjoining a building shorter in height but wider in circumference. Both have windows carved into stone high up the walls. Rounded at the top, the narrow windows were perhaps openings meant for watching and waiting, in a time of feudal lords galloping into a town such as this without warning. The stone is of an extremely light brown color, almost a dusty dull gold, and worn so smooth that I cannot detect the lines between bricks and mortar.

Thanks to the terrible fire that struck nearly a century past and King Henry VIII's destruction of the Catholic faith a century before that, we've not many structures such as this in London. Although it's not a beautiful structure, and forbidding with only those dark slits for windows, the church awakens my curiosity. I wonder if before the Huguenots rose up, my ancestors would have joined the line of worshippers filtering inside, when France was of a single faith.

Thomas taps me on the arm, breaking the spell, for the church is not our destination. It's a white-washed inn and tavern across the street.

I hear a hoarse, high voice: "Madame — Madame — can you help us? Help my children?"

With a start I realize the woman must be speaking to me, for I am the only female in our party. Standing a few feet from me, she wears a worn, frayed dress, her face that of a gaunt old woman, though the boy and girl on either side are younger than ten. Taking a closer look, I perceive that she is not old but suffering has aged her; she is hollow-faced, her eyes dull and lips white. Her children too have sunken faces.

"Help you?" I repeat in French.

"We are hungry," she says, and one of the boys stares up at me, tears brimming

"Bread," wails the boy.

The girl takes up the plea, though she is so weak it's more of a groan: "Bread."

Just as I step toward them, the fury of the men around me explodes. "Get back! Get back!" shouts a man, whether he's of the town or of Sir Gabriel's party, I don't know.

"Shame!" cries another. "You know you should never come to the square." The woman and her children stagger off as Joshua pushes me toward the door to the inn.

I'm reminded how I've seen the poor in London; I walked among its beggars every day. I witnessed a food riot this year, a crowd of 500 women surging through the streets, its gaunt leaders holding black poles with bread as effigy.

What is this war doing to the common people of both our countries?

The innkeeper leads Thomas, Joshua, and myself to a smooth oak table in his crowded chamber. No sign of Sir Gabriel. A moment later a platter of freshly baked bread materializes.

The smell of it makes me recoil as I think of the family on the square.

"Would Madame care to retire for a moment?" asks the innkeeper, his thick eyebrows nudging in concern. "We have a privy closet — my wife can take you."

Joshua frowns but says nothing. How could he reasonably object?

"Yes, thank you," I reply.

A moment later, the innkeeper's young wife appears. During that time, Joshua peers meaningfully at Thomas, sitting next to me. As long as Joshua has one of us in his grasp, he has control over both. I know it all too well, and Thomas must too.

I follow the innkeeper's smiling wife, her striped skirts rustling, her curly russet hair escaping from a white lace cap, toward the privy closet.

"Have your travels been wearying?" she asks.

"Yes, we've come far," I answer. I wait for a reaction, but evidently my French does not sound strange to her. I'd wondered if the ordinary French people would recognize my lack of belonging: a discordant accent, a lack of familiarity.

But she seems to perceive nothing amiss, and it makes me want to seize her arm and say, "I'm held prisoner!"

As if that would work in our favor. We are English, France's most hated enemy. Even worse, I am a despised Huguenot. Even if we could be wrested away from Sir Gabriel, who would take up our cause? The innkeeper's wife could no more help me than I could do anything for the beggar woman in the street.

Inside the privy closet, I gather myself; there is nothing to be gained from showing weakness to Sir Gabriel or his men. Taking deep breaths, I still my panic. When I emerge, the innkeeper's wife is no longer there. She must assume I can find my way back alone.

I retrace my steps, following the sound of cheerful voices that grow louder until I reach the doorway to the eating chamber. Another, wider doorway is to my left, the one leading to stairs to the second floor. Sir

Gabriel stands there, absolutely still. His clothing is fresh and unwrinkled, his face clean. Upstairs, the privations of travel have been wiped away.

Sir Gabriel does not notice me, his eyes fixed on a point across the room. Following his gaze, I realize he's watching Thomas.

The helpless panic of moments earlier is nothing compared to the terror I feel now, for Sir Gabriel's face is so altered that he is almost a stranger. I've seen him poised and calm, amused, annoyed. I've seen him angry, contemptuous, lustful, and sorrowful. But at this moment he is studying Thomas with a loathing that turns his patrician features to ice. Worst of all, his eyes: in that frozen face, they blaze with hatred.

And I remember, as if it were yesterday, his words as we looked at the mural along the wide staircase at the British Museum. "For daring to challenge a god, Apollo flayed Marsayas alive, slowly, inch by inch."

Sir Gabriel's expression is so striking that a short, slight Frenchman passing him pauses to peer up at him nervously. That triggers something. Like a shutter slammed down, the hatred disappears. His face composes itself into his usual calm expression. With a tug of his waistcoat, Sir Gabriel strides to the table.

I hurry after him, my heart pounding madly. I had thought that Sir Gabriel had nothing but professional feelings toward Thomas, a pride in his capture perhaps. Where is the hatred coming from?

Sitting with all of us at the table, Sir Gabriel is all smiling politeness once more. The innkeeper's wife brings us a platter of roasted rabbit, and everyone except me dives into their meal. I watch Sir Gabriel as carefully as he watched Thomas, but his mask never slips, nor does he seem to take notice of my scrutiny.

Fingering his glass of port, Thomas says to Sir Gabriel, "I wonder if you could tell me the history of Sèvres."

"No," I say, loudly. I am dismayed by this request.

Thomas tosses me an apologetic glance.

Sir Gabriel says, "Mr. Sturbridge wishes to understand his situation, which is quite natural, Genevieve. And the porcelain manufactory has an intriguing history, well worth knowing." He dabs at his mouth, delicately, and says: "It began much as all the successful porcelain workshops do, with a scoundrel and a dreamer."

I interrupt with: "*You* would know all about the scoundrel."

"As would you, my dear," he shoots back.

Thomas shifts in his chair, his eyebrows furrowed. Our sparring pains him, for some reason. I force myself to be quiet. Like it or not, I will listen to the story of Sèvres.

CHAPTER THRTY-FIVE

"It began with two brothers, Giles and Robert Dubois, employed at the Chantilly porcelain manufactory," Sir Gabriel says. "This was long ago, you understand. The secret of how to make porcelain seeped across Europe in 1710, thanks to the French Jesuit spy who spied on the Chinese workers. Little workshops sprang up everywhere, but their owners all soon realized that they could not survive without wealthy sponsors. Creating exceptional porcelain is expensive. Many ventures failed within months. Chantilly survived because it was sponsored in 1730 by Louis Henri, Duke of Bourbon, prime minister of France."

"And this duke, with such responsibilities, chose to devote his wealth to porcelain?" asks Thomas.

"The duke was the richest man in France for a time, so the money he poured into it was by no means a strain," explains Sir Gabriel with a tolerant smile. "He had lost favor with King Louis, and once Louis turns away from someone, there is no coming back. The duke had an insatiable thirst for 'white gold' and was determined that his creations would rival those of the Orient. He built the manufactory in the park of the family home, the Château de Chantilly. Only a Bourbon could take aim at a venture with such confidence."

I shudder at the name Bourbon. This is the royal family that seeks the destruction of all Huguenots, that wages war on England.

"At Chantilly, Giles Dubois was a sculptor and his brother Robert was a decorator," Sir Gabriel continues, oblivious of my misery. "They had artistic ability, yes, but they were also drunkards and liars, mired in debt. They managed to steal the most important formulas for the Chantilly porcelain, in particular the secret of its milk-white glazes, and one day they disappeared, to create their own business and thus make their fortune. To get what they dreamed of, such immoral measures were thought necessary."

Sir Gabriel's gaze alights on me, and I make sure to return it with my most ferocious scowl.

"They built a laboratory in secret. Once they had pieces of beauty to show, they carefully approached various men of means who would be so eager for a stake in porcelain, they'd not condemn the brothers for their lack of morality. They finally found such a patron in Orry de Fulvy."

"Another prince?" asks Thomas.

Sir Gabriel's eyebrows arch. "Hardly. Orry de Fulvy was a man of finance, with many connections. He persuaded seven men of good circumstance to join him; together, they raised 90,000 livres. It was all very secretive; they used a false name as head of the enterprise: Charles Adam. De Fulvy was also a friend to the Marquis de Chatelet, governor of the Château of Vincennes. He persuaded his friend to allow the workers to make use of the buildings. It was in the ruins of Vincennes that they hired their workers, set up their workshop, and first created the most exquisite porcelain of France, strange as that may seem."

Sir Gabriel looks at us expectantly. I fidget with my fork; Thomas shrugs. He is as uninterested in royal castles as I am.

"You have never heard of Vincennes?" Sir Gabriel asks in disbelief. "The fortress of France?"

We shake our heads.

"When King Louis IX, Saint Louis, went on Holy Crusade in 1269, never to return, he departed from Vincennes," Sir Gabriel says.

Any trace of hunger I might have had is gone. Before the Bourbons, before the Valois dynasty, were the Capets. Louis IX was the first French monarch to favor blue, to have himself painted in blue robes. Four hundred years ago, the royal family wore blue. To my humiliation, I actually *knew* that. My interest in the history of color once led me to a book that described the Capets' passion for blue. I hadn't needed an Englishman, Sir Humphrey, to tell me blue was the color of France. But stupidly I'd not made that last, most vital connection, between France and its royal family's favorite color and the porcelain factory of Sèvres.

"Kings of France were born at Vincennes, married there, died there," Sir Gabriel is saying. "But once Louis XIV focused on Versailles, the château fell into disuse. The Dubois brothers set up their laboratory there."

"And what makes their porcelain so special?" asks Thomas.

Sir Gabriel considers for a moment, and says, "I think, in the beginning, it was its delicacy. The Vincennes formula was partly stolen from Chantilly but partly based on innovations made after the brothers began. It was soft paste. You know this, I'm sure. The problem was, the porcelain was so fragile that five-sixths of the pieces had to be destroyed. But that sixth one? Breathtaking. The Dubois brothers guarded the formula with their lives. They were devious enough to fool everyone but François Gravant, who joined them in the laboratory. He was a man who embraced the punishing hours, who had the mental strength to create not just any porcelain, but the porcelain of Vincennes. He had a vision so strong that it overcame all."

I wonder if Thomas is thinking what I am. That this description summons up a comparison to a certain Englishman we know: William Duesbury. The director of Derby Porcelain Works has never treated me with kindness, but I suddenly miss his homely face and flapping arms.

Sir Gabriel sips his port and continues, "The Dubois brothers ran through the investment of Orry de Fulvy with not much to show for it. One night when Giles and Robert Dubois were passed out on the floor drunk, Gravant found their hidden papers and he stole their stolen formula. He took control."

Sir Gabriel sips his wine and continues. "Gravant attracted the sculptors and artists that fashioned objects beautiful enough to lure Madame de Pompadour, who in turn brought in Jean Hellot. Monsieur Hellot turned the porcelain-making into a scientific enterprise and the manufactory had its breakthrough."

"Which is?" Thomas asks.

"That it is not just shape but color that commands excitement, and only a marriage of art and science can create never-before-seen colors."

I watch Thomas nod thoughtfully. This is what worries me — the scientific appeal of the work being conducted at Sèvres. Sir Gabriel is doing his best to entice him, as he did months ago with me at that dinner on Fournier Street.

Sir Gabriel continues, "Monsieur Hellot understands that what is most effective is not just a dabbling of a color, a border, a painting of a flower or person, but an entire color background. This is what Madame de Pompadour supports, and what attracts the patronage of the King. Do you know that when King Louis expressed his first official support of the Vincennes porcelain factory, he was at the front in the last war, the one against Austria, and he turned away from the battle?"

"What do you mean by 'turned away'?" asks Thomas.

"The King retreated to his camp and read through twenty pages before signing the royal privilege for Vincennes in 1745, granting them the power to make porcelain 'in the Saxon manner' and investing his own money. After signing, the King returned to the front in his chariot."

They are all mad, I thought. *Completely mad.*

Sir Gabriel says, "Each time that they needed to raise capital to produce porcelain, King Louis increased his shares. Four years ago, the King paid for a magnificent new building in the town of Sèvres, closer to Versailles — it cost him nearly 1,000,000 livres. The name was changed to Sèvres. In this building, under the guidance of Madame de Pompadour, the staff has grown to 250 painters and gilders and sixteen chemists..."

Unable to stop myself, I say, disgusted, "And this is what the King lavishes money on — when the people starve before our very eyes."

"Quiet, Genevieve," orders Sir Gabriel, glancing around.

"Do you know why, with a country as large as France, the money runs out?" I ask Thomas, ignoring Sir Gabriel. "Because no king has the power to tax his nobles or his church, and they own the vast majority of the land, obviously. The common man must meet the tax burden, and..."

Sir Gabriel rises from his chair to say in a lacerating voice: "Not another word, you little fool. Do you fancy yourself in one of your London coffee houses? This is not England, where such radical drivel is tolerated. You could be arrested based on what you've said at this table, and welcomed into the Bastille. You do not know the governor of the Bastille — I do — and may I assure you, it's not a comfortable prospect."

Sir Gabriel throws down his napkin. "Dinner is over," he declares.

*

Within minutes, Thomas and I are once again sitting in a carriage hurrying to Sèvres, the loathsome Joshua with us.

"I told you on the ship, it achieves nothing to antagonize him," Thomas says to me.

"I couldn't bear his efforts to lure you in," I say.

"Do you think that I would forget myself simply because I have learned that Sèvres is well staffed? I am not so easily swayed as…" His voice trails off.

"As I am?" I finish.

Thomas turns away from me to look out the window, though there is little to see in the deepening dusk. Joshua chuckles in his corner. It is a humiliating moment.

In the tense silence of the coach, I try to understand why Thomas became angry. I think back over the meal. Could it have been my arguing with Sir Gabriel that distressed him? Thinking over our sparring, I fear we revealed our intense feelings for each other, many of them hostile, but not all. No, not all. So much has happened. I've wanted to kill him, and I believe he's wanted to kill me, too. It's a tangle of distrust and desire, if I am completely honest. "My weakness" were Sir Gabriel's words. Has he been mine, too?

It is a most uncomfortable night, rocking back and forth in the carriage, catching snatches of sleep. I desperately want to talk to Thomas, but not with Joshua listening. If I could, I'd throw him out of the carriage.

Dawn reveals a gray day of low, thick clouds and a changed landscape too. There are fewer open fields and more towns; the buildings grow taller. I fear we are nearing Paris and, with it, Sèvres.

No longer caring about Joshua's presence, I reach for Thomas' hand and he takes it. I lay my head on his shoulder, adoring that groove between bone and muscle beneath his coat. This is the man I love, there is no doubt. Each moment I feel those long fingers intertwined in mine is a gift, though one wrapped in pain. I dread arrival at Sèvres so much that I feel lightheaded, and faint with nausea.

Before noon, the carriage stops. Peeking out, I see a small stone house, a bank of tall trees on one side, a muddy stream on the other. I can't imagine why — this obviously isn't the prestigious Sèvres Porcelain Manufactory, a building that cost 1,000,000 livres.

Sir Gabriel taps on the carriage door. "Out, Genevieve."

Thomas is the first one onto the ground, demanding answers, with me tumbling after him.

"Genevieve will stay here while you work," explains Sir Gabriel.

Two people step out of the house, a man and woman in middle years. They are an unusual sight, for they are much alike: the same height, sallow and long nosed, with close-set dark eyes. The woman drops a quick curtsey to Sir Gabriel; the man bows and then wipes rain from his glistening forehead.

"Victoire and his sister Sophie will look after you, Genevieve," Sir Gabriel says.

These are my jailors. It may not look like a prison, but that is what the house surely is.

"And when will I see her?" asks Thomas.

"Not for a while," says Sir Gabriel. "Not until you have produced work deemed satisfactory. Then it will be considered. Until then, your lodgings are elsewhere."

I had not expected that we would be separated so soon and so completely. I'm unable to speak, for once. Thomas is the one who finds his voice.

"This is unacceptable, Sir," he says, his hand slicing through the rain-fringed air.

"Given the trouble you have both caused, it is extraordinarily generous," says Sir Gabriel. "Mr. Sturbridge, you have a choice. Oppose this separation and I'll have you put in the carriage by force. Accept it with dignity and you may say your farewells."

Sir Gabriel turns away, as if he knows which choice Thomas will make, and indeed, rather than fight, Thomas turns to embrace me more tightly than he ever has before. My ribs ache, and I welcome it. He kisses my lips, my cheeks. I long for the world to vanish around us, but I hear the muttering of Sir Gabriel's men, the squawk of birds above, and the steady patter of rain on the stream.

"No," I say, brokenly. "I can't do this."

He buries his face in my hair spilling down my shoulders, and whispers in my ear, "You must believe in me. Remember your promise? You will do nothing — nothing — before hearing from me. I will preserve our lives. No reckless acts, I beg you, Genevieve."

It's a promise I don't want to make, and I don't wish to keep.

"Mr. Sturbridge, if you will?" calls out Sir Gabriel.

Thomas pleads, "Genevieve!"

"I will do nothing," I whisper, forcing the words.

He pulls himself away, and Joshua nudges Thomas back into the carriage. The door slams, and I can't see him any longer.

The rain quickens, spattering my head and my body as I stand, numb, watching the carriages and horsemen hurry up the road, leaving me behind. Sir Gabriel rides a bay horse and his is the last face I see. He turns in the saddle and holds up his hand, I think for a second as a wave for me, but it's to serve as a shield from the rain. He turns back around, kicks his horse, and is gone.

CHAPTER THIRTY-SIX

Trying to conceal my trembling and my tears from this silent, watchful brother and sister, I step over the threshold. The largest room has a table and stools at one end and a massive fireplace on the other. Adjoining it is a bedchamber, with one window — my sleeping quarters, evidently. The third room is a pantry. The door to the road is always locked. As for the spacious garden, locks are unnecessary, for it is completely enclosed by stone walls ten feet high.

It does not take long to get the feel of the house or of the keepers of the keys, Sophie and Victoire. They live in rooms on the second floor, the door to the stairs closed to me. The siblings don't mistreat me. In fact, it is just the opposite. From the beginning, Victoire is cordial and scrupulously correct, if wary; Sophie is nervous and eager to please. At times I feel as if she is afraid of me. When we are in different rooms, or she thinks me asleep, I hear a much different side to her. Sophie sings and hums, and calls out remembrances, little jokes, to Victoire, that make him laugh in response. They have their own light-hearted code, built on growing up together. Whenever I appear, they instantly turn quiet and vigilant.

I would like to know what they've been told about me and Thomas, but questions do not get me far.

"How far are we from Sèvres?" I ask them the first day.

"We are *in* Sèvres, Mademoiselle," Victoire answers. "This house is on the outskirts of the town."

"And how far is this from the location of the porcelain manufactory?" I ask.

He shakes his head, his brown eyes guarded. When I try again later, he says he can tell me nothing about the porcelain factory of Sèvres.

But all in all, I'm treated better than I expected. Sophie cooks with skill and supplies me with clean clothes and bedding. Books are sent to the house, though they are frivolous novels not to my interest. Victoire is taken aback when I ask for a newspaper, but a few days later, one appears: *Mercure de France*. Each article in it relates what is happening at the Court of Versailles in bland, respectful prose. Nothing about the war. Not a sentence about an invasion of England. I absorb every word, and end not feeling I have any better understanding of France. Or at least, nothing that could help me here. I spend most of my time in the garden, surrounded by tall, flowering trees and rectangular plantings of budding peonies and white lilies.

This does not mean I am content, by any means. I ache to escape, and I quickly come up with a way to do so. I'll climb a tree, jump from branch to wall, and scramble down the other side. No filching of keys required, or tricking of Victoire and Sophie.

Yet I *can't* take action, because of my promise to Thomas. If it weren't for that, I'd have escaped already. Or would I? I've not a coin in my possession, nothing to sell. How would I survive long enough to find my way out of France, not to mention pay for passage? It's a daunting prospect, yet I know that, had I free will in this, I would escape nonetheless.

The days go by and I have no idea what Thomas is experiencing at the porcelain manufactory. I think of Sir Gabriel's chilling tale of the chemist-alchemist Bottger, trapped in Saxony until he performed his miracle. Wasn't he imprisoned for ten years?

This can't go on for years. I refuse to consider that possibility.

I am not allowed to see Thomas until he produces work, Sir Gabriel says, but I have no idea how soon that will be, since I assume he is postponing production for as long as possible. The war will surely have bearing on our fate.

I can't decide if France winning the war would make our situation better or worse. To know nothing and to worry about everything, it is a form of torture, and to be respectfully treated within these stone walls doesn't take the fear away. I have my suspicions of Victoire and Sophie. Despite their courtesies, I am watched so very closely. At the end of the day I sometimes hear the two of them talking about what I did, making a list of my movements. I decide they're composing written reports. I would hope it's Thomas who reads the reports, though it's far more likely to be Sir Gabriel. Still, he must have to tell Thomas *something*, or else he'd rebel. If only the information ran this way as well.

The days lengthen into weeks; it turns warm during the day while staying cool at night. And then the nights turn warm in my bedchamber with the one window and the only door locked.

When I ask that they leave the door open at night to permit air to flow, Victoire agrees after some hesitation. He remains so cautious. But I haven't given them any trouble whatsoever — how can he refuse?

"Very well, Mademoiselle," he says.

That night it is less stuffy in my room, but I still cannot sleep. I do little during the day to tire me.

Wide awake, I pace the room, thinking of Thomas, as always. Worry gnaws at me, and something else. A resentment hovers. Why was he insistent I do nothing? Does he think so little of my judgment and ability?

I pause to peer out of the bedchamber window. I spot Victoire, sitting in the garden, alone, his face tilted skyward as if basking in the moonlight. Next to his chair gleams a wine bottle.

This is an opportunity. I put on my dress and make my way to the garden.

When he sees me, Victoire rises quickly, saying, "Are you unwell, Mademoiselle?"

"I cannot sleep, but I'm well apart from that. Would it be possible for me to take some wine with you?"

Victoire says nothing, plainly uncomfortable with the idea. Yet finally he nods, and goes into the house to fetch another chair and a glass for my wine. He also lights a thick candle shoved into a brass dish and sets it down on the ground between us.

The wine is dry, with a trace of spice. I sip it slowly, carefully, wishing to keep my head clear.

I enjoy the breeze on my cheeks, whispering through the trees. In the last few days the trees' white blossoms have lost freshness, crumbling and falling, to be replaced by vigorous green shoots. There is just enough left to lend the air a tint of sweetness.

My purpose is to wheedle information from Victoire, but our wordless enjoyment of the garden gives me a bit of peace. I'm reluctant to break the mood.

It is Victoire who speaks.

"Perhaps you will sleep better after this respite, Mademoiselle? It would be helpful to us if you could do so."

"How helpful?" I ask.

"Our continuing to work here depends on you," he says. "The worst thing would be if you attempted to leave, but if you sicken or fall into a melancholy, that is bad for Sophie and me, too."

"And you wish to continue working here, I take it."

Victoire chuckles. "If you knew where we were employed before coming here, you'd not need to ask."

I sip more wine, my thoughts going round and round. He has no idea that I'd promised Thomas to never attempt escape. Perhaps I can make use of that. Victoire is speaking more frankly than ever before — perhaps it's the wine.

"So you fear that I will try to leave?" I ask.

"I've been told to expect an attempt, that it is in your nature to do so."

I stifle a bitter laugh. That could only be coming from Sir Gabriel Courtenay.

"We could make a contract, you and I," I say. "I won't make any effort to leave this house if you will answer some questions of mine."

He thinks it over with his usual deliberativeness. I half expect him to refuse me. "I can't speak to my orders or the details of your confinement," he says. "But perhaps other questions?"

My heart soars at the triumph. "Of course, of course."

I sip more wine. I cannot leap into this with a difficult question or I'll scare him off.

"Where did you and Sophie work before this?" is my first question.

He says haltingly, "In a private establishment... favored by the King. It is on the grounds of the palace of Versailles but it is separate and the people who... *occupy* it, do so in the greatest secrecy."

After a moment I say, "You're talking about the Deer Park."

He sits straight in his chair. Victoire is genuinely startled. "You have heard of it?"

"I think that throughout Europe everyone knows about the house where young women are brought, in shuttered coaches, to entertain the King," I say.

He presses his finger to his lips, looking fearfully around the garden as if the banks of white lilies harbored spies from Versailles.

"It was a misery for Sophie," he says. "She's so much happier — as am I — serving a proper Huguenot lady rather than the dregs of Paris."

Now I am the one who is shocked. "You *know* I am a Huguenot — and it doesn't offend you?" I ask.

He shakes his head.

"I've not met a Huguenot before, but I've heard a great deal," he says. "I'm curious, I admit to it."

And so, instead of my drawing out of him information that would help me in my plight, our night-time conversation turns to his questioning me. He asks about my family history, of the decision to leave France, of the difficulty in building new lives in England. He finds it interesting, that my mother's family is from the south of France, while my father's is from Picardy. I describe Spitalfields to him, and the silk weavers' businesses and the importance of our church.

"It sounds like quite a decent place," he says.

Something shifts within me that night. Victoire is still my guard in this house, I am still a hostage to Thomas' work, but the fear of the French people I've harbored all of my life begins to lessen. I was taught that in Paris, during the massacre of St Bartholomew, it was not just the nobles and their soldiers who killed helpless Huguenots, but ordinary men and women. Yet this man sitting in the garden does not think my faith makes me his enemy.

I did not realize that the grief of the refugee was a weight on me until it eased. Not completely, of course — Victoire could be an exception to the rule. Or he could represent the thoughts and feelings of many others. Impossible to know. But it is a step for me, an important step.

I tell Victoire, "I think I will sleep well now."

"Very good, Mademoiselle. That is beneficial for Sophie."

Pausing at the door to the garden, I say, "I think the reason I am often not tired or hungry is because I do nothing here. Since I was very young, I've held employment or at least gone to market. To be idle is difficult."

Victoire chuckles. "We've been servants at Versailles since we were children, observing many, many ladies. Idleness was their natural state. It did not occur to me you'd wish to have an occupation."

*

A week later, when I rise from my bed, something new awaits me. Laid out on the table is a collection of supplies. I run my hands over thick paper, an easel, oil paints, pastel chalks, brushes. Victoire must have communicated what I said, and Thomas insisted I receive this wonderful bundle.

What to paint? The garden? It has possibilities... but no.

That afternoon, I take out a piece of chalk and sketch shapes and outlines, my fingers moving eagerly. A narrow, curved street in a town, a man in a window.

The next day I stretch canvas and set up in the garden, where the light is best. I'm so excited that I have to focus on keeping my fingers calm and still. I paint a sky darkening with a coming storm. A man in a second floor window holds a candle as he watches a boy leap between cobblestones.

I enjoy painting Thomas, his Titian red hair loose on his shoulders, but it's the boy who obsesses me. I need to capture his spirit in not just his face but his arms, his legs. I'm not finished then. I paint a few other people in the foreground, those who live in this town, busy on

385

the streets. When I master all of the details of human flesh, as well as brick and sky, I lay down my brush.

The next day I sketch again. Another scene of Derby that I feel compelled to bring to life. I mount a fresh canvas on the easel. In the foreground, men and women scramble across a grassy riverbank, each of them moving with purpose. In the background, on one side I paint the edge of a giant wheel dipping in the river. On the other I paint the old stone house, looking abandoned.

Without any planning, as if the brush is leading me, I paint a face in the window of the stone house. I don't know yet if I should make it a man or woman, young or old.

I slowly realize what is happening. I've found my way in painting, my place in the world of art. I longed to bring the turmoil, the passions and injustices of London, to the canvas, as Hogarth did. He scorned the society portraits and ancient-world tableaux for something more vital to the people of England, and it has been a source of intense frustration that I could not follow in his footsteps. But my purview is not the gin craze or the crashing of investments. It is the life of Derby, with all of its complexity, and the other towns that will spring up just like it, and how they lead to our future.

I'm working on the riverbank with my smallest brush when I hear a soft footfall behind me. I expect it's Sophie, come to tell me that dinner will be ready soon.

I turn around to find a thin, wrinkle-faced man, in his seventies at least, impeccably dressed, watching me with sharp, gray eyes.

"Oh!" I say, the breath catching in my lungs. I haven't seen a stranger in weeks.

He does not name himself. He bows, and says, gesturing at the painting, "May I see?"

I nod, wonderingly.

"This is most promising," he says after a moment. "Excellent composition and use of light. Thomas was right about your talent."

"You know Thomas," I gasp. I realize who this is, in a flash. "You are Monsieur Jean Hellot?"

The old man bows.

"Is Thomas coming today? Will I see him?" My heart gallops as I look past him, hoping Thomas will be next to materialize.

"No, alas. I wish I he could see you. Believe me, he wishes it. I have no say in it."

"Then he sent you?"

"He doesn't know I'm here, although I will tell him of our meeting later today." He hesitates, as if reluctant to say something but finally pushes himself to do so. "Thomas is a fine young man and a gifted scientist."

"I'm glad you think so," I say. So Thomas has done it, he has brought about this meeting of the minds. How he managed to win Hellot's respect while delaying production of blue, I can't imagine.

"I've made a study of color my life's work," he says, gazing up through the tree branches in the garden. "The understanding of light, and how man is able to see color, to perceive it; that is the mystery, the challenge. I'm humbled before this question every day of my life. Only Thomas understands. And to create a color from an entirely new source, an undiscovered metal? The future of science belongs to the bold, like Thomas Sturbridge. I've begun the procedure of nominating him to the Royal Academy of Sciences. I think that the blue will be but his first triumph."

"His triumph?"

"Yes. We've been working on his formula day and night. Thomas would not stop to eat or sleep if I didn't insist."

And with that I plunge into a nightmare. How could Thomas do this — how could he rush to help them at Sèvres with production of blue? Delay and prevarication were supposed to be his strategy. If he is so occupied, if he's made definite progress, then why haven't they let him see me?

Somehow I manage to ask Monsieur Hellot when the new color will be ready.

"We should be able to produce our first line of blue porcelain for King Louis within weeks."

CHAPTER THIRTY-SEVEN

Monsieur Hellot does not linger, for it's obvious I'm distressed. I can see the puzzled concern in his eyes as he makes his last bow, and a moment later hear him speaking to Victoire through my door. That's where I've retreated to. In this instance I am the one to close the door, and I'd lock it from the inside if I could.

As I lie on the bed, I try to remember what Thomas said to me. The more I piece it together, the more I realize I've been a fool. Thomas never shared my deep hatred of France; instead, he spoke of his admiration for Hellot and the country's superior scientists. I perceive now that he sought to calm me and extract promises of my cooperation at every turn. Sir Gabriel dragged me to France as a means of forcing Thomas to do Sèvres' bidding. What a supreme joke. Such force was never needed. They could have left me behind in the inn at Devon, or that crate on the pier of Portsmouth, and Thomas Sturbridge would still have created the most beautiful blue the world has ever seen.

"Will Mademoiselle be having dinner?" Sophie's nervous voice trembles through the door.

"No, I want nothing," I respond.

There's silence after that. I'm left alone, in my misery, the entire night.

I resolve on one course of action. I will escape this house and leave France, on my own. If I have to steal, beg, and smuggle my way across the kingdom, I shall do it. Daphne escaped from the Constance Tower of Aigues-Mortes, making it all the way to London. I can break free of this house, surely.

I dig into a bowl of gruel. I've no appetite, but I'll need all of my strength for this endeavor. Out of the corner of my eye, I spot my easels and paintings and supplies, carefully arranged against the wall, despite what I said yesterday. I try hard not to look in that direction again.

My hand, gripping the spoon, freezes halfway to my mouth as Victoire slides onto the stool across from me. He's never entered my chambers unannounced like that before.

"Don't do it," he says.

"Do what?"

"Attempt to escape. We made a contract, you and I. Or have you forgotten?"

I take a deep breath. "I've not forgotten."

"I have no wish to keep you a prisoner of your bedchamber, or to hurt you," Victoire says, and with slow, deliberate movements, withdraws a narrow blade from his left sleeve, where it had been concealed.

I pull back from the table. "You armed yourself this morning, I see."

Victoire says bitterly, "I have been so armed since the day you arrived, Mademoiselle. I am a man not unaccustomed to violence; we were chosen for this employment for good reasons. I beg of you, do not make me take up such violence here."

I open my mouth to speak, and close it again. I cannot lie to him.

I hear the key turn in the lock once I'm in the room. Now I am truly imprisoned. Victoire and Sophie bring me my meals and take them away, barely touched, their faces worried. I know that they hate treating me in such a way — and that they have no choice but to go on treating me this way.

When I brood over Thomas, my mood veers from anger to puzzlement to shame, with teary moments too. The third afternoon of my confinement, when I'm stretched out, fully clothed, on the bed, Victoire knocks, a new urgency to his voice.

"You have callers, Mademoiselle."

I should have expected it. Victoire reports daily on my well-being. My distress must have set off some sort of reaction.

Through the door, I hear Victoire say, "Monsieur Hellot." Resentment surges. Why is he back? I pin up my hair and pinch my cheeks. I may feel dreadful but I don't want to arouse the pity of my enemies.

The instant I step out of the now unlocked room, I realize that I face a true challenge. Monsieur Hellot stands before me, yes, but crowded behind him are a half-dozen figures. Women and men. I blink at the sight of them, dressed in such intense and uncommon colors — lavender, yellow, apple-green, and dark cream — as they stare back at me. Feathers and lace flutter. A diamond flashes in a woman's bosom, a sapphire gleams atop a man's shoe. To see such rarefied creatures in this humble kitchen parlor is almost ludicrous.

"Mademoiselle, I understand you've not been well," says Hellot, his voice a question.

"I am well," I say quickly.

A woman says, her voice melodic, "We are happy to hear it."

The group parts to allow her to walk toward me: The woman is somewhere about thirty, of slender frame, dressed in a shimmering embroidered silk dress of cream, pink, and blue that billows from a tiny waist out to wide hoops. Her hair is powdered white and teased to a tower, but her delicate eyebrows are chestnut brown. She has a heart-shaped face with a delicate chin sloping to a long, willowy throat draped in a diamond necklace. Most dazzling are her eyes: light golden brown, fringed by long eyelashes.

She does not introduce herself; nor does Hellot name her. It's unnecessary. I am in the presence of the most famous — or infamous — woman in all of Europe: Madame de Pompadour.

Hellot says, "May I present Mademoiselle Genevieve Planché."

She tilts her head to one side. Everyone seems to be waiting for something. Am I to curtsey to the mistress of King Louis XV? That will not take place. I stand my ground, not moving or speaking.

Undaunted, she walks up to me, until we are but a few inches apart. Her eyes travel from the top of my unwigged head to my feet clad in the plainest of shoes.

With a brilliant smile, she extends her gloved hand. For a split second of horror, I fear I am meant to kiss it. But no, she shakes my hand, her touch delicate, almost fragile.

"It is lovely to make your acquaintance," she says, and then spins around, calling for the berries. A lovely young woman sidles forward, carrying with both hands a silver tray. In the middle is a gleaming porcelain dish with freshly washed strawberries and raspberries arranged across it.

"If a woman is feeling poorly, I say the cure is freshly picked fruit," says Madame de Pompadour in that voice like a snatch of song.

I've always had a weakness for strawberries. Staring at the tray, my stomach comes close to growling. I cannot stop myself from reaching for them, eating two that are bright red and perfectly ripe: not too hard, not too pulpy soft. Hellot and a few others join me, everyone murmuring thanks. Madame de Pompadour does not join in; in truth, her lips, carefully covered with cosmetics, appear unsuited to such earthly pursuits as eating.

"May I see your paintings?" Madame de Pompadour asks, gesturing to the door of the garden. There my two paintings are mounted, no doubt to prepare for her arrival.

I feel my face flush. "They're not ready to be viewed."

She laughs for the first time, a rich tinkle. "Do you know how many artists and sculptors besiege me, day and night, to see their work? I can't remember the last time I was refused."

I bite my lip. She is making obvious efforts to charm me. I can feel Monsieur Hellot's eyes on me, apprehensive. But why should I care about upsetting him and the rest of the Versailles rabble? I'm about to refuse to show my work a second time when I catch a glimpse of Sophie behind him, stricken with fear that I will say or do something wrong and pitch her and her brother into disaster.

"Very well," I say shortly.

I lead her out into the modest garden, to my easels, and wait for the insincere flattery to bubble from her lips. Fortunately, her entourage does not follow.

She regards my work in silence for a few minutes. At one point, she squints, and I see lines crinkle under her face paint.

"Few women have achieved mastery with oils, the 'weaker sex' is commonly relegated to watercolor," she finally says. "But he was correct in saying that this would be your medium."

"Thomas told you that?" I say. I don't remember discussing technique with him to that degree.

She levels a sharper look at me. "No. Not Thomas." Madame de Pompadour returns to my paintings. "Whom will you place in the window?" she asks, studying the old stone bridge. "It should be you, I wager. You have the eyes and hair for it. And it is your part. Are you not someone who watches?"

Without waiting for a response, she beckons to Monsieur Hellot.

"We could try a stone bridge over a river in the country, perhaps as decoration on the side of a tall pitcher? I've not seen that before. I think some additional ivy would help carry it off."

"I'll see to it," Hellot says.

Madame de Pompadour directs her sparkle at me again. "Mademoiselle Genevieve, would you care for an outing? An hour or two away from this house, in my company?"

An outing. She is the woman whom I blame for much of what has gone wrong in my life. Spend an hour with her?

I inhale Pompadour's fragrance, a disconcerting mixture of heavy musk and light tuberose. Oh, but I ache to leave this tiny house. I'd accept an invitation from Catherine de Medici herself. More pragmatically, if I am to escape from France, I need to better understand the stage of events, and the players. She seems curious about me. I'm curious about her.

"Yes," I say.

"Tomorrow," she breathes, her dainty hand caressing my shoulder. "And I have a gift for you to keep — I understand you are a dedicated reader. I've given all of my friends Voltaire's new novel."

A cold-eyed dandy presses a package in my hands, and with that, the King's mistress and her party sweep out of the cottage.

Voltaire? The French philosopher in exile because of his dangerous ideas? I unwrap the package. It smells like a book printed yesterday. The pale gray cover says: *Candide, ou l'Optimisme.*

Suspicious, I say to Victoire, "But isn't it illegal in France to read this book?"

He shrugs. "If it is, they'll have to build a new Bastille. I see this book in everyone's hands."

The rest of the day and half of the night, I read without stopping. It is a novel like no other, a fantastical tale of an idealistic young man's dire adventures, yes, but also a witty and biting attack on war and priests and tyranny. The story travels from Westphalia and Bulgaria to France and even to England.

Why did Madame de Pompadour give me such a book? How could the mistress of an absolute monarch possibly agree with its ideas?

In the morning, a note arrives that Monsieur Hellot will arrive at eleven with a carriage. It seems he is to be my escort. Along with the note is a dress, nothing like the frilly gowns, the confections that Madame de Pompadour and her friends wear. The last time I was given a dress to wear for a special occasion, it was at Sir Gabriel's home and for a dinner I'd prefer to forget. But what I've been sent by Pompadour is simple, of rich green, almost a dark forest green, with gathered skirts and a square bodice — like a very well made version of a dress a proper Huguenot woman would don.

Her comments on my painting, the gift of Voltaire's book, and now this dress. I sense that Madame de Pompadour is trying to tell me something. But I've no idea what.

Exactly on time, Monsieur Hellot appears. It promises to be a hot, cloudless afternoon. Looking at his elderly profile in the doorway, it occurs to me that it might not be too hard to escape if Monsieur Hellot is my only escort.

Victoire follows us down the path to the sleek waiting carriage and jumps atop it, to sit next to the driver. So much for that idea.

As I settle into the back of the carriage and it rattles up the dusty tree-lined road, I say, "I would think Sèvres Porcelain a demanding employer, but you've managed to visit me three times in a single week, Monsieur."

"I must try to mend what I have broken," he says.

"What is broken?"

His mouth works, twisting this way and that, as if he's trying to decide what to disclose. Finally, with a sigh, he speaks. "Thomas is most distressed by the reports of your unhappiness. He has not stopped asking questions about you, what I said to you, word for word, and then what you said."

"I see." My stomach churns. So Thomas knows that I am aware of his willing collaboration and that I disapprove. Well, what did he expect?

"And I take note of the fact that you have not asked me questions about Thomas' welfare," says Hellot, his voice edged with disapproval.

"You told me all I need to know," I shoot back. "Thomas is busy, day and night, perfecting the color blue that will be used in every flag and uniform and porcelain piece of France."

Hellot frowns and says, "Flag? Uniform? What do you mean?"

"Isn't Thomas finalizing the formula for his color blue? That's what you told me."

"Ah. I see. No, his blue, what he called Derby blue at the outset, does not translate to fabric. We discovered that at once. It is much too dark — and the mixture cannot be adjusted. Only when the blue is used on porcelain does it reach its transcendent potential."

It's warm in the carriage, but that is not the only reason I feel my forehead dampen and sweat trickle down my back. Did Thomas trick them into believing his color could not be used on fabric? Perhaps I was wrong to doubt him. But even if he's deceiving them on the fabric, he's busily perfecting the porcelain blue without question.

I try to hide my turmoil, and look out the window with unfeigned interest. Oceans of green greet me: sprawling fresh meadows, dotted with wildflowers.

"Where are you taking me, Monsieur Hellot?"

"To Versailles, where else?"

The center of power of the French king. My throat closes.

"Madame de Pompadour will receive you at a little house near the gardens, built just for her. She enjoys great privacy there with the King. It's called the Hermitage."

In panic, my nails dig into the flesh beneath the folds of my dress. "The King is there now?"

A dry laugh fills the carriage. "No, Mademoiselle."

While I hate being laughed at, I'm relieved beyond words that King Louis will not be present. Peering out, I say, "We seem to be traveling to the country, not a royal palace."

The carriage reaches the top of a rolling hill, pauses a few seconds, starts down on a bit of a descent, and at that moment...

I see Versailles.

CHAPTER THIRTY-EIGHT

As a Londoner, I've seen my share of grand buildings. The Tower of London sprawls on the Thames close to Spitalfields, and I've long thrilled at the sight of its medieval white tower, its greens endowed with ghoulish legends. I'm familiar with the silhouette of the Houses of Parliament in Westminster. And just last summer, Grandfather and I made a day of walking in Kensington, peeking at the trim palace containing the cantankerous George II. In London, the city is the master; the houses — be they for the royal family or the ministers of government — have been tucked here and there, wherever space could be seized.

Versailles is something so completely different.

Miles away from Paris, they built a royal palace on a field. Versailles is completely uniform, the endless wings and pavilions of its many buildings fashioned in one ornate style. Approaching the front gate, so tall and glittering it suggests a portal to heaven, I'm overcome with admiration. Not for King Louis XIV or any Bourbon, but for my Huguenot forefathers who possessed the courage to defy the monarch responsible for this torrent of brick and marble and paint and mirrors.

Will I have need of some of their courage today?

Our carriage is one of many in line to Versailles, heading toward the gate. But when we reach the front, we do not pass through and join the masses. Our driver swings to the left, skirting a series of buildings until the gardens and shimmering ponds materialize.

Monsieur Hellot clambers out first. I notice, for the first time, something frilly in his hand. It's a green and white parasol, and he hands it to me. I'm to hold it over my head as a shield from the sun on our walk to Madame de Pompadour.

Victoire also jumps down, his eyes on me. When Hellot takes my arm and we begin our walk, he falls in behind. Apparently Victoire thinks me capable of slipping away behind the shrubbery. He's not wrong.

The day has grown very warm indeed, but the famous gardens of Versailles leave me as cold as if it were a January midnight. Everything is beautiful: the rows of flowers, the spreading trees, the vivid green hedges. To me, though, the garden is not truly alive. I'm looking at nature whipped into submission. The hedges are sculpted so precisely it is as if every leaf and twig were trimmed with individual shears. Though I see no streams or other sources, the air bursts with the noisy white spray of many fountains, as if to proclaim Versailles' superiority to nature: *we control the water itself.*

What unnerves me the most are the golden busts and statues. They gleam everywhere. Men, women, and children, some nude and some in togas or other classical garb, writhe in ponds the size of lakes, or pounce from planting boxes, or loom at the top of ivy-edged steps. Their perfect golden faces are strangely unhappy. I wonder what it must be like at night, to wander through this garden and be among the golden people trapped in the sternly beautiful groves.

"Madame de Pompadour lives at Versailles?" I ask.

"She has her own permanent apartments within the palace, as well as a house in the garden," Hellot confirms and is then silent for a time.

"Her position is not an easy one. She has been the King's favorite for fourteen years and during that time her enemies' numbers have grown and grown."

"Are they envious?" I ask.

"There is some of that," Hellot says. "But most of Versailles has been set against her from the start."

"Because they disapprove of the King having a mistress?"

At that, Hellot stops in his tracks and laughs.

"I don't see what amuses you," I say coldly.

"The king of France is expected to have mistresses," he explains. "It would be a crisis if he *didn't*. Regarding Madame de Pompadour, they disapprove because she has no noble blood. She is of the bourgeois class." He sighs. "The fact that she brings the King happiness can never compensate."

"How do you know that she brings him such happiness?" I say, challenging him. I think of the Deer Park, elsewhere in Versailles, where King Louis stores his young conquests.

"Because I have known the King for many years," Hellot responds, wiping from his face the exertions of heat. "He is a man burdened by his position of leading monarch of the Western world, a man made melancholy by it, even, to be honest, bored by it. Madame dedicates herself to his comfort, his entertainments. Everything must be perfect. She will never permit herself to be anything less than perfect in every aspect."

We enter a wood providing shade, giving relief to Hellot, whose steps are starting to flag. Glancing over my shoulder, I see Victoire still follows.

My dread growing with each step, we make our way through the wood in silence, until the trees thin again. "Our destination," says Hellot, pointing ahead. "The Hermitage of Madame de Pompadour."

In England, the words Madame de Pompadour are synonymous with decadence and a display of frivolous, sensual luxury. Yet here I am, invited to her private retreat and it is… a farm?

Nestled between a bower of trees and a barn stands a wooden house with a thatched roof. The windows are flung open, with white cotton curtains fluttering in a puff of a breeze. On the lawn flowers bloom everywhere, instead of marching in the rigid lines of the palace gardens. I spot a riot of roses and beds of peonies and gardenias.

On the walkway to the door, I see it is not a single barn to the side of the house but a collection of buildings, a henhouse and a hothouse included. A farmhand herds two goats into the barn. I hear chickens squawking.

A young maid opens the door to Hellot's firm knock.

It doesn't take long for me to understand that this rustic dwelling is more than it seems. The floor is parquet, not dirt. Hanging on the wall in the little antechamber is a painting of exquisite detail.

Hellot has gone on ahead, and I hear the soft voice of Madame de Pompadour.

In the main room of the house, overflowing with flowers and books, the marquise is twirling, just as she did yesterday. This time she's showing off a dress with a large bow at the bodice and a nipped waist. Its most outstanding feature is its color — all pink, with no print, no embroidery or embellishment. This shade of pink is brilliant, not too bright nor too pale, and sets off her complexion to perfection, I must admit.

"My dear Hellot concocted this color just for me, what do you think?" she asks me, smiling.

I nod; it's obviously beautiful. She doesn't need me to say it.

Madame de Pompadour suggests that Hellot have a walk in her rose garden in the back of the house. "We will be talking as women now, leave us," she says with a playful push.

Yellow cakes and chocolat appear, not exactly the everyday repast at most country cottages. Over the mantle of the small, unlit fireplace I spot something else that gives away the true nature of the Hermitage's owner: a golden clock with a white enamel face, the slender Roman numerals taking their places in the circle. Studying it, I realize that the clock's golden swirls along the rim are in the shape of seashells.

Following my gaze, Madame de Pompadour says, indulgently, "The King adores his clocks. He could not spend any time, anywhere, without one in the room. When he came to the throne, the English horologists had surpassed the French. He made sure to correct that and now, I'm happy to say that French clocks are the best again."

"I suppose," I say, "that is why Thomas and I are here, in France. You must be foremost in everything, in porcelain too."

"In porcelain *too?*" she says with a pained laugh. "Porcelain is first in everything. Nothing is more important."

She studies me and then says, "There is nothing on earth that transforms itself like porcelain."

I remember the slats in the floor in Derby filled with dark clay smelling like rotting vegetables, and I cannot disagree.

"My belief is that those who work with porcelain, bent on bringing forth its exquisite qualities, are themselves transformed. Do you understand my meaning, Genevieve? Do you?"

I look away from her lovely face, her imploring yet imperious gaze, as I struggle against the force of her will.

She says, "I know you do not like being confined at the house in Sèvres, though I have made sure you are completely comfortable. I would like to remove all the constraints and welcome you as a true guest."

"Why?"

She says bluntly, "To make Thomas Sturbridge happy."

Answering her with my own bluntness, I say, "So that he will create his blue for you. But isn't he doing that already?"

"I want more from him than the one new color, as spectacular as it is. Jean Hellot is old, he wishes to retire. Thomas is young; he has the talent and knowledge to take this position, to guide Sèvres Porcelain to the next stage with his vision."

Thomas has succeeded here more than I — or possibly he — could ever imagine.

"How could an Englishman hold a key position in a French business concern?" I demand. "We are at war."

"There are many things about to occur, things you would have no way of knowing," says Madame de Pompadour, with the authority of someone who has seen correspondence with royal seals. "He would do well to accept a position in France, and having a French wife would smooth things over."

I feel as if I've been slapped in the face. "Yes, I suppose that would solve your problems, if Thomas married a woman you found for him here."

"A woman I have found?" She laughs. "I'm talking about *you*, Genevieve. You may have been born in England but you are French to your fingertips."

"No," I say.

She says, "You are intelligent, both artistic and pragmatic, with the spirit only a Frenchwoman could possess. And the passionate nature that drives men to distraction."

I feel my face turn fiery red.

"Oh, don't be embarrassed," she says, waving her hand. "I said we must speak woman to woman."

Fighting for dignity, I say, "Madame, I may be of French descent but I am Huguenot."

"Yes, of course I know that. But I am a friend and patron to many philosophers, including Voltaire, who believes in tolerance. A protégée of mine wrote a paper saying that France suffers without the talents and industry of its Protestant people and they should be welcomed back. I am not unsympathetic, Genevieve."

"And the King?" I say. "Is he not unsympathetic? By his laws, I should be in prison right now, not eating cake at Versailles."

"Oh, no one is sending you to prison. I cannot think of anything more absurd." She looks around the room, unsettled, before saying, tartly, "My, my, my, he is right! Forthright does not begin to describe you."

"Who is this person describing me?"

"Gabriel, of course," she says. "He knows he went too far in how you and Thomas were treated. But you made his life so very miserable."

"*I* made *his* life miserable?"

Madame de Pompadour takes a final sip of champagne. "Gabriel, when he first came to Paris, was the most beautiful young man anyone had ever laid eyes on. So brilliant and charming." Catching a look from me, she says, "Do not imagine I imply *that*. Since the day I first danced with the King, I have loved him with my entire heart. But Gabriel... ah, he is always mournful. So alone. And now that he is in disgrace..."

"He is disgraced?"

"Yes, well, Gabriel is an established traitor now in England. He did not handle his assignment well. There was indiscretion. Lives lost. I did what I could to defend him, but I was under a cloud myself for my role in it."

"I don't understand."

Madame de Pompadour hesitates and then says, "Le Secret du Roi report to the king alone and I honestly know nothing about it or any of their names, except for Gabriel's. He was a favorite of the court when he came here as part of his Grand Tour. We formed a friendship. He has been invaluable in England for at least ten years." She fidgets, twisting the bracelet around her wrist. "I should not have asked him to get me the new blue that was rumored to exist in England."

As the truth of what she's saying sinks in, and all of its implications, I feel as if the room spins.

"It was *you*," I say. "Not King Louis. Sir Gabriel admitted to me the blue was for Sèvres and I thought, everyone thought, it was to obtain the blue for the King. The color of France."

Madame de Pompadour says firmly, "It was for Sèvres and also for the King. How could we in France be expected to endure the creation of a superior blue in England, of all places?" Shaking her head, she says, "But Gabriel took it all so seriously. He became obsessed. He has an obsessive character, as you of course would know."

Looking into my eyes, all grave sincerity, Madame de Pompadour says, "I did not want anyone to be killed or kidnapped as part of obtaining Thomas' formula. Not that, no, no, no. It is all regrettable."

I am not sure I believe her, or much of anything else she has said.

"I will redouble my efforts to rehabilitate Gabriel with the King, but so far, no success," she says. "He tells me he may go to Italy."

"To Venice?"

"Yes." A shrewd, assessing glance from Madame de Pompadour. "You know about this plan, I see." She leans forward. "Let us be practical. I will keep trying, but Gabriel is most likely finished. Thomas is the future. Spies are easily found. A genius is something else entirely."

A shiver runs through me at her ruthlessness.

"Thomas Sturbridge will be the next chief chemist of Sèvres, succeeding Jean Hellot, and he will make history with his creations," she says with complete assurance. "Thomas loves you, he says he can't stay in France without you. I can't lose my creator. So we need to make an accommodation with each other, Genevieve."

I cannot bear to speak to her right now, I am so angry and confused.

She says softly, "Think of this. You can get married, have children. I'll give you a beautiful house — I hear that Victoire and Sophie Lemanteau are attached to you. They can work for you permanently. And you do not have to sit in the house, Genevieve. I know you do not fancy idleness. You can paint. You can be one of the chief decorators at Sèvres. Or I will hire for you a history painter and develop your talents. You can exhibit your work in Paris, Genevieve. I can make this happen for you."

I close my eyes. The scent of the sea of flowers outside, mingling with that of the gathered bouquets inside, creates one fragrance, luxuriantly complex and yet fragile. This particular fragrance will never live again after this afternoon. And I sense that this offer from Madame de Pompadour will not come again. But my pulses race with anger, too, with how she's sought to learn my most intimate thoughts and desires, my wishes for my future, to carve out some significance, and taken it all and put it into a neat package of temptation. And I resent that Sir Gabriel has fed her these personal details — or was is Thomas?

Suddenly the face of my grandfather appears before me, and my eyes fly open.

I say, "And again, I tell you this cannot happen if I am Huguenot. I would have to convert, and it's impossible."

"Genevieve, I will tell you something not widely known. A few exceptions have always been made, for certain Huguenot bankers, ministers, or military leaders. They have not been arrested, or punished, because France needs them too much. For you, the same exception could be quietly made."

"So for me you would look the other way, but any other Protestant would be subject to persecution?"

She shrugs, as if to say that is the best she can do. That shrug seals it for me.

"Madame, I cannot participate in the freedoms of France until they are available to all Huguenots. When the laws against all of us are changed, I will happily take up your offer."

The pupils within her shimmering hazel eyes widen in fury. Madame de Pompadour seems to be on the verge of an outburst. With visible effort, she subdues herself. As frustrated as she is, she's not going to punish me — not yet. She is still determined.

"I see," she says.

I say, genuinely baffled, "How can the color blue be this important to you, to anyone? You cherish porcelain, I understand that. But why this color?"

"Blue is the sky and the sea, it is eternity. Yet it eludes us in art. No one has made its elusive beauty tangible like this before — no one. When I look at Thomas' blue porcelain, I see art that will last forever. I will be gone, as will you, Thomas, Gabriel... but the blue remains."

Well, I asked a question and she answered it. How can I or anyone stand in her path when she's grasping toward eternity?

With that far-sighted, otherworldly gaze, she murmurs, "Do you believe in magic, in destiny?"

"No."

"When I was nine years old, a prophetess told my family that my fortune was to one day win the heart of a king."

"And this was taken seriously by your family?"

"Completely. I was educated in every possible art and science.

Dancing, singing, drawing, writing, acting. First, of course, they sent me to the Ursuline Convent in Poissy, for best advantage."

To learn your child will one day be a courtesan — to exult at this news, and not only that, to send the child to a *nunnery* to prepare for eventual seduction? She said I was a true Frenchwoman, but I could live in this country 100 years and not understand the French.

"You will think over everything I've said?" Madame de Pompadour says.

I nod, and she stands, signaling it is time for me to be gone. In the last moment, her more pragmatic, assessing eye on me again, she eases the bracelet off her wrist. "That color suits you as I knew it would — it brings out your eyes, Genevieve — but you are in dire need of accessories," she says sweetly.

And with that, I am ushered outside, clutching the bracelet. What she cannot know is that this is finally in my answer, my salvation. With such a piece of jewelry to sell, I can pay for travel expenses; success is at last possible.

And Madame de Pompadour's campaign of charm has accomplished one more thing: I know Thomas is lost to me. She will never let him go. All that keeps him from becoming Sèvres' complete creature is me, and my departure is the only thing left to do. It is best for both of us.

Back inside the house, I pace the floor, back and forth, thinking about everything Madame de Pompadour said, cursing her for what she's done to me, to Thomas... and to Sir Gabriel, too. I can't help but feel a pang of sympathy for Sir Gabriel, who was used and abandoned.

A steady rap on the door means they've most likely brought me a late dinner.

When the door opens, it's Victoire, not Sophie, and he beckons for me to come out. "If you please, your dinner will be served at the table," he says.

Tonight may be the night I will go, I think with grim determination, and hurry out the door.

Standing by the table, his head slightly bowed, is Thomas.

CHAPTER THIRTY-NINE

Neither of us moves. Neither of us speaks.

Here is the man I fell in love with. But in crucial ways, he is different. I take careful note of his light gray coat and fitted embroidered waistcoat, types of clothing I've never seen him wear before. His face has filled out a little, and a sprinkling of freckles warms his cheeks. Apparently, Thomas' grueling schedule for Sèvres Porcelain has included visits to the tailor, fine cooking, and walks in the sun. Part of Thomas' fascination for me had always been how he stood apart from other men: Good looking but oblivious of it, dressed carelessly, which speaks to my rebel soul, and always a bit ravaged in health and the demands of genius, which speaks to heart. But now he resembles a handsome gallant, impeccably groomed, dressed, and polished, like other men of society. Like… Sir Gabriel Courtenay.

"I have trout prepared for dinner," Sophie says shyly. "Victoire cleaned two fish."

"Thank you," Thomas says to Sophie. Taking a step toward me, he says, "I would very much like to dine here, if Genevieve is willing."

I would prefer to boot Thomas back to his new masters. Yet another part, which is also making it hard for me to draw a full breath, longs for him to stay.

I shrug. "You're here, you may as well have something to eat."

I spot Victoire in the corner, frowning at my churlishness.

Thomas takes a seat at the table. I choose a place opposite from him. Sophie and Victoire retreat to ready the meal.

He places his hands on the table and says in English, very rapidly, "I've been going mad. I heard you had stopped eating, Genevieve, that you were distraught, in despair."

I say, coldly, "Do I appear to be in despair?"

"You look exquisite, truth to tell." He smiles that mischievous smile that I have missed desperately, the same smile I saw in the Dolphin when we first met. But anger is still there.

"This dress is a gift from your great patroness, Madame de Pompadour," I say, pulling at the sleeve. "I paid her a visit today, which you must surely be aware of, since you're here at long last."

"I have asked, pleaded, threatened them, over and over, saying I must be permitted to see you," Thomas says, vehemently. "I was refused. They showed me reports on your welfare, to prove to me you hadn't been harmed."

"Harmed? No, no one has harmed me. Not yet."

Sophie sets down the plates of food: the trout, cut into pieces, cooked in wine and butter and rosemary, the asparagus, the radishes. Her eyes spark with curiosity.

Attempting to break the tense mood, Thomas scoops up forkfuls of the trout and then calls out praise to Sophie. She and her brother beam. I think about Madame de Pompadour's offer to set Thomas and me up in a house, with Sophie and Victoire.

I say, "I wager that the true reason they've kept us apart — it was so that I would not interfere with your work, weaken your progress. I'm sure Sir Gabriel said I would be an opposing influence. He knew things would proceed better without me."

"Yet now we are allowed to meet?" he says, frowning as he considers.

"Because now the pressure is to be put on me," I say. "Madame de Pompadour thinks I will agree to her proposals, if I see you like this. That's why you were sent over."

"And what gave her that idea?"

I spear a chunk of trout. "I don't know," I lie. I am not ready to tell him of the promises Madame de Pompadour made. But then I toss down my fork. "How could you do it, Thomas?" I demand. "How could you work with Monsieur Hellot to produce Derby blue?"

"I did everything I could to contain the damage," Thomas says, glancing sideways at Victoire and Sophie. I'm certain that Sophie can't understand English and I doubt very much Victoire can, but it's a mistake to underestimate him, always. I suspect that Thomas is trying to convey to me that he sabotaged the production of blue for fabric. He is right to be cautious — that is explosive information.

"But Hellot told me the color blue for porcelain is nearly ready," I say. "Why didn't you put them off? Bottger kept the King of Saxony waiting for ten years. You lasted two months!"

"Now, Genevieve, that is hardly fair. No one else in Saxony knew a single thing about porcelain when Bottger was trying to break the Chinese formula. While I was, within hours of saying goodbye to you, face to face with Jean Hellot, the chemist with the most advanced knowledge of porcelain color production in all of Europe. Not to mention, he had in his possession a piece of porcelain stolen already and the basic premise of my formula, which you had passed along to

Sir Gabriel Courtenay in the spring!"

When he presents the facts like this, I have to admit that evasion would be difficult.

I pick up my fork again and attempt to eat Sophie's dinner, and Thomas does the same. "Where do you live, where do they keep you?" I ask.

"At the porcelain manufactory. There are living quarters there for many of us, within the main building."

I say bitterly, "How nice it must be for you to work under such splendid conditions."

Thomas blinks and says, "There are a great many workers, yes, but there are also problems. The money that is earned from sales of porcelain does not come close to paying for the running of the manufactory: the large staff, the expensive materials."

Surprised, I say, "When I was at Derby, Mr. Heath was most grieved by Sèvres, and envious, because he thought its success could not be matched."

"In England we none of us had any idea of the true situation at Sèvres. I overhear them fretting. The loans have reached 200,000 livres. If the bank notes were to be called, and they may be soon, the porcelain manufactory would be ruined."

Sipping the wine, I say, "Well, one thing is certain, Madame de Pompadour can coax funds from a certain royal person to make up the difference."

"I don't know how easy that would be. The country is straining under taxes it can barely pay. The war is devouring."

I set down the wine. "Is it possible," I say slowly, "that for all her talk of the infinity of blue, the reason Madame de Pompadour was so desperate to get her hands on your formula is to pour money into Sèvres' coffers, to save it from ruin?"

He says quietly, "It's possible."

Money. When it comes to porcelain, whether England or France, the answer is always money.

Thomas clears his throat. "I understand that you're painting again. When I heard that, I was very, very happy."

"Wasn't it you who arranged for the canvas and paints to be sent?"

"No, it was not me," he says. He frowns, but then pushes forward. "I'm very happy about it, I know how much your work means to you."

His kindness, his support, always warms me. What would it be like to live with Thomas, while painting, exhibiting my work in Paris when it was ready? Every day we'd eat like this, we'd talk over our day, laugh together. At night we'd sleep in the same bed. I can almost see the outlines of two little heads peeking over the top of this table. Our children.

I can't bear this agony any longer. My face sinks into my hands.

"What is it, Genevieve?"

"Why don't you admit it, you want to live in France and be the next head of chemistry at Sèvres Porcelain," I say. "The time has come for honesty."

His face reddens. "Honesty? You call for honesty? You?"

"At last!" I hurl back. "The patient and understanding Mr. Sturbridge shall tell me what he really thinks."

"Let's begin with the fact that your entire presence at Derby was a façade — you went there at Courtenay's bidding to acquaint yourself with me and learn the formula. To pretend friendship, and more besides."

It is like a slap across my face, to have him put into words the disgusting truth of what I had done. His condemnation hurts me — while I had demanded it, had in fact long craved it.

Thomas says, "And the entire time, you were his… his *creature*."

"No. I am no one's *creature*. Not Sir Gabriel's — and not yours, either."

Victoire appears at the table, scowling at Thomas. He plainly does not know what we are saying but our quarrel triggers his protective instinct.

"Perhaps you should leave," I say to Thomas.

"Yes, certainly. I will not trouble you any further." He shoots to his feet. In a few quick strides, Thomas is at the door.

His hand on the doorway, he turns to take a last look at me, his eyes bright with pain.

"Thomas, no," I say, pushing past the table, running to him. "No, no, no."

He enfolds me in his arms, not kissing me, just laying his cheek against mine and hugging me. The strain and confusion, the loneliness and fear, break inside me and I sob as Thomas holds me.

"It will be all right, it will be," he says. I am grateful for his soothing words, his strong arms, but I know that things will not be all right.

I take him by the hand and lead Thomas to the garden. "I will tell you everything Madame de Pompadour said to me," I say, wiping my eyes with a kerchief.

Thomas stays silent throughout, listening closely, as I begin with her first visit, her compliments and gifts of strawberries and Voltaire, and relaying all I can remember of our conversation in her hermitage. When I come to the marquise's telling me that Thomas and I could marry, I flush.

Thomas reaches for my hand and kisses it. "I would marry you tomorrow, of course. You know how much I love you."

"And I love you." I look down. "That is why I can't insist that you spurn her offer, it means so much to you."

Thomas says, "Do you think that I wish to serve King Louis? That doesn't enter into it at all." He sets me down in the one chair in the garden and then kneels at my feet, his elbows on my knees and hands clasped, as if he were praying. "I dream of a world beyond nations and their brutal wars over faraway lands, their insane thirst for conquest. I have no respect for Louis XV. Nor do I respect George II. To me, they are all the same. Our society is rotted; man is without liberty. It's as Rousseau said, 'The fruits of the earth belong to everyone.' Science is the only master I can ever have."

"They seek to use you, Thomas, for their benefit. They're working to own you — body and soul by use of your ideals."

"What a lofty-minded, benevolent, foolish sort of man you think me," he says, smiling fleetingly. "I hate to disabuse you, Genevieve. But you don't perceive that it is *I* who am using *them*?"

I shake my head. "You can't. They have all the power. It's wrong — you can't imagine how much I agree with you that this is wrong, a rotted system. But do not underestimate them."

His dark-auburn eyebrow arches. "I don't, not for a single second."

I take his face in my hands. "Thomas, I cannot be a Huguenot benefitting from Madame de Pompadour's patronage, which means King Louis' patronage, even if an exception were made for my faith. Not while my beliefs are illegal for other Protestants. She wants me to be a happy bird, singing in a cage. I can't do it."

"I understand. But then…"

Victoire clears his throat behind us. "It is time for Monsieur to leave," he says. "The carriage will take him."

"Yes, thank you very much," Thomas responds in French, rising to his feet, and pulling me up to him for an embrace. He whispers in my ear, in English, "I told you I would preserve our lives, Genevieve, and I have, haven't I? I'll find a way out for both of us. You must trust me. You haven't — not entirely."

He's right. I haven't. I love him, but trust is far more difficult. "I shall try," I whisper back. "But you must trust me too. And if it comes to it, you'll do this my way. Escape."

With Victoire watching and waiting, I kiss him, and with that he is gone, absorbed into Sèvres again, like a bee returning to its hive.

*

If there was any hope that his visit was the first of many, the following days prove otherwise. In the next week, I do not see Thomas again, nor do I receive any word from him. There is only silence. How are we to make plans? But I cannot give in to my nerves, and raise the suspicions of Victoire. We have returned to a more lax arrangement; my door is not locked at night. Should I decide to escape, I need to lull him into a false sense of security. I make myself eat, I struggle to paint.

On a hot afternoon, I paint my own watchful face in the window of the stone bridge, in Derby. Madame de Pompadour is right, I think sourly. I do belong there. That night, after I finish the painting, I peer outside and see Victoire enjoying the garden. Hoping to learn something, anything, I join him.

"The war is no longer going well for France," he says. "The news crossed the Atlantic. We've lost Martinique. The commander of the island surrendered to the English."

"Ah, I see," I say, rejoicing inside. "Are you certain that there's no word of any invasion effort? Using ships built at Le Havre?"

He shakes his head.

So hostilities between England and France come to a full boil, with England poised to triumph. There couldn't be a worse time for Thomas to try to extricate himself from Sèvres Porcelain. His departure would fatally weaken the manufactory's earning potential at a time when the King could not possibly increase investment.

What will they do to Thomas should his plan go wrong — and to me?

A potential answer arrives, and it comes in the form of a thick cream-colored page of vellum addressed to me, sealed with a large, red wax ornamentation and a white flower above. Victoire's somber expression when he hands it to me is worrying

"What does this mean?" I ask, touching the initials raised on the red seal: two "L"s with a "B" between them. It is familiar, but I can't place the origin.

"Those are the marks of Sèvres Porcelain," he says.

It must be from Thomas then. But why the formal presentation?

"And this?" I point at the three petals, which, the more I study them, look familiar too. "It looks a bit like the fleur de lis."

"That is the personal mark of King Louis XV," Victoire says.

I drop it on the table as if it were hot enough to burn me. Victoire draws out his knife and slices the seal, handing the paper to me.

"Mademoiselle Genevieve Planché is cordially invited to attend a presentation to be held at Sèvres Porcelain at seven o'clock, on the tenth of July."

That is a fortnight away. Everything about this screams a warning, even a trap. Is Sèvres Porcelain where my fate will be decided? I have to say, it does not come as a surprise.

No, it was always inevitable.

CHAPTER FORTY

As the sun lowers in the sky on the tenth of July, 1759, I step into the light carriage bound for Sèvres Porcelain. I've no idea what will unfold there, still less why my presence is desired. I wear the dark dress Madame de Pompadour sent me weeks ago as well as her bracelet, and I carry a determination to fight my way out of this morass, one way or another.

Victoire leaps up to take the seat next to the carriage driver, the same as he did when I was taken to Madame de Pompadour. I do not know if he will closely shadow me tonight. If he does not, then there may be a way for me to slip away. In my many weeks in this house, chatting with Victoire and Sophie, I've gleaned the knowledge that we are quite close to Paris. Tonight, I wear the bracelet.

Once again, the countryside beckons, grassy fields and brilliant flowers, and making our way there it's hard to believe we approach the most sophisticated porcelain maker in all of Europe. In a short time we follow a drive that curves around a bank of trees, and the carriage reaches a clearing. I lean out the window to take in the sight of the building rising before me.

Four stories high and hundreds of feet long, Sèvres is not a manufactory but a castle, the last rays of sun glowing in its upper windows. Two long wings terminate in pavilions. Nestled behind it, I spot the outlines of twenty ovens that fire the wares. This is Madame de Pompadour's greatest triumph. But also her greatest risk. How does a woman who lives for perfection, who demands it of herself, cope with the collapse of a world-famous business?

The drive widens and my carriage joins a line of others. In the central courtyard in front of Sèvres, lanterns flicker. I hear the fluttering music of violin and harpsichord. A group of people, perhaps twenty dressed in silks and satins, mill about. The women flutter fans before their faces. There's no sun shining on them now, but the air is hot and still. One man, wearing a tightly coiled wig, leans back, overcome with laughter, and others join in.

It's most definitely a party, with no sign of Thomas among the guests.

I step out of the carriage, and suddenly I can go no farther. I find my legs rooted to the ground. I hold an invitation in my own name for once — the Christmas gathering of Hogarth's seems a lifetime ago — but this is a party I do not want to propel myself into.

I turn back toward Victoire. "Is the King here?" I ask, nervously.

He shakes his head. "His Majesty goes nowhere without his personal guard for fear of assassins, and there's no sign of them."

I turn, take a deep breath, and walk in the direction of the courtyard. Victoire does not follow. Two guards with swords swinging from scabbards stand at the courtyard entryway. One beckons for the invitation, and after a scrutiny of me, my dress, and my paper, delivers a courtly bow.

"Welcome to Sèvres Porcelain, Mademoiselle."

I quickly realize that the other people in the courtyard could not be employees at the porcelain manufactory. They are surely from Versailles or Paris and, while strangers to me, are well known to one another. The way they talk, laugh, grimace, and lean close for a whisper speaks of intimacies gained over years. One group of older men cluster in serious conversation; another group of men is lighthearted. I take note of the presence of a priest; he stands with the light-hearted. As for the women, their clothing is more elaborate, their jewels brighter and their hair higher than I've ever seen in London. They powder their hair and cover their faces with paint so thick that their true features are hard to discern.

While I observe all of them, no one examines me. I stand alone at a party of society, but in this instance I'm not regarded disapprovingly. They simply look through me, incurious.

The paneled door to the porcelain manufactory opens and two men slip out to join us.

My pulse quickens. Thomas is not one of them, but Monsieur Jean Hellot is. The pair are immediately the center of attention.

"What is the grand secret, Jean-Claude Dupleisse, why were we summoned here?" calls out a lady, her hair teased to a point one foot taller than her skull and red rouge in the shape of upside-down triangles startling her cheeks.

"You will learn soon enough," says the man standing next to Hellot, replying not just to her but to everyone, holding up his hands and smiling, though to my eyes he looks uneasy.

There's a burst of laughter as a young wigged man wearing a cream-colored waistcoat fidgets with some object. I slide closer to get a look. The object is a large, lanky doll, dressed like a Harlequin trickster with its black eye mask and black-and-red checked suit. The young man, by holding strings and levers, makes the wooden doll dance.

"Tell us, Dupleisse, tell us, oh, won't you please," the young man calls out, in a sing-song voice. The pantin dances, crazily, as the guests clap. Pleased by the applause, the man widens his circle of performance.

He whips around and makes his doll dance in my direction. Its dead marble eyes behind the mask glitter with the reflection of light from the glowing lanterns, making his eyes seem to roll in his head. It's coming to life. I clench my fists. I feel like the pantin is laughing at me, mocking my plan to escape, that everyone here joins him in mocking me. My rage shifts to a hollow terror, for every person's eyes turn to me, and they bare their teeth.

The young man pivots again, and the crowd shifts, and I realize that there is no predatory malevolence targeting me in this bizarre dance. It was my imagination.

I must get hold of my feelings, arrange my priorities. *Concentrate.*

I need to speak to Hellot to find out where Thomas is, but the director of chemistry and Dupleisse are engulfed by guests competing for their attention. I've no choice but to bide my time.

"Would you care for champagne?" a servant asks, bending from the waist as he slides a gilded tray holding four brimming glasses my way.

"Thank you, no," I say.

"A few months in France and you still haven't developed a taste for wine."

The smell of jasmine drifts over me as Sir Gabriel Courtenay smoothly snatches a glass of champagne from the tray. He wears a deep russet coat, his waistcoat cross-stitched with tiny gems. The odds that Thomas and I will leave tonight just plummeted.

"Why are you here?" I ask.

"I think the more interesting question is, why are *you* here?"

"I was invited." Sir Gabriel didn't know? It's possible he's not in complete control of events. That's an interesting prospect, if a bit unnerving.

"So you do not approve of my being freed from confinement?" I say.

"I do, when you come appropriately dressed," he responds.

There's a stir behind me. Madame de Pompadour, in a gown of shimmering lavender, a matching ribbon around her slender white throat, makes her way through the crowd, greeting well-wishers. I have no wish to be in her company, but, unfortunately, she wishes to be in mine. The Marquise heads for me and Gabriel with that determined, graceful step.

"There are many surprises for me here," she says to Gabriel. "Although you finding your way to her side" — she gestures in my direction — "is not one."

Sir Gabriel looks away, his jaw tightening.

"Could it be Hellot at the root of this?" she says to him, her voice low so that no one else can hear except for Sir Gabriel and myself.

He nods, saying, "I've determined it has nothing to do with the director. Dupleisse is in the dark."

"But would Hellot dare?" she demands.

At that moment, the woman with hair teased highest, who I suspect is inebriated, storms Madame de Pompadour in a fit of excitement. The King's favorite is swallowed up by her admirers.

"What do the two of you think Monsieur Hellot has done?" I ask Sir Gabriel.

"Organized all of this," Sir Gabriel says, gesturing toward the crowd. "He's found a path directly to His Majesty, arranged something, without including Madame de Pompadour or Dupleisse. It's an unimaginable tactic."

"But doesn't Sèvres Porcelain offer its pieces for sale at presentations?" I ask. "Why is this one unusual?"

"Because these people aren't potential buyers, they're investors," he says, his eyes roaming the courtyard. "Everyone here either holds shares in Derby Porcelain or is a friend of Madame de Pompadour's. Something big is happening to the manufactory itself. And she has no idea what."

Madame de Pompadour herself smiles in the center of her fawning circle, as if she had not a care in the world.

"Well, why doesn't she just ask the King what this evening is all about?" I ask impatiently.

"You don't understand Versailles, Genevieve."

"So I've been told."

A female guest turns to stare at Sir Gabriel, then leans over to others to whisper, and they, too, survey him; not with the usual appreciation he inspires in women, but with the smiles of shared unpleasant gossip.

Sir Gabriel stands taller than ever; I can see in his face and stance his effort to achieve nonchalance. Perhaps no one else could detect the signs but me. Being a pariah among the privileged is of no concern to me. But the order of society, the right of a certain class to rule while others are condemned to oblivion and poverty, is so important to Sir Gabriel Courtenay. What is he left with, when they turn on him?

Something stirs inside me. "So you are planning to leave France?"

"Nothing is decided."

"And aren't you angry?"

He peers at me, guarded. "What do you mean?"

"Madame de Pompadour used you and then abandoned you."

"Ah, Genevieve, always so dramatic," he says, but bereft of sarcasm.

"And I don't think you'll be returning to England at the head of an invasion fleet," I say quietly.

"That would be made especially difficult by the fact that five days ago the English burned the fleet of the French navy gathered in Le Havre," he says. "The English appeared out of nowhere and bombarded the ships with heavy fire before a defense could be mounted. Very few men were killed, but the ships are wrecked. It was a most audacious feat."

I am nearly certain that there is admiration in his voice. Sir Gabriel has a high regard for the country of his birth, even though it's a country he has betrayed and will most likely never see again. All because of the blue — and me.

"I think," I say, "I shall never understand all of your invisible circumstances, Sir Gabriel."

"Oh?"

"Was it you who sent me the canvas and supplies so that I could paint?" I ask.

He nods.

I swallow, and say, "Thank you."

I'm not sure what I expect but it is not this. Sir Gabriel laughs, shaking his head.

"What is so amusing?" I demand.

"Do you know that is the first time you've thanked me, Genevieve, for anything? And for it to be voiced now, here, at Sèvres? The gods are surely having their sport with me."

I'm not sure how to respond to this. But before I can answer, a new commotion ripples through the party.

"The King... the King... the King," they whisper.

Louis XV has arrived.

CHAPTER FORTY-ONE

The lethal enemy of every Huguenot is here. My legs tremble as I watch a phalanx of guards, wearing blue and gold livery, stride into the crowd. Above their heads appears the white wig of a tall man.

There is a break in the crowd, all curtseying and bowing, and I glimpse King Louis XV, a glittering figure with a proud visage. He is nearing fifty, dark eyes, a hawk-like nose, and the lips that to some may suggest carnality but to me shout cruelty. For the first time in my life, someone whom I've heard about for years is before me in the flesh, and he's exactly as I always pictured him.

The King strides toward Madame de Pompadour, who has not moved since he arrived. When he's a foot away she sinks to the floor in a deep curtsey. Coming up, her smile is radiant. He kisses her hand, and they draw together.

"Very well, Hellot," the King says in a deep timbered, weary voice. "On with it."

Hellot, now revealed as the impresario of the event, announces that we are to all move to the presentation room of Sèvres Porcelain for what next occurs. I fall in behind the others. I must find an opportunity to talk to Hellot, to ask him where Thomas is. Failing that, I will find him myself. But how will I do that, with Sir Gabriel at my side?

As we walk up the wide stairs, long corridors stretch on either side, candlelight spilling from dozens of doorways. A few people peek out at us with curiosity. Finding Thomas in this building will be supremely difficult even if I can manage to slip away from Sir Gabriel.

We reach the high-ceilinged presentation room, lit with candelabras everywhere. There are small platforms erected throughout the room, at shoulder height, and at the end of the room a larger, lower raised platform.

Thomas Sturbridge stands next to that platform, alone.

I gasp, drawing back, at the exact same time Sir Gabriel sees him and says, "What the devil?" Thomas' eyes scan the crowd until he sees me and nods, but grimly. He looks quite nervous.

Sir Gabriel turns to stare at me. I shake my head slightly. I don't know what is happening.

Hellot walks to the platform, climbing the three steps to stand before us. He clears his throat, glancing down at Thomas, as if for reassurance.

Whatever is about to happen, they are in it together.

Hellot calls out, "Your Majesty, ladies and gentlemen, may I present our new color... the blue!"

A line of servants proceed into the room, each carrying a porcelain object that is painted Derby blue.

My first emotion is disbelief. I knew that Thomas was nearing completion, that he would have to try to keep them happy to survive. The blue was inevitable, yes. But to arrange my being invited here so that I could witness his submission? And in the presence of Madame de Pompadour and King Louis? I see Thomas across the room, talking to Jean Hellot, the older man looking at him proudly, as if he were his son.

The color causes a sensation. One by one the finished objects take their places as the invited guests stare, open-mouthed, the supercilious attitudes gone. The blue is either the entire object or a background or part of a smaller decoration. All of these people can see its intrinsic superiority, its peerless beauty.

A tureen with a resplendent goddess gracing the side.

A delicate bouquet of blue flowers.

Two blue-and-gold goblets meant for the finest champagne.

A snuffbox with a nobleman's proud sneer painted atop.

It goes on and on, all the pieces painted with a blue so delicate and so bold, icily perfect and excitingly sensual at the same time.

The piece of porcelain closest to me is a pot-pourri à vaisseau, a two-foot-tall potpourri vessel, shaped like a ship, with a small sailboat painted in a white circle. I draw closer, studying the boat, beautifully sculpted, knowing that its sails, rigging, and puffy clouds were painted with a tiny brush. It has been decorated with superb skill. A great many people, highly trained, incredibly talented, spent countless hours creating it.

I move closer still, my fingers close to touching it. My breath coming quick, I reach for the pot-pourri à vaisseau. It is exquisite, yes. And it also represents everything that I most hate, everything that I have fought against. I want to push it off the platform. Here, in front of a king, I ache to smash it into a hundred pieces.

I had thought that tonight, if events turned a certain way, I could slip away in the crowd, out of Sèvres Porcelain, melting into the streets of Paris as I did when I escaped from my grandfather's house in Spitalfields all those months ago. But right now I don't want to disappear. I long to destroy, to show everyone what I think of their creations of beauty, the creations they obsess over that have cost me so much. I'll destroy myself in the process, and I don't care.

I feel his eyes on me — I look up at Thomas, frowning. He understands me better than any other man. He loves me. He would not bring me here to trick me, or devastate me.

Trust. He asked for it. More than any man living, he deserves it.

My hands drop to my side.

Hellot ascends the raised platform at the end of the room. He says, "His Majesty King Louis XV wishes to take this opportunity to inform all assembled that he has made a decision. Papers have been drawn up to make the King the sole stockholder of Sèvres. This place of creation will now officially be designated the Royal Porcelain Manufactory. The King of France owns Sèvres."

Madame de Pompadour says, "Oh!" and covers her mouth. Even with all of her control, she cannot conceal her shock. A few seconds later, as the implications sink in, she looks at the King across the room, with unmistakable joy and gratitude. The threat of bankruptcy is over. The leading porcelain factory in Europe is safe.

Hellot says, "His Royal Highness has something to tell you all."

Now they all look at one another in surprise. It seems that the King of France does not often speak in public.

Once he surveys the crowd, he says, gazing at only one person, "I hope I have made you happy today, Madame."

She curtsies, her eyes filling with tears. "Yes, Sire," she breathes.

"Then you will indulge me." He points at Thomas and says, to seemingly no one in particular, "Is that the English chemist?" The way he says *English* is with distaste.

"He is," says Hellot, and beckons Thomas to come forward.

Thomas Sturbridge walks to a place directly below the King, his every step marked by courage. My breathing comes quicker; I can hardly bear standing here.

"Your blue porcelain is quite… good," says King Louis. "However,

I have by this action made Sèvres a manufactory of the crown. You understand that to produce porcelain painted a color invented by an English chemist, it will not do. We are at war with England. Blue is the sacred color of France."

"Yes, Your Majesty," says Thomas.

"We shall make use of our own people, who are the most gifted in the world, to create all of our colors," says Louis, glimpsing at Monsieur Hellot, nodding firmly in response.

"It is possible that actions to recruit you were made in error," the King says, his gaze searching, and finding, Sir Gabriel Courtenay in the room. For a moment, king and spy regard each other and I feel the room hum with a decade of secrets flowing between them. "And I believe that these actions were initiated by those who had the intention of pleasing me." He turns to Madame de Pompadour, whose face flushes. "And you should realize, Madame, it does please me. I will forever be pleased with you."

In the way he speaks to her, some deep question between them is resolved. Madame de Pompadour nods, and I see her long fingers tremble around her fan as she struggles to hide her emotions from the gawking partygoers. It is their affair, its intertwined needs and emotions unfathomable to me, that sent into motion everything that happened to me, to Sir Gabriel, to Thomas.

Louis XV speaks again: "But this blue will only be on display a single night and that is tonight. Tomorrow these objects will be destroyed, the shade will be destroyed, never to be resumed in its production at Sèvres."

I look at Thomas, and he stares back at me, his eyes blazing with triumph. This is his solution, a drastic one to be sure, and something of which I never dreamed. He must have brought the idea to Hellot, or they formed it together. For whatever reasons — and Hellot's affection for Thomas surely did play a part — a way was found to release Thomas Sturbridge from Sèvres, to make his contribution unwanted.

"Where is the English girl?" asks the king, again addressing the room.

"I am here," I shout, raising my hand.

Disapproval shudders across the room. Clearly this is not the way to address royalty. I push my way forward.

Before I reach the King, Thomas hurries to meet me, and bring me to the front of the room. He takes my hand as he looks sideways at me, smiling, as we approach King Louis.

Louis XV called me "the English girl". Is it possible he does not realize I am a hated Huguenot? Then I realize: to him I am English — and I *am* English. Born there, raised there, and I passionately wish to return there, if a way can be found.

In the last few seconds of my approach, Louis XV's eyes move up and down my figure.

"You are an artist, I hear?" he says.

"I am," I say, raising my chin.

"Hmmm," the King says, permitting himself a smile. He is enjoying himself. "And I take it you would both wish to return to England?" he says.

"Yes," Thomas and I say at the same time, very clear.

The King says, "France broke off diplomatic relations with England years ago, of course, so we have a bit of a difficulty. However, I received an audience earlier today from the Dutch ambassador. His country remains neutral, and he may be willing to assist the two of you in returning to England and smoothing over the difficulties. Is that acceptable?"

Thomas stammers that it is, as I nod, speechless.

"If the Dutch balk, we will make them a porcelain dinner setting in one of your finest colors, Hellot."

"Yes, Your Majesty."

"We know the Dutch have nothing like Sèvres," says the King, and the room laughs. Thomas and I stand before him, unsure of whether our 'audience' is finished.

Louis XV eyes Thomas. "It would be… unfortunate if this color were to appear in England," says the King.

"I intend to devote myself to other areas of scientific research," says Thomas. "My work with blue is finished."

"Good," says King Louis. "Very good."

He turns his proud head toward Madame de Pompadour. "I would ask you, Madame, if you alone would care to remain with me, admiring this particular blue. We will not have it long, but while we have it, we may enjoy it."

She walks to the King, drops another deep curtsey, and rises with tears glistening on her eyelashes. "Yes, Sire."

She has won her most fervent desire — the public devotion of King Louis and the triumph of her porcelain — and yet I doubt she will ever understand what set in motion Thomas' plan, executed by Jean Hellot. If it were not for his love for me, none of this would have taken place. It is my love story that changed the destiny of Sèvres, not just hers.

The King comes down the steps of the platform to take her by the hand, and the rest of us are ushered out of the room. Louis XV and Madame de Pompadour shall have their privacy.

As for us, Thomas grips my hand tight, and I clutch his arm. Neither of us can stop smiling, not even while experiencing the baffled scrutiny and haughty hostility of some of the other guests. What do they matter? Not a whit. We are free — we have won.

"I can leave with you," Thomas says.

"We leave for England now?" I cry, ecstatic.

"No, no, travel arrangements must be made with Hellot's help," he laughs and then whispers in my ear: "But I'm no longer expected to reside here. I can go with you to the house, tonight. We'll be together from now on."

Out in the courtyard, guests do not leave but seize newly filled goblets and resume the party. I see more than a few happy faces. I suppose being bought out by a king would put one in a celebratory mood. Hellot appears, and Thomas says, "Would you mind if I settled a few matters with him tonight?"

"Not at all," I say. "There is something I need to do as well."

I spot Sir Gabriel striding toward the line of carriages next to the brightly lit lamps. He seemingly has no wish to linger at this party. I hurry toward him, calling out his name.

He turns slowly. I expect to see rage or sorrow. The destruction of the blue porcelain must be a blow. He may very well suspect that despite all his efforts to keep us apart, I did influence Thomas. If anyone is responsible for the destruction of the transcendent blue, it is me.

But Sir Gabriel is calm. In fact, I see that, for him, something is resolved.

"You are leaving France?" I say.

He nods.

This serenity is unbelievable.

"Sir Gabriel, all that you went through…" I pause, and correct myself. "All that we went through for the blue, the lives that were lost and ruined, it was, ultimately, for nothing."

"Not for nothing," he says vehemently.

I look at him inquiringly.

"It was and always will be the most beautiful color ever seen," he says. "Something that beautiful couldn't last long. Remember the butterfly?

If it exists for one night, and then it vanishes forever, like…" He pauses, searching for the word.

"Magic?"

"Yes." His dark eyes gleam. "Like magic. So be it. It still existed. I must seek a more lasting answer for myself in all things."

"A purpose?"

"If you will."

Sir Gabriel takes my hand in his, kisses it, and bows.

"Goodbye, Genevieve."

With that, he disappears into the night.

For me, I already know my purpose — to create, to love, to trust — and I turn back to find Thomas Sturbridge

He's finished his conversation with Hellot and sprints toward me, a riotous smile on his face, his eyes bright, as I run into his arms. "Would it shock all assembled if I kissed you?" he says.

"Let's find out."

And so we do, before finding our way out of Sèvres forever, and beginning the journey home.

AUTHOR'S NOTE

I came up with the idea of a spy story set amid the rivalry of eighteenth century porcelain factories while, with my sister Amy, I toured Hillwood, the Washington, D.C. estate of heiress Marjorie Merriweather Post. There I admired Post's large collection of exquisite porcelain, much of it created in Sèvres, the French factory sponsored by Madame de Pompadour, mistress of King Louis XV.

The atmosphere of high stakes and stolen formulas depicted in *The Blue* is factual. One English factory that stood out from the rest was Derby Porcelain Works. While Genevieve Planché and Thomas Sturbridge are fictional creations, Andrew Planché, William Duesbury, and John Heath existed. In reality, Derby Porcelain was such a success that it was recognized by George III and became Crown Derby in 1773, followed by its designation of Royal Crown Derby. It is in business today, celebrated for its craftmanship. For purposes of drama, I added to the life stories of the original founders, but their dedication to excellence was real. As for Sèvres, the manufactory has been in continual existence since 1740, with Louis XV becoming its principal shareholder and financial backer in 1759. It survived the French Revolution intact, and Napoleon Bonaparte turned out to be as proud of Sèvres porcelain as were the late Bourbon kings.

Discoveries in pigment of color have a long and fascinating history, and none more so than in blue. A scientist named Georg Brandt was the first person to discover a new metal after he realized that the color of a blue pigment came from cobalt. I have taken some liberties with the timeline of experiments in the German mines and caves in order to give Thomas Sturbridge his breakthrough. Fittingly, English, Viennese, and French scientists have a claim to official discovery of cobalt blue as a pigment, with the evidence pointing to Frenchman Louis Jacques Thenard as holding the honor. What is not debated is the color's value to artists such as Vincent van Gogh, J. M. W. Turner, and Jean Renoir. The toxicity of cobalt blue is also based in reality.

The lives of the Huguenot refugees in Spitalfields are well documented, and there are several groups dedicated to preserving the details of their lives in the Georgian period. I researched the Huguenot experience deeply, while also drawing from the history of my own family. The name I gave to Pierre—Billiou—is the original version of my name, although in my case the Huguenots headed for America in the 1660s and a city then called New Amsterdam. The Billiou-Stillwell-Perrine House still stands on Staten Island, New York, and is on the National Register of Historic Places.

Genevieve Planché's experience as a painter who worked for Anna Maria Garthwaite, a pioneer in textile design, is based on women who held those positions. During this time, women were blocked from becoming 'serious' artists. Fortunately, by the late eighteenth century, women were taking their rightful place in the art world, particularly in France.

The eighteenth century was also a time of crucial developments in espionage. Sir Gabriel Courtenay may not have existed, but Louis XV's

Le Secret du Roi is a fact. For some twenty years, a group of elite operatives reported to the French king alone. The spycraft that was developed in different parts of Europe during the Seven Years War played an even more crucial part in the American Revolution.

ACKNOWLEDGEMENTS

The Blue would not have found its way to a novel were it not for my literary agent, Nalini Akolekar, and for Alice Rees, publishing director of Endeavour Quill. I thank Alice for her enthusiasm and for her knowledgeable and careful edit of the book.

I am grateful to Russell Rowland, my longtime writing teacher, for his notes on the manuscript, and to Emilya Naymark and Harriet Sharrard for their insights. Special thanks also to Kris Waldherr and E. M. Powell. I appreciate the help from Peter Andrews on the history of chemists and Sophie Lechner on France. Other people to thank: Evelyn Nunlee, Elaine Devlin Beigelman, Dawn Ius, Christie LeBlanc, Sophie Perinot, Barbara Claypole White, Stephanie Jones, Adam Rathe, Natasha Wolff, Rhonda Riche, Daryl Chen, Mark Alpert, Donna Bulseco, Faye Penn, Ellen Levine, Michele Koop, Max Adams, Beth von Staats, Heather Lazare, Patricia King, Richie Narvaez, Jeff Markowitz, Laura Curtis, Karen Park, Radha Vatsal, Victoria Mckenzie, Theresa Defino, Dana Kennedy, Bret Watson, Bruce Fretts, Ricardo Martinez, Stephen Handelman, and my wonderful Queens writers group: Laura Joh Rowland, Jennifer Kitses, Mariah Frederick, Shizuka Otake, and Triss Stein. A special shout out to Sue Trowbridge, for her work on my author website.

Finally I thank my husband and best friend, Max, and my two amazing children, Alexander and Nora.

ENDEAVOUR QUILL

Endeavour Quill is an imprint of Endeavour Media

If you enjoyed *The Blue* check out
Endeavour Media's eBooks here:
www.endeavourmedia.co.uk

For weekly updates on our free and discounted eBooks
sign up to our newsletter:
www.endeavourmedia.co.uk/sign-up

Follow us on Twitter:
@EndeavourQuill

And Instagram:
endeavour_media

ENDEAVOUR MEDIA